Praise for

Off the Menu

"Readers hungry for cleverly written contemporary romances will definitely want to order *Off the Menu*." —*Chicago Tribune*

"Another fabulous and soul-satisfying meal . . . With the perfect blend of humor and heart, Ballis's writing is powerfully honest and genuinely hilarious."
—Jen Lancaster, *New York Times* bestselling author of
The Tao of Martha and *Jeneration X*

"Enticing. Ballis writes a bit like Emily Giffin and Isabel Wolff, and the recipes will please gal foodies as well." —*Booklist*

"Smart, sexy, and delightfully buoyant . . . In a word, scrumptious."
—Quinn Cummings, author of *The Year of Learning Dangerously*

"Interesting characters and a satisfying plot . . . Fans of Stacey Ballis will devour her latest book." —Examiner.com

"A great contemporary romance about a chef striving to find balance in her life and enjoying both her man and her career."
—*Parkersburg News and Sentinel*

Good Enough to Eat

"*Good Enough to Eat* is like a perfect dish of macaroni and cheese—rich, warm, nuanced, and delicious. And like any great comfort food, Stacey Ballis's new book is absolutely satisfying."
—Jen Lancaster

continued . . .

"Witty and tender, brash and seriously clever, Stacey Ballis's characters are our friends, our neighbors, or, in some cases, that sardonic colleague the next cubicle over . . . Her storytelling will have you alternately turning pages and calling your friends, urging them to come along for the ride. And in Stacey Ballis's talented hands, oh what a wonderful ride it is."

—Elizabeth Flock, *New York Times* bestselling author of *What Happened to My Sister*

"A toothsome meal of moments, gorgeously written, in warmth and with keen observation, *Good Enough to Eat* is about so much more than the magic of food; it's about the magic of life. Pardon the cliché, but you'll devour it and wish there was more to savor."

—Stephanie Klein, author of *Straight Up and Dirty* and *Moose*

The Spinster Sisters

"Readers will be rooting for Ballis's smart, snappy heroines."

—*Booklist*

"A laugh-out-loud hoot of a book. Jodi and Jill are amazing characters. They are challenged by balancing their business lives with style, charm, and grace. A must-read." —*A Romance Review*

"Filled with characters so witty and diverse yet so strong in their passion for friends and family that they could easily be our best friend or favorite aunt . . . Women of every age will relate to Ballis's clever yet unassuming story about sisterhood, dating dramas, and the bonds of friendship and family." —*RT Book Reviews*

Room for Improvement

"For those who say 'chick lit' is played out, all I can say is think again. Stacey Ballis proves the genre can be funny, honest, clever, real, and, most importantly, totally fresh."   —Jen Lancaster

"More fun than a *Trading Spaces* marathon. One of the season's best."   —*The Washington Post Book World*

"Rife with humor—always earthy, often bawdy, unwaveringly forthright humor."   —*Chicago Sun-Times*

"A laugh-out-loud novel that will appeal to HGTV devotees as well as those who like their chick lit on the sexy side. One of the summer's hot reads for the beach."   —*Library Journal*

"In her third outing, Ballis offers up a frothy, fun send-up of reality TV. Readers will have a blast."   —*Booklist*

Sleeping Over

"Ballis presents a refreshingly realistic approach to relationships and the things that test (and often break) them."   —*Booklist*

"Fans of relationship dramas will appreciate this fine, character-driven tale."   —*The Best Reviews*

"*Sleeping Over* will have you laughing, crying, and planning your next girls' night out."   —*Romance Reader at Heart*

"This engaging story delivers everything you ask from a great read: it makes you laugh, it makes you cry, it makes you *feel*."   —*Romance Divas*

Berkley Books by Stacey Ballis

ROOM FOR IMPROVEMENT

THE SPINSTER SISTERS

GOOD ENOUGH TO EAT

OFF THE MENU

OUT TO LUNCH

Out to Lunch

STACEY BALLIS

BERKLEY BOOKS, NEW YORK

THE BERKLEY PUBLISHING GROUP
Published by the Penguin Group
Penguin Group (USA) LLC
375 Hudson Street, New York, New York 10014

USA • Canada • UK • Ireland • Australia • New Zealand • India • South Africa • China

penguin.com

A Penguin Random House Company

This book is an original publication of The Berkley Publishing Group.

Library of Congress Cataloging-in-Publication Data

Ballis, Stacey.
Out to lunch / Stacey Ballis.—Berkley Trade paperback edition.
pages cm.
ISBN 978-0-425-26549-9 (Berkley trade paperback)
1. Administrative assistants—Fiction.
2. Celebrity chefs—Fiction.   I. Title.
PS3602.A624O98 2013
813'.6—dc23
2013031071

PUBLISHING HISTORY
Berkley trade paperback edition / December 2013

PRINTED IN THE UNITED STATES OF AMERICA

10 9 8 7 6 5 4 3 2 1

Cover photos: "Spaghetti" by Silvia Rico/Getty Images; "Dogue de Bordeaux" by
Erik Lam/Shutterstock.
Cover design by Rita Frangie.
Interior text design by Laura K. Corless.

For Bill, always

Acknowledgments

I want to thank, as always, my amazing family of Ballises, Thurmonds, Hirts, and Surrats. I am a lucky girl.

My agent Scott Mendel, for being exceptional in every possible way.

The extraordinary team at Berkley/Penguin, most especially my editor Wendy McCurdy for always seeing the book I mean to write and helping me uncover it, Leslie Gelbman for sticking with me, Katherine Pelz for all the details, and everyone in marketing and sales for keeping me employed.

My core group of writer pals who keep me sane and remind me that we have the best job in the world and write the books I love reading most: Elinor Lipman, Amy Hatvany, Sarah Pekkanen, Laurie Notaro, Laura Caldwell, Elizabeth Flock, Eleanor Brown, Quinn Cummings, Alison Pace.

The incomparable Jen Lancaster, for many more reasons than I can put here, most of them hilarious.

Tracey S. and Gina B., who are so much more than lunch buddies, and Lisa L. and Amy G. for being the best girls to vacation with. And Wayne G. for knowing that I wrote this book before I met him, and didn't mean to borrow his name.

Penelope, whose strength and determination and courage were a huge inspiration in the writing of this book.

And of course, my insanely dreamy Charming Suitor, who still thinks most of my crazy is adorable and makes my life thoroughly delightful every single day.

1

I take a deep breath and look out at the sea of faces. Friends, family, colleagues, clients. I'm weirdly calm, in spite of the fact that when it comes to the public speaking part of our business, Aimee has always been the voice of our company. Today is my turn, since Aimee can't exactly come up here and talk about herself. Even if it were possible, it would be "very bad form," and Aimee is nothing if not a stickler for good manners.

Over the years as we built first our own separate businesses, and then the company we founded together, Aimee was always better at the investor meetings, the panels we were asked to sit on for Women in Business conferences, the guest lectures at local colleges and high schools. I'm a behind-the-scenes girl from way back. Aimee was always the hostess, I was always the cook. Didn't matter if it was one of our early dinner parties in our first little crappy apartment off campus in Hyde Park, or one of the seven-figure weddings or galas we produce for the rich and famous. Aimee is the front-and-center mover and shaker, and I'm the kitchen workhorse.

But this space is full of love and kindness, and I can feel Aimee's faith in me, and I face the room to say what needs saying. There is stillness in my chest, the tightness that has been lurking there all day unfurls, and I take a deep breath and begin.

"Thank you all for being here today to honor the extraordinary Aimee Brand, my best friend, my soul sister, my business partner, and in many ways the one true love of my life." Everyone laughs a little at this, and that warm sound bolsters my resolve.

"My name is Jenna Stewart. Aimee and I met when the wise team at Student Affairs at the University of Chicago placed us together as freshman roommates. From the moment we first talked on the phone the summer before classes started, it was clear that we were a perfect pair. We couldn't have been more different, me an only child, Jewish, who grew up in downtown Chicago, and Aimee heading to the big city from her boisterous Lutheran family on their Indiana farm, with too many brothers to count!" There is a chortle from the front row, where five of Aimee's six brothers are shaking their heads and smiling. Jordan, the youngest, is staring off into space. He was an oops baby, born after Aimee was already off at college, and now, at twenty-three, he's clearly uncomfortable about his lack of connection to the older sister who was always more like a distant aunt, around in a whirlwind for occasional holidays.

"Aimee had been a Young Republican, I had organized my high school's field trip to the Democratic Convention. She had the Amazonian height, the blond curls, the legs for days, and I . . ." I trail off and gesture impotently at my short, round self, my dark wall of straight hair. Supportive chuckles and smiles. "But none of this mattered. We shared deep passions. John Hughes movies, the New Romantics, the Chicago Bears. We both loved chicken-flavor Ramen and hated the shrimp flavor. We liked thin-crust pizza over deep dish, and wine over beer, and gin over vodka. From the moment we met,

Aimee and I dreamed all our dreams together. Our company is the result of years of conversations over bowls of Sunday cereal, and bottles of cheap sauvignon blanc, and late-night whispers in the dark. We started our first businesses separately, but as soon as we were established independently, we merged them into one entity. Yes, it was a smart thing to do from a business perspective, a catering company and an event-planning company becoming one-stop party shopping. But the truth is, if Aimee and I were going to work so many long hours, we wanted to do it together.

"Aimee has always been the source of my best and deepest laughter. She has been my secret-keeper for more than half my life. The sister I never had, my conscience, my sounding board. We have traveled the world together, literally and figuratively. She is my hero."

I look up and catch Wayne's eye. He's nodding constantly, his big square head strangely fluid on his thick neck, like some odd bobblehead doll on a dashboard. My heart sinks. Because the one thing I've never been able to understand about Aimee is why she married this loaf. But today is not the day to question her sanity or motivations, and lord knows I'm the last person to be able to pass judgment on anyone's romantic choices. At least Aimee has a husband who's crazy about her, sitting here in support today. He might not be the guy I would have chosen for her, but as odd as he is, as annoying as I find him, I don't ever question his love for her or hers for him. But I can't think about that now.

"No one I have ever known personally or professionally can come close to Aimee's passion or perseverance. It doesn't matter if it was doing the Chicago Scavenger Hunt and Urban Race, in record-breaking time I might add, to raise money for cancer research in memory of her Mom, Jean; and her Dad, Thom; or negotiating the buyout of our company, or teaching her nieces one of the cheers from her days on the high school squad. Aimee is a one hundred percent effort, one hundred percent of the time woman.

"Aimee taught me how to tip a maître d' for the best table, and how to tip cows. She gave me the best birthday presents, and the best life-coaching. Her unflagging honesty and fearlessness in every area of life meant things as simple as I never went out in public in unflattering pants on her watch, and as complex as our taking some calculated risks with our business that ended up ensuring our futures.

"Aimee always believed in hard work and harder play, and in generosity of spirit and pocketbook. She is the one who made sure that our company had established significantly reduced not-for-profit rates for our services, and a commitment to both pro bono work for smaller charities and a profit percentage devoted to charitable donations. Aimee told me once that you couldn't be completely proud of your work unless it was benefiting others and not just yourself.

"Aimee taught me patience; she taught me that every person, even the most hateful, has something to teach us, and there is always something about them to like. She taught me that you should face the day with more hopefulness than despair, and more mascara than lipstick."

And good underwear. I can hear what Aimee would add, as loudly as if she had actually said it.

Everyone laughs, and the sound almost drowns out Aimee's voice in my head, but I know she's behind me, approving.

The laughter around me swells.

"Nothing in my life has ever made me prouder, happier,

or more full of joy than to have the honor and privilege of being Aimee's best friend, sister by choice, and business partner."

Everyone in the room is nodding, and I know it's time for me to wrap this up. Aimee always said that you could feel in a room when your audience was at a good place to stop listening, plus my knees are suddenly a bit weak. So I know it's time to say the words.

"And nothing in my life will ever be harder than facing every day without her."

I turn behind me and face the simple mahogany coffin, place a hand on its shiny smoothness, and let the tears come.

2

I have no idea what to wear. What on earth do you wear to your first ever therapy session followed immediately by your best friend's will reading? Conservative, obviously. Non-itchy, nonpinchy, since you're going to be uncomfortable anyway. Aimee would know what to wear. She'd know in a heartbeat. I stand in my closet in my underwear, sensible black cotton briefs on my ever-expanding tush and simple bra locking and loading the girls, for whom gravity is an endless enemy; hair in a towel turban on my head. Volnay, my twelve-year-old long-haired dachshund, sighs deeply, her elegant head resting on her stumpy crossed front paws.

"I know, girl, I'm figuring it out."

Aimee loved this closet. To be clear, Aimee designed this closet. She specifically had me buy a four-bedroom house, despite my lack of either romantic partner or offspring, because, and I quote, "You need an office and a walk-in uber-closet and a room for me when I sleep over." I always did what Aimee said, and called my Realtor back and said to stop looking at the two-bedroom condos, and start looking at four-bedroom houses.

"You have the money, indulge," Aimee had said when my Realtor, Deborah, showed us the gorgeous house on Maplewood three years ago. A two-story Arts and Crafts gray brick place on a lot and a half, wraparound yard, two-car garage with deck on top, huge master bedroom suite, and three decent-sized bedrooms on the second floor. It was more than I had thought of paying, but Aimee had a point. We had recently sold our company, StewartBrand Events, to a New York–based company, Peerless. Peerless is THE full-service event planning company on both coasts and had wanted a Chicago office, but decided that they wouldn't be able to compete with the company Aimee and I had built together, so they made us an offer we couldn't refuse. It wasn't Gates money, but it was eight figures cash plus stock and salary for a five-year commitment as consulting partners. Enough eight figures that it was still eight figures for each of us even after taxes.

I'm forty-two years old, wealthy by almost anyone's standards, and semiretired. I could be fully retired, but Aimee and I had kept one piece of our business separate from the sale altogether. The Larder Library was our gift to ourselves almost seven years ago, a sweet little store in a large converted Victorian house where we sell cookbooks, nonfiction food books, and foodie fiction; as well as a small selection of well-chosen kitchen gadgets, some vintage and some new; and a few impeccable ingredients. It has a demo kitchen on the first floor and event spaces on the second, with offices and storage on the third, so when cookbook authors are on book tour, they have a place really designed to highlight and test the recipes from their books. Local chefs do special classes, we do private parties; it is, or was, our clubhouse.

My face gets hot, and I sit down on the chaise that is in the middle of my closet. Volnay gets up, stretches her squat little body and schlumps over, licking my shin and collapsing back down on my foot. I reach down to scratch between her silky ears.

"I'm okay, girl. Just a little sad."

"Well snap out of it." I can hear Aimee's voice in my head. *"Wear the damn Eileen Fisher dress with the black boots and use some blush for a change; you look like a zombie. And then eat something."*

I look across the closet and spy the dress. A burgundy wrap dress that hides a multitude of physical flaws. I grab the dress and put it on, tying it in a simple knot at my hip. I slip on my tall black flat riding-style boots with leather in the front, but ankle-to-knee elastic in the back, the only kind I can fit over my wide calves. Years of standing on my feet behind a stove or prep table, added to thick legs predisposed to a Polish-peasant roundness, makes any other kind of boots enviable, covetable, and sadly, impossible.

I wander out of the closet and across the hall to the bathroom, Volnay clicking on the hardwood behind me. The pup, named for the wine that had been our favorite, was my thirtieth birthday gift from Aimee. I'd never had a pet, not so much as a goldfish, growing up. The Stewarts are an allergic people, or so they claim. I've secretly always believed that my mom just didn't want hair on the furniture and my dad was resistant to anything that might disrupt his work. So I was pet free, and not unhappily so, until Aimee showed up the morning of my last day of being twenty-nine with a teacup-sized, deep red, wriggling puppy. It was love at first sight, and I'm grateful for her serene and placid presence. Not to mention the fact that she is the perfect dog. Never naughty, never sick a day in her life, never has an accident in the house or chews anything she oughtn't. She is essentially the non-dog dog, practically a person, and I can take her anywhere.

Volnay jumps up gingerly on the closed toilet seat to watch me do my hair. She loves perching there, and we have many of our most important conversations here in the bathroom.

"Okay, girly girl. I'm going to go meet the nice lady doctor to see if I can't maybe score us some excellent pharmacology, and then to see the lawyer with the chin, and hope upon hope that Aimee did not leave us that enormous ghastly sculpture she bought in Miami."

Volnay tilts her head to the other side as I finish blowing out my hair, which has only two states, wet and dry. My hair is thick, very dark brown, and stick straight. Women are forever asking me if I have had a Japanese or Brazilian straightening treatment. They always seem sort of pissed off when I tell them it's just my hair. Aimee, who had a corona of frizzy blond ringlets she was forever struggling with, was always jealous of my hair. I told her I would trade for her legs anytime she wanted.

The Aimee Voice in My Head, or the *Voix* as I have come to think of it, since Aimee always said everything sounds elegant in French, is right. I do look a little bit like a zombie. My usually cream-pale skin has taken on sort of a greenish-gray pallor of late, the result of weeks of bedsitting with Aimee. I swipe on some blush and waterproof mascara; since my ex, Jack, once told me that most therapy is either crying therapy or whining therapy, and I've never been much of a whiner. I believe very strongly in chocolate therapy. Champagne therapy. Massage therapy for sure. But *therapy* therapy? Of either the crying or whining variety? Keep it.

My kitchen is the only room in the house that is a departure from the Arts and Crafts style, essentially a large home version of a restaurant kitchen designed for pure functionality.

I open the fridge, still filled with well-meaning sympathy casseroles going dry and/or fuzzy, and reach for the half tub of fried rice from last night's take-out Chinese from Orange Garden, eating it in cold, slightly greasy chunks standing over the sink. Volnay huffs at me; I haven't cooked properly for myself in weeks, and she misses her little bits and nibbles.

I throw some kibble in her bowl, put on a long charcoal gray trench coat, grab my purse, and head out to the garage.

Dr. Nancy Schmidke is a psychiatrist specializing in grief counseling. The head nurse at the hospice where Aimee spent her last few weeks slipped me her card as Wayne and I were taking Aimee home for her final nights. "She's the best, and it will help."

I kept the card, and the day after the funeral, after weeks of never being able to sleep more than a few fitful hours full of nightmares, and enduring occasional mini–anxiety attacks during the day, I called, figuring that the therapy part might at least get me a scrip for Ambien and maybe some Xanax.

Dr. Schmidke isn't at all what I was expecting. She is a statuesque, light-skinned African American woman with striking hazel eyes, and a mass of shiny, light brown skinny dreadlocks shot with gray that go halfway down her back. She's wearing a sort of deep orange caftan with a mandarin collar, and a large necklace of chunky amber beads and silver nuggets lying with ponderous weight on a bosom of epic proportions. Tiny gold-rimmed oval Ben Franklin glasses perch on the tip of her nose, and her hands are warm and strong when she clasps my hand in both of hers and welcomes me into an office that is all warm dark wood and plush rug and leather and tribal art. I sit in one of the two deep chocolate brown velvet chairs in the bay window. Chicago is bright and sunny today, one of those wonderful early October days where the sun seems to glitter off of every yellow leaf.

"So, I'm Nancy, if that's okay for you," she starts. I nod. "Good. I've been a therapist for twenty years. I tend to begin work with people who have been through a recent trauma, but I don't like to think of this process as a Band-Aid for some new wound. The way we grieve or deal with an unexpected tragedy or difficulty is informed always by who we are, where we came from, and what other unfortunate things we have experienced."

Uh-oh. I want the Band-Aid. I need the Band-Aid. The minute I hear "where we came from," I can sense that this is about to get much more involved than just a quick meeting and some magic from the prescription pad.

"So just like beginning any therapeutic process, there's no timeline, no restrictions. We can meet as often as you need, for as long as you need. We may start with what is most current or present, but I hope you will also be willing to explore some things from your past so that it will help us best figure out how to manage what you are going through today. How does that sound?"

Crap. That is what I was afraid of. How does it sound? It sounds annoying, frankly. I'm mostly here to talk just enough to get myself a little chemical assistance. I mean, of course I'm sad, I just lost my best friend. But it doesn't mean I need to go all Woody Allen for the rest of my life. But I figure I'd better play along for now. After all, I'm a grown-up. This isn't court mandated. I can stop coming whenever I want.

"Okay," I say.

Nancy smiles, a broad smile, with even, white teeth. "Good. Why don't you tell me a little about yourself, Jenna."

"You mean why I'm here?"

"I mean who you are. Let me get to know you a little bit. You can bullet point it for me if you would prefer."

I think about that. "Okay, I guess. I'm Jenna Stewart. I'm forty-two. I'm a chef, or I was, but I'm sort of retired now. I co-own . . ." I stop myself. The Larder Library is all mine, Aimee signed it over to me the week before we went in for our surgery, when I gave her part of my liver. Just in case. I'd asked her what if I was the one who died on the table? She said she knew that she was already my primary beneficiary. And she was right, of course. I didn't really have anyone else. This reminds me that now I have to change all of my estate stuff. I guess the University of Chicago and the Lynn Sage Cancer Research Foundation are going to really love me when I am dead. Good thing I'm going to the lawyer next. "I mean, I own a small bookstore and event space in Logan Square, but I don't run it day to day, and I sit on the board and consult with an events company."

Nancy nods, makes some notes, looks up to me to continue.

"Um, I'm an only child, my folks are retired and live in California. They're older, in their early eighties, so that's starting to be a challenge. I mean, they're good and very independent, but starting to show their age. I've never been married, so no kids. I mean, I suppose I could've had kids and still never been married, but, um, you know, neither. No boyfriend right now. I was engaged a few years ago, but it didn't, I mean I couldn't . . . we called it off. No one special since then. Um, I guess, that is the big stuff?"

"Okay. And what brings you here?"

I take a deep breath.

"My best friend and business partner passed away two

weeks ago. She was like my sister, we've been inseparable since we were eighteen, and she got sick about three years ago, autoimmune hepatitis. It was pretty fast and very debilitating. I gave her part of my liver two years ago, and her husband and I really thought she would get better, and for over a year she did, but then she had complications and then she just got sicker and sicker and then she died. So that has been hard. I haven't been sleeping very well, and sometimes for no reason I get all hot and sweaty and nauseated and dizzy and my heart races, and so I thought maybe I might need some sleeping pills and possibly something to calm my nerves, you know, just for a few weeks while I get over this . . ." I drift off, not sure what else I could possibly say.

"Do you think this is something you get over, this kind of loss?" Nancy asks.

"Well, of course, I mean, you always miss people when they are gone, but you have your memories and you move on."

"I spoke with Carla, who referred you to me, a little bit about your friend, it was Aimee? She filled me in on what your friend went through, and how much time you were with her. And from what I can gather, Jenna, this isn't just losing a best friend. The closest thing I can compare it to is the loss of a spouse. Not that you and Aimee were in any way romantic, but in terms of history and connection and emotional intimacy and dependence, not to mention that you were intertwined in your business as well, the magnitude of this loss is no less than if you had been widowed. So to a certain extent, that is I think the best way for us to proceed, to treat this loss for you as that significant. That life changing."

Suddenly my dress seems too bright and cheery. Like this woman thinks I should be shrouded in black, rending my clothing, shaving my head. But that's a little extreme. I had three years to face Aimee's health issues, and almost six months to prepare for the inevitable end. Of course it sucks, but I knew it was coming. My best friend is dead. So are a lot of people. And since throwing oneself on the funeral pyre isn't really done anymore, you pick yourself up and go on. Besides, I don't have time to be all broken about this. I have a business to run, and another that requires I at least check in now and again. I have employees and people counting on me. I can't let myself be all wallow-y and woe is me-y.

Nancy seems to take my silence for concern about my meds. "I'm not averse to prescribing some things to help get you through this time, but only in small amounts and only connected to talk therapy. I'll give you enough medication to get you through to our next session, but no more, not until we determine how the drugs work or don't work for you, and making sure they are a tool and not a crutch. For starters, I want to see if just getting you more restful sleep might not eliminate the other events before we try any antianxiety medication. Because to a certain extent, at this part of the process, you need to feel your feelings. Numb is not going to help long term. And since, as you said, you do not have pressing business or family obligations, let's get your sleep regulated first and then work on the other stuff."

Great. If I were a mom or had a real job, I'd get the good drugs. But being semiretired and childless means I get to "feel my feelings." Fuck my feelings. My feelings suck. I'd like to be able to sleep for more than three contiguous hours, and not worry that I might pass out or crap my pants in the middle of the grocery store for no reason. But I don't say that. I say "Okay."

"Okay, good. And what about Aimee's husband? It must be important for you two to lean on each other right now; how are you handling this together?"

Wayne. Half-Brain Wayne I always secretly think of him. Wayne of the epic Star Wars collection, the massive library of comic books, the laundry list of failed get-rich schemes. Wayne who has had an endless series of two-year corporate employments that read like Middle Management 101, all of which end in either amicable layoffs or quitting to pursue his next "surefire" opportunity. Wayne says "surefire" a lot. Wayne also says "you betcha" and "that's the truth, Ruth." Wayne. Wayne said he wished it were him and not Aimee at least once a week for the last three years. I never contradicted him.

"Wayne and I . . . how can I even explain this? Wayne is the only thing about Aimee I never understood." That seems fair. And I should stop there. But I don't. "Wayne always felt like the only time Aimee ever betrayed me. It was bad enough when she started dating the guy, but when she called from their trip to Mexico to tell me she married him on the beach, without asking me, without even talking it over, it was the only time in our life together things ever got strained. And Aimee thought I was just hurt that I wasn't there, that there wasn't some big wedding to plan and showers and parties and I didn't get to be maid of honor and all that, but that wasn't it."

And it really wasn't. When I was engaged to Jack, we were planning a tiny, private ceremony. Aimee and I spent enough time dealing with other people's parties and celebrations. I didn't resent not being a part of her wedding, I resented not being a part of her decision to marry Wayne.

I take a deep breath. "Wayne wasn't good enough for Aimee. He wasn't smart enough or handsome enough or elegant enough or ENOUGH enough. He didn't deserve her, and she deserved so much better, and I just never got it, and now she's gone and he's here and it makes me hate him. I know it isn't his fault that she got sick, and he was actually amazing with her every step of the way, a really good caregiver, and I was grateful for that. And I know that he truly loved her and she loved him, but I just never got it and now Aimee is gone and I feel like she wasted all these years on this guy who I. Cannot. Stand." I have never, ever, said this aloud to anyone except Volnay, and it feels horribly, deliciously, wonderful. And it just keeps coming, eight years of built-up resentments and snark and choked-back commentary flooding out of me.

"Wayne is a geek with no chic. He is weird and odd and socially awkward. He can't hold his liquor. He only eats eleven things. ELEVEN. Total. And he's proud of it, like it makes him some special cool guy to sit at a dinner party with a shitty take-out burger that he brought with him while the hostess cringes. Wayne can't keep a job, but he can keep all his strange Dungeons & Dragons friends from high school, with their nonironic, crusty Rush concert shirts and huge 1980s wire-rimmed glasses. Wayne can spot a stupid investment from eighty paces and hand over his life savings, but Wayne can't ever see that his pants are always an inch too short. Wayne was supposed to be the blind date Aimee and I laughed about and made fun of, he wasn't supposed to be the one she married, and now she's gone and he's here and I sort of hate that he is alive when she is not." I deflate back into the chair like a morning-after party balloon.

Nancy looks up at me. "Did you and Aimee talk about how you felt?"

I shake my head. "She didn't know."

Nancy looks at me over the tops of her glasses, one perfectly groomed eyebrow raised in disbelief. Her tone is that of a gently chiding parent. "Jenna, of course she knew. Friends know these things, and you and Aimee were more than just friends. She knew. And next time, I think we should talk about what it means that she knew and you never spoke of it. Okay?"

Aimee knew. I guess I probably knew that deep down, but it sounds sort of awful coming out of Nancy's lips. Like an admonition.

Nancy hands me a prescription for a week's worth of Ambien, and we schedule our next appointment.

I leave through the second door to Nancy's office, and duck into the small powder room to pee. This requires struggling out of and then back into my Spanx, because I do not care that there is that little split-crotch thing going on, I have never been able to go commando under my girdle. And the one time I tried, I both peed on my hands trying to keep the split open, AND ended up with my skirt stuck in my junk when I stood up from my chair. There is just no classy way to pull your clothes out of your kitten as you leave a restaurant. I'm an all-underwear-all-the-time girl. By the time I am done wedging my butt back into its spandex prison, I am flushed and a little sweaty. But the pink actually takes some of the green tinge from my face, and once I pat the little sweat-bead Hitler mustache off with a paper towel, I don't look terrible.

Which is good, because in precisely forty-seven minutes I have to be at the lawyer's office.

Handsome Lawyer Brian, Aimee always called him. I always call him the Lawyer with the Chin. He is Central Casting chiseled attorney guy. Tall, dark hair, square chin, broad shoulders. He's been handling our business and personal legal stuff for the past five years. I find him annoyingly attractive. Aimee always said he was all face and no heart. He's not overly warm, very businesslike, the consummate professional. We always liked that he wasn't a schmoozer, no fakey cheek kissing or outfit praising like some lawyers we've met. Just straightforward, clear legal advice and support. For an exorbitant hourly wage. In five years I don't think I've met with him more than once or twice without Aimee, and I know we've never had a conversation about anything but business.

But apparently there are things about Aimee's estate that I have to deal with; I know she made me the executor, but luckily according to Brian, she was very specific about bequests . . . educational trusts for all her nieces and nephews, lump sums for her brothers, jewelry to her sisters-in-law, local charities that get their share. I'm assuming that this meeting is about whatever she might have left me, and after everything I have been through, and the emotional drain of my meeting with Nancy, I just want to find out if I have to find a place for that horrible sculpture or not.

Brian's office is in one of those monolithic downtown marble and glass monstrosities, and I always get lost trying to find it. Luckily for me, Brian's assistant, Dawn, happens to be coming in from a Starbucks run just as I arrive, and she ushers me right to his door.

"Jenna." He reaches out a hand, warm and strong, which envelops mine briefly, and then retreats. "How are you doing?"

"I'm fine, thanks for asking."

He looks a little puzzled, but what does he expect? Should I burst into tears?

"It was a lovely service, and your eulogy was very moving." There seems to be very genuine concern in his voice and manner, and it disconcerts me more than a little.

"It was so nice of you to come." Like he wouldn't attend a six-figures-a-year client's funeral.

"Of course. And you're hanging in there?" And then, it happens. The fucking head tilt. At once patronizing and paternal. I've had THREE YEARS of fucking head tilting and it makes my ass twitch. If one more person head tilts at me, I'm going to start making everyone strap on a neck brace before they can speak to me.

Good grief. Literally! Can't I just be okay? "Of course. You know, it's hard, but it is what it is, and I'm just glad she's out of pain." Which is the truest thing I know. The last couple of months were ugly and horrible and I wouldn't wish it on anyone who had not committed genocide.

"Well, that must be a comfort."

"Yep."

There is a weird pause. I find myself staring at his hair. He has politician hair. That hair that is so perfect it is almost creepy. Stepford hair. I must really be staring because he suddenly runs his hands over it, as if worried that it's somehow out of place. Like that could happen.

"But you seem to be hanging in there," he says.

"Yeah, you know, it's been weird, but you just do what you do."

"Well, if you need anything . . ."

Um? Emergency legal advice?

"I'm good, really, thanks."

"Good. Staying busy?"

"Not so busy, things are pretty quiet." Not really sure what he is aiming at here.

"Well, maybe we can have dinner or something sometime soon."

Oy. He must really want to be sure he keeps all the business. I guess I can't blame him. In this economy, keep the clients happy. Maybe there is a new mandate from the other partners to wine and dine more.

"Yeah, sure." What else can I say. We pause again, and I wait for him to move things along.

"So, Jenna, I think you know that you're the executor of Aimee's estate."

"She told me she was going to set that up."

"She did. And the good news is that mostly, it is very uncomplicated and straightforward. I know you already know about her bequests for her family. Her remaining shares in Peerless SBE revert to you, so you now vote those shares in combination with your own as a larger partner. She has also left you her handbags, jewelry, and other personal effects to keep what you want, and distribute the rest to her sisters-in-law and nieces. She has made small cash gifts for all of the employees of The Larder Library, and has bequeathed ownership of the Lincoln Square apartment she rented to your employee Benjamin to him outright. The house, and its contents, as well as the rest of the money, the life insurance payout, all go to Wayne."

Hallelujah. No sculpture abomination for me! Dodged a bullet on that one. And I get both of her Birkin bags, the big chocolate brown one and the smaller taupe one, which I have to admit I've always coveted. Of course I don't really have anywhere to carry them, but that is beside the point. They are so much better than neon artwork.

"But . . ."

Oh crap on a cracker. There's a but.

"The way she set up Wayne's portion of the estate is a little bit unusual."

And suddenly, looking at his uber-Grant (Cary meets Hugh) face, with its furrowed brow, and such kindness in his impossibly teal blue eyes, something tells me that *unusual* is code for *you're utterly fucked.*

3

The letter is on heavy cream cotton paper, with Aimee's beautiful, rounded, swirly handwriting in charcoal gray ink, one of her signatures. Aimee was a fountain pen girl from the minute we got to college. Part of her transformation from rural Indiana cheerleader to elegant city sophisticate. I've read the letter six times since Brian gave it to me yesterday.

Jenna,

Well, isn't this just a huge bucket of suck? I'm so sorry to have gone off and left you, and in such a terrible, ugly way. Awfully inelegant of me, I know. We were supposed to grow old (but never gray!) together. We were supposed to take amazing vacations and have indulgent spa weekends, and if you had left me like this I would be so fucking angry with you that I would be red-faced and impossible forever.

Since you're already mad at me, I'm going to do something that will make you even madder. And no, I'm not giving you that sculpture from Miami that you hate so much.

I'm giving you custody of Wayne.

If I'd had kids of my own, you'd have been their fairy godmother, and I'd have needed you to be there for them, to be their memory of me, and go all Beaches for me. I just have Wayne, and I need you to take care of him for me. I know that you never really understood him or liked him very much or got why I loved him, and that we never talked about it. On the one hand, I'm so grateful that you never made me defend him, you were never snarky or eye-rolly about him and you never once said "What the hell were you thinking?" even though I know you thought it more than once.

And on the other hand, I wish that during my life you could have gotten to know him enough that you would have never even thought that to begin with. I always thought we'd have plenty of time to talk about it, or that one day it would just click and that would be that. But then this stupid thing happened and there were just no words and no time.

Here's all you need to know. I loved him with all my heart. He made me laugh every day, and I could always be completely myself with him. He was the best man I ever knew, after my dad, and my deepest wish for you is that someday you will find someone with whom you can have a love affair like I had with Wayne. We were real and powerful and deep and true, as real and powerful and deep and true as you and me, and it's time for you to start to comprehend that. He needs you now, and now that I'm gone, I need to know that the two people I loved most in the world stay connected to each other. And selfishly,

I need to know that you finally understand the only part of me that you never did. For the things that will be annoying and frustrating and maddening, I'm sorry in advance. I know he isn't perfect and that I'm the only thing you have in common. But I love you. And I'll be watching out over both of you forever.

Handsome Lawyer Brian will tell you the legal details, but essentially, Wayne is your new charge. The regular household bills, Noah's support payments, and all of that stuff is on automatic with the accountants. You don't have to worry about any of that. But any expense over $1,000 that Wayne wants to make has to be cosigned by you. His one credit card has a maximum $999 charge limit per month, and the banks won't let him open a new one using my accounts, so he'd have to get a job if he wanted more. But I have no-limit cards in your name that you can use on his behalf. The bank knows that there is a $999 maximum monthly total check approval, anything bigger you have to cosign. I worked my ass off to create this business with you, to leave this legacy. You were there when the dream first began; I need you to be there to ensure that our dream continues.

And while it makes me very happy that I can give Wayne the gift of financial independence, you and I both know that he doesn't have a lick of business sense. I don't worry for his being able to support himself and Noah while he can work, but I need to know that when he's old, he's taken care of. That he will never lack for health insurance or proper care or a decent roof over his head. I want him to find love again, but I need to know that he isn't taken in by some bimbette with champagne wishes and caviar dreams. Someone sane needs to be there to tell him that his buddy's new restaurant concept is crappy and won't last a month, that independent movies are never a good investment, and that Noah needs a Honda and not a Hummer when he turns sixteen.

All I ask is that you really listen to him when he comes to you for something, and that every decision you make about how you deal with things takes into account his current happiness as well as his future security. You know me. You know how I handled Wayne and his desires, when I said yes and when I said no. You can't just say no all the time and leave it at that; if you know I would have approved, even if I would've thought it ridiculous, you have to say yes.

Brian has all the details, but the gist is this: You have to save Wayne from himself; you have to be there for him, you have to stay connected. And if after a year, you really truly can't take it anymore, you can hand him back over to the estate lawyers.

I know it's a lot, I know your head is spinning; I know this is the last thing you think you need. But you do need it. Like it or not, Wayne is the only person in this world that knows me the way you do, that gets me the way you do, and no one else is really going to understand what you are going through.

I love you with my whole heart, and I miss you already, and I am so, so sorry for the pain you are in right now. In the meantime, take a deep breath, make a big batch of your carbonara, and prepare to

be strong. Be strong for yourself and strong for Wayne.
I'm watching.

Your Aimee

Wayne. She gave me custody of Wayne.

So much worse than the horrible Miami sculpture.

If she weren't dead, I'd fucking kill her.

And she's right about one thing. I'm making a double batch of carbonara, and I'm going to eat every bite right out of the goddamned pan.

4

Volnay whines at the door, deep and insistent.

"Okay, okay. I'm coming." The morning walk is very important. I think somehow she knows that her arthritis loosens up after some exercise, and she's so stiff these days when she wakes up that she's less and less patient with my dawdling. I don't know what it is; I was always the on-time-with-Swiss-precision girl. Aimee was the one who never managed to get out of the house at the right time. It used to make me nuts, her assing around when we needed to be somewhere. But she had personal magic for avoiding traffic and finding parking. I could leave a half an hour before her and arrive somewhere at the same time, because whatever route I take? Traffic and construction and street closures and detours and endless block circling, looking for a parking space. Arriving at my destination to see Aimee's huge Audi SUV parked right in front. Maddening.

But apparently I have learned how to ass around the house myself of late, puttering and futzing and finding strange projects to obsess about. I'm not really sure what it is, maybe it's that I generally sort of have nowhere to be, not in any serious way. And my self-imposed errands and life maintenance that are supposed to get me out of the house, I plan for certain times or days, and then suddenly I have to clean out the freezer or redo the spice rack.

Volnay gives a little bark, and I pop out of my head, look-ing at her sitting by the door, her little blue leash in her mouth. Poor thing.

I lean over and attach the leash, and open the door. She pulls me outside, down the front stoop, and out to the gate. I turn right, but she growls and I look back at her. She is lean-ing back into the leash, pulling me to the left.

"C'mon, NayNay, this way." I give her a little tug. She tugs back. And I know exactly what she wants.

If we go right, we take a long winding stroll through the quiet neighborhood side streets, looking at the houses, seeing the occasional dog or a mom out with her kids. But if we go left, we head up the boulevard to the Square, and that is where The Larder Library is. It's been almost two weeks. And my dog misses her friends and the home-baked dog treats and her comfy sleepy spot in the sunny window. I give one more halfhearted tug in the other direction, but she will not be moved. She has a lot of gravity for a thirty-pound dog.

"Fine. Let's go see everyone." We head up to Logan, walk-ing by the big houses and towering trees. Volnay is prancing, head up proudly; her squat little bowlegs producing a smooth gait that would make the dog show people preen. She carries herself like a supermodel. Weiner dog or no, she is a fairly perfect specimen of her breed. And I know I'm supposed to be all about the rescue mutts, and I give money to PAWS every year, but there is something about having a dog with a pedigree that makes me smile. Her AKC name is The Lady Volnay of Côte de Beaune. The French would call her a *jolie laide*, "beautiful ugly," like those people whose slightly off features, sort of unattractive and unconventional on their own, come together to make someone who is compelling, striking, and handsome in a unique way. I'm always so proud that I'm her person.

As we get close to the Square, which is oddly really more of a circle, my chest tightens. My breathing gets shallow. My palms slick over with sweat. My stomach turns over.

I pull back on Volnay's leash and walk over to one of the outdoor chairs in front of La Boulangerie on the corner. I try to get a deeper breath, so annoyed with these little attacks that come upon me out of nowhere. It's ridiculous. I thought it might be perimenopause, but my doc said my hormones are fine, and that it sounded to her like panic attacks. Which is ridiculous because I have nothing to be panicky about. But they keep happening, out of nowhere, my bowels turn to liquid, and my legs go all noodley. Volnay puts a paw on my knee. I sit and wait for it to subside. Finally my breathing gets smoother, and my rib cage unclenches.

Frankly, I want to go home. To crawl back into bed and go to sleep and not wake up for a year. But I know that as much as Volnay wants to go to the Library, deep down, so do I. Eloise and Andrea have called and sent e-mails, and little Benji keeps sending the funniest snarky e-cards, and poor Lois keeps leaving tins of pastries on my porch. We are a strange little family, but I know they are worried about me, and I didn't have much time at the funeral or at the house after to do more than hug and accept the usual banal sentiments of condolence, and the last two weeks have been full of paperwork and phone calls and business crap, and with not getting good sleep, I've just had very little energy.

I stand up, less wobbly, and, pretty sure that pants-shitting is not in my future, head in the direction of the Library. Weirdly, I want to be able to see Nancy tomorrow and tell her that I did it, even though I know that she cares less about what I do and more about how it makes me feel to do it or not. But it will feel like a small victory.

The Voix pipes in. *"Good lord, just get there already. It will make you feel better. Or it will make you feel worse. But so the fuck what? Put on your big-girl panties and do it, because we always had brave faces for the team, and like it or not, they need to see you and be with you and know you are okay."*

As soon as we turn the corner onto Kedzie, Volnay starts to pull on her leash, half dragging me down the block. We zip past Lula Café and City Lit Books, waving at Teresa, the proprietor, who is doing a display in the window as we pass.

Just on the next corner sits The Larder Library, a three-story gray stone Victorian lady with a wide stoop leading to the porch, the dark green sign with its gold lettering carefully weathered to look like it has been here forever. The heavy dark wood double doors are open to let in the soft unseasonably warm autumn breezes, and the sweet vanilla scent of something delicious is wafting out into the street.

I let go of the leash and Volnay tears up the steps ahead of me like a bat out of hell, careening into the shop, and skidding on the worn wooden floors, tumbling ass over teakettle and landing in a wriggling lump at Lois's feet in their ubiquitous clogs.

"Well, my word, look who's here!" Lois bends her round form down and scoops my pup up in her arms like she is a mere feather, snuggling her to a Teutonic bosom and letting the dog lick her wrinkled cheeks.

"Hello, Mrs. Piggle-Wiggle." I go over to accept the bone-crushing embrace. Lois is only barely five feet tall, but is strong as an ox with a milkmaid's peaches-and-cream complexion, water blue eyes, and the pinkest Cupid's bow mouth I've ever seen on a grown-up. Her hands and arms are strong from years working in her family bakery, kneading vast lumps of dough into submission, and whisking dozens of eggs to fluffy clouds by hand. Two of her sons run the bakery now; the third is a butcher at Paulina Market. But Lois was never one for retirement. She had been a widow for over twenty years and a neighborhood resident her whole life; we hadn't even gotten the sign up before she wandered by with a strudel to offer her part-time services. One bite told us all we needed to know, and we hired her on the spot. She treats us all like errant nieces and nephews, and we dote on her.

"Liebchen." She cradles my face in her strong hands. "I'm so happy you're here. Sit. I'll make tea."

She wanders over to the kitchen, tossing Volnay a biscuit on her way with perfect efficiency of motion. Volnay takes the treat and clicks after her, a kitchen-floor dog if ever there was one.

"Hey, Jenna, how are you?" Eloise floats out from behind the antique library table that serves as the front counter.

I remember when Aimee called to tell me that a small neighborhood library on the South Side was getting a makeover and that she had snapped up a ton of beautiful old furniture, including card catalogs, tables, chairs, shelves, even a pair of ancient carrels which we put in the back of the store for the local writers who like someplace a little quieter than New Wave Coffee for their free Wi-Fi. She nailed the "Library" part of our name in one fell swoop, furnishing nearly 80 percent of the store with that one adventure.

"Hi, El, I'm okay."

She reaches out with her endless slender arms, bending at

the waist to envelop me in a brief hug. As short and round as Lois is, Eloise is a lithe expanse of waif, at least six feet tall with a ballerina's body and a mane of pre-Raphaelite auburn curls that she keeps twisted into a complicated bun, little ringlets escaping around her forehead that she is always blowing out of her green eyes with their pale lashes. She is elfin-featured, has impossibly long fingers, a tiny button nose, a pointed chin. A retired dancer at thirty with a degree in library science and an epic supply of insanely delicious cookie recipes, she glides around the store in an endless series of long, flowy skirts with leotard tops, and with her calm grace, teaches all of the children's classes and does story time. She is also in charge of research and assists with book buying.

"Well, it's about fucking time." Andrea wanders down the staircase.

"Well, hello to you too."

She grabs me by the shoulders and looks me in the eyes.

"How. Are. You? Are you beyond shitty? Because we are all beyond shitty, so you must just be beyond the beyond. You must be Losing. Your. Mind. Are you losing your mind?"

Andrea is the store manager, and after Aimee, probably the person I have been closest to the longest. She was my first sous-chef when I opened Fourchette, my catering company. She and I met doing a weeklong intensive chocolate course right after I got back from France. She is a brilliant self-taught chef, and was my right hand at Fourchette until the merger with Soiree, Aimee's company. Then she became Vice President of Food and Beverage for StewartBrand, and when we sold to Peerless, took the generous buyout they offered to employees who did not want to stay, and asked us to install her at the Library, where she could stop dealing with demanding clients and vendors. She is store manager and head chef for the cooking classes and special events, and keeps the menagerie in line.

She and I are the same age, both native Chicagoans, although she is a Southsider and I am a Northsider. But as long as we stay away from each other during the Cubs/Sox crosstown series, we are very similar. Both only children of driven working parents, mine a therapist and an academic, hers both doctors. Both public school educated. Both single. In many ways we have much more in common than I had with Aimee. She and I are the same height and generally the same build, which makes shopping for clothes with her much easier for both of us. She has the most gorgeous caramel skin and keeps her chestnut hair in a close-clipped natural style, accentuating her beautifully shaped head and swanlike neck.

Andrea's dad is African American, and her mom is Dominican, and they sort of adopted both Aimee and me over the years . . . Aimee, who lost both her parents within a year of each other in our late twenties; and me, with my folks in California for the past decade. We always spend Thanksgiving and Christmas Eve with them. Mother's Day we always have a ladies' lunch, and Father's Day we have a BBQ.

"Hey, will you give your folks my love, and tell them thank you so much for the note and flowers?"

"You'll tell them yourself on Sunday. You are coming to dinner."

"Oh, that's sweet, but . . ."

"You. Are. Coming. To. Dinner. Family dinner. Sunday night. Mom is making lechón and pan de coco, and Dad is making Nana's mac 'n' cheese. I'll pick you up at six."

There is no arguing. And if I am going to feel beyond

shitty, as Andrea says, I ought to be full of delicious slow-roasted pig and mac 'n' cheese and coconut bread.

"Thank you. Tell them I'll bring that green slaw they love. Get a vegetable in us so our arteries don't freeze solid before coffee."

She leans over and kisses my cheek. "Good girl. They'll be delighted."

Lois comes over, handing us each a steaming cup of tea. She always remembers that I like mine with milk and one sugar, Andrea takes hers black; Aimee was a honey and lemon girl.

"Go, sit." She motions to the sitting area in the bay window, a pair of extrawide and extradeep down-filled gray linen reading chairs, with a small side table for each, and a low coffee table in between. Andrea and I settle into the chairs; Volnay jumps up to share my space. Lois comes back over with a plate of vanilla shortbread, barely cooled from the oven, with a small pot of grapefruit curd to dip the crisp, buttery fingers in. Eloise slides the doors closed, and flips the sign to "We'll be back in 20 minutes." She and Lois grab tea for themselves, and bring over two of the wood armchairs to join our circle. We have no sooner flicked the first crumb off our laps, when there is a clattering at the door. Benji is having a fit on the porch, scratching at the door like the stray tomcat he is. Eloise glides over to let him in.

Our prodigal adopted son, Benji, came to us at sixteen as an intern. He'd been in a group home, taken from his addict single mom when he was fourteen, and was something of a problem child. But as he likes to say, cooking saved his life. The woman who ran the kitchen at the group home took him under her wing, and he found that he loved being in the kitchen and had a natural aptitude. He found a calling, discipline, and people who treated him with care and respect. Shavon, his mentor, served on the board of a small not-for-profit for which we were planning a pro bono benefit, and mentioned him to me. I met him the night of the party and immediately offered him an internship. He was one of the hardest workers I had ever met, and frequently saved the day when my team was in the weeds.

When he graduated from high school, he won a scholarship to Kendall Culinary School. Aimee and I gave him a monthly stipend to cover books and equipment, and Aimee bought a small one-bedroom apartment in Lincoln Square and rented it to him cheap. Now twenty-two, and fresh out of culinary school, he's having the classic struggle of figuring out whether he wants to focus on fine dining or casual; hotel work or restaurant or catering; whether he wants to open his own place someday, and he changes his mind every day. The fact that Aimee left him his apartment means that he has the freedom to continue training and exploring, since he just has to cover his bills with no rent hanging over him.

Benji flies into the room and throws his arms around my neck.

"Auntie Jenna! You're back!"

"Hello, darling." I kiss the cheek he brandishes at me, trying not to poke my eye out on his heavy black-rimmed hipster glasses.

He makes the rounds kissing the rest of his "Aunties" and collapses in Andrea's lap, folding his long gangly legs up over the arm of the chair, and nuzzling in her neck. Volnay immediately abandons me and jumps into his lap, licking his face emphatically like he is a dirty puppy. Which, considering that he is twenty-two, completely adorable, and "sexually flexible" as he says, he probably is. I don't understand the whole bi or "pansexual" thing, I'm old enough to think you just pick a side, but he seems happy and comfortable with himself and is having a good time.

"Well, this is a sight," Lois says.

We all fall silent, take sips of tea, reach for more cookies.

"This SUCKS," Benji says, gray-blue eyes flashing behind thick black lashes, and blushing to the roots of his artfully mussed dark hair.

"Ben . . ." Eloise admonishes.

"No, THIS SUCKS. I miss Aimee. I hate that she isn't here. And I'm really mad about it." Tears swim in his eyes. Benji has received a lot of group therapy over the years, is very in touch with the immediacy of his emotions, and something about this circle of care has clearly put him in a sharing mode.

"Ben, this isn't . . ." Andrea starts. I put my hand up.

"Yes. This is. If not here? With us?" My voice breaks a little, surprising me. "He's right, it sucks and we all miss her, and we all hate that she isn't here, and we're all angry at how unfair it is. And I'm sorry I haven't come sooner, I just . . ." I trail off.

They are all weeping. Lois reaches for my hand, and squeezes, pulling a hankie out of her bosom and blowing her nose like a foghorn. Eloise puts her hand on the back of my neck like a cool compress, and then gets up to find tissues for the rest of them. I'm just sort of cried out. I did a lot of late night sobbing when Aimee was first diagnosed, and again when she took her final turn for the worst. And again when we had to move her to hospice. I'm fairly well desiccated at this point.

Andrea and Benji snuggle on the chair, and Volnay rests her chin on Benji's shoulder.

"We're all miserable, and sad and pissed off, and we are just going to have to lean on each other and ask for what we need and make it okay. Because no one is more angry at this whole thing than Aimee, and if we don't figure out how to live without her, she will never forgive us."

"There's my girl," the Voix says.

I look at these people, my odd family, and make a decision.

"I'm making lunch. Who wants pasta?"

"We have leftover caramelized cauliflower and some cannellini beans soaking," Lois says.

"There's a chunk of pancetta in there," Benji pipes in.

"I roasted a mess of garlic yesterday," Andrea offers.

"Perfect," I say, smiling, the dish coming together in my head.

Andrea smiles and nods. Benji raises his head and grins through tears. Eloise smiles a little, and Lois slaps her meaty thigh as if an important decision has been made. I stand and head for the back of the store. Because if I'm going to help these people heal at all, it's in the kitchen.

5

Making dinner for Wayne is either the easiest thing or the hardest thing on the planet, depending on how you look at it. After all, Wayne's famous Eleven are neither difficult to procure nor annoying to prepare.

They are just.

So.

Boring.

Roasted chicken
Plain hamburgers
Steak cooked medium
Pork chops
Eggs scrambled dry
Potatoes, preferably fries, chips, baked, or mashed, and
    not with anything fancy mixed in
Chili, preferably Hormel canned
Green beans
Carrots
Corn
Iceberg lettuce with ranch dressing

That's it. The sum total of what Wayne will put into his maw. He doesn't even eat fricking PIZZA for chrissakes. Not including condiments, limited to ketchup and yellow mustard and Miracle Whip, and any and all forms of baked goods . . . when it comes to breads and pastries and desserts he has the palate of a gourmand, no loaf goes untouched, no sweet unexplored. It saves him, only slightly, from being a complete food wasteland. And he has no idea that it is strange to everyone that he will eat apple pie and apple cake and apple charlotte and apple brown Betty and apple dumplings and fritters and muffins and doughnuts and crisp and crumble and buckle, but will not eat AN APPLE.

But a good chef knows that food is supposed to be about pleasure, a gift you give to your diners. I've never been one of those ego-driven chefs, offended if someone asks for salt, implying my seasoning palate isn't perfect, as opposed to acknowledging that they might just like things saltier than I do, and are entitled to that opinion. I've never wanted to teach my diners a lesson of some kind. I appreciate the current trend of nose-to-tail; I do think there are undiscovered pleasures to introduce to a broader market. I have converted many a guest to the joys of oxtail and halibut collar. But I hate the chefly smugness that seems to come with it, that attitude of "you aren't a real foodie unless your desert island dish is blood sausage."

I suppose it's because so much of my career was spent catering and not in a restaurant. Successful catering is a thousand percent about giving the customer something they want at a level beyond what they dreamed possible. It's about tapping into their deepest desires and delivering it perfectly to everyone at the same time. Restaurant chefs can often sneer at caterers, thinking that so much of what we do lacks creativity, isn't as badass as working the line in a churn and burn;

we don't have the pressure of the critics or the next hot Top Cheftestant's new place to deal with.

But chefs who really know their shit know that the exact opposite is true. We don't have a handful of critics or Yelpers and bloggers who may or may not like what we do, we don't have places full of people who have chosen on purpose to come dine at our establishments; we often have five hundred people at one time who did not choose us, who love to stand around and snark about whether the tuna tartare is spicy enough or chopped too coarsely. We have to deliver an exceptional dining experience where we usually have no control over space, flow, timing, equipment, or audience. We can't, most often, craft a perfect menu that we know will wow and flow, because menus come together by committee and the bride is afraid of anything with a sauce because it might get on her dress, or the eightysomething gala chair still thinks filet and salmon are the only two possible elegant entrée options, and no amount of prodding will get her to pick the skate wing and hanger steak instead.

We sit through endless tastings where people with Naugahyde for palates pick apart our dishes and offer suggestions and changes that we? HAVE TO MAKE. I happen to love a braised pork cheek garnished with crispy bits of fried pig ear, or a smoked bison tongue salad. But I have yet to meet a client who wants me to make that for their daughter's sweet sixteen.

And at the end of the day, if I can bring integrity to one more chicken breast dinner, to the "trio of salads" ladies' luncheon, to the surprise hot dog cart at the end of the wedding, perfectly snappy grilled Vienna Beef beauties with homemade steamed buns and all seven of the classic

Chicago Dog toppings, then I have done my job and might get another.

What's the task that all those TV cooking competition folks fall down on? The ones that knock out the favorites and even presumed winners? The Wedding Challenge. The Quinceañera Challenge. The Fundraiser Challenge. Even the Masters, already famous and multi-restauranted and Michelin starred, competing for charity? The cake falls, the apps aren't hot enough, the salad wilts. Because those are the CATERING challenges, and catering is just fucking hard.

Dinner parties are just small self-catered affairs. Some people, whether chefs or just passionate home cooks, make dinner parties to show off their prowess, trying to turn their homes into restaurants with fancy plating and things assembled in ring molds, trying to replicate something they ate at some fabulous new hot spot.

Not me. Sure, I adore the edamame dumplings at Buddakan in New York. But I don't try to make them, because stuffing and steaming dumplings while trying to keep glasses full and dinner on schedule would make me insane. So I figured out the filling and turned it into a dip for crudités that I can put out and be done with it.

When I have a dinner party, I want to sit with my guests and not worry about whether the caramel spirals for the dessert garnish are sagging in the kitchen humidity. I want every dinner party to feel like Thanksgiving. I want a ton of delicious food, something for everyone, with one comforting thing and one surprising thing. And this means knowing my audience.

You're diabetic? I'm making low-carb for everyone.

Vegetarian? The whole party will be meat free.

Eating Paleo these days? We're having a caveman party with plenty of steak and veg and no dairy or legumes for anyone.

Gluten-intolerant vegan?

I'm making reservations somewhere you like, because seriously, some things I just cannot manage. Sorry. I'm not insane.

Dinner parties with Wayne aren't hard. I make a great roast chicken. Burgers can be fun and unexpected. I can always save his portion of beef and cook it medium and still serve everyone else medium rare. I love the challenge of making things he will eat for a whole table and not feel like some 1950s housewife serving up banal Tuesday dinner. And I can always go all out on the dessert, which helps.

But tonight it's just the two of us. No buffering friends or joyful noise. And no Aimee to keep him from going off on a Star Wars tangent, or asking a mortifying and inappropriate question. First time he met Andrea, he asked her if African Americans could get acne. I'm not kidding. I wanted to crawl into a hole. Aimee laughed it off, smacked him in the arm and told him to refill her wineglass and that was the end of it, but that moment haunted me for months.

Wayne called yesterday and said he thought we should get together, so I have a couple of fat pork rib chops brining in cider that I will throw on the grill. Crisp wedges of iceberg lettuce with a homemade buttermilk ranch dressing spiked with fresh herbs. Buttery glazed carrots, steamed green beans with lemon and a little bit of chili. On the sideboard in my enormous walk-in pantry, I have fresh fig tarts cooling, shiny with fig jam glaze and ready to be dolloped with a pistachio whipped cream. A meal that Wayne will eat, and I will actually enjoy. As much as I can enjoy a meal with Wayne.

"*Suck it up, buttercup,*" the Voix spits in my ear. "*Get your head in the game. You have one year. One year to be his pal, to keep him from blowing through my money, and to learn why I thought he was the bee's fricking knees, so how about you put on your game face.*"

Sigh. It was bad enough that Aimee was always right when she was around; being right AND dead is sort of monumentally annoying. But it is what it is. And the fact is that the only time I ever have spent with Wayne alone in the eight years he and Aimee were together was in my hospital room after the transplant. Aimee was in the ICU; neither of us could be with her for the first few days, so Wayne hung out in my room. And if I'm going to be honest, he was mostly pretty awesome. Always went on a coffee run when my folks were there or other people came to visit, quick to fetch me a Popsicle or more ice water. Checking with my doctor to see what I was allowed to eat, since while you are recovering from donating part of your liver, stuff can really disagree with you, and then going out to find delicious versions so that I didn't have to eat the hospital food. He brought me an iPod full of audio books so that I didn't have to keep my eyes open to read, and an iPad with the entire *Buffy* and *Angel* series loaded in, since he remembered I once confessed that I had never seen them, but was somewhat curious.

Of course, he also managed to knock over my tray table at least once a day, usually right after I had fallen asleep, used my bathroom with loud frequency, which totally squicked me out, and had to be asked to leave the room every time a doctor came by to check my incision or discuss my progress.

Deep breath. One day at a time. And a year isn't so much. Aimee thought that this little experiment would work, but

I know better. Wayne lived in her blind spot. I just have to get through this year. Not even a full year, just have to get to October first of next year. Eleven months and sixteen days. Do I have a calendar in my closet with red Xs on the days? You had better believe it. That's the truth, Ruth. You betcha.

I take the chops out of their brine, pat them dry and leave them on a tray on the island to come to room temp. I feed Volnay, who eats in her unusual way, delicately removing one piece of kibble at a time from her bowl, placing it on the little rug that serves as her dining room, and then eating it before going back in for a second piece of kibble. It takes her the better part of thirty minutes to finish her bowl. I'm sure if she had thumbs, she'd be patting her chin with a linen napkin after every morsel. When she finishes, she hits the water bowl. Silently. No one can figure out how she drinks, she sort of purses her lips and sucks, none of that slurping and splashing that accompany most dogs' drinking. She is a stealth drinker. When she finishes, she heads to her little bed in the corner of the kitchen to groom her fur a bit. Lovely girl.

I've got my entire mise en place, en place. Prep trays next to the cooktop, ready to be put into quick action. There is a six-pack of Miller High Life chilling in the fridge. Bet you can guess whom that is for. I've got a bottle of Raveneau decanted and am working on my first glass, letting the wine relax my shoulders a bit. The doorbell rings, an old-fashioned ding-dong sound that was not only hard to find but ridiculously expensive by doorbell standards. I shake my head, steel my spine, and head to the door.

Wayne fills my porch. The ultimate bull in a china shop, Wayne has a presence much larger than his physical person. His six feet tends to feel more like six four or five, since he is often smacking his head into low-hanging light fixtures or shelves. He is probably only about 230 pounds, but he carries it in what feels like enormous bulk, enhanced by clothes that are neither expensive nor fit well. He borders on schlumpy. His hair is thick, dark brown, sprinkled with gray a little more prominently over the past year, with a serious widow's peak. He isn't handsome, but would be considered cute in a baby-faced way, like a giant eight-year-old. Which he sort of is. When clean shaven, he looks like Eddie Munster, so his face is an endless experiment in facial hair, mustaches thick and thin, goatees, full beards, sideburns of various configurations. He was full bearded at the funeral, the last time I saw him, close-trimmed and neat. Today he has only one strange half-inch-wide stripe down the center of his weak chin. It looks like a face Brazilian. Oy.

"Hey Wayne," I say, stepping aside to let him in. He grabs me in a bear hug and I'm doused in Drakkar Noir. Hello 1984, how I have not missed you.

"Hello Jenny." He snuffles into my hair. He has always called me Jenny. And I have always hated it. I am Jenna to most, Jen only occasionally, schnookie to my parents. Miss Jenna to Andrea's folks and Auntie Jenna to Benji. But I am not now, nor have I ever been, a Jenny.

Some other odor is cutting through the miasma of cologne. Wayne steps back and thrusts an enormous bunch of white and pink stargazer lilies at me almost violently. My least favorite flower. They stink to high heaven. Every florist Aimee and I ever worked with at StewartBrand knew that stargazers were a firing offense. And these, grocery store flowers if ever I saw them, still have their pollen pods attached. I look down. Yep, the front of my pale blue cashmere sweater is now sprinkled with yellow dust from the force of Wayne's imposition of the bouquet on me. He sees me looking down.

"Oh, sorry, did I do that?" he says, reaching over and trying to brush the pollen off my stomach.

"No! Don't . . ." Too late. The pollen is now streaks of saffron yellow, and from experience, this sweater is now ruined forever. This particular pollen is as bad as beet juice in the stain department. Many a perfectly good tablecloth has met with an early demise when a florist forgets to remove the pods.

"Uh-oh. That's bad, huh?" He continues to swipe at me absentmindedly with his hamlike hands, ensuring that the pollen smears are well distributed. But I am not going to let this faze me. It's a sweater. I ruin half a dozen a year myself with cooking spatters when I'm too lazy or overconfident for an apron, and god knows how many over the years because practically everything I eat eventually ends up landing on my chest.

I reach down and grab Wayne's hand to stop his mauling. "I'll get it cleaned, don't worry. I'm just going to go change quickly; why don't you grab a beer from the fridge."

I head up the stairs and pop into the little laundry room off the closet, and dump the sweater in a sink of cold water with a little Woolite to see if it is salvageable. Then I pull one of my endless black turtlenecks off a shelf, figuring I might as well guard against the probability that I will be spattered with something else before the night is over, and head back downstairs.

"Be nice."

I'm always nice.

"What's up with the pup?" Wayne is hunkered down on the floor petting Volnay. "She wouldn't jump in my lap and when I went to pick her up she whimpered?"

Oh, poor thing, it's a damp day, her arthritis must be bad. I go to get her a pill. "She's getting old, she has arthritis. The weather must be making it worse tonight."

Wayne hauls his ungainly carcass off the floor. "Aw. That's sad. Are you going to have to put her down or something?"

My heart catches in my throat. I've always known conceptually that pets by nature are gifts with an expiration date, but since I've never had one before, that's always been someone else's problem. I can't begin to think about actually making that decision, and certainly not within a month of putting my best friend in the ground. "No," I say, trying to keep my annoyance out of my voice. "She's fine, just takes some extra medications and is a little slower, that's all. Vet says she is otherwise in good health."

"I have a friend who has a dog like that," Wayne says, taking a pull on his beer and waving off my offer of a glass. "He just got a puppy. The puppy makes the old dog feel a little younger, the older dog sort of helps train the puppy, and he knows when he has to let the older dog go it will be better because he'll still have the puppy."

"I've heard that. Sounds like it must be a good plan for a lot of people," I say, heading to the stove to work on dinner. My cooktop is actually in the kitchen island, since I like to cook with company, and I hate having my back to people when I cook for them. This way I can talk and visit while I putter. The island is enormous. When I rehabbed the building

I bumped out the back, losing part of the backyard in favor
of a much bigger eat-in kitchen, so the island is a full twelve
feet long and four feet deep. One end is a four-by-four square
of foot-thick custom larchwood butcher block, the six-burner
BlueStar cooktop in the middle, with a dark gray soapstone
counter behind, with room for four people to sit, and more
soapstone to the right of the cooktop, where I have my prep
trays all set up.

Wayne perches on a chair on the other side of the island.
"So look at all this!" He gestures to my prep trays energeti-
cally, promptly knocking over my abandoned wineglass in
his flailing. Here is the thing about really good wineglasses.
First? They actually do change the taste of the wine. I'm not
a wine snob, but my ex-fiancé Jack was pretty knowledgeable,
and he showed me the importance of proper stemware, gift-
ing me a complete set of Riedel stemware for both Burgundy
and Riesling, my two favorite types of wine. Second? They
don't just break. They EXPLODE. Into teeny tiny miniscule
little shards of crystal. I look down at my prep. The trays are
now aglitter with glass and doused in wine.

"Oh, shit, Jenny, I'm so sorry, I just . . ." Wayne starts to
get up, and I reach across the divide and place my hand on
top of his head and push down.

"Do. Not. MOVE," I say through gritted teeth.

He looks up at me, and I can swear I see his chin with its
ridiculous landing stripe quiver.

*"He's all you have left of me. Don't lose it. I broke more than
one wineglass in our time together, as did you, and we always
laughed it off."*

I look at this grown man, hazel eyes not quite tearing up,
but definitely extra shiny. I can see the mortification in his

face. And I realize that the Voix is right, the only thing I can do is make it better for him. I take my hand off his head.

"So, I'm thinking we go out instead?" I say with as light a voice as I can muster.

Wayne breathes and smiles widely. "Orbit Room?" he says, his favorite place for burgers, and very close to my house.

"Absolutely. We can come back here for dessert." I gesture across the room to my kitchen library, a sort of a pantry nook that houses all my cookbooks and equipment, where the tarts sit on the counter, safe from Hurricane Wayne. Hurriwayne. Have to remember to tell Nancy that one.

Wayne sits quietly while I dump what would have been dinner in the trash, and clean up the spilled wine and glass bits. I toss Volnay a bully stick to keep her busy in our absence, feeling bad that there will be no delicious bones for her to gnaw on later, and grab my jacket.

Wayne and I head out to his car, a massive black Escalade with the license plate MLMFLCN. And before you ask, this is not some Roman numeral for a year when something interesting happened. This is Wayne. It stands for *Millennium Falcon*, Harrison Ford's spaceship in Star Wars. Between that and the horrible gangsta vibe of the car itself, I'm loath to get in. But I haul myself up into the beast, and off we go. The sooner we get there, the sooner I get the remains of my evening back, and I have very specific plans that include a long hot bath, the latest Sarah Pekkanen book, and an eventual Ambien.

The Orbit Room is a nondescript neighborhood bar on California, just north of my neighborhood. They have sassy waitresses, bartenders with generous pouring hands, and truly killer burgers. Hipsters and capital F Foodies might flock to

Kuma's, with the endless waiting and the loud music. And Kuma's makes a heck of a burger, I cannot lie. But at the end of the day, if I want a burger, I want it soon, hot, and in a place where I can hear the person across the table from me. The Orbit's burgers may not have the street chic rep, and there aren't the same volume of topping options, but they are juicy, beefy, cooked perfectly to your preferred temp and served with mounds of either fries or onion strings, both of which are the perfect pairing of crisp and salty.

We're halfway through dinner when Wayne puts down his "plain burger, medium, with fries, please," and looks me deep in the eyes.

"How are you?"

"Fine, thanks." On autopilot.

"Not fine, I know you're not fine, I'm sure as hell not fine. How ARE you?"

I put down my "American cheese and bacon, rare, with onion strings, please" and look back at him. I take a swig of my Blue Moon and wipe my mouth.

"I'm okay, really, Wayne. I mean, I miss her, of course, and it's sad. I pick up the phone to call her at least four times a day. But that isn't so unexpected. We had all that time to process, you know? So it's more disconcerting than debilitating. I'm mostly just trying to figure out a little what my life is supposed to be about now."

"Well, apparently your life is about making sure I don't send all Aimee's money to a Nigerian prince." To his credit, Wayne says this with total good humor, and not a hint of resentment.

"Well," I say, trying to stay in the same vein, "you know how tempted you are by those overseas lotteries. And so many of your friends end up stranded in Spain with no money!"

Wayne laughs. I have to begrudgingly give him a little credit; a lot of guys would be enormously pissed about being financially babysat by their wife's best friend. "Well, I get it. I mean, Aimee always said that the only reason the business was worth as much as you got for it was because you guys didn't just plan cool parties; the food was always as extraordinary as the décor and the details. Even more, she said. Because at the end of the day people left your parties raving about the food, not just flowers and table settings. So essentially, I have you to thank as much as Aimee for my lifestyle, and you to answer to as much as her. That's the truth, Ruth."

I suddenly realize that whatever Aimee may have said to me about this weird arrangement, her explanation for Wayne must have been much different. Because of course, Wayne has no idea that I've never really liked him. Oh, boy.

"Well, I think she just wants us both to have time to heal and for us to help each other get through this."

"Exactly."

"How's Noah?" I ask, desperate to change the subject. Wayne's big face lights up.

"He's great! I mean, he's sad too, obviously, but I think it is more that he's worried about me. He calls me every night to check up on me. I went up to Madison yesterday to see his soccer game, and he scored a goal, so that was amazing! He definitely gets his athleticism from his mom." Wayne laughs, his pride obvious and unabashed.

Noah is a sweet kid. Polite, relatively low maintenance, the perfect stepson, Aimee always said. "Well, good for him. When do you get him next?"

"He'll be with Josie and her family for Thanksgiving Day,

but then I get him for the rest of the weekend. Then I probably won't see him till Christmas break."

Every time I hear Noah's mom's name I can't help but think of Josie and the Pussycats. Figures Wayne would knock up someone from a comic book. At least she didn't let him name the kid Luke. A lifetime of "Luke, I am your father," and the bugger would be in a clocktower with a rifle by his fifteenth birthday.

"Well, that will fly by, I'm sure."

"Yeah. I guess. What are you doing?"

"For the holiday? I'll be with Andrea and her family for Thursday, the potluck at the Library on Friday, and probably working at the Library on and off the rest of the weekend to give the team a break."

"That's nice of you. Maybe Noah and I will stop by!"

"Absolutely. That would be great."

"You're doing terrific. See? This isn't so hard."

"I do need to bring up our first money discussion. There's something I want to do."

Oh. No. Too soon. I swallow the mouthful of burger that has suddenly turned to lead on my tongue.

"You know how Aimee donated a bundle of money to U of C a couple of years ago, to fix up the theater and the quad where they do the plays in the summer?"

"Yeah . . ."

"I want to commission a statue of Aimee for that quad. Right now there's just a little plaque on a wall that no one can really see."

"Um, I dunno, Wayne, the university might not . . ."

"They're totally in! I talked to them today. I even get to pick the artist. And they'll have an unveiling ceremony and stuff. We'll have to make an additional donation, and pay for the statue, but I think it will be a great way to honor her, you know?"

"Did Aimee ever say anything about something like this that would make you think she would want it?" Because I know she would be MORTIFIED. Can you imagine? Some hulking bronze statue that undergrads can dress up for holidays, rubbing a boob for luck on their way to their Russian Lit class? Every summer having to either cover it up or incorporate her into the set design for the plays? Ugh.

"Well, not specifically, but she always really liked sculpture. And the guy that did the piece in the living room, the one we bought in Miami? He said he would be available to do it."

GACK! The heinous sculpture of death. I try to stay calm, after all, this may set the tone for the rest of these discussions, and I have eleven months and sixteen days of them to get through.

"Well, how much are you thinking it will cost?" What the hell, if it is just four or five grand, I might as well let him do it.

"The artist said it would be sixty grand for the commission. And then there would be some installation costs, et cetera. Plus the extra donation for the university. Probably one fifteen to one twenty-five all in."

One hundred twenty-five THOUSAND DOLLARS??? Hell. To. The. No. I try to keep my face impassive. "Well, Wayne, I think we want to be very careful. After all, that is a lot of money and the piece will live forever. And I never knew Aimee to want big public acknowledgment of her generosity like that, that's probably why the small plaque. But why don't you have this guy send you a drawing and some specs so that we know what we are really dealing with, and then we can make a final decision."

This will at least put it off a bit. And since Wayne has the attention span of a deranged hummingbird with ADHD, he might forget entirely.

"Yeah, that's a good idea! Don't want to do something that doesn't do her justice. I'll talk to the artist tomorrow."

"Great. How are you doing otherwise?"

"I'm okay. My guys have been really good; they check in on me all the time, stop by so I'm not alone. And Aimee's brothers have been pretty great about calling and stuff. But the house feels really empty. I mean, I was used to being there alone a lot, because of the crazy hours you guys worked, but it's just different now that I know she's not coming home . . ." His voice catches a little. "But I'm hanging in. Day by day, you know. You betcha."

"Good."

"The accountants said that Aimee told them I could sell the house if I was too haunted by her memory or something, as long as the sale covers whatever I buy to replace it. But I dunno, if I move someplace she never was, then it's like I won't feel her there, and I like feeling her there."

I can't imagine Aimee's house with someone else living in it. It's hard enough to imagine it with just Wayne. Aimee built it from the ground up, every detail was hers; no one else could ever fully appreciate the things she agonized over. Another of the places we diverged, I wanted old history and quirky and patina. Aimee liked shiny and new, ultramodern and sleek and flawless. I wanted to stay in Logan Square, quiet and off the beaten path, and she wanted Lincoln Park.

"You shouldn't really make any big decisions about any-thing for a while. I think it must be like AA, you know, they tell you not to make any big life decisions or start any new relationships or anything until you've been sober a year, you know? You just need to take your time and figure out what life looks like for you now that Aimee is gone." This is actu-ally a good tactic, maybe I can convince him that he should spend this next year grieving and not doing much, and he will mostly stay out of my hair and then I can hand him back to the lawyers and they can babysit.

"Yeah. You're probably right."

We finish our burgers, and Wayne heads for the bathroom. I wave for the check when a voice at my elbow startles me. "Well, hello there."

I look up. Lawyer Brian of the Chin. Looking casual in dark jeans and a Chicago Bears logo thermal shirt under a worn brown leather jacket. Five-o'clock shadow on his chiseled mug. Yowza.

"Hi, Brian, how are you? What are you doing here?"

"I'm well, I was having a quick bite with a buddy, but his kid has the flu, so he just left, and I saw you here."

"Small world. I'm having dinner with Wayne."

"How is that for you?" A smile plays around the corner of his mouth.

"Awkward. But okay."

Brian winks at me. Or he has something in his eye. Hard to tell. "Well, good," he says, still smiling.

"And how are you?" This man sort of makes me generi-cally stupid.

"I'm pretty good. Things at work are cranking along. Everyone gearing up for the impending holiday season."

"I would think that your business would be slower around the holidays?"

"It is, but as a result these last weeks before the holidays are a little insane. But you must love this time of year!"

"Why is that?"

"Well, I assume that for years you'd have spent all this time doing everyone else's holiday parties and making their holidays special and important, and now you can just focus on your own."

This is very astute, and thoughtful, and makes me feel a little warm. "True enough." Most people forget that when you are a caterer and event planner, the holidays are awful. Office parties, Christmas fetes, New Year's galas. The cobbler's children have no shoes, and Aimee and I always laughed about the fact that we always showed up to Thanksgivings and Christmases exhausted and brain-dead and never actually hosted our own.

"BRIAN!!! Dude? What are you doing here?" Wayne has returned. He claps Brian on the back with such force that the beer Brian is holding showers me from head to toe.

"Ooops. Sorry Jenny!" Wayne leans forward, but Brian stops him, takes a napkin from the table, and gently wipes my face.

"Sorry about that, we lawyers are notoriously unbalanced, the slightest wind will knock us over." He looks in my eyes in a way that says that he has some opinions of Wayne that aren't dissimilar to mine.

"Good lord," Wayne says. "I'm a disaster, and that isn't even the first time tonight." Nor probably the last, I think. "Hey, Jenny made some amazing dessert back at her place, it's not far, you should come have some with us!"

Yeah. And perhaps I should book a ticket on the *SS Titanic*. Luckily for me, Brian is way too professional to accept that invite.

"Sounds great, if you have enough . . ." Brian says. Crapalicious.

"There's ALWAYS enough when Jenny's cooking." Wayne is effusive. I hate that it makes me sound like I make huge amounts of food, since Brian knows I live alone and can certainly see the current magnitude of my ass.

"Well, if you're sure." Brian looks over at me.

What can I do? At least he'll be a good Wayne buffer. "Of course. The more the merrier."

"Great! Let's go!" Wayne shepherds us out of the bar and into the brisk evening air.

6

The snoring is different. Volnay is often a little bit snuffly when she sleeps, which, I admit spinsterly, is on the second pillow on my king-sized bed, but it sounds weird, somehow harmonic. I roll over to give her a nudge and my arm stops midway.

That is not Volnay.

That is Handsome Lawyer Brian. Rattling with his mouth open and an arm thrown over his head. Volnay, to her credit, is keeping time tunefully, nestled in the crook of that same arm.

The night floods back so fast, my head spins. Brian coming back to my house with Wayne and me, breaking out a bottle of port, decimating the tarts, making meaningful eye contact every time Wayne said something stupid or geeky. Wayne leaving and Brian refilling our glasses. My liquor-loosened tongue giving voice to every Half-Brain Wayne story I can remember, to keep Brian laughing. Thinking that I had never heard him laugh, and wanted to listen to it on endless loop and make it my ringtone.

And then the kissing and the hands in my hair and the dizzying rush of blood to tingly girl parts long unattended. The brazen way I took his hand and took him to bed, relieved that there were still condoms in the nightstand; dusty, but not expired. It would have been, by anyone else's standards, perfectly acceptable sex. Nothing overly acrobatic, no particularly special skills on his part. He has a nice body, not amazing; well-cut suits hide the fact that while his shoulders are broad and hips slim, long hours behind a desk have made him somewhat doughy and undefined. Absolutely average in the package department, nothing weird, nothing notable. A very good kisser, which is always nice.

But you know the old saying, hunger is the best sauce; and I was a very hungry girl. So while back in the day when I actually had sex on a reasonably regular basis it would have been considered a good start but not fireworks, last night it rocked my world. Twice.

I look up at the time, which my bedside clock conveniently projects on the ceiling in a pale blue light. 5:47. I peek over at Handsome Lawyer Brian. He is out for the count.

"Nice work! That's the ho I know and love. And good for you. Mazel tov!"

Great. Aimee approves. I notice she didn't pipe in when I was Wayne bashing for the better part of an hour as part of my seduction.

I slowly begin to slide sideways away from Brian, slipping through sheets and blankets that are tangled and akimbo. I get a leg out, flailing it a little in the brisk air before letting its weight pull me down and I slide out of the bed, landing in a soft lump on the rug. I hold my breath and listen. Brian's snoring is steady. Whew.

I thank God for my architect, who conveniently put the bathroom across the hall from the bedroom instead of directly connected, and gave it, at my request, a fairly soundproof door. I crab-walk naked out of the bedroom and into the bathroom, shutting the door with a barely audible click. I turn on the light and see the hot mess that is me.

My hair is matted on one side of my head, turning me into a startled cockatoo, and it reeks of old beer. I have whisker-burn on my chin, making me look like I dipped the bottom half of my face in cherry Kool-Aid. My mascara has migrated southerly, effectively rendering me half raccoon, and my eyes are pink with lack of sleep and contacts left in, and a little too much booze. There are sheet wrinkle marks on my cheek and chest. My breath, based on how my tongue feels, must be somewhere between dead warthog and sweat sock dipped in blue cheese. I brush my teeth, even using the stupid tongue scraper Jack insisted I buy "for my oral health." I grab one of my MAC makeup remover cloths and get my face clean. A little bit of tinted moisturizer tames some of the violent pink on my chin, and a brush returns my hair to mostly normal; some dry shampoo spray tempers the beer scent. Well, now it is like beer and citrus, but it is all I can do. My cheek still looks like a topographical map of Indonesia, but I'm forty-two; my skin is just not as elastic as it used to be, there isn't much to be done. I pee for about seven minutes, sure that Brian is waking up in the other room, gathering clothes, and sneaking out, and I'm not so sure that isn't a hope and not a worry on my part. Would it be so awful if he just skedaddled? I turn the light back out, and open the door slowly. I listen. Still snoring. Thank goodness.

I tiptoe back into the bedroom, and Volnay raises her head. I shrug, and I swear she raises one eyebrow at me before letting her head return to its place nestled in the crook of Brian's arm.

"Stop staring at me and come back to bed," Brian says without opening his eyes. Busted.

"Don't give yourself that much credit, I was looking at the dog."

"She smells sort of like graham crackers, did you know that?"

"I'm aware." I climb back into the bed, and Brian, eyes still closed, throws his other arm open for me to snuggle into. Boy, I wish he had just snuck out. I'm not good at this part. I don't want the closeness; I don't want to be held. I needed sex, not tenderness, and usually guys are just phoning in this part anyway. But it is a dance as old as time, and at least I know my part. I lay down with my head on Brian's chest, and feel his arm settle around me, hand resting on my hip. He leans down and kisses the top of my head.

"I may have to pass you on to a colleague for your future legal issues," he murmurs into my hair.

"Why is that?"

"It is going to be ethically ambiguous for me to keep you as a client."

"Just because we slept together?" Oh lord.

"No," he says, reaching around and putting a finger under my chin, lifting my head to meet his eyes in the early morning blue light. "Because I intend for us to keep sleeping together. And doing other things together." He leans down and kisses me, and while my head is giving me a million reasons that I should not start actually dating anyone, especially Brian, the rest of me buzzes so loud that I can barely hear my own objections.

You slept with The Chin?!" Andrea says, handing me her plate.

When I finally woke up after Brian left, I needed to dish.

In the past this would have meant calling Aimee. And this morning, in my postcoital haze, I blindly reached for the phone and pressed number one on my speed dial, and the message hit me like a punch in the stomach.

"Hello, darling, whoever you are. This is Aimee from beyond the grave. If you are a loved one, know that I adore you and miss you. If you didn't know I had passed on, I'm sorry for the shock. If you have a business matter, please call my attorney Brian Casswood at 312-555-1755. And if you are a telemarketer, know that in my time here in heaven I have not met ONE person who was a telemarketer in life; so get out before you doom yourself to the fires below for eternity. Cheers!"

It took me five minutes to stop giggling, and then ten to stop sobbing, all the time Volnay stomping around my head on the pillow trying to lick my tears and make me okay. And when I finally got my emotions in check, I picked up the phone again and pressed number two on the speed dial and told Andrea to come over for breakfast on her way to the Library.

"Yep," I say, cutting a large slice of the Dutch Baby pancake and sliding it onto her plate along with two pieces of thick-sliced bacon. Then I serve myself, the fluffy pancake, doused in butter and lemon and confectioners' sugar, the bacon perfectly crispy and salty.

"What happened? 'Cause that is some full-service lawyering; I'm clearly with the wrong firm. Damn this thing is delicious," she says in a rush, forking a large piece of pancake into her mouth and rolling her eyes.

"I know, right?" I take a small bite, letting the flavors mingle, the light pancake, the tart lemon, the sweet sugar.

Perfection. "So you know last night Wayne was coming over for dinner."

"Yeah, how was that?"

"He broke a wineglass all over my mise."

"Not really."

"Really."

"You were doing the cider pork chops?"

"Yup."

"Tragic. So then you had to go out?"

"Orbit Room for the burger king."

She takes a large bite of bacon. "Wayne and his food bullshit."

"Exactly. So we eat, and all of a sudden Brian was there, and Wayne invited him back here for dessert . . ."

"And he thought he'd have you, you little pastry, you."

"Sort of! I'm an insane person. Right? I've lost the plot. Only an insane person would have random sex with their attorney. It's a problem, isn't it? Are you going to have to commit me for my ridiculous insanity?"

"Um, you wanna put some of that pancake in your face so that noise stops coming out of it? First of all, the day ANY single woman DOESN'T have sex with a single man THAT good-looking the moment he asks her, I don't care if he is her lawyer or her freaking PRIEST, that is the day the world stops turning. You are a grown-ass woman, and you are single, and he is single, and there is not a damn thing wrong with it. Unless it was bad. Was it bad? It was bad, wasn't it? Please tell me it wasn't bad. Is he really small? Teeny weenie? Cocktail frank? Hooks to the left?"

I nearly spit my coffee at her I'm laughing so hard. "Relax. He was fine. Perfectly adequate in every way. And while he wasn't a frankwurst, he was a solid five to the pound." Andrea always uses Vienna Beef hot dog designations to stand in for penises. Aimee and I adopted it immediately. Thank god they have every size in their arsenal, from the cocktail frank up to the full-pound Homewrecker.

"That is enough real estate for anyone." Andrea nods. "So what? Why are you all crazy pants? Give me more of that pancake." She waves her plate at me.

"Okay, here's the thing. He's my LAWYER. If I'd met him randomly, one-night stand, hookup after a party, whatever. I'm a big girl. But he works for me. I pay him. A LOT. And he knows all my personal financial business and stuff, and it's sort of like, why now? You know? I mean, look at him, he could have ANYONE. And he has never once in five years ever expressed the least bit of interest. So it just seems weird, like, does he think I'm vulnerable now because Aimee is gone and he can just . . . what?"

"I'm sorry, have you seen my friend Jenna, because I'm pretty sure she was around here somewhere." She slips Volnay a small piece of bacon under the table, despite my raised eyebrow. "First of all, who the hell cares what HIS motives are. YOU are smart and not exactly a pushover. Does it matter if somehow he thinks he can make you his girlfriend and you'll buy him shiny objects with all your millions? It only matters if you are suddenly feeling like you want to put him in your will or hand him the keys to his new birthday Bentley. I mean, are you really in the market for a boyfriend right now, or are you just getting a little TLC at a tough time?"

"No, I'm probably not really thinking about any sort of long-term relationship."

"Then go on with your badass self! Hit it again! Sleep with that man until he bores you or it gets strange or he annoys you and then stop sleeping with him. If he gets weird, fire him and get a new lawyer; they are easy to come by in this town, if you hadn't noticed."

"Seriously. Just . . ."

"Just don't even think about it."

"Wow. That never even occurred to me."

"That's why you have me."

"And that's why you get the last piece of bacon."

"You know I'm eating that."

"I know."

"Jenna, in all seriousness, unless you don't like him or didn't like the sex or whatever, don't freak about this. I think it's a good thing."

"You do?"

"I do. It's not just that it's been a few weeks since Aimee died, it's been three years of stress and sadness and two years since Jack, and I know there hasn't been anyone since him, and I just think it is time for your life to be about your life, because the last three years of your life have been about Aimee's death."

"That's not fair."

"No, honey, it really isn't. But it's true. Ever since the diagnosis it was about preventing Aimee's death. And then the ultimate gift you gave her to try and make that happen lost you a fiancé. Granted, better to know he was that guy before you married him, but still a not insignificant loss, and one you didn't have time to deal with because it was about Aimee's recovery. And then her not recovery. And then the inevitable end. This is the first thing I have seen you do just for yourself in over three years, and I want you to revel in it and not question it and just have some damn fun."

"Not that you've thought about it at all."

"Nope. I love you, you know."

"I know."

"And Jen?"

"Yeah?"

"Thanks for calling me. You know you can do that anytime day or night, right?"

"I do."

I walk her to the door and head back to the kitchen to clean up. And to eat the last piece of bacon that I held back in the oven for myself. Because a good hostess will always let her guest have the last piece of bacon on the platter.

But a smart hostess will make sure that there is another last piece that somehow doesn't make it on the platter.

"You learned that from me."

You bet your ass I did.

7

And how did it make you feel, to hear that he wanted to pursue a relationship?" Nancy asks, all judgment and opinion carefully stripped from her voice.

"Annoyed. Worried. Confused."

"I see. Not at all happy or excited." It's a statement more than a question.

"Look, I know it should have made me all wiggly and giddy and wanting to call all my girlfriends and summon them to cocktails to dissect it or something."

"Sex and the City Syndrome," Nancy says, almost parenthetically. But it makes me laugh.

"Exactly!"

"But you did call Andrea."

"Yeah, but that was more because hearing that message on Aimee's voice mail freaked me out, and the Brian thing seemed like a better excuse to ask her to come over than I accidentally called Aimee and she answered and I lost my shit."

"I see. But her thoughts about Brian didn't reassure you."

"Not really. I mean, I keep thinking the whole thing over. I had a long night. It's exhausting trying to stay upbeat when hanging out with Wayne. I had some drinks to numb it a little, and a good-looking guy kissed me. I'm single, and it had been a very long time since I had sex, and I went to bed with him. All of that was fine. It didn't need to become a whole, you know, *thing*. I didn't need him to become my boyfriend or something. And he probably just said it because he wanted me to feel okay about it, like a grown woman doesn't get the whole one-night-stand thing."

"What about the possibility that he just likes you and is attracted to you and wants to spend time with you, get to know you."

That idea just floats in the room. Because not for one minute did it ever occur to me.

The pause is not lost on Nancy. "Jenna, you've said that you find this man attractive. That you have always thought him smart and competent. That last night you found him to be charming and funny, and you enjoyed his company, especially since he shares your opinions of Wayne, which made him feel like an ally. And you enjoyed your intimate time with him. Why is that not someone you think might be worth dating? He didn't propose marriage, he asked you to have dinner with him."

I have to think about this. "I haven't dated anyone since Jack."

"Why do you suppose that is?"

"Aimee was sick."

"Aimee was pretty good for almost a whole year, by your account, and over two years is a very long time."

"I just wasn't up for it. The breakup with Jack was difficult. I wasn't ready. My focus was elsewhere. Aimee was sick. I know that isn't an excuse, but it is what it is. I'm in my forties, I don't want kids, I have plenty of money . . ."

"So for you, a man in your life needs to be about either fathering children or supporting you financially." Again, a statement, not a question, and devoid of editorializing.

"I don't know. Maybe."

"What about love and support and companionship."

"I have . . ." Crap.

"You had Aimee for that," she finishes for me.

"Guess I'm pretty fucked up, huh?" I laugh.

"You're human. And I think we are getting at some of the root of your grieving, the magnitude of your loss. You don't have to go out with Brian if you don't want to. But I want you to make that decision for yourself thoughtfully. Would it be so bad to just have dinner with him and see how you feel, about him, about you with him."

"Maybe not." I do hate that she keeps making points about the "magnitude of my loss." It feels a little judgey, like I should be in bed twenty hours a day staring at Aimee's picture and wailing.

"Oh come off it. No one thinks that. Besides, being strong for everyone is what you do. What you always did. You wouldn't have the first clue how to fall apart."

Nancy breaks through Aimee's lecture. "This seems like a good place to stop. I'll see you next week."

"Okay. Thanks."

"Jenna, if you don't like him or don't think you could like him, there is no shame in a grown single woman getting her physical needs addressed and leaving it at that. Your friend Andrea is right on the money about that. But be sure that is all you wanted, all you needed, before you completely dismiss the idea out of hand."

"Okay. I will."

I head home, determined to take Volnay for a long walk and to stop by the Library. But the long day, the lack of sleep, and the slight hangover interfere. I sit down on the couch for just a moment, and fall into the sleep of the dead. When the doorbell wakes me, the sky is already just starting to darken.

I drag myself up off the couch and head for the door. Peeking through the window, I see a short man nearly obscured by a large floral arrangement. Maybe this Brian thing isn't so bad . . .

"Hi, I'm from Fleur. Delivery for Jenna Stewart?"

"That's me." I sign the clipboard and receive the flowers, a gorgeous antique silver champagne bucket filled with deep pink roses, accented with pink and white sweet peas, Mexican tuberoses, and pink calla lilies. Not a stargazer in the bunch.

I stick my nose in the fragrant blooms, and smile to myself. Maybe Nancy is right. Maybe I do need to give Brian a chance. Last night was fun, before I got all in my head about it. And this morning was kind of nice, if slightly awkward. I just need to get out of my dark thoughts and go with the flow. He is a smart, kind, very attractive man, and I'm frankly shocked he is remotely interested in me. But so what? Why shouldn't I just let it go and see what happens? It doesn't have to be a big deal; I could just date him and see how it goes. Andrea's right, he can't make me be more involved than I want to be, I should just go with the flipping flow. Resigned, I pluck the card from the bouquet, and open the little envelope. Wayne's weirdly tiny handwriting stares back at me.

Hey Jenny, just wanted to say sorry for all the klutziness and thanks for a great night. It was really nice to be with you and talk. I'll call you later. Wayne.

Oy.

"I did give him SOME training, you know."

"Seriously, Aimee. Not fair."

"Hey. That man just spent about a quarter of his monthly allowance to apologize and do something to make you smile. And you and I never subscribed to the whole Rules *bullshit about sex and flowers anyway."*

"I know."

Volnay looks up at me from the couch, cocking her head to the side, wondering what I am doing speaking to a bunch of flowers. I sort of wonder the same thing. I pick up my phone.

"A long time ago in a galaxy far, far away, I stepped away from my phone . . . so leave me a message!" Good grief, he doesn't make it easy.

"Hey Wayne, it's Jenna. I just wanted to say thanks for the lovely flowers; it was very thoughtful and totally unnecessary. But it was nice to, um, see you last night, and we'll have to do it again soon. Take care."

I pause, and then dial a different number.

"Brian Casswood."

"Hi, Brian."

"Hello there." I can hear the smile in his voice. "Please don't say you're calling to cancel on me . . ."

"Nope, just wanted to confirm our timing." Deep breath, Jenna, it's just dinner.

"I'll pick you up at seven thirty, does that work?"

"Perfect. I'll see you in a bit."

"Looking forward to it."

"Me too." And I almost am. I replace the phone and look at the dog. "C'mon girly girl. Let's take a quick walk and then figure out what on earth I am going to wear on my date."

I manage to take a power nap, shower, make up, and then I decide on an olive green dress that Aimee always said made my eyes the most extraordinary color. Brian is exactly on time, looking amazing in dark jeans, a V-neck sweater in heathered charcoal, with a white T-shirt underneath, a perfectly broken-in leather blazer. We head to Mythos, one of my favorite places, a BYOB Greek joint with amazing food.

Brian opens the first of the two bottles of rosé he brought, and once we decide to just order a meal of all appetizers and do a small-plates dinner instead of entrees, I find that the conversation is much less stilted than it was yesterday.

"So Aimee comes back from her spa afternoon and finds Wayne sitting in the middle of their huge suite on the floor . . . playing with Legos."

"Wait, how old is this guy?"

"FORTY-FOUR!!! Of course, he was only thirty-nine at the time . . ." I'm going to have to figure out how they make these featherlight zucchini fritters. I wonder if they whip the egg whites?

"Seriously," Brian says, refilling my wineglass, and placing another piece of house-made grilled loukaniko sausage on my plate. "He's in Vegas, he has an afternoon to himself, and instead of hanging by the pool, or going to sit in the sports book, or hitting the tables . . ."

"He walked the strip till he found a toy store, bought himself some Star Wars Lego kits, and spread them out on the floor in a million tiny pieces."

"I gotta ask, what the heck did she see in him? I mean, I don't want to speak ill, but she always seemed so together and she was certainly gorgeous and smart, I just assumed she would have been with some elegant intellectual architect or venture capitalist or think-tank guy or something."

"I know. I sort of don't really know how it happened. She met him at a holiday party we did for a company he worked for. I was in the kitchen, so I missed the whole thing. When the party was over, Wayne saw her standing outside when he drove by, and he offered her a ride. They ended up going out for a drink and then they were just sort of inseparable."

"And insufferable," Brian pipes in around a mouthful of chewy bread spread with tzatziki.

"Yeah, that too."

"Surely you have something else you can talk about besides Wayne. You are starting to go a little mean girl."

My hand, halfway to the calamari, stops in midair. Damn you, Aimee. I realize that now that the floodgates have opened, between Nancy and Brian, eight years of pent-up complaining and poking fun have all come right to the surface and I'm very much in danger of becoming both boring and cruel. I don't want to fall into that trap.

"So, enough about Wayne, what's your story?" I ask.

"Um, what do you want to know?"

"I don't know, you said last night you grew up out east, came here for school and liked it. Been with the firm since an internship in law school. But what about personal life? Who are you, what do you like, what do you do?"

"Ha. So, the whole thing, huh?" He smiles, one dimple popping out charmingly. "Okay, let's see. I was married once, for seven years. Law school romance, didn't survive our mutual ambition as associates. I bought my condo when I made partner, South Loop, love the area."

He gestures to the last piece of house-made grilled loukaniko sausage, and I nod to let him know he can have it. He spears it with his fork and continues.

"I genuinely like my work, so I probably let it consume me more than I should. I like to ski and scuba, so I tend to split my vacations between Colorado and the Caribbean. I collect contemporary photography. Mostly interested in food and wine as a spectator, but always thought it would be fun to actually learn how to cook. Know anyone that would like to teach me?"

"I might be able to put you in touch with someone."

"What about you? What is your story? Quid pro quo."

"Not much to tell that you don't know, I'm pretty sure." It is a little weird that Brian already knows so much about my financial situation, my work history. It's also refreshing that he is delighted to talk shit about Wayne and reference Aimee, but hasn't asked me how I am "doing."

"Well, I don't know, how is it possible you are single?"

Do men truly have no idea how horrific a question that is? I know you think it makes you sound complimentary, like how did you get so lucky to catch me between suitors, but really? To women it just sounds like you are asking what sort of scary undateable shit we are hiding from you. What shall we say at this juncture? I'm emotionally unavailable? I bite my toenails? I'm a secret Satan worshipper who dabbles in blood sport? I'm a lousy lay? We say the stuff we have learned to say. Men are intimidated by my brains/financial success. I'm married to my work. I don't want kids. I just haven't found the right match, and I don't want to settle.

We don't say the stuff we fear is true, which is that there just isn't a right match out there for us. That we aren't young enough, pretty enough, thin enough, sexy enough. That we are too broken. That we blithely discarded half a dozen men in our youth that might indeed have been The One if we weren't so focused on our careers, or if we hadn't been so glib or superficial about what was important.

Instead I shrug and go with as much honesty as I can muster. "I was engaged a couple of years ago, but Aimee got sick, and when I decided to give her part of my liver, I didn't talk with him about it; I just booked the surgery and told him later when it was already decided. And he said that he couldn't spend his whole life competing with Aimee, and I realized he was a selfish douchewaffle, so we broke off the engagement."

He nods. "And now?"

Oy. Isn't it a little soon for this kind of deep? Technically we are on our first date.

"I know, how about do what you NEVER do with guys and just go for total honesty. No glossing over, no adjusting who you are to fit what you think they want you to be, just be all 'take it or leave it this is who I am' for a change."

Why the hell not?

"Brian, I can't really answer that. I like you, I do. I've never thought about you or us with any romantic potential, which doesn't mean it isn't there, but this is very unexpected. So I guess all I can say is that I'm here, and I'm having a nice time, and I hope that we can just be a little loose and let it be whatever it is going to be without thinking too much."

"I get it. And I can do that."

My shoulders relax. He raises his wineglass to me and I clink it with my own. And then I smile at him. "You can still spend the night tonight if you want."

He grins with the perfect amount of sparkle in his eye.

"You betcha."

8

The alarm goes off, and I smack it to make the ringing stop. But it doesn't. I open one eye and look at the clock. 7:06. I haven't set an alarm in ages, and today is no different. Volnay lifts her head from the pillow and begins a low growl. I realize the sound isn't my alarm, it's the doorbell. Ping-ponging insistently.

At seven o'fucking clock in the morning.

I jump up and grab my robe; a lovely featherlight knitted gray cashmere beauty Aimee gave me as my recovery present when we had our surgery. Aimee was a big believer in cashmere. Tying it at my waist, I slide into my slippers, and Volnay uses her little staircase to gingerly get down from the bed. I yell down the stairs.

"I'M. COMING." This had better be good.

Volnay and I head down, and I peek through the window. Sweet mother of crap. Wayne.

"Deep breath, sleepyhead, if he's here at this hour it is probably important. And lord knows you can take a nap when he leaves with your big day full of nothing planned."

I really hate you right now, Aimee.

"I know. But you hate everyone at seven in the morning; I don't take it personally."

I open the door.

"Jenny! I brought you breakfast!" He holds out a bag from Dunkin' Donuts and a large cup of something that smells like a Yankee Candle. "Donuts and a Pumpkin Spice Latte!"

I throw up a little in my mouth. I want coffee to taste of coffee. Maybe a little cream and sugar. I do not want coffee that tastes of potpourri or fruit or nuts or like licking the bottom of my spice drawer. And while I should not be eating donuts to begin with, I REALLY don't want to waste precious donut-related calories on Dunkin'. If I want to be bad, I'll head to the Doughnut Vault for a pistachio or coconut old fashioned, or maybe grab a Chocolate Bacon from Fritz Bakery for a real treat. Wayne thrusts the bag and cup at me, and I take them before I end up wearing them.

"Thanks, Wayne, that's very sweet." He follows me in, scooping up Volnay and whispering sweet nonsense at her in a guttural language. "Are you speaking to my dachshund in her native German?"

"Nope, Huttese," Wayne says.

I look at him, too early for this to register.

"Like Jabba the Hutt," he explains further.

"Don't throw the shitty coffee at him."

Sigh. "I don't know that she speaks Huttese."

Wayne laughs, a sort of girlish giggle that belies his bulk. "I know, it's kinda stupid, but for some reason most dogs seem to like it."

Volnay does seem to be happy as a clam, snuggling under Wayne's chin. *"Maybe she speaks Huttese."*

Oh, you need to shut up right now.

"Sorry."

"Come on." I head for the kitchen, trying to think of a graceful way to dump the coffee.

Wayne follows me, and settles on the little love seat in the window that overlooks my backyard. I reach into the bag and grab the donut. Strawberry glazed. Not even going to get a chocolate fix today. I put it on a plate, and pick at it a bit. Sweet on sweet, slightly stale, and yet, weirdly comforting, everyone's first donuts. I leave the offending latte on the counter, exuding a scent of burnt coffee and pumpkin pie and artificial cinnamon flavoring.

"So, Wayne, were you just in the neighborhood?" Haunting me?

"Nope, but I woke up early with the most amazing idea and I just couldn't wait to tell you about it!"

Super. I take another piece of the donut. The glaze is gritty in my unbrushed teeth.

"What sort of idea?"

"New business."

"Hear him out. Let him explain."

You are so lucky you are dead.

"Yeah, a real lottery winner."

"That is exciting, but I thought you were taking a break from working."

"Well, I was, and it was good when Aimee was still with us, you know, I could manage the house and all the life maintenance stuff, be the house husband and the nurse, drive up to see Noah, but with Aimee gone . . ." He trails off, and despite the shitty pastry in my mouth, and the early hour, I feel for him.

Peerless has essentially asked nothing of me in my role as consultant for the last six months since Aimee took her turn for the finish line, and as there are only two annual meetings of the board, my "job" is essentially nonexistent. Andrea and the team have everything cranking along over at the Library, and while I'm better about stopping by, my days are sort of filled with futzing. Little projects I invent for myself. Puttering in the back garden. Organizing closets and drawers and cabinets. Polishing silver and entering piles of the old family recipes into the computer. Sharpening my knives by hand, which I frankly haven't done since culinary school. Long walks with the dog. Dinners and sex with Brian once or twice a week, still casual and nice but undefined. He was semiserious about wanting to learn to cook, so we mostly stay in and make something simple together and then go to bed. I get the unmoored part. The dichotomy of a desire to have something to do to keep you busy and not thinking too much, and a total lack of energy to figure out what that should be. Except Wayne seems to have plenty of energy.

"So, you're thinking about going back to work?" If he was making his own money he might not need to come see me as often; that could be good.

"Thinking about starting a business."

This cannot be good.

"What sort of business?"

Wayne grins as if he is about to tell me his plans for the next Apple or Facebook. "Wax and Lube."

"A car wash?"

"Better. A car wash, quick oil change, and spa."

"Car spa?" Actually not a terrible idea if the neighborhood is right, Simon's detailing place does pretty well in Lincoln Park, and there are a couple up-and-coming neighborhoods that might be ready for that.

"No, silly, girl spa." Wayne drops Volnay on the floor, and she schlumps down on top of his foot. Et tu?

"Girl spa."

"Yeah. See, my buddy Georgie was over last night playing Gran Turismo 6, and so we were talking about cars and stuff and how his business partner's wife was always complaining because it takes so long to get an oil change and a car wash and you have to sit there. And you know, those are like the only thing that most women sort of have to do for the family cars while guys are at work and stuff." Of course, here in 1954.

"You and I know plenty of stay-at-home moms and work-at-home women who end up taking on the bulk of that sort of stuff for the family."

I'm not speaking to you right now.

"Fine, just hear him out."

"Okay, so they are sort of time sucks, because you have to just sit there and wait for your car." I'm really trying to get through the sleep haze to figure out his thought process.

Wayne lights up like a Christmas tree. "Exactly! So then I thought about all the stuff women would like to do, instead of just sitting and waiting, you know, and it came to me. Wax and Lube. A play on words. Come in for an oil change and get your personal waxing done at the same time. We could have all sorts of packages, you know? Car detailing with a lip and eyebrow wax. Full oil change with a Brazilian . . ."

"Okay, yeah, he's lost the plot."

You think?

"Um, Wayne, you are thinking that a woman would bring her car in for service and then get waxed while she waits?"

"EXACTLY! Isn't that a great idea? I mean, wouldn't you love to come out after your waxing and have a nice clean car?"

Sweet Mother McCreary. I put on my most impassive face, as if I am not being presented with the world's most inane idea. "Wayne, spas and salons are very personal things. It can take a woman years to find the aesthetician she trusts. Those are not a walk-in-off-the-street impulse thing. And the whole point of a spa is that it is a relaxing, soothing environment. That doesn't smell of motor oil."

His face falls. "Oh. I just thought, two birds . . ." Poor guy, I do feel badly for him. And then I remember that he felt the need to wake me up at seven in the morning, and I feel more badly for me. A year of this is going to be a huge pain in the keester.

"Jesus, Jenna. He didn't shit in your bed. He woke you up to share an idea that he thought was great. Because usually he would roll over and tell me and I would listen and we would talk about it and I would gently tell him it wasn't such a great idea, and then make him feel better with a quickie."

Seriously? Are you suggesting I give him a little morning delight on your behalf?

"I'm suggesting, Mrs. Snarky Pants, that he does not have his wife to tell his brilliant ideas to anymore, all he has is you."

Okay. Dredge up supportive Jenna.

"Wayne, it isn't that a twofer is a bad idea, actually, those kind of things can be great. I just think this is the wrong combo. But it's exciting that you're thinking about what you want to do; I think that's terrific. Maybe you might not want to start as big as launching your own business, maybe just getting a regular job?" Which would be AWESOME. Forty hours a week of Wayne being someone else's problem, and a steady income that wouldn't require my oversight.

His whole face falls, and I can see that now I've actually hurt his feelings. "Could you go back to a normal job for someone else now, after where you have been?"

"Probably not, you're right. I didn't mean . . ." Great, now I'm a total asshole.

His smile returns, king of the bounceback. "I know you didn't! No worries. I have a dozen ideas a week, eventually one of them will be the right one." A hundred monkeys at typewriters. I give him points though, he does snap out of things quickly.

"Of course you will." And I will have to hear every last ridonculous one of them. Whee.

"That's the truth, Ruth! So, what's on your agenda for the day?"

"Um, have to get dressed and take the dog for a walk, head over to the Library to check in, and do some prep for the stuff I'm bringing to Thanksgiving this week."

"Cool. You need any help?"

ACK! I can just see him chopping off his fingertips on the mandolin, shattering my vintage Emile Henry roasting pans, and blowing us both sky-high with the gas stove. "I'm good, Wayne, thanks for the offer. I really appreciate that. Are you going to Indiana for Thursday?"

"Yep. Big bash over at the Brands'. Then I go pick Noah up Friday morning."

"Tell everyone I send my love and that I will see them at Christmas."

"Of course. Maybe I can bring Noah by Friday afternoon or something?"

"I'd love to see him. We're decorating the Library that day, just bring him there, he can help with the tree. And thanks for the breakfast."

"You betcha! I'll talk to you later, Jenny." He kisses me awkwardly on my temple, and I walk him to the door. Then

I go back to the kitchen to dump the coffee and the rest of the donut, and head back upstairs to bed, hoping I can pretend it was just a bad dream.

Except I can't fall back to sleep. I check the clock. 7:55. Hmmm. I reach for the phone.

"Good morning, beautiful." I do have to say, I'm getting more comfortable with the fact that Brian genuinely likes me, despite being the type of guy who never paid the slightest bit of attention to me historically. Nancy keeps reminding me that he is actually an individual person and not personally representative of every classically handsome boy who ever ignored me in high school and college. And after.

"Good morning. What are you doing?"

"I'm just getting ready to go to work. What are you doing?"

"Up early, thought you might want to stop by on your way to the office. Breakfast meeting with a client?"

Brian chuckles. "I don't have anything horribly pressing this morning. On my way."

I leap back out of bed and jump into the shower for a quick rinse off, brush my teeth, brush my hair out, change out of the oversized men's V-neck white T-shirt I usually sleep in, and into a cute bra and one of the endless sets of lounging pajamas Aimee was forever giving me.

"I love a lounging pajama."

You also love a marabou mule slipper and a satin robe with a train.

"It is elegant."

It is insane.

"It is sophisticated."

Sure, if you're Nora Charles. It isn't 1940.

"Yeah, but look at yourself."

I look in the mirror. The silk and cashmere blend fabric has just the right amount of drape to conceal the lumpier parts of me without clinging, but enough weight to seem more substantial than sleepwear. The color is somewhere halfway between cream and ballerina pink, a color I would never pick, but is a lovely counterpoint to my pale skin and dark hair. All in all, I look fairly adorable for this hour, certainly good enough to warrant a little morning attention.

"Told you so."

Yeah, yeah.

"Didn't I give you a matching robe for that?"

Don't push it.

"I'm just saying."

Fine. I grab the matching robe. It has a wide band of gathered elastic in the back that hits right above my tush, giving me shape, even though the robe isn't tied. Made of the same fabric as the pajamas, it doesn't add bulk the way most robes do, but instead almost serves as the same elegant look a long trench provides.

"HA!"

You are such a bad gloater.

"Too bad. You look utterly shaggable."

Well I hope so, since I'm pretty sure Brian doesn't think he is coming over for an actual meeting.

"My work here is done. Go forth and lay the lawyer. Get some action from the attorney. Jump the jurist. Bang the barrister. Climb the counselor. Solicit the solicitor . . ."

I'm laughing so hard; tears are streaming down my face.

Volnay is looking at me like I have gone completely off my nut. Which I suppose I probably have, since the imaginary voice of my dead bestie is making me giggle myself apoplectic.

Cut it OUT!

Lucky for me, the doorbell rings before the Voix goes off on another tangent.

I pop downstairs and open the door. Brian is standing there with a grin on his face, two steaming cups from New Wave Coffee in a cardboard carrier, and a bag in the other. I don't smell anything that remotely makes me think of air freshener. He leans in and kisses me softly.

"Hello there."

"Hello yourself." I relieve him of his burdens, and can tell by the scent that the bag is full of croissants from La Boulangerie. I stand aside so that he can come in. He drops his briefcase on the floor by the door, hangs his black wool overcoat and gray scarf on the coatrack, then turns to me.

"You look awfully delicious this morning."

"Thank you."

"You're welcome."

Shut up.

"Bitter, party of one."

"There is something a little fabulously glamorous about you today." He smirks at me, then steps forward and slides an arm around my waist, and begins to waltz me around, my hands occupied with coffee and pastries, while he whirls me with firm control around my living room.

"Dancing with Darrow. Monkeying with Matlock. Partying with Perry Mason. Boogieing with Brandeis."

This last one makes me snort laugh, and Brian looks down at me, giggling like an idiot in his arms.

"Well now, I do love to see you laughing. I like that I can entertain you." He leans down and kisses me deeply, so proud of his ability to amuse me. And I place the coffee and croissants on the console table at the foot of the stairs, and take his hand, leading him upstairs where he can indeed entertain me. Which he does. And blissfully, the Voix does not provide color commentary.

While he's in the shower, I head back downstairs to reheat the coffee and pop the croissants in the oven to heat up a little, grabbing butter and homemade apricot jam out of the fridge.

Brian comes into the kitchen, pink cheeked and sloe-eyed, coat and tie over one arm, crisp white shirt unbuttoned at the neck.

I hand him his coffee, and gesture to the pastries and condiments.

"You are going to have to take the rest of these croissants to work with you, I cannot be trusted alone in the house with a half-dozen buttery, crispy pillows of deliciousness."

"Well, I wouldn't have brought so many, but that place will only sell them if you buy eight or more!"

I laugh. A Logan Square conundrum. "I know. One of the neighborhood quirks."

"You hipsters with your crazy convolutions."

I laugh. The transitional predominantly Latino neighborhood I moved into almost fifteen years ago has indeed become hipster central. Full of young men in skinny jeans and ironic T-shirts and scraggly facial hair, and young women in cotton sundresses with motorcycle boots, all blithely riding about on their vintage Schwinns with earbuds in, making motorists stabby.

"What can I say. We have our own ways."

"Indeed you do. I hate to um, eat and run . . ." He blushes a bit, in light of the recent activities. It suits him.

"I know, you have very important legal things to attend to."

"That I do."

"Well, at least one of them won't be helping Wayne with his new business."

"This should be nutrient rich."

I fill Brian in on the whole Wax and Lube proposal while he finishes the last of his coffee and pops the final morsel of croissant in his mouth.

"Did he really say an oil change slash Brazilian package?"

"Yep."

Brian stands up, wipes his mouth, and brushes a stray couple of crumbs off his shirt before coming over to kiss me, tasting of coffee and apricots.

"Well, it is just another ten and a half months."

"That it is. I do feel a little badly for him, though. He's pretty lost and doesn't have much of anyone to turn to for this stuff."

"He's an overgrown man-child who needs to get his shit together. I get that he is grieving, but dumb ideas are not exactly in any five stages I've ever read about. I don't think I am ever going to understand what Aimee saw in that guy." Brian slides into his jacket, and drapes his tie around his neck.

His statement makes me feel weird in the pit of my stomach. But I ignore it, and walk with him to the door.

"Thanks for the visit and breakfast," I say as he puts on his coat and grabs his briefcase.

"Thanks for calling. A lovely surprise. We still on for the Bears game Sunday?"

We both have holiday-related plans for the rest of the week, but Brian snagged two seats for the game from the firm's season tickets and invited me to join him.

"You bet. I have all my layers ready, and double hand and foot warmers. I warn you, I'm a Chicago girl, and a die-hard fan. Your date is not going to be all cute and perky in a little jacket and high-heeled boots, she is going to look like a navy and orange Stay Puft Marshmallow woman with Franken-stein feet."

"I'll look forward to that. And trust me, I will take Stay Puft and not bitching about being cold, over a fashion plate who begs me to leave at halftime any day." Something tells me this is a very specific reference, but I'm going to ignore that.

"Good."

"I'll call you later to check in."

"I'll be here."

Brian leans in and kisses me softly. "Good-bye sweet girls." He leans down and gives Volnay a quick head rub.

"Good-bye."

I watch him head down my front stoop before closing the door.

"You know NayNay? I do believe that now, I could actually do with a little nap before we have to do all this cooking." She nods up at me seriously, and we pad up the stairs together for a short rest before the work begins.

9

Andrea is coming to pick me up in about thirty minutes to head to her folks' house for Thanksgiving. I've got buttery yeast rolls from Aimee's mom's old family recipe, my cranberry sauce with port and dried cherries, and a batch of spicy molasses cookies sandwiched with vanilla mascarpone frosting. I also have the makings for fried shisito peppers, which I will make there. Andrea's mom, Jasmin, is making turkey and ham, and braised broccoli and an apple pie, Andrea is doing a potato and celery root mash and a hilarious Jell-O mold that contains orange sherbet and canned mandarin oranges and mini marshmallows, and her dad, Gene, is making his mother's candied yams and sausage corn bread stuffing. Benji is cooking and serving most of the day at the group home where he grew up, and will come join us for dessert, bringing his chocolate pecan pie with bourbon whipped cream.

Jasmin and Gene always have a great event, with a few orphans they collect, usually exhausted and grateful residents from Northwestern Hospital where they both work, Jasmin in orthopedics and Gene in cardiothoracic surgery. There is football on the TV, all of us rooting against the Lions, classical guitar music on in the dining room, a warm and welcoming buzz of conversation, and the noise of a busy kitchen.

My phone rings and I reach for it, just as I put the last container of cookies into the insulated bag that holds all my offerings. Mom.

"Happy Thanksgiving!"

"Hello sweetheart. Happy Thanksgiving. How are you doing?" Oy vey. I can hear the freaking head tilt over the phone.

"I'm fine Mom, really." Subject change, please. "How are you and Dad?"

"You know, sitting up and taking nourishment." She always laughs off their advancing years, but the fact is, they are both in their eighties and neither of them is in particularly terrific shape. Dad has already had one open-heart surgery and a pacemaker, and Mom has high cholesterol and is in need of a double knee replacement, but she won't admit it. They live in a small ranch house in Berkeley, and Dad spends most of his time gardening, and Mom does what all women of her age seem to do, lunches and good works and cards. She is a serious bridge player and apparently something of a ter-ror on the northern California circuit. "We are going to our friends the Osbornes for the day."

"That sounds like fun."

"That is a nightmare, they have eleven grandchildren under the age of nine. Everything will be sticky."

I laugh. My friend Alana always said she didn't want kids because they were sticky, and Aimee and I co-opted the phrase. It was more complicated than that for both of us, but at the end of the day, the fact that we both were childless by choice was a part of the strength of our bond. Especially as we got older and all of our friends started becoming parents and speaking that language that you vaguely recognize as English, but still feels like you need subtitles. Wiggleworms and *Back-yardigans* and Graco and Britax and attachment parenting and helicoptering, and Aimee and I would smile and nod and look at pictures and go to showers and then head somewhere just the two of us and have a cocktail and toast the fact that we were in the no-kid thing together.

"Well, at least they're good cooks." Mr. Osborne is a whiz with the Big Green Egg smoker, and Mrs. Osborne was raised in Kentucky, and between them they can knock out a heck of a meal. We had dinner there the last time I visited my folks, and it was spectacular. He did a slow cooked brisket that was meltingly tender, and I'm still trying to figure out her recipe for cauliflower gratin.

"Why do you think we put up with all those little fingers in the appetizers? Dinner will be spectacular, and then all the kids go home to go to sleep and Daddy and I help clean up and drink a good bottle of Madeira with them."

"Sounds like you will have a good time."

"As will you."

"Is Daddy around?"

"He ran to the store to get me some lemons."

"Lemon cream pie?" My mom hates most pie, especially the holy trinity of Thanksgiving pies, pumpkin, apple, and pecan. But she makes a killer lemon cream, which is actually one of my favorite things to eat on Thanksgiving, a welcome bit of tart and bright after so much richness.

"Of course. So, what are you doing with your time these days?"

My parents are very confused about my work life, or lack thereof. I think they believe I should either still be working or doing some sort of major volunteering or something. And they aren't entirely wrong, which of course puts an undertone of disapproval on their part and guilt on mine into all of our conversations.

"You know, just doing all the stuff I have to do."

"Okay." She knows I'm deflecting. "I'm sure you know what is best for you, sweetie." Which means that I have no idea what is best for me, but she doesn't want to argue about it today.

"I do, Mom." Which means I probably don't, but the one thing we agree on is that neither of us really wants to go into more detail.

"We are both so sorry for what you are going through, and we love you very much, and we are here if you need us."

"I know, Mom. Thank you."

"Love you to the moon."

"And back again." I'll make a point to call when I get home tonight so I can talk to my dad. The older they get, the more the age issue complicates our relationship. By the time I was born, they were both forty. I never had young parents. I never had parents like Andrea who were cool and hip and even though they are older, don't feel fuddy-duddy. The four-decade gap between my folks and me is a chasm, and since they live so far away and I only see them once or twice a year, it doesn't ever seem worth it to be terribly confessional about my life with them. We keep things simple and surface. But I do sometimes wish that they were younger, more able to connect with me. I adore them and we have a great time when we are together, but it isn't as intimate as it might be if they had had me in their twenties or thirties.

I feed Volnay and finish getting my stuff together. Brian texts me that he'll be insane all day, but wishes me a Happy Turkey, and says he'll call tomorrow. It still feels a little weird with him, and I'm realizing that this is the first time I'm dating someone new since we sold the company, and for the first time in my life, I am wondering if the person I'm dating might have ulterior motives. Not that I really think Brian would be with me because of the money, but it still feels weird how much he knows about my personal finances.

"Who cares if he wants you for your money, you aren't going to marry him; as long as he also seems to want you for sex, enjoy! Isn't landing hot partners supposed to be one of the perks of money? Pretend you are an old man, and you'll be fine."

The Voix finishes her speech just as the bell rings. Thank goodness.

"Happy Thanksgiving my soul sister!" Andrea envelops me in a big holiday-sized hug, wearing a terrific-looking wool coat in a fabulous shade of deep poppy orange, and a knitted brown mink infinity scarf Aimee gave her last Christmas.

"Happy Thanksgiving to you. And I thought you hated that, what did you call it? Shroud of dead weasels?"

Andrea looks sheepish. "I did. I mean, I thought I did, but then that last cold spell in February? I put it on, and, um, I kinda actually love it. I get all kinds of compliments on it, my dad says it makes my eyes sparkle, and it is really warm . . ."

"And I am a GENIUS. Why does no one trust my geniusosity?"

Of course. "Aimee Knows Best. Let me tell you about my

morning a couple of days ago. It involves pink lounging pajamas with a matching robe . . ."

Honey, hand me that last platter, would you?" Jasmin
gestures to the lovely silver tray that held a glistening
pile of candied yams dusted with toasted praline pecans, it
seems, mere minutes before.

I pick up the tray, sneak a last bit of crispy pecan topping
from the corner as she swipes at me with a towel.

"Leave the girl be, Jazzy, she can't resist my momma's
yams." Gene reaches over me and picks his own little crumb,
and Jasmin swipes at him as well.

Dinner was amazing, the turkey moist and savory, all the
sides appropriately rich and filling, the wine free flowing, the
conversation light and fun. Jasmin and Gene sparring lov-
ingly. Their neighbors, empty nesters John and Sophie, who
do their own thanksgiving on Fridays so that their kids can
be with in-laws today, are a lovely couple, and she is originally
from France, so I get to practice my French with her. Andrea
engaging in some serious flirty banter with a new doctor from
her mom's group, a cute single guy in his midforties named
Law, recently moved here from Cincinnati, who specializes
in sports injuries and made us play "name the Cub" whose
knee he recently scoped. Mike and Mark, two very sweet if
somewhat sleepy residents from Gene's department, both coming off of twenty-four-hour shifts with semibedhead and dark
circles, and so strangely interchangeable in look and manner
that I can barely tell them apart.

The guys are all crashed out in the den watching football,
John and Sophie begging out early to do their own prep for

tomorrow, and Andrea, Jasmin, and I doing a first round of cleaning up to help digest before the onslaught of desserts.

Jasmin shoos Gene out of the kitchen with some mutterings in Spanish, the only word I caught was *loco*. He grabs her around the waist from behind, kisses the side of her neck loudly, and goes to join the boys.

"Okay, Missy." Jasmin points at me with the scrub brush, flicking some bits of foam in my general direction. "How are you doing?" This is not head-tilty. This is not patronizing or condescending or even presumptuous as these questions seem to be when you have lost someone close to you. This is pointed, specific, knowing.

"I am doing fine, I think."

"Mami . . ." Andrea says in that tone that indicates this is delicate.

"Mami nothing, *niña*. There was an empty seat at our table this year."

"Two," Andrea says, reminding us all of the times Aimee and Wayne would come to Thanksgiving. Wayne is surprisingly unobtrusive at holidays. I think the crowds make him uncomfortable, and certainly at Jasmin and Gene's house, the conversation leans fairly intellectual. Wayne would usually put his head down, pick around a plate, trying to convince himself that turkey is just a big chicken, and mostly eating rolls and mashed potatoes and waiting for dessert. I always sort of appreciated him at holidays, because he stayed out of the way and was quiet, and rarely did anything too annoying.

"You're right, two. Thank you, honey. Wayne is doing okay as well?"

"He is," I say. "He's spending as much time as he can with Noah, and his friends have really rallied around him."

"Andrea told us about the arrangement Aimee put you both in."

I smile at Andrea to let her know that I'm fine with her having shared this information. She winks at me.

I try to find the right words. "It's unusual. But we're finding our way."

"Well, it makes sense to me."

"It does?" Andrea asks, incredulous.

"Of course! Aimee wants you to see him the way she saw him, and she isn't here to make that happen. I understand that. Do you think your Dad was everyone's top pick for me? Completely from outside my community, a surgical resident working insane hours, distracting me from my own residency, who knocked me up and eloped with me to Las Vegas? On a TUESDAY?"

"MAMI!" Andrea says in mock horror.

"What? We were working a million hours, and were constantly exhausted. I barely remembered to eat, let alone take my birth control pills regularly." This? Right here? Is the kind of thing that would never come out of my mom's mouth.

Andrea shakes her head and takes the platter Jasmin has now finished washing to dry it and put it with the others on the counter.

"I'm sure everyone loved Gene," I say, reaching for a gravy boat from the dish rack to dry it off.

"Everyone did not love Gene. There was a language and culture barrier. It was still shocking to some to see an interracial couple. My family thought he was a gold digger, a know-it-all, and a corrupter of their perfect child and ruiner of the American Dream."

"Gold digger?" Andrea laughs. Her maternal grandparents

were hardworking middle-class Dominicans, who always had their tiny house full of recently emigrated cousins crashing on couches and floors. They owned a small bodega in their neighborhood on the northwest side, and would never have been thought wealthy by any standard. Gene, on the other hand, was raised in Bronzeville in a huge gorgeous brownstone by parents who were leaders of the black bourgeoisie, owners of over a dozen local businesses including five banks, three grocery stores, two clothing stores, and a popular soul food restaurant chain run by Gene's Aunt Bettie.

Jasmin laughs as well. "They were immigrants. They had their prejudices."

"They thought any black man must be a poor, nappy-headed thieving Negro from the housing projects, on welfare with ten illegitimate children and a heroin habit," Gene pipes in, having wandered in to get a round of beers for the football crew.

"So there was that," Jasmin says.

"I'm just saying," Gene says, heading back out of the kitchen with an armful of bottles.

"I never knew that," Andrea says.

"By the time you came along, you were the great peacemaker. My family loved you so much, and they could see that your dad was a good father to you, and they met his family and could see they were good people. Just like you can see Wayne is good people, even if he is not the person you love most in the world."

"Of course Wayne is good people. It's just . . ." I don't know how to explain. Or if I should even try.

"I know. He doesn't fit. But your Jack didn't fit so well either, as I recall."

Andrea smacks her forehead.

I turn to her. "You didn't like Jack?" News to me.

"No one liked Jack. We called him Jackass. He was a putz. And SOOOO BOOORING."

"I thought he was a little, um . . ." Andrea stammers a bit.

"Um, dull, dim, uninteresting . . ."

"Self-involved," Jasmin offers.

"Exactly!"

"That's a good way to put it, Mom, self-involved. He seemed to always interrupt you when you were talking to tell about something related to himself."

"I didn't really notice."

"BULLSHIT!"

"Well, you loved him, but that is the point," Jasmin says. "To you, he was probably just telling interesting stories, sharing about himself and his life, because you loved him. To us, it looked like he only wanted to talk about himself all the time to the exclusion of you being able to speak. But that's the whole point. Not every person we love is immediately lovable to everyone else. But that doesn't mean we are wrong to love them. Aimee was a brilliant, wonderful woman and an amazing friend, and she loved Wayne. So I have to trust that he's lovable, even if I don't love him."

"Jasmin, you rock my world, girlfriend! Can I get a WITNESS!"

"I'm trying." Which I really am.

Jasmin comes over and clasps my face between her hands. She is still a strikingly beautiful woman, despite being near seventy, her olive skin practically unlined, her dark hair not unlike mine in color and texture, shot with white that sparkles instead of dulls. "I know you are, *niñita*. And I know that

Aimee knew what she was doing when she made this decision. I also know that you are doing a great job of convincing everyone, especially yourself, that you are okay. I hope you know that when you stop being okay, we are all here for you. Including Wayne. Probably especially Wayne. And I hope that when that time comes, you come to all of us. And I do mean ALL."

I flinch. Because she is so serious, and Andrea is looking at me with the goddamned head tilt, and suddenly my colon clenches and I can feel one of my attacks coming on. "I will," I promise, moving away so that she can't feel the clamminess that is sprouting on my face. "And now I have to use the powder room." I force myself to smile and walk casually out of the kitchen and down the hall to the bathroom. I run the water in the sink full tilt to hopefully cover the sound of a complete and rapid intestinal evacuation, my heart beating half out of my chest, sweating like I've just run a four-minute mile, and clenching my teeth against the wave of nausea. It takes ten minutes for my pulse to slow, for the sweating to abate, for me to feel like I can move without being in danger of revisiting my recent Thanksgiving feast in reverse.

"It's okay to be okay. I'm not insulted."

It's not that . . .

"It's that you feel like the world expects you to be broken."

Maybe I should be.

"What would happen?"

I don't know.

"Maybe that's the problem. If you knew what would happen, you could decide if it was worth it."

Worth it to be broken?

"Worth it to miss me differently than you are doing now."

Jasmin clearly thinks I'm going to have some sort of breakdown. So does Andrea probably, probably everyone. And who am I to argue? I'm in the bathroom sweating like a pig, being chastised by my dead best friend.

"So what if you did break down?"

I don't want to.

"Then don't."

What if I can't help it?

"Then do."

You suck, you know that?

"Hey, I'm dead. The dead cannot suck. It's in the handbook. For what it is worth, Wayne has not once implied you are doing it wrong."

That's true. He hasn't.

"I'm not saying, I'm just saying."

I find the air freshener and give a thorough spritz to the small room that I have violated. Flush again. Wash my hands. Pat my face down one last time, and head back out to the kitchen.

"Auntie Jenna!" I don't have time to look at their faces to see if I was gone too long, if they are worried, because my arms are full of gangly twentysomething.

And something about Benji arriving makes my shoulders unclench. "Hello, boy. Happy thanksgiving."

"Yes it was. Shavon let me exec chef the whole meal, and everything turned out awesome!"

"Congrats, kiddo. I'm sure it was delish."

Jasmin comes up and kisses me on my cheek. "You ready for dessert?"

I smile at her, giving my best imitation of cheer. "There is always room in the dessert compartment."

"That is what I want to hear, because I put some LOVE in this pie," Benji says.

"Pretty sure that's bourbon," Andrea says.

"God, I miss pie."

"I don't care what it is, I'm about to eat it without you," Gene yells from the dining room.

And we all head in the direction of sweetness.

10

By the time I get to the Library, the table is set, and the kitchen island where we do the cooking demos is half-full of casserole dishes and containers. Lois is poking at something in a saucepan, and Eloise is arranging what appear to be forty different types of cookies on a platter.

"Happy Thanksgiving, ladies," I say, dropping my bag on the counter. Lois immediately turns to put out my offerings, a bag of the rolls I made yesterday, some of the cranberry sauce. Lois reaches down and offers Volnay a piece of turkey, which she takes gratefully and retires with it to her little dog bed in the corner.

I drop my coat on the rack in the corner, and go to receive my kisses from Lois and Eloise.

"Liebchen, how was your day?"

"It was lovely. Too much food and wine."

Eloise stops arranging cookies. She hugs me with one willowy arm, and kisses the top of my head. "Happy Thanksgiving, Jenna."

I squeeze her back. "Happy Thanksgiving, Weezy."

Leftovers Brunches were one of the first traditions Aimee and I came up with at the Library. We were always closed the day after big holidays, which we originally thought would give everyone a day to recover from parties. But it became clear that we all just sort of wanted to be together to share the cheer, and so we started having everyone bring all their leftovers to the Library for brunch the next day, so that we could taste what everyone else made and get the stories out while they were fresh. We have them for Thanksgiving, and Easter, and they are always enormous fun. We tried doing them for Christmas, but it never seemed to work out so well, so we gave up and instead do a late-January brunch to talk about the upcoming year and for everyone to show off recipes they've been playing with.

The buffet already has leftover turkey, which Lois makes by first steaming it and then roasting it, and her traditional bread dumplings in rich turkey gravy. I spy Eloise's potato gratin with prunes, and Andrea must be upstairs; I recognize the ham and sweet potatoes from last night. I can smell the unmistakable scent of brussels sprouts caramelizing in a hot oven. Eloise puts my cranberry sauce and rolls on the buffet, and returns to arranging cookies.

When we are done eating, we will decorate the store for the holidays, setting up the menorah with the orange light-bulb "flames" in the front window, and next to it, Aimee's favorite tree, a small tabletop vintage German one made of white turkey feathers. In the far corner, Lois's sons have already set up an eight-foot blue spruce, and Benji brought the boxes of lights and ornaments up from the basement on Wednesday. Every year Eloise has a class where kids make and decorate ornaments out of either stiff bread dough or a cinnamon paste that gets baked to rock hardness. She has them each make two, one to take home and one for our tree. It's always fun to see kids who have been with us for the past few years come back to find their ornaments on the tree and show them off, or bring younger siblings to class to introduce them to the tradition.

The door flies open, bringing with it a wild gust of wind that ruffles my hair and raises goose bumps all over my arms. "Do. I. Have. The. Delicious?" Benji yells to the room. "Hell to the yeah, I do!" His long arms are full of bags and boxes, and it looks as if he has decided to make the entire meal again on his own. I remember that feeling. When I was first out of culinary school, I would leave restaurants and dinner parties and holiday dinners and run to the grocery store to go home and try to recreate or improve on the favorite dishes. Even at my own parties, I'd have a flash of how to make a dish even better, and pop out of bed in the middle of the night or the wee hours of the morning to see if my vision was real.

I look at Benji unpacking casserole dishes and Tupperware containers on the buffet, and smile, thinking that he must have been up at the crack of dawn inspired and nearly feverish with the adrenaline of cooking flat out from the deepest part of your heart. No different than an artist frantically slapping the paint on the canvas, or a writer in the middle of the night typing with sparks shooting out of their fingers to get the story down. When you are possessed by food as chefs are, and the muse calls, you head to the stove.

Benji is explaining his offerings to Lois and Eloise, who are looking at him bemusedly. "I hacked an old Crock-Pot and turned it into a sous vide machine, and did a turkey breast, and then seared the skin on the stovetop, so it is totally crispy, but the meat is BEYOND juicy. And the stuffing is a combination of homemade corn bread, homemade buttermilk biscuits, and brioche, with sage and thyme and celery and onion and shallot. And I tried the Robuchon Pommes Puree, and thought that there was no way to put **THAT** much butter into that much potato, but holy moley is it amazeballs! And I did a butternut squash soup with fried ginger and almond cake with apple compote." All the bustle has roused Volnay, who wanders over to greet Benji, and receives a dog biscuit for her trouble from Eloise.

"Honey, breathe a little," I say, laughing.

"It's just . . . I . . . I mean . . . THANKSGIVING!" he says, which cracks us all up.

Andrea appears from upstairs and comes over to give me a hug.

"Nice outfit," I whisper, looking her up and down pointedly. "Looks just as good as it looked last night."

Andrea blushes. "Yeah, um . . ."

"Dr. Law from Cincinnati?"

Her skin burnishes even deeper, going absolutely copper. "Yup."

"You fabulous Jezebel, you!"

"All my bitches getting LAID."

"We didn't . . . I mean, not really, we just had a drink, and we talked and . . ."

"You have nothing to apologize to me about, I took my lawyer to bed. More power to you."

"Deck the halls with boys and con-doms . . . fa la la la la."

"I actually kind of, I dunno, LIKE him?"

"Good. He seemed likable. If he sticks, maybe we can double-date!"

"Yeah, you can go for malteds after the sock hop."

"Let's see if I get a solo date first before we make reservations."

"Good plan. But regardless, I think you have something extra to be thankful for!"

"Stop whispering in corners, you two, and help us get this food organized," Lois calls out to us.

"Wait till you taste Benji's soup," Eloise says, a steaming mug in her hands and a proud smile on her face.

"'Cause Benji is a ge-nius," Benji singsongs.

"Oy. Let's go eat before these people lose their minds." I take Andrea's hand and we go to load up our plates.

So then we're getting all the food out, and guess who comes in the door?" Benji says, working on his second enormous plate of food. Where he puts it in his scrawny body is beyond me. His metabolism is the thing on earth I covet the most. I skipped seconds yesterday and today and tried to limit desserts to just tastes, but I'll still end the weekend four pounds heavier, and will barely get it off before Christmas puts it right back on.

"Elton John," Andrea teases, since we heard this story last night.

Lois smacks her arm. "Who, *Schatzi*?"

"The MAYOR," Benji says.

"Mayor McCheese?" I say, teasing.

"The Mayor of Casterbridge?" Eloise jumps in.

"Rahm freaking EM-AN-U-EL, you evil women. And you know what was really cool? It was just him and his family and the security, no press, you know? No photographers, no posing. It was like, 'Hey! I'm your mayor. Sort of sucks that you don't have parents, but I've got your back, and how is your Thanksgiving?' He was badass. And his wife gave me her card because she wants me to send her my recipes! And he told me I made the only pecan pie he ever actually liked, and I totally didn't even flinch when he shook my hand and I felt that weird little nubbin finger!" Benji dips his finger in gravy and puts his hand down for Volnay to lick. Spoiled dog.

Andrea and I are laughing so hard that tears are streaming, and Lois is holding her sides while her astounding bosom heaves, and Eloise chuckles behind her delicate hand.

"And was your dinner that exciting, El?" Andrea asks.

Eloise shakes her head. "Nothing special. We went to my aunt's house in Rockford, me and my folks and my sister and her kids. My brother-in-law is still deployed, but he was able to Skype in and say hi, so that was good. We had sent a care package for him and his unit, and it arrived in time, so they all kept walking by to thank us over his shoulder, made us feel really proud. My cousins were all in for the weekend with all of their kids, so there was lots of noise and laughter, and my aunt is a great holiday cook, all the classics, so it was a nice day. And my team won the touch football, so we didn't have to clean up, which is always nice!" For being the world's most maternal, nurturing, supportive person on the planet, Eloise HATES cleaning. She isn't slovenly, more just messy, leaving a wake behind her of bits from craft projects and half-read magazines, and half-drunk mugs of tea. When she cooks, she does so with wild abandon, and then faces the pile of dishes and sighs deeply, as if it is a Sisyphean task that will kill her.

"God forbid you wash a dish, *Mausi*," Lois says, giving her arm a pinch. Lois loves cleaning up. Eloise is an endless source of fabulous cleaning-up opportunities for Lois, who teases her good-naturedly about it, and adores every pot she can scrub spotless and every surface she can clear and organize.

"And how was yours, Lois?" Benji asks around a mouthful of stuffing.

"Ack, *gut*. My daughters-in-law, you know . . ." she shrugs her rounded shoulders resignedly. "They are such sweet girls, good mothers, kind to me . . ."

"And such bad cooks!" we all say in unison, the refrain of every Leftovers Brunch in our history.

"Tell us," Benji says, all of us relishing the litany and details of failed dishes.

"Well, Gina, you know, she is Italian, so she brings sausages in peppers, which smells like feet. And she takes the beautiful sausages that Kurt makes at the butcher shop and cooks them until they are like hard little rocks. Ellie, she is afraid of getting fat, so she makes cheesecake with no-fat Greek yogurt and Egg Beaters and fake sugar that tastes mostly of petrol. Lisa wanted to do stuffing, and it was so dry that you could barely choke it down. I had to make a second batch of gravy in the middle of dinner because everyone was trying to soak it so that it didn't kill us."

"But you made that beautiful turkey, and those dumplings are like pillows," Andrea says.

"And your famous German potato salad," Eloise says.

"And all of those desserts from the bakery," I say, dreaming of crispy, sweet pastries, oozing custard and homemade jam and dolloped with whipped cream.

"A good meal in spite of the girls." Lois beams, knowing that we all really mean our compliments. "Now. I clean up while you start the tree." None of us argue, she loves to do it, and we are in divide and conquer mode.

Benji and Eloise untangle the lights and get them strung on the tree, while Andrea and I set up the menorah and Aimee's tree in the window. Aimee always liked the feathers lit with pink fairy lights, and dangled with vintage silver mercury glass balls. We just leave it decorated year to year, so all we have to do is plug it in. The menorah is a kitschy silver plastic number with nine orange lightbulbs that you screw in as the nights go by. Since Chanukah is still a couple of weeks off, we just light the center Shamash light until the holiday arrives. A couple of garlands around the base of the window, and stacks of cookbooks tied with ribbons and topped with whisks go around the bases.

We are just heading back to help get the ornaments on the tree, when there is a knock at the door.

Wayne and Noah are grinning and making nearly identical faces in the window, and I go to let them in.

"Happy Thanksgiving!" Wayne says, throwing his arms wide and smacking Noah right in the forehead. "Oh, hey, sorry little man." He ruffles Noah's hair. Noah cracks up.

"Dad, you are such a klutz. Try not to concuss me. Hey Jenna."

Noah is a roly-poly kid, all cheeks and poochy tummy and little round butt sticking out. But this is just Wayne's genetics peeking through; he's a pretty good athlete, a fast runner, good soccer player, and my guess is that when he hits puberty, he'll shoot up like a beanpole and lose the baby fat. I'm wishing a total Jerry O'Connell for him. His hair is light brown with a hint of strawberry, and has a major cowlick right over his left eyebrow that always makes him look as if he has had a recent surprise. Bright blue eyes, freckles on his nose, smart as a whip, and about the most easygoing kid you can imagine. I reach out to give him a hug.

"Hey kiddo, how's it going?"

"He's still working on that ark," Wayne says, making the crazy sign with his finger next to his temple. "Talks to God." Wayne never gets tired of the Noah jokes. I have no idea why Noah doesn't tell him to shut up already, but I guess after ten years of it, he just lets it slide.

"Yup. Anyone seen a pair of aardvarks around here any-where?" Noah asks. He drops his coat on a chair, and goes to give Volnay a cuddle. Aimee and I always said that when it came to kids, Noah was like winning the lottery.

"He was better than winning the lottery. That kid never broke anything, spilled anything, pitched a fit or complained. And more importantly, he never once got sick when he was with us."

Aimee was fearless about everything except puking.

"Cannot. Do. It. Not mine. Not yours. Not anyone's."

Even when she got sick, with all the pain and fatigue, she was nauseated a lot, but never threw up.

"'Cause that is how I roll. I am a vomit-free zone. Also? In heaven, no barfing. You have my word on that."

Noah leaves Volnay to return to her nap and heads over to say hello to everyone, and gets hugs and kisses and high fives before Lois squires him over to the buffet, where we have left all the desserts set up. Noah carefully chooses one of Elo-ise's spicy gingersnaps dipped in white chocolate, one of Lois's poppy-seed cookies, and one of Benji's pecan squares and brings his plate over to the tree.

"We saved all your ornaments for you," Eloise says, hand-ing him the small box where we have always kept his orna-ments, since he has come to every ornament class since the very first one and always makes at least four or five to leave here. It is fun to see the progression of his skills, from the lumpy, spattered sloppy ones from his first class, to last year's fairly precise renditions of all of the Angry Birds characters.

"Excellent," Noah says, putting the poppy-seed cookie in his mouth whole and taking the box, beginning to place his ornaments randomly all over the tree. "A little bit of Noah wherever you look," he says.

"What is your theme this year?" Eloise asks. The ornament class is in two weeks; we always schedule it on Wayne's weekends.

"I think I'm going superhero logos this time. Batman and Robin. Superman. Captain America. Wonder Woman. Spiderman. Maybe the Incredibles."

"Sounds very awesome," Andrea says.

"You doing the Punisher?" Benji asks.

"Don't know that one, is it cool?"

"Yeah, he's a good one from the '70s. Marvel. Logo is a really amazing stylized skull."

"Hey Dad! When we go to Elliot's can we look for the Punisher?" Noah yells out to Wayne, who has been silently demolishing the desserts. He must have eaten at least a dozen cookies in the last six minutes.

"Yeah, totally!" Wayne says, cookie crumbs flying out of his mouth in a spectacular spray.

"Way to win the hearts of the ladies, Dad." Noah laughs.

Wayne smiles and takes a napkin to shield his mouth. "Oops."

"We're going to Elliot's store later. Are you coming, Jenna?" Elliot is Wayne's best friend since grade school. Aimee always called him Frumpty Dumpty.

"Because he looks like a Weeble."

Elliot is a nice enough guy, definitely in need of a total makeover, shares the whole Star Wars/sci-fi/Dungeons & Dragons thing with Wayne, and owns a small comic book store in Andersonville. What I do know is that he has really been there for Wayne since Aimee got sick, checking in, dropping off groceries, taking Noah out to movies and arcades when Wayne needed to take Aimee to the doctor.

"Can't buddy, have to finish decorating here. Besides, that is guy time. No girl cooties allowed at Elliot's."

"You don't have girl cooties. You could be like our Batgirl."

"Spoken like a kid who has no idea how bad you would look in a rubber catsuit."

Thanks.

"I'm just saying they are unforgiving. I couldn't pull one off on my best day. And your Polish-peasant tush? I think not."

"I appreciate that, Noah. Maybe next time."

"Hey Dad, Jenna says she'll come next time. When I'm back, that's Elliot's store party right?"

"Yep."

"Cool, Jenna, you can come with us. It is going to be AWESOME."

"That will be great," I say, smiling.

Super. I now have agreed to attend some sort of party at Elliot's store. I smell a night of Chex Mix and Taco Bell catering, cases of Schlitz and the Star Wars soundtrack on the record player while the overgrown geek patrol wanders around looking for a bargain on Batman comics. Fab. Going to have to figure out a way to avoid that.

"C'mon kiddo, finish getting your stuff on the tree so we can skedaddle. Elliot is going to leave early so we can go have movie marathon at his house."

"'Kay Dad. Almost done." Noah begins to deliberately and thoughtfully find places for his ornaments on the tree, with Eloise and Benji helping.

"How was everything yesterday?" I ask Wayne.

"Okay," he says. "Subdued. It was hard to not have her there, and noticeable. But the nieces and nephews were all in good form, so that kept us laughing. We had a tough moment during grace, saying how much we missed Thom and Jean and Aimee, and something is going on with Jordan; he was really just off to himself most of the day. But it was pretty good, all things considered. They all send their love to you and say they can't wait to have you for Christmas. I figure you and I can drive together."

Terrif. Three hours each way trapped in the car with Wayne.

"Sure. That will be good." And then pigs will fly out of my butt.

Wayne reaches for another cookie just as Noah finishes up.

"I'm going to hit the head before we go, buddy," Wayne says, striding toward the little powder room in the back of the store.

"How are you doing, Jenna?" Damned if the little bastard didn't just head tilt at me.

"I'm okay, Noah. How are you doing?"

He shrugs. "I miss Aimee. She was always really nice to me, and she wasn't ever a stepmonster like some of my friends have. And I'm really sad for my dad. He tries to pretend he is okay, but . . ." Noah leans in conspiratorially, and whispers, "I hear him crying sometimes in the bathroom or when he thinks I'm sleeping."

"We're all really sad because we all loved her so much,

especially your dad. So it is pretty normal that he might be upset. Does it scare you when you hear him crying?" I know that sometimes it is really traumatic for kids to see weakness or vulnerability in their parents.

"No. I know he feels bad and he just misses Aimee."

"That's right."

"And I know that he has you to be his bestie and make sure he is okay, so that makes me feel better."

And makes me feel worse.

"I promise I'll try."

Noah leans forward and gives me a hug.

"Ready to go?" Wayne returns.

"Just as soon as you zip up your fly, Dad."

"Ooops!" Wayne says, looking down at his gaping khakis.

Noah shrugs, as if to say, "what can you do?" and goes to put his coat on. Wayne and Noah make the rounds to kiss and hug us all good-bye, and head out to their next adventure, hand in hand, and looking pretty happy.

"Now that is enough to make me pretty thankful."

Indeed. Indeed it is.

And I turn around and head back to our friends to make things festive. Maybe if I put enough light and color and sparkle around me, some of it might just seep in a little.

"Fake it till you make it."

"Jenna! Come be in charge of tinsel, Andrea is clumping," Benji says in a tattletale whine. Volnay stretches in her dog bed, and comes over to get some love from Andrea, who is starting to look like her long night with the new doctor is taking its toll, and I sense that there is a serious nap imminent as soon as we finish.

Lois hands me a steaming mug of spiced cider, with a small shot of bourbon I can smell, and winks at me.

Eloise offers up the box of ornaments for me to choose, and I grab an odd-looking reindeer that looks more like a cat, and find a good bough.

And pretty soon I find I don't have to fake it after all.

11

Volnay nudges me with her nose. Probably because I've been standing in my closet in my underwear for the better part of a half an hour, staring blankly at a wall of pants.

"They're pants, not brain surgery. Pick a pair before you get pneumonia."

Except these days, most of my pants are fitting tight, if they're fitting at all. You know all those stories about the ladies who grow pale and wan and all skinny in their grief? The ones who wake up a size 6 without noticing? I am not one of those ladies. I've probably gained at least eight pounds since Aimee died.

"It's not your fault Hostess announced bankruptcy; you had a moral obligation to revisit those childhood treats."

Yeah, just what I needed, a massive three-day Hostess binge, followed by a week of trying to replicate recipes so that if no one decides to buy and reissue Twinkies and Suzy Q's, I'll be all set. It was a ridiculous endeavor, since most of the experience of Hostess is in the slightly plasticky tastes and textures, which cannot be replicated in a home kitchen. You can make a delicious moist yellow cake and fill it with a marshmallowy vanilla cream, and it will be spectacular, trust me; I ate at least a dozen. But it won't taste like a Twinkie.

The cake won't have that springiness, the filling won't have the fluff, and it is impossible to get those three little dots in the bottom. Which should be fine, since I hadn't actually eaten a Hostess product for the better part of a decade, hadn't missed them either. But that little news item hit, and in a Pavlovian fit of nostalgia, I was off to the local gas station to load up on white boxes with blue and red details. Twinkies, Sno Balls, Ding Dongs . . . even a cherry Fruit Pie. All of them the flavors of my youth, and proof that there are certain things you should leave as fond memories, since they don't really hold up.

Case in point? *Real Genius.* Trust me. Don't watch it again. It will make you sad. Hold the memory in long-time-ago soft focus, when you thought Val Kilmer was HOT and that the movie was edgy and the popcorn scene hilarious. It is a 1985 movie and needs to stay there. If you're feeling itchy, go *Sixteen Candles.* It hasn't lost a thing.

The Hostess Insanity, after the binge of Thanksgiving, and the fact that I was already generally off the rails diet-wise, and that the only time I felt like I had a good reason to use the "my best friend died" excuse was to avoid the gym, and here I am. Pantless.

"Wear the J. Jill flowy ones. Elastic waistband."

Sigh. My official Fatter Pants. Since, let's be honest, all those size 14/16s I'm not squeezing into so comfortably are not exactly Skinny Pants. Good idea. I reach over and pull the black loose-fitting pants, one step up from pajamas, off their hanger. An oversized gray sweater will mask the fact that even these are clinging around the thighs more than they are supposed to. I just can't bear the thought of Spanx today. Mama needs to breathe. Plus I can wear my black Frye motorcycle boots, which have taken the last decade to break in "just right."

"There you go. Now slap on some jewels and lipstick and get out of here already. You want Brian to beat you there?"

The Voix has a point. I'm debuting Brian as "the guy I am seeing" at a very special event at the Library, and he is meeting me there straight from work. I definitely don't want him to get there before me and face the team alone. Thomas Keller and his pastry chef Sebastien Rouxel just released their amazing cookbook, *Bouchon Bakery*. They are in Chicago to do some events, one of which is a tasting and signing at the Library, a huge coup for Andrea, and an event that has been sold out for weeks, even at one hundred dollars per person, which includes a copy of the book.

We have seventy of Chicago's most passionate foodies descending on us in an hour, the maximum our space can handle. Lois and Eloise and Benji have been cooking from the book all week in preparation, making everything from homemade marshmallows and chewy pâtés de fruit, to homemade Oreos and Better than Nutter Butters. Caramels, macarons, miniparfaits filled with apple compote and vanilla custard and olive oil cake. Insane little chocolate tarts. Shortbreads and chocolates and my personal favorite, the Chocolate Bouchon, essentially a cork-shaped brownie that is one of the most delicious things I have ever tasted.

"You are going to be diabetic by the end of the night."

I will not. You know I never eat at events.

"Because you are queer. All that yummy just sitting there."

Because I invariably have a mouthful when someone needs to talk to me, or walk around with kale in my teeth all night that no one tells me about.

"ONE TIME. One time you had kale in your teeth. You are going to have to forgive me for that, I apologized fifteen times. Oh, and I DIED. So I'm off the hook."

I'm getting really sick of the whole "I'm dead" excuse.

"Well, I'm sick of being dead, so we're even."

I put on a chunky clear Lucite cuff bracelet, my granddad's old Rolex that I always wear as my good watch, a pair of dangly drop earrings with pear-shaped aquamarines surrounded by teensy tiny black diamonds. Aimee taught me that some stones that you might not like usually, like the aquamarine, which I always found watery and fake looking, can actually be really gorgeous if you buy really bad quality. Cheap aquamarines are opaque, not clear, and somewhere halfway between turquoise and teal in color, rich and interesting, not to mention about ten times less expensive. Aimee was very proud of me when I bought these earrings, which I found in a hole-in-the-wall pop-up store in SoHo. Despite being over ten total carats of aquamarine, they were less than ninety bucks.

"Love those. They make your eyes pop."

So you have told me.

It's still been unseasonably warm, so I just throw a large black wrap around my shoulders, and head out. I'm grateful for the weather, in the 50s today, so that I can walk to the Library, since parking over there will be a nightmare with the event going on. Plus it means Brian can drive me home and hopefully spend the night. I've been enjoying his company, and the fact that while it feels regular and mostly comfortable, it doesn't feel fraught with pressure to be anything other than what it is, for which I am deeply grateful. He is the man I am dating. Not boyfriend; I'm still not ready for a boyfriend.

"He isn't boyfriend material."

By which you mean?

"You don't sparkle enough. He is perfect for now, a little sumptin' sumptin' to keep you relaxed. You can boyfriend later."

You mean when I'm better.

"I mean when you meet someone worthy."

I toss Volnay a treat as I head out the door, and enjoy the walk down the boulevard, all lit up. I pass by the famous Christmas house, lit up from top to bottom in a way that I am sure can be seen from space, and for the millionth time wonder what their electric bills must be like.

By the time I get to the Library, there is a wonderful buzz in the building. The event is spread over both of the two floors of the space; on the first floor people are shopping, nibbling from the main buffet and getting glasses of champagne and sparkling water, and then they are sent upstairs where there are the two small rooms with more formal tastings, and the larger event room where Thomas and Sebastien are signing at a big table. People are milling around, buying lots of books and some small cookware, and the staff seems to be relaxed and having a good time interacting. We have brought in a duo from The Paper Source, who are doing spectacular wrapping for a small fee, and Eloise and Benji are both ringing up customers while Lois is meeting and greeting and working the floor.

"Hey, you." My friend Alana comes over with her husband RJ, and they both kiss me simultaneously on my cheeks. They live in the neighborhood, and we sometimes have doggie play-dates with Volnay and their dogs Dumpling and Pample-mousse.

"So much love. How are you guys?"

"Good," Alana says. "Busy. But considering the alternative, we can't complain. How are you doing?"

"You know me, I'm fine."

Alana and RJ seem to not really know what to say after that. I help them out.

"Have you guys been upstairs yet?" I ask. "Met the man?"

"Oh yes," RJ says, beaming like a true fan. "So cool."

"We haven't seen him since I took RJ to the French Laundry for his fiftieth. It was great to catch up a little," Alana says.

"He is a great guy, very genuine," I say, having met Chef Keller a few times over the years.

"Very."

And then we are all looking at each other. RJ jumps in.

"You have to come for dinner soon. Alana seems to have perfected this insane braised chicken with chorizo and chickpeas that is perfect for this weather," he says, bragging about his wife. Alana is a terrific chef, best known for her role assisting Patrick Conlon on *Master Chef Battle*, and her own new show, *Abundance*, both staples on my TiVo. I've known her since I catered a cocktail party for her former boss Maria De Costa, the talk show host, about fifteen years ago, and we have stayed in casual touch ever since. When she moved into the neighborhood, we got a little closer, but since Aimee got sick I haven't been as good about staying in touch. But considering that was around the time she met RJ, she's been too busy to really notice.

"Yes! Andrea says you have a new man in your life, you should bring him to dinner!"

Dinner parties at Alana's are awesome, and for the first time in a long time, I feel in the mood to be social.

"Anytime. Shoot me some dates, and I'll bring the dessert."

"Mmmm. Will you make the dark chocolate pudding?" RJ asks. The man is addicted to pudding. The last time I went to their place for dinner, over a year ago, I brought a recipe I'd been working on and he clearly approved.

"Of course."

"Good. Honey, we're going to go, but we will see you very soon. I'll e-mail you dates this week." Alana leans in to give me a hug, and RJ kisses my temple, and they head for the door.

I make the rounds, checking in on the team, all of whom are glowing with the excitement of having a true culinary icon in the house. So far so good. I check my phone, and there is a text from Brian saying he should be here by seven thirty or so, about a half an hour from now. So I head upstairs to see how Chefs Keller and Rouxel are doing.

"Hello, Chef," Keller says as I approach the table, winking at me over the head of the person whose book he is signing with practiced flourish and a felt-tipped calligraphy pen. "My goodness. I don't think I have ever done a *J* like that before," he says to the woman in front of him. "You have a rare and special book now, with a one-of-a-kind *J.*" The woman preens and begins gushing about her experience at Per Se the month before.

"How goes it?" I ask him.

"Okay. I have a little headache . . . caught a shelf in my hotel room with my head earlier, but this is helping." He gestures to the glass of bourbon at his side.

"It doesn't cure the pain, but it makes you not care," I say, smiling.

"Exactly. Thank you, Jenna, this is a very lovely event. And . . ." He pauses, and reaches a hand out to squeeze mine. "I'm so sorry about Aimee. She was a firecracker."

"*Yes I was.*"

"Thank you, Chef."

"Thank you for having us." And then he turns to the next person in line.

"Bonjour, Chef," I say to Sebastien, coming around the back of the table. "*Ça va bien?*"

"*Oui, Chef. Tout va bien. Et vous?*" he says smiling, looking about twelve years old, and not what you would expect of one of the world's finest pastry chefs.

"*Pas mal. Avez-vous tout ce que vous avez besoin?*"

"*Oui, bien sûr.*" He raises his full glass of champagne at me.

"*Bon. Je retour.*" I love speaking with Sebastien in French; I rarely get to practice these days. I leave them to their work, knowing we will get a brief chance to catch up when they are finished. Andrea is posted in the room, making sure that they have water, that the line moves along, and keeps a watchful eye out for anything funky.

All in all, I'm enormously thrilled. It's a lovely event, and I'm so proud of my staff, and our little store. I spot Allen and Ellen Sternweiler in a corner chatting with Paul Kahan, probably about burgers. Chris Pandel from The Bristol is talking to Naomi Levine from TipsyCake and Jason Hammel from Lula Café a few doors down, who must have scampered over in the middle of service, wearing his chef's whites, spattered with something presumably farm to table and delicious.

It's a rock star kind of night, just enough star power to make the civilians feel like they are going to have plenty to Facebook and Tweet about and make the rest of the foodies jealous. Which means they will come back for future events, even if the headliners are not quite this megawatt.

And then I hear it. The unmistakable sound of something

big and messy crashing to the floor. Oh no. Please let no one be hurt. Keller and Rouxel look up at me quizzically, and I wave them off with a smile and scurry out of the room and back down the stairs.

The crowd downstairs is gathered around something, and I push my way through to discover the buffet table in the center of the room completely upended. The floor is awash in champagne and fizzy water and a zillion shards of broken flutes. A week's work for three people in meticulously crafted small desserts has been reduced to crumbs and spatters, mingling with the spilled beverages and glass in an epic sludge of horribleness. And sitting in the middle of this catastrophe, is Wayne. Cookies on his shirt, pants soaked, hands bleeding.

"Wayne?" I say.

"Oops," he says.

Eloise and Lois are shuttling people away from the mess, sending most of them upstairs, while Benji has a few people, the ones who obviously got caught in the cross fire, off to the side, getting names and addresses so that we can reimburse dry cleaning costs.

"Upsey daisy, big boy." Brian, who has appeared out of nowhere, steps up gingerly behind Wayne and grabs him under the armpits to help him stand. As soon as he is up, Lois, ever the mother, motions for him to follow her to the back staff bathroom, first aid kit under her arm.

I'm paralyzed. I can't move. I'm staring at the floor. It looks like high tea exploded in here.

"Hey, honey. Sorry I'm late." Brian comes around, wiping his hands on a napkin and leaning in to kiss me. I can't even kiss him back.

"I hate him."

"Careful, Princess."

"I HATE him. He ruins everything." My whisper is violent, vehement, the bile rising in my throat. Benji, finished with the spattered guests, sends them upstairs and quickly runs to get the mop and bucket.

"No prob, Jenna, I'll get it clean in five minutes. Time me," he says, trying to be light, clearly shocked by my face.

"He is the most ridiculous, oafish, stupid asshat, and he fucking turns everything he touches into shit. I wouldn't be surprised if Aimee's fucking disease was because of her constant proximity to that complete monumental waste of space." The tears prick at my eyes, and Brian reaches out and hands me his napkin, a sweet gesture that completely sends me over the edge, the tears spilling loose and an enormous lump taking up residence in my throat.

"I'm really sorry Jenny, I had no idea the table would go over like that if I leaned on it," Wayne says, having come back in the room god knows when and having heard god knows what. And I? Don't care.

I spin on my heel and face him with every bit of my venom. "Get. OUT," I spit at him.

"Let me help clean . . ." he starts.

"GET OUT! You have done enough. More than enough. Just get the fuck out of my store. You are not welcome here." And then I am done. Sobbing like an insane person, hiccuping and snorting, snot on my upper lip, crying like a four-year-old and finally burying my face in Brian's chest.

"You'd better just go, okay buddy?" Brian says in a tone that is firm and essentially says *get out or I will throw you out.*

"I'm so sorry Jenny, I'm . . . I'm going."

I can hear the catch in his voice, and I know he feels like hammered shit, and all I can think is, *Good.*

Benji is true to his word, the mess is dealt with in five minutes, and the buffet table put back on its feet. Lois and Eloise have gotten the last of the baked goods, the ones in reserve to restock platters, out on the table, and while it has lost some of its glorious abundance, it isn't horrible and there is still plenty to nibble on. Jason, who came down to head back to Lula to finish service in the middle of the cleanup, sends two of his busboys over with crates of clean champagne flutes, and I thank god that we didn't have bottles on the table, just filled glasses, so there are still bubbles to put in them.

I finally calm down, apologize to Brian for my outburst, and head to the staff bathroom to put myself back together. My face is red, my eyes are puffy. I have that horrible hitch in my throat that makes me feel like I could start crying again at any time.

"He's sorry."

Fuck you.

"I'm sorry."

Fuck you twice.

"It isn't the end of the world. It's all cleaned up. Accidents happen."

Wayne is an accident. Your biggest.

"You don't mean that."

Then you don't know me at all. Go away. Go haunt Wayne if you are so keen to make someone feel better about this. I have no desire to talk to you.

Before the Voix can lecture me about how hateful and awful I was to her precious Wayne, there is a knock at the door.

"Jenna? Lemme in," Andrea whispers.

I lean forward and unlock the door.

"You okay?" she asks. I shrug, because if I try to speak, I'm gonna lose it all over again.

"It's all fixed out there. And except for the fifteen people downstairs when it happened, who are all being supercool about it, it didn't even really register to the people upstairs. Everyone up there just thinks someone dropped a tray of glasses or something, no worse than what we have all heard dozens of times in a restaurant. Thank god for Lois and Eloise going overboard as usual; they couldn't stop playing with the recipes all week, so we still have plenty of food. And the chefs seem very pleased." She gets this all out in a rush, eager to make me feel better, to make it right, to be the fixer.

I nod. "Good." It's all I can get out.

"You know, if you want to . . ."

"Go home? Yeah. I'm going to go home."

"I'm so sorry, Jenna, but it'll all be fine."

"I know. Thank you for taking care of it. Tell everyone . . ." What can I tell anyone other than I need to run away? That I won't be able to muster a fake smile, to pretend to be having a good time. That I am fresh out of positive thinking and false bravado. "Tell them thank you. Tell them something I ate for lunch hit me funny or something plausible, and apologize to the chefs for me for not saying good-bye."

Andrea hugs me, and I walk past her. Brian is waiting for me, a look of grave concern on his face.

"I'm sorry. I can't . . ." I touch his arm, and head for the door, desperate for the cool night air, for home. But he follows me out and stops me at the bottom of the stairs.

"Come with me," he says.

"I'm sorry, Bri, I'm just not . . ."

"I know. But come with me anyway."

I don't have the energy to argue, so I follow him to his car. And to his credit, he doesn't speak, he doesn't offer any platitudes, he just shoots straight down Milwaukee to Armitage, and then turns left and parks.

I look up and laugh.

"Margie's?" We are parked in front of the legendary old ice cream parlor, the place my parents used to end most of their dates, since my mom has eaten a bowl of ice cream nearly every day of her adult life.

"I find that even if hot fudge doesn't make everything better, it doesn't hurt," he says, smiling at me.

We get out of the car and go inside, sitting down in a saddle-colored worn booth. Brian orders us both Grandpa's Turtle Sundaes, a classic with vanilla ice cream, hot fudge, caramel sauce, whipped cream and nuts, topped with a house-made turtle candy instead of a cherry. Sigh. So much for getting out of the elastic waistband pants anytime soon.

But the thing is, it works. Decadent, insane, over the top, but so freaking delicious. Cold ice cream, fluffy whipped cream, the mingling richness of fudge and caramel, perfectly tempered with the salt and crunch of toasted pecans and peanuts. A weirdly perfect food. I make it about halfway into my enormous bowl, totally focused on making each bite balanced, careful to not drip anything gooey down my bosom, before I drop the spoon.

"Tilt," I say. "I'm tapping out."

"Nah," Brian says. "You're just taking a break. A couple sips of water, a few minutes, and it will call you again. I always think I'm going to stop at half, but I never do."

"Thanks for bringing me here."

"No worries. I know when someone needs a sundae." He grins.

"I need something," I agree.

"Like a Waynectomy?" he says wickedly.

"GOD. He just makes me INSANE. And I don't really understand why."

"Because he is an idiot?" Brian says.

"I dunno. I try to think about it, if you or Benji or Andrea had accidentally dumped over the buffet, my main concern would have been to make you feel better about it, to make it no big deal. But Wayne does it and my blood pressure shoots up and I start dreaming of large-caliber weaponry."

"Why do you think?" Brian says, biting into his turtle candy, long strings of caramel pulling out of the chocolate shell.

"I wish I knew." I take another spoonful of my sundae; apparently Brian is right about getting a second wind. "I guess I'll have to talk to my shrink about it. In the meantime, I don't want to talk about or think about Half-Brain for the rest of the night."

"Not a problem. I have some ideas that don't involve Wayne in the least."

I think about this for a moment. "Um, you do realize that stuffing a girl full of a sundae the size of Montana is not smart as a foreplay move. I'm not going to be feeling acrobatic for at least ten hours after this."

"Dirty mind, you have such a dirty mind. I wasn't talking about ravaging you. I was thinking maybe a snuggle movie at your house. Something stupid funny. Maybe from the '80s. Something Brat Packy." He knows about my secret stash of '80s filmography.

I laugh. "You're on."

"And Jenna?"

"Yeah?"

"Thanks for inviting me tonight. Before the Waynado, it was a really lovely event and I liked your store. Maybe one of these days I can really meet your crew."

"I'd like that. And I know they would."

"Excellent. It's a date. In the meantime, let me tell you about the partner at my firm who got so drunk at the holiday party last night that he mistook an office for the bathroom. Not HIS office, mind you . . ."

And before I know it, I'm actually smiling and scraping the bottom of my bowl.

12

I find it interesting that you are so painfully aware of how much harder you are on Wayne than you are on the other people in your life. How much slower to forgive or give the benefit of the doubt. What do you think that is about for you?" Nancy says.

I think about this. "I can feel it when it's happening, I can feel myself go immediately to anger and annoyance, but the whole time I'm thinking that I'm such a horrible person because I know if someone I loved did the exact same thing, I would brush it off."

"So you are not just hard on him, you are hard on yourself for being hard on him."

"I'm my own Doublemint Twins of psychosis."

"You aren't psychotic, you are human. But I wonder where it comes from. Originally. When is the first time you remember being annoyed with Wayne?"

I think back. "The first time I met him. He and Aimee had been dating for a few weeks, and Aimee brought him to a dinner party I was having. He showed up with a bag from McDonald's, announced that he heard I was a great cook, but there was just a lot he didn't eat, so he brought his own."

"Not a great first impression."

"To say the least. And then all night he kept just jumping

into the conversation with weird non sequiturs and asking strangely personal questions. Mostly it didn't matter. It was Andrea and her current boyfriend, my friend Alana with a date, and another couple I can't remember right now . . . and I had a guy there, a friend of a friend I had a crush on, a wine consultant, and Wayne was sitting next to him. By the end of the night, Wayne was fixing him up with some woman he worked with."

"So not only did he come to your home with his own food, snubbing the thing that is most important to you, but he, um . . ." Nancy reaches for the right words.

"Twat-blocked me."

She laughs. "Not the phrase I would have used, but the sentiment is correct."

"It felt like every time we were together the first few times, he was just, so weird or did or said something so wrong. He asked Andrea's mother if she made good Mexican food; not the best thing to ask a Dominican. He asked Lois's husband if he had been recruited for the Hitler Youth back in Germany, which was ridiculous not just because he would have been about three years old at the time, but also because both his and Lois's family were part of an underground movement that hid Jews. At his first Christmas weekend at the Brands', not only did he do a McDonald's run for lunch and dinner for three days straight, he kept challenging the kids to games and then BEATING THEM. I mean, you know, winning, not like, *beating* . . . oh, and he knocked over their Christmas tree. Twice. By the time the weekend was over, all the kids were pouting and the tree was down to lights and tinsel and a couple of plastic ornaments. Eventually he figured out how to fit in better with them, the extended Brand family is very easygoing and forgiving, but it just irked me to no end. And I like to think of myself as tolerant, open, but it felt like every conversation I ever had with Wayne was just a nonstarter. In the early days he would ask me horrible questions about my lack of a dating life, and then when I met Jack they didn't connect at all either . . ."

"So you never found the right opening to really get to know him. I mean, if the person after Aimee who was most important to you wasn't a Wayne fan, then it goes to reason that while you were together it wouldn't be terribly easy to reverse your opinion."

I think about this for a minute, wondering if Jack's anti-Wayne stance helped build this wall I'm trying to dismantle. "I guess that was probably part of it. Jack was the kind of guy you could take into any situation and he would figure out how to fit in. Wayne, not so much. So they didn't really ever bond."

"You know what we therapists say about people who fit in in every situation?"

"What?"

"They have no inherent genuine personality. They aren't themselves, they are only who they think the current audience expects them to be. Flawed though some of Wayne's actions may seem to you, at the end of the day he sounds like someone who isn't afraid to just be himself, all day, every day. That takes a fairly strong sense of self, to not go against your natural instincts, to not try to make yourself into something you aren't in order to be better liked or more homogenous."

"I never thought about it that way."

"Most people don't. But if you look at some of the truly great minds and artists of our history, they are often people who didn't necessarily fit, who were outside the norm. Some of them had actual disorders, many of the great minds are now presumed to have some level of Asperger's or low-level autistic tendencies, but a lot of them were just left of center."

"Are you saying that Wayne is a secret genius? Do I have a Jobs or Spielberg or something on my hands?"

"Of course not. I'm just saying that fitting in, or caring about fitting in, isn't necessarily in and of itself the world's most desirable trait."

"So I should try and think about Wayne's 'outside the boxness' as a good thing."

"I think anything you can find to appreciate about Wayne, you should. Maybe for next time you could come with a list of eight to ten things you like about Wayne, and we can explore more. In the meantime, maybe it is time to think about the beginning of your relationship with him and acknowledge that there might have been some very minor things that sat wrong with you that were the genesis of this enormous negativity you have about him."

"You're probably right. I was sort of quick to ignore the reality of him in the beginning. Aimee and I were so busy with work, and I wrote him off as a total nonpriority. By the time I realized that Aimee was really serious about him, I just was too far down a path of dislike to turn myself around. And then they up and got married and that was that."

"People talk about inheriting family when you get married, but friends are just as important, sometimes more so. After all, even if you are close to family, you spend far more time with your friends."

"Exactly. Suddenly this guy that just didn't fit anywhere was involved in almost every aspect of my social life."

"And how was Aimee with you and Jack?"

"I thought she liked him, but now I think she didn't."

"What makes you think that now?"

I haven't mentioned the Voix to Nancy, since I have no desire to be institutionalized. "Some things that Andrea and others have said recently."

"How does that make you feel?"

"Okay, actually. I sort of thought that maybe people thought that I had missed my chance when we broke up, let a good one get away. It weirdly feels nice to know that actually they didn't like him for me, so it makes me feel like I dodged a bullet."

Nancy looks at her watch. "We're almost out of time. How are you handling the current situation with Wayne?"

"You mean post-Waynepocalypse? I'm dealing best as I can. He is stopping by tonight with Noah. I'm having a small Chanukah party to introduce Brian to my friends since he didn't really get to meet them last week. Thank god Wayne and Noah are going out to dinner, but coming over just for dessert. He called and apologized a zillion times, asked me to please charge his account for the damage at the party and all the dry cleaning costs, sent me a cookie bouquet . . ."

"And have you forgiven him?"

"Mostly. I think out of self-preservation I need to just let it go. I know intellectually that he never means to do anything to hurt me or make me angry, it is totally unintentional, and I just have to get to a place where that is enough to keep my emotions in check."

"Good. I'll look forward to hearing how this goes next time I see you."

"Okay."

I head out of the office and out to my car. Everything at

home is in good shape, I'm picking up rotisserie chickens from Feed, I have homemade latkes with applesauce and sour cream already prepped, chilled steamed asparagus dressed in a lemon caper dressing, Andrea is bringing roasted root veggies, and Benji is bringing predinner nibbles. Eloise is bringing cookies, I'm sure. Lois can't make it, it is one of her grandkids' birthdays, but she usually makes excuses for evening events anyway. I think she just likes to be home and without the tumult of people thirty to fifty years her junior. Brian is bringing wine, and I'm interested to see how the gang takes to him.

I get home and Volnay limps over to greet me. I wonder if there is snow coming; her arthritis seems to be really acting up, so I slip her a pain pill in a spoonful of peanut butter.

The bell rings.

"Hello beautiful. Happy Chanukah!" Brian comes in carrying a bag with six bottles of wine, which he immediately goes to drop in the kitchen. He leans over and gives Volnay a rawhide chew toy in the shape of a dreidel. "Couldn't resist." He grins. He's very early; ostensibly to help set up, but it becomes quickly clear that he is of a mind to sneak in a little romp before the party. Not that I'm complaining. It doesn't always have to be flowers and romance; sometimes a girl just needs a skirt-up quickie on the island in the kitchen library. I wait till Brian goes to put himself back together in the powder room to wipe the island down with a bleach-based spray.

"You might be a ho, but you are still a stickler for food safety."
True enough.

Brian is still in the bathroom when the team arrives en masse, having come straight from the Library. After hugs and kisses and coat dumping, everyone comes to the kitchen. I have a lovely formal dining room, but for tonight, we are setting up the food on the kitchen island and eating at the large farm table in the kitchen.

"This is a happy sight," Brian says, appearing from the back hallway and surveying the scene in the kitchen. There is a quick round of introductions, and then Brian works on getting everyone a glass of wine while Benji puts out some elaborate snacks.

"So," he explains. "Take the piece of bread, dip it in the olive oil and then in the spice and nut mix, and then smear some of the spicy carrot dip on top."

The appetizer is complicated to assemble, but absolutely delicious. The bread, a hearty baguette from La Boulangerie, is a chewy, crusty foil for the buttery oil, savory crunchy nut mixture, and sweet and spicy carrot puree. An explosion of flavor and texture. He also has some creamy local chèvre, and marinated olives.

"So, Brian, are you very busy at this time of year?" Eloise asks, licking a rogue bit of carrot off one elegant finger.

"Not too terrible," Brian answers, gratefully accepting the appetizer I have assembled for him. "A lot of my clients are in vacation and holiday mode, so hopefully things will stay relatively slow until after the New Year."

"That must be nice," Andrea says. "Will you be doing any travel to see family for the holidays?"

"I'm off the hook this year. My folks are on a Christmas cruise, and my brother and his family are in Disney with their kids for the holidays. I'm actually heading out on Christmas Day for a skiing trip. I have some friends who have a house in Snowmass."

"Ooooo. Fun!" Benji says, making Brian another bite, and handing it over. "Is Jenna going?"

"BENJI!" I say, slapping at him.

Brian grins. "Funny you should mention that . . ." Brian reaches into his sportcoat pocket and hands me an envelope. "Happy Chanukah . . . I hope."

Inside, a homemade coupon. Oy.

"Good for one trip to Snowmass, preferably on Christmas Day," Brian says.

Eloise claps. Benji smacks Brian on the back. Andrea whispers, "Excellent."

"We'll talk about it later, thank you." I lean forward and kiss him, and everyone ooohs and aaahs.

The dinner is casual and very tasty, and everyone talks easily of their upcoming holiday events while I bustle a bit, keeping the latkes frying until everyone is bursting at the seams. Brian is charming with everyone, asking Benji about his plans, telling Andrea he wants the recipe for her root veggies. Turns out he actually likes ballet and had seen Eloise perform, which made her go all giggly. It actually feels nice to have him here, and I think they all like him. But I do wonder a little bit about what Nancy said, the whole fitting-in thing. Brian suddenly reminds me a little bit of Jack, easy in a new situation, finding the right thing to say to everyone to make them happy. I can't help question the genuineness of this. Is he really ever going to cook those root veggies, or does he just know that asking for the recipe is the way to Andrea's heart?

Plus, I have to admit; the ski trip thing is more than a little scary. I haven't yet confessed to him that I have never skied, and have no intention of starting at this age. Strapping my unathletic fortysomething self to a pair of planks and hurtling down the side of a mountain on purpose seems like a stupid way to die. And a whole week together, that seems too soon. We haven't even done a whole weekend yet. But it was very sweet of him to want it, to want me, especially since he has old friends who will be there. We have settled into such a pattern of cooking at home and staying in, as much my preference as his, but still . . . any girl might wonder if she were something of a secret guilty pleasure.

We all clean up, and then set up Eloise's cookies on the coffee table in the living room for dessert. While I'm in the kitchen making tea for everyone, I hear the bell and then voices. I close my eyes and take a deep breath. I haven't seen Wayne in person since the Library debacle, and despite the numerous phone apologies, my spine is still a little clenched at the prospect of him being here. Then I hear giggles and shrieks of delight, and some very happy barking from Volnay, the same kind she uses in the dog park. I leave the teapot on the stove and head out to face the music.

As soon as I get through the door from the kitchen, I see a copper-colored blur heading my way, and then it levitates off the floor, hitting me full force in the stomach, and knocking me right on my ass. My breath shoots right out of me in one powerful *whoomph*, and before I can even register what is going on, my face is being attacked with enormously wet licking. My first thought is that Volnay's pain pill contained some sort of amphetamine, but then I realize that Volnay, who is not averse to the occasional delicate kiss, has a much smaller, less sloppy tongue, not to mention a much less monumental weight. I reach down and grasp the wiggling blur to see what I'm dealing with.

There, in my lap, all legs and huge paws and mouth and floppy jowls, tongue lolling out of the side of his mouth, is a puppy.

"Surprise!!!" Noah is jumping up and down.

"Happy Chanukah, Jenny," Wayne says, his hands on Noah's shoulders, both of them beaming at me.

"Holy shit."

"Um, what?" I say, not registering, while the puppy begins to gnaw on my arm with shockingly sharp little puppy teeth.

"He's for you," Wayne says. "A Dogue de Bordeaux. You know, like the wine. A French dog named after a French wine region, you know, because you love France and you love wine and everything." I'm noticing that he is working on a soul patch. The least funky man I know.

"Dad says you were thinking about getting a puppy for Volnay to play with, and my mom's friend Josh breeds these, and someone backed out of buying him for Christmas, so we thought that it would be perfect!" Noah is so excited. "Look, she loves him!" Volnay has come over, and immediately begins cleaning the puppy, who wriggles in joy, flips over on his back, and begins to maul my shoe absentmindedly while submitting to her strangely efficient ablutions.

And despite my every fiber wanting to scream out *You idiot, I don't need a puppy! I don't WANT a puppy. Especially not this slobbery monster!* I don't. Weirdly, I just start to laugh.

Noah gets down on the floor to play with the puppy, and Brian comes to help me up. "Oh boy," he whispers in my ear. I look at him, eyes wide, and nod.

"Wow, Wayne, Noah, that is a REALLY big surprise." I

feel like my heart is beating about four times per minute, everything seems to be in slow motion.

"He's adorable!" Benji says.

"So sweet," Eloise says.

"Isn't that Hooch? At least it's a good '80s dog."

"HOOCH!" Andrea says in shocked recognition.

"Oh, god, it IS Hooch," Brian says.

"Who's Hooch?" Noah and Benji say in unison.

"God, to be born after Turner and Hooch. You're going to have to show those boys that movie ASAP."

"Maybe you should name him Hooch," Wayne says.

"I'm not naming him Hooch," I say, because really, what else can I say.

"Let's get the rest of the stuff, Dad!" Noah says.

"Bri Guy? Give us a hand, will you?" Wayne says. Can't wait to hear what Brian thinks of being called Bri Guy for the rest of his natural life.

"Hey, dog! Quit it," Benji says, going to save the cookie platter from a clearly interested puppy. Volnay nips the puppy's ankle, as if to say, *Not on my watch, mister.*

"Oh boy, he really is doing everything possible to prove me wrong about this whole thing, huh?"

You THINK?

Eloise and Andrea move everything edible to the taller console table, while Benji holds the beast back, and I can look at him fully for the first time. He and Volnay are two shades of the same color, her deep auburn a complement to his brighter, brasher cinnamon. He has light hazel eyes, squished-up floppy ears, and a large square head atop a body that is built like a little tank. He looks a lot like a miniature orange mastiff. His paws are enormous. Not to mention some other obvious parts of his anatomy. This isn't going to be some elegant little thirty-pound girl. This is a serious BOY dog. And he's going to be HUGE.

But he does have the advantage of being a puppy, and all puppies are adorable so that you don't kill them. He's curled up in Benji's arms, licking his ear, and I can't help it, he is pretty goddamned cute. I'm in real trouble.

Brian, Wayne, and Noah come back in, laden with a box that says it contains an extralarge dog crate, and half a dozen bags from Petco. I give Wayne credit; he didn't miss a thing. While he and Brian and Noah set up the crate in the kitchen, the girls and Benji and I unpack the rest of it, puppy food, bowls, toys, leashes and collars and blue bags, endless things to chew on. The puppy immediately co-opts Volnay's bed, and I think I'll have to order another one from Ayers, my favorite company for home accessories and furniture, which makes dog beds so beautiful and elegant that they look like they are a part of your interior design and not accidents. And then I watch as he begins to chew the leather off of the corner of Volnay's little perch, and think, maybe I'll go with Costco instead.

"What are you going to call him?" Noah asks.

"Well, he's a dog from Bordeaux, so I guess, maybe Latour or Lafite, the best wines in Bordeaux?" I say.

Noah looks disappointed. "Oh."

"What were you thinking, buddy?" Clearly he has something in mind.

"Chewbacca! Because he likes to chew stuff!"

Oh, hell no. But then I look at his sweet, eager face. Oh

well, in for a penny. "Chewbacca it is. Thanks Noah, perfect name."

"AWESOME! DAD!! She liked my Chewbacca idea for his name!" Noah runs back to tell his dad the good news.

"You are a serious menschette."

Yeah, and a complete pushover. With a puppy I didn't want. Who now has a name I hate.

"Well, maybe now Nancy will cough up the Xanax."

Maybe. Or the ECT.

Over the course of the next two hours, Chewbacca knocks over a plant, eats a dish towel and half of a glove, and pees on Benji's backpack, which is thankfully waterproof, and demolishes Volnay's dreidel rawhide, which he promptly throws up, along with the previously consumed textiles, on the living room rug. By the time everyone leaves, I am coming out of my shell shock and the reality is beginning to set in.

Puppy. A fucking puppy. A puppy that is going to become a huge dog, and probably eat my whole house in the process.

At the very least, according to Wayne, the twelve-week-old dog has already been crate trained and partially house-broken, and that the peeing was likely nerves and territory marking, and the throwing up just excitement. And to his credit, after an energetic last walk around the block with Volnay, who is already fussing over him like a mother hen or a British nanny, he goes right into his crate with a chew toy and schlumps down to go to sleep. And Volnay, who usually comes upstairs to sleep with me, lies down in her bed across the room and curls up, looking up at me with a face that says "I'm the night nurse. Scat."

Brian and I head upstairs.

"So, were you really thinking of getting a puppy for Volnay?" he asks.

"NO. Wayne thought I should get a puppy because he's heard it is good for older dogs to have younger ones around."

"Yeah, sounded like his logic not yours. You gonna keep him?"

"What can I do? Forget Wayne, I don't really care about what he would think, but Noah would be crushed. And he is sort of cute. It isn't like I have a lot on my plate, there is plenty of time on my schedule for training."

"He is cute. But he is going to be a bruiser."

"I know. Did you see those paws?"

"Oh yeah."

"Well, you're a better person than I am, if that guy gave me a dog I had no interest in or plans for, I'd have read him the riot act."

"I dunno. I'm working on trying to see beyond my knee-jerk reactions to him, and see the good behind what he does. After all, he knows that Volnay is getting older, and how much she means to me. He thinks that having this puppy will be good for her, but also good for me for when she is gone. So I have to focus on the part of this gift that is really very thoughtful and sincere."

"As opposed to the part that is really inappropriate and annoying and presumptuous."

"Exactly."

"Well, better you than me. Oooofff!" Brian says as something flies onto the bed and lands on his stomach.

"CHEWBACCA!" I say. The dog is practically grinning ear to ear as we chase him around the bed and then around the bedroom.

Over the course of the night, the puppy escapes his crate four times, making Brian check him half sincerely for thumbs, and sending me searching in the middle of the night on my iPad in the dark for a puppy-proof crate.

I think the Voix may in fact be correct, Nancy is going to have to admit that this new development is even more Xanax worthy than Wayne. And that is saying a lot.

13

I'll pay for the kennel," Brian says, exasperated.

I'm trying to explain that I can't possibly go with him to Snowmass for Christmas. Despite the fact that it would get me out of going to Indiana with Wayne, which I want more than world peace, it would not be good for Chewie's training for me to be away for any length of time right now. And I'm still not ready for a whole week away with Brian, especially if skiing is involved. "It isn't about that, it's about needing to be consistent with his training so that I don't end up with a hundred-and-twenty-pound dog I can't control. By the time a dog is twenty weeks old, something like ninety percent of their habits and things are set and really hard to undo. Besides, I can't put him in a kennel till he's had his sixteen-week shots anyway. I'm sorry Brian; we can make plans to go away after the New Year sometime. But I just can't do Christmas."

"Okay. Sorry. Didn't mean to be petulant. I'm just disappointed. I really wanted you to meet my friends, and I thought it would be nice for us to get away." He is saying the right words, but his voice is still annoyed, and for the first time since we began dating I feel on strange and uncertain ground.

"Trust me, I would love to meet your friends and be away with you. But I'd already promised Aimee's family I would be there for Christmas, I think it would be bad form to go back on that this year."

"I get it. Truly. We'll make plans for a long weekend away in the New Year. How is the pup doing?"

"Well, he continues to Houdini himself out of his crate every night, but so far he can't get past the wall gate I put up in the kitchen, so other than methodically eating Volnay's dog bed a little bit at a time like he's whittling it with his mouth, and the loss of one pair of boots, it's okay. He's a sweet boy, and actually very trainable, even if he is something of a natural disaster for the moment. He's the star of his puppy kindergarten class, and can sit, lie down, roll over, and high-five. But *stay* and *heel* are hard for him because he has so much playful puppy energy. He's also gaining about ten pounds a day, and I think maybe I should have named him Clifford, because I fear he's going to be bigger than my house by the end of the month."

"Well, at least Volnay likes him."

"Whatever else is wrong with him, Wayne was right about one thing. Volnay seems to be happier and perkier. She's helping train him, which I think is the only reason he hasn't eaten the entire neighborhood by now, and she has absolutely adopted him. Which is hilarious, because she is so alpha, and he is already bigger than she is. When he's full size, it is going to be pretty funny!"

I'm glad we were able to turn the conversation around, but still have a small knot in my stomach from having to say no to him, and how much it upset him. And I know part of the knot is guilt because of how relieved I am to not have to go.

I go back to the kitchen and lead Volnay into the kitchen library and slide the door shut. I now have to feed her in here because she takes so long to eat and Chewie can't stand it, so he just pushes her aside and demolishes her food if I leave them both in the kitchen. Once she's set up, I leave her in there with the door closed and go to feed the beast.

He hops up and down, butting my calves with his big head, and licks my hands. He is very affectionate in a Lenny "I didn't mean to hurt her, George" kind of way. I get his bowl full of kibble and put it down on the floor.

Three . . . two . . . one . . . empty. And that heart-wrenching puppy look that says "Please, sir, can I have some more?" Lord love him. I take the bowl and rinse it out. It's one thing to not have my weight under control; I refuse to have overweight dogs. Breaking the cycle.

I go upstairs to change, and when I come back down, I let Volnay out of her private dining room, and she immediately pushes Chewie out of her bed and settles in for a nap. I toss him a bully stick, and close the kitchen gate. Might as well get this over with.

Jenny!" Wayne throws the door open for me, and grabs me in a big hug. The soul patch is gone, and in its place, the beginnings of a Fu Manchu mustache.

"*Sweet mother of crap, what the hell has he done to my house?*"

Why did you never tell him to stop doing that stupid shit with his facial hair?

"*It's his face.*"

Well, now it's his house.

Aimee's impeccable wide foyer is full of garbage bags that seem to have strange plastic weapons sticking out. I can see past him into the living room, which looks like a video game convention has exploded.

"Hey Wayne, how are you?"

"I'm good. Had the guys over last night for a big games party, so things are kind of a mess."

"No worries."

"Worries! Many worries! My poor house . . ."

"Come on in, I've got the drawings in the kitchen."

I follow Wayne down the hall into the kitchen, where the remains of a major guy party are in evidence. Empty pizza boxes and KFC buckets. Open bags of Doritos and packages of Oreos. A zillion empty beer bottles. It looks like a frat house, not the elegant home of a forty-four-year-old man.

"I'm weeping. WEEPING IN HEAVEN."

"Right over here," Wayne says, motioning me to the dining room table.

I wander over and take a seat at the table, which Wayne has thoughtfully cleared off. There is a large folder in the center of the table, which I presume has the exciting new sketches in it.

"So, how's Chewie?" Wayne asks, handing me a can of LaCroix grapefruit flavor, which my friend Alana got me hooked on a couple of years ago. Aimee hated it. But she always had it in the fridge. It's sweet of him to have remembered to have it on hand for me.

"He's doing pretty well. Still having plenty of puppy moments, which are to be expected, but the training is going okay, and Volnay has taken to him like she was born to be a mother."

Wayne beams, I can practically feel the joy coming off him in waves. "I'm so glad. When Noah told me about the puppies he had gotten to meet and that one of them had been rejected, everything just clicked!"

"Well, it was very unexpected, but very thoughtful."

"So, I thought if it was okay with you, I would drive us down to the Brands' next week? My car is big enough to hold all the gifts."

Last week I had gotten the pleasure of spending the better part of three hours on the phone with Wayne searching on Amazon to get the holiday shopping done. Between Noah and Aimee's family, there was no way to stay within the December budget, especially since he had blown a decent chunk on my new family member and all his accoutrements. For every gift, for every person, there were at least five ideas that were terrible until we finally found something rational for everyone. The ensuing headache was epic, and lasted nearly a whole day.

But apparently everything has arrived intact, and Wayne has been wrapping like mad; I can see a stack of gifts on the dining room table, covered in bright paper, awkwardly done with lots of what appears to be packing tape, and ribbons with floppy bows. Poor guy. Aimee was always in charge of gift wrapping, her impeccable packages crisply covered with pristine paper, invisible tape, and perfect bows. That is a tough act for anyone to follow. But the wrapping doesn't matter, it will be shredded and garbage in thirty seconds, and I do think it is sort of sweet that he put so much effort into it.

I'm predominantly a "gift cards for anyone between age twelve to twenty, books for the younger set, and booze for grown-ups" kind of gift giver. Aimee was the one who loved finding the perfect thing for everyone, searching for just the right thing. I'm a boring and unimaginative gift giver.

"Not true. You gave great gifts."

Sure, to you. Because you always said, *This is exactly what I would like.* often with coupons to get it on sale, or a link to the right website. But for people who are less forthcoming, I'm dullsville and predictable.

"Looks like you've been a one-man wrapping center," I say, gesturing at the table in the other room.

Wayne laughs. "Don't worry, I'm not going to tell you that I want to open a personal wrapping business. Which three days ago I actually thought might be a good idea, but after all of that, I don't even want to think about wrapping anything ever again. I don't know how Aimee did it! She made it look so easy."

"Aimee made everything look easy."

"Well, except laundry."

Now it's my turn to laugh. "True enough, she was really terrible at laundry."

"Hey, now . . ."

"Remember when she shrank the alpaca throw blanket?" Wayne says, shaking his head. "Turned it into a five-hundred-dollar dishcloth."

"No one told me alpaca was essentially fancy wool. How did I know it would shrink?"

"Or when she missed that one blue sock in the bottom of the hamper after your anniversary party and turned all your good white table linens pale blue!" I say, remembering the frantic phone call the next day.

"I remember the first time she did laundry after we got married, she didn't realize how much more laundry two people make versus just one, and just put it all in one load the way she usually did, and broke the machine. Suds everywhere, and soaked clothes we had to wring out in the tub and then schlep to the laundrymat." Sigh. He always says *laundrymat*. It is second only to *supposably* and *nucular* in my list of annoying mispronunciations.

"I'm very uncomfortable with this discussion."

"Thank god you took over." Wayne, from Aimee's reports, is a laundry guru. "Or the two of you wouldn't have had a towel or pair of pants left."

"Or socks! Every time she did laundry she lost at least seven socks. I don't know how she did it."

"THE DRYER EATS THEM! I'm sure of it."

"I remember the first time we did laundry in college, Aimee had never done it before. EVER. Jean always did laundry for the kids, and never thought to teach Aimee or the boys to do their own. So we grab all our stuff to take it to the machines in the basement of the dorm, and Aimee just stood there, and burst into tears. She had no idea even where to begin."

"Yeah, she told me that story. I just told her that even the world's most perfect woman couldn't be amazing at everything, or she'd be boring. That's the truth, Ruth." We smile at each other, and for the first time, I'm only feeling warmth toward him. I always idolized Aimee more than a little, she seemed to be everything I wasn't. But it is easy to forget that she was also human with foibles and quirks and some of her own annoying traits.

"I don't know what you could be referring to."

Um, do you really want me to make a list?

"Yeah, never mind."

Thought so.

"So, Wayne, let's see these sketches."

"You betcha." He pulls the folder over and takes out three sheets of paper. My whole heart sinks.

"What on God's green earth is THAT?"

"I think he did an interesting job," Wayne says. "He thought he would bring in the proscenium aspect of theater that is missing in outdoor space, and represent Aimee sort of coming through that proscenium, breaking the fourth wall in the way that outdoor theater does sort of by nature. So you have this rectangular frame and Aimee is both framed by it, but also coming through it."

I'm looking at these sketches, and something is sitting weirdly. It is clearly going to be bronze. A large rectangle with a full-body representation of Aimee sort of half in the frame, with her arms and torso reaching through in a manner that I assume is supposed to be her reaching out to the people in the quad. It reminds me of something. Something annoying. Something awful. Something Aimee . . .

"AAAAAUUUUGGGGGHHH!!!! Nononononono. Is he insane?"

Would hate.

"Um, Wayne, what do you really think of this sketch. Deep down. As it relates to Aimee."

"Well, I dunno. I mean, it's an artist she loves, for the university you guys went to, for a space that meant a lot to her . . ."

"Holy crap, I'm goddamned Han Solo in carbonite."

THAT'S IT! That's what it looks like. Jesus, involve Wayne, and somehow Star Wars is in evidence.

"Wayne. Does this remind you of anything?"

He looks at it closely. "I don't know, it seems a little familiar, but I can't place it specifically."

"Well, let me ask you this. Could you see it hanging, um, I don't know, in Jabba the Hutt's lair?"

"Oh my god. She's carbonite Han." I can almost see the lightbulb over Wayne's head.

"EXACTLY!"

"That is SO COOL!"

"Oh, hell no."

"Um, Wayne . . ."

"I mean, that is awesome! And I didn't even think of it! But total rock star. Good eye, Jenny, look at you knowing your SW references!"

"Wayne, I want you to look me in the eye and tell me that Aimee, our Aimee, would want to spend eternity referencing Han Solo in the middle of a college quad."

Wayne doesn't look up. "She might love it . . ."

"Wayne."

"Wayne Randolph Garland, you look her in the eye."

Wayne doesn't move.

"Wayne, please . . ."

He raises his head, looking like a kid who just found out he cannot have ice cream unless he eats all his peas. "No, she probably would not think it is as cool as I do."

"Wayne, I promise, if someday YOU would like to be immortalized in this way, if I'm around I will try and make it happen. But Aimee . . ."

"Would DIE OF MORTIFICATION."

"Would hate it. You're right." He sighs deeply. "Well, back to the drawing board! Ha, literally! I'll call him and say we are looking for something more traditional. Never fear, we'll get it right."

I had hoped the failed sketch would mean the complete end of the project, but at least we have more time again. "Okay, Wayne. Sorry."

"It's okay. I wouldn't want to do something Aimee would hate."

"Okay, I have to go home, walk the dogs."

"Good plan, Stan. So I'm picking up Noah Friday afternoon, you still available to come with us to the holiday party at Elliot's store?"

I had forgotten I agreed to that. I swallow every instinct to back out of it. "Sure. What time?"

"It goes from five to eight, but we are shooting for seven, hang at the party for a bit, grab a bite after. Want us to come get you?"

"Nah, I'll meet you there."

"Perfect. Should be a blast."

"I'm sure it will be." A nightmare. "I'm looking forward to seeing Noah, and I know Eloise is excited for the ornament class Saturday."

"He's got all his printouts of the superhero logos. I think he's very happy with his theme."

"Well, he comes by it right!"

"True enough."

I walk to the door, grabbing my coat off the rack and putting it on, retrieving my purse from the console table next to the door.

"See you Friday, then."

Wayne moves forward and grabs me in a big hug. "Bye, Jenny," he says into my hair.

"Bye," I say, into his shoulder.

I get home, clean up the remains of what I believe used to be a leather pot holder that Chewie appears to have mistaken for a snack, and take both dogs for a long walk. Once we get home, I change into my cooking blacks. I get the chef's whites when you work in a restaurant, and I used to wear them for events. But home cooking? I have an endless set of black leggings with black T-shirts. Because cooking is messy, and I'm a slob, and no amount of bleach will really salvage whites once you spatter them to hell with demi-glace and chocolate and beet juice.

I head to the kitchen to get set up for my annual holiday baking. I used to make a million different cookies and treats, never fewer than a dozen different things in every gift box, but by the time the holidays rolled around, I was exhausted and cranky. And now that I'm out of the business, I don't have the same need in terms of holiday giving. No big clients to impress or huge staff to acknowledge. I bring stuff to Christmas Eve with Andrea and Jasmin and Gene, and some to bring with to the Brands' on Christmas Day. Some for the Library, where we keep the buffet full of our favorite holiday treats to keep customers high on sugar and shopping. I send some to my parents, who I won't see till I go visit for Passover in March. Some for Noah and Wayne. I used to send some to Brian, but now that feels weird, so I sent a plant for his office instead. I learned the hard lesson a long time ago to just make one or two things that I can do in bulk. This year I am doing praline pecans, an old family favorite, easy and addictive. And a festive holiday dark chocolate loaf cake, with pistachios and dried cherries and white chocolate chips.

I get out my huge seven-quart KitchenAid mixer, and head to the basement, where I have ten pounds of gorgeous halved pecans in the chest freezer, and a pallet of organic eggs from Paulie's Pasture in the commercial refrigerator I use for entertaining and overflow. Upstairs, I focus on separating eggs, reserving the yolks for making pasta or custard later. Beating whites, melting butter, I can feel my shoulders unclench as the scent of toasted sugared pecans caramelizing fills the house. Volnay and Chewie are curled up together sleeping after their exercise.

"Looks like you are getting the holiday spirit after all."

I'm trying to.

"Well, I promised you I wouldn't die within a week of a major holiday, so at least you don't have to be maudlin."

You also promised we'd have the rooms next to one another in the old people's home.

"Well, one out of two."

Yeah.

"For what it's worth? Nothing makes me happier than to see you actually having some holiday cheer in your life."

For what it's worth, I'd trade all the holiday cheer in the universe till the end of time to have you back.

"I know. And I love you, schmoopy. But you're hanging in there. As well you should."

I love you too, schmoopy.

I salt the still-warm pecans with some flaky sea salt, and a little bit with a few tears I hadn't realized I still had in me.

14

Elliot's store, Cosmic Comix, is in a storefront on Clark Street in the Andersonville area. Which makes it an even bigger pain in the ass, since parking is notoriously difficult in this bustling Chicago neighborhood to begin with, but even more so during the holiday season. I circle the area no less than a dozen times before I finally find someone leaving a spot about three blocks away. The unseasonable warmth we've been enjoying has continued, and no snow yet, which is a blessing for everyone except those who believe more in White Christmases than they do in being able to get around. I'll take this, myself. Especially when I have to walk a quarter of a mile to get from my car to my destination. This whole semiretired-homebody thing has spoiled me when it comes to being out and about. I run my errands during the day midweek when normal people are working, and my social life tends to focus on hosting at my house, especially now since that mostly consists of hanging out with Brian, who always sleeps at my place because of the dogs.

I get to Cosmic at around seven fifteen, noticing that Wayne's Escalade is parked right in front.

"I bequeathed him my parking karma."

Couldn't have shared a little with me?

"Nope. Having bad parking karma keeps you humble."

I open the doors, and head into a surprisingly large space. The small storefront belies a fairly enormous store, as these places tend to go, this is no six-hundred square foot hole-in-the-wall. The place is very deep, and duplexed up with a large central staircase leading to the second level. And unlike the somewhat dingy place I imagined, with bad fluorescent lighting and dusty boxes of dolls and toys on warped shelves, this place is bright, clean, and appears to be very smartly merchandised. There are about thirty or forty people milling around, looking in the glass locked cases at mint condition action figures, signed memorabilia, and authenticated movie and television props, as well as what I assume are the more valuable older comics. The walls are lined with the newer comic books, and I'm overwhelmed at the sheer volume of them.

I personally went through a brief *Archie* thing in kindergarten, and a serious *Doonesbury* phase in high school and college. And I still love a good *Calvin and Hobbes* collection. But other than that? Comics were never my thing. Nor sci-fi or fantasy or video gaming or any of the associated genres. I have seen some of the more famous movies; obviously, you can't grow up in the '70s and '80s without being aware of the original Star Wars series, Christopher Reeve Superman movies, and the original *Batman* TV show. I even had a crush on Adam West when I was little. But it isn't something that stuck, and by the time Dungeons & Dragons hit the scene and Atari moved beyond Pong, I was out. I've never read the Harry Potter books. I wouldn't know *Star Trek: The Next Generation* from *Stargate*.

A shapely woman with jet-black hair in a high ponytail and severe bangs revealing a swath of tattooed stars down the back of her neck that complement the tattoo sleeves she is sporting, wanders over.

"Can I take your coat?" she asks.

Flabbergasted, I hand it over and receive a chit in the form of what appears to be some sort of eight-sided space currency. She disappears into a side room that is emitting an eerie blue glow, and I head in search of Wayne and Noah.

"Jenna!" A voice behind me calls out. "You made it!"

I turn around. "Hi, Elliot." He comes forward to give me a hug. Elliot is maybe only three or four inches taller than I am, five eight or five nine at the most. He's wearing old, ripped jeans that sag, being entirely without ass to hold them up, an ancient T-shirt from the old *Heavy Metal* animated movie, and a black sportcoat that is somewhat threadbare. But to his credit, despite being a little disheveled, he smells good. Like a combination of baby powder and cookies.

"How are you?" he asks, concern in his pale green eyes. Elliot, like Wayne, has something of a baby face, but luckily he embraces it and doesn't festoon it with ridiculous facial hair. He's clean shaven, looking about sixteen except for the slightly thinning sandy brown hair in a classic Gary Sandy feathered cut that takes me back to my roller disco days. He always reminds me of when you see a teen idol all grown up, there is a little of the not-young-anymore Shaun Cassidy around the edges, and despite his youthful demeanor, there are some tiny lines beginning to appear in the corners of his eyes.

"I'm okay. Hanging in there. You?"

"Good, good, you know. It's that time of year we retailers love and hate in equal measure. But can't complain. And our boy seems to be keeping his chins above water."

"He does at that."

"I know he's very lucky to have you right now."

"Well, I think I'm probably more a pain in his ass, but it's nice of you to say. I think he's far luckier to have you and Georgie and the boys supporting him."

"Well, hell. None of us have ever had much luck with ladies to start with, and certainly not the kind of luck to be with someone like Aimee. To land her and then lose her? That is a colossal tragedy for geeks everywhere." He smiles, and his eyes sparkle wickedly.

I can't help but laugh. "Well, regardless, it's great that he has you guys to keep his spirits up."

"We do what we can. Can I get you a drink?"

"Sure, what are you pouring?"

"For the masses? Various things in bilious colors served over dry ice for appropriate sci-fi effect. For you, I have a secret stash of Buffalo Trace bourbon in my office, which I am serving over ice with the merest splash of ginger beer and a lemon twist. But only for my friends."

"That sounds great, thank you."

"No problem. And between us, stay away from the buffet and stick to the passed hors d'oeuvres. These monkeys double dip and manhandle the cheese."

"Good to know. Thanks for the heads-up."

"Wayne and Noah I think are upstairs; I'll find you with your drink momentarily."

"Thanks, Elliot."

I make my way through the crowd, bypassing the buffet, where a crowd of bearded and bespectacled men of indeterminate age are indeed manhandling the cheese and eating as if they will not see another meal till the second coming of

Yoda, and head up the stairs. The second floor appears to be more regular books and graphic novels, DVDs and video games. There is a large-screen TV set up with various game stations, and Wayne and Noah appear to be engaged in an epic battle of some sort.

"Hey Jenna! I'm almost winning!" Noah says.

"He's getting better. He might actually beat me this time," Wayne says. I stand behind them, not at all sure what I am seeing, and absentmindedly accept a little phyllo triangle stuffed with a savory and sweet chicken mixture from a passing tray. It isn't as piping hot as I might like, but it is crispy and well-seasoned, sort of reminds me of a Moroccan bisteeya.

"Ah HA! Gotcha!" Noah yells, and he and Wayne high-five. "Did you see that, Jenna? I won! I really won!"

"So you did, congrats." Noah gets up from the chair and comes to give me a hug.

Wayne gets up and ruffles his hair, leaning over to kiss my cheek. "Hey Jenny, this guy really nailed me on that one."

"I saw."

"Never beat him before, that was the first time!" Of course it was; god forbid Wayne would let a kid beat him at some game.

"Well, I hope you make it a habit," I say, trying to leave any judgment out of my tone.

"Yeah, me too!" The kid is wiggling with excitement.

Behind me I feel a presence. "Hey Wayne, Noah, um, Jenna." Georgie. Who is exactly what you would expect a nearly fifty-year-old man named Georgie would be. Georgie is tall and gangly, with the most pronounced Adam's apple I've ever seen outside of a Disney cartoon villain. His thinning, mousy brown hair is kept long. He wears a long black trench coat with an extralong red and yellow striped scarf everywhere. And his teeth are a shade I can only describe as gray. Not yellowed or brown, but actually gray. With sort of a hint of lavender. He is Wayne's second best friend after Elliot, and while I've met him no fewer than twenty times over the years, to my knowledge we have never exchanged more than ten words.

"Hey Georgie," I say.

"How are you?" He head tilts. The bastard.

"I'm good, thanks. You?"

"Good. Work is busy, so that's nice, considering. But I'm ready for a break. Heading home to Michigan for a week for the holidays, see the family, play with the nieces and nephews, you know."

This is officially more information than I have ever known about Georgie in eight years of his acquaintance.

"Sounds great." Not really sure what else to say.

And then? Georgie turns and walks away without another word. Lord, the strangeness.

"Noah, stay with Jenny, I have to go to the little Jedi's room." Wayne heads for the restrooms.

"You know what is so cool, Jenna?"

"What's that, little man?"

"My friends? All their dads let them win all the time. Board games, cards, video games, sports. My dad? He always tries his hardest because he says he wants me to try my hardest, and because he only wants me to know what it feels like to really win for real, and because he says the only thing better in the world than a winner is a gracious loser."

I am gobsmacked. First of all, the fact that Noah appreciates the fact that his dad has never let him win all these years; and second, that it was actually a conscientious parenting decision as opposed to a juvenile need to win that drives Wayne's actions.

"Yeah, I bet it feels really good to know that you won even though he was trying his hardest to beat you." I hope no one else can see the lightbulb over my head right now.

"It. Is. AWESOME."

"A beverage, milady?" Elliot comes over and hands me a short tumbler, and I accept it and take a sip.

"Delicious, thank you."

"Hey Elliot! I just beat Dad at Hitman: Absolution!"

"No way! You really did?"

"I totally squooshed him."

"That is amazing, dude. I still haven't beaten him on that one. Congrats." Elliot and Noah high-five. I take another sip of my drink, which is perfect, smoky bourbon, sweet heat from the ginger beer, a little brightness from the lemon twist; the ideal thing for a brisk evening.

"Hey, El, awesome party, man." Wayne returns, wiping his hands on his jeans. I hope from having washed them, thinking of Elliot's earlier buffet comment.

"The dryer broken in there?" Elliot gestures with his head at the bathroom. "Or you just trying to shrink those floods of yours to capris?"

"HA! That's a good one, he totally burned you, Dad!"

Wayne grins. "What can I say. I was raised by wolves."

"That you were, my friend, that you were." Elliot laughs. "Well, we are about ten minutes to shutting this party down. Jenna, are you joining us for dinner?"

"Oh, I don't . . . I mean . . ."

"Pleeeeeese, Jenna? Come with us! We're going to Hamburger Mary's and Dad said we can get the fried mac 'n' cheese fritters."

"Pleeeeese, Jenny? Come with us! We need a fourth if we're getting the chili cheese Tater Tots," Wayne pipes in, perfectly imitating Noah's voice and inflection.

"Pleeeeese, Jenna?" Elliot is not to be left out. "Come with us! You're the only one who will eat the fried pickle spears with me."

"Okay, okay, uncle. I'll come." I can't say no to all of them, and the bourbon is making me pliable.

The three of them high-five one other. High-fiving appears to be an essential part of guy communications.

"You guys go get a table, I'll be there in fifteen," Elliot says.

"Don't you need help cleaning up?" I say, looking around at the party, which still seems to be in full swing. There is an hour of work at least once he gets everyone out."

"That, my dear, is what twentysomething staffers are for. Once the party is officially over, I am off the clock and free as a bird. You guys head on over and order, and I will join you in mere moments. And Jenna? You order for me. This idiot will get me a medium well plain hamburger, and that will make me cry."

He smiles at me and winks, and heads over to chat with a customer. Wayne, Noah, and I go downstairs and retrieve our coats from the be-inked girl, and head out in the direction of fried pub food, Noah wiggling in between me and Wayne, grabbing both of our hands, and swinging merrily.

Y ou get that boy home to bed, I'll walk Jenna to her car,"
Elliot says. Noah has hit a wall. The long day, the drive
from Madison, the excitement of the party, the enormous
amounts of food . . . ten minutes ago his head hit the table,
and he can barely keep his eyes open.

"Thanks, man. I'll talk to you tomorrow. G'night Jenny,
thanks for coming," Wayne says to me over an armload of
exhausted ten-year-old.

"'Night, Jenna," Noah mumbles.

"Bye, guys."

Wayne gets Noah strapped into the backseat, his head
lolling back with pure exhaustion. He claps Elliot on the back,
and heads around to the driver's side.

"Nightcap? There is still some bourbon in the office. And
I just want to do a quick check to make sure all is well, but I
can walk you to your car first if you don't want to come in,"
Elliot says, gesturing at the now-dark store.

"No more bourbon for me, I'm driving," I say. "But you
can check the store if you want. I'd actually love a water."

"Of course. Nothing like the salty fried goodness of Mary's
to suck all the spit out of your mouth."

"Exactly."

Elliot unlocks the door and slips inside, turning off the
alarm and turning on the light. He steps aside so I can come
in, then relocks the door behind me. Dinner was actually a
good time. I hadn't been to Hamburger Mary's before, but
the food was terrific versions of pub grub, great burgers, and
a cool atmosphere. It was actually fun to be there. Noah is

always funny, and Elliot good-naturedly ribs Wayne and calls him on his crap, and they all defer to me in very old-school gentlemanly ways. I don't think I've ever spent an entire evening without being annoyed by Wayne, and even when he dropped the open ketchup bottle into my purse, I just couldn't get it up to be overly annoyed at him. That is probably the bourbon. And the fact that I never really loved this purse anyway.

"Hey, I gave you that purse."

They can't all be winners.

"Come on in, I'll grab you a water," Elliot says, heading for the door marked Office. I follow him, and again am shocked. Elliot's office is clean, elegant; English Arts and Crafts desk, old barrister's bookcases, sleek computer system, chocolate leather couch, more like a professor's office than a comic book store owner. I was expecting toys and mess.

I sit on the couch, and he hands me a bottle of water from a small fridge in the corner.

"I'll just be one second," he says, powering up the computer, and pulling out a small pair of reading glasses. He scans over something, smiles, types a little, and then shuts down the computer. "Sorry, I have a client in Japan who needed to check in."

"Wow. What did he want?"

"I've been helping him build his private collection for the past few years, there is a specific item he has wanted me to track down for him, which I finally acquired earlier this week. He was quibbling a little about price, but finally agreed to what I wanted, so I had to send him the account information for the wire transfer."

"Doesn't he have a credit card?"

"Not that he can charge four hundred and fifty grand on."

I almost do a spit take. "Um, four hundred and fifty THOUSAND dollars? Are you selling him black tar heroin?"

Elliot laughs. "No, I tracked down a Detective Comic number one from 1937 for him. Very rare, and this one is in amazing condition."

"That is insane."

"Lucky for me."

"So what is the markup on something like that?"

"Well, this time I actually got it in a big lot from an estate, we didn't even know it was in there, just knew the guy had been collecting since he was a kid, and he was in his eighties. It was over three thousand books, so we knew we'd make our money on it. But this was a huge, important find."

"So, if it isn't too presumptuous . . ."

"I bought the lot for about 70K. This one is the only really ridiculous item, the rest will go for between fifty and twenty-five hundred each, which is what I figured when I bought them."

"Congrats, that is really fantastic."

"A good day." He nods. "So I think Wayne seems to be hanging in there. How do you think he's doing? Really?"

"I think he's okay. I think we're all okay. It sucks, but we had time to face it, to prepare. He has you and the guys and Noah."

"And you."

"I think I'm less support and more of a babysitter, but it's nice of you to say."

"You're more support than you think. And let's be honest, he needs a babysitter. The man raised himself, it's a small miracle he walks upright."

"Wayne doesn't really talk about his family, Aimee never

said much except that he wasn't in communication with any of them."

"I knew Wayne back in Missouri; we grew up together. He was other-side-of-the-tracks trailer trash. Mom was a drunk, essentially a hooker who got paid in drinks and the occasional bit of cash or wad of food stamps. Never knew his dad, who took off after knocking Mom up, never to be seen again, but he had a couple mean drunk biker uncles who liked to beat him up for grins."

"That must have been awful. Did you know it was going on at the time?"

"He didn't really talk about it till we were older. I knew he hated his house, just didn't know specifics."

"Wow. How did you guys get to be friends?"

"I was one of those sickly kids, asthma that I eventually grew out of, but held back a year because I missed so much school. We bonded like geeks bond. Best friends since fifth grade, his mom finally drank herself to death when we were seniors in high school, and he lived with me and my folks to finish out the year, and then he and I ended up at Wash U together."

Now I feel shitty. "I had no idea it was so hard on him growing up."

"He doesn't talk about it. When his mom died he just said that now his life could start, and he was never going to look back. I think he looks for the positive side of everything because he knows what really crappy looks like."

I take a sip of water. And suddenly every nasty little thing I've ever thought about him feels like salt in a wound I didn't know existed. "It's kind of amazing when you think about it."

"Look, Jenna, it isn't like Wayne is perfect. Our crew is a

bunch of overgrown misfit children. Wayne had it the worst growing up, but we all had the unpopular weirdo freak thing in one way or another. I like to think that a combination of decent brains and a fairly good sense of humor kept us all from becoming tragic statistics."

"You mean criminals and meth heads?"

Elliot laughs. "Exactly. And at a certain level, I think we all cling to our weirdness because it insulates us from trying to fit in and failing. My brother is really fat, like four hundred pounds. Last time I tried to get him to lose weight, he said he deep down didn't want to know what would happen if he was thin. Because if you are forty and four hundred pounds and single with a crappy job, no one expects much. He said he didn't want to get thin and find out that still no one wanted to date him or hire him, because then he would have to know that it wasn't the weight, it was just him."

"That is really sad."

"Yes it is. And I always thought it was pretty amazing that Aimee was one of those rare individuals who was secure enough in being A-list normal that she could afford to see the awesomeness that is Wayne, and was always very cool with the rest of us. She never tried to change him or make him fit her world, she never cut him off from us; she just let him be and loved him and let him love her. She was a great, great lady."

And suddenly I am weeping, for my friend who is gone, for her spirit which was even more amazing than I knew, for Wayne's horrible childhood, for me being small. Elliot comes over to the couch and puts his arms around me.

"I'm sorry, I know how much you miss her. Shhhh." He holds me and rubs my back and lets me cry.

"Sorry. Sometimes . . ."

"Sometimes you just gotta cry. I get it. Totally." He hands me a Kleenex.

"Thanks, Elliot. For seeing her. Her specialness. And for sharing that with me about Wayne."

"Hey, I like to think we are all friends. And you really are the only one who will eat the fried pickles with me."

I laugh. "Anytime."

He smiles. "You okay?"

"Yeah. But I have two dogs at home with their legs crossed."

"Let me walk you to your car."

He locks up again, and we walk the three blocks in silence.

"Thanks Elliot."

"You betcha." He grins wickedly at me. "Hey, I'm having a small do for New Year's Eve. Wayne is coming; if you don't get a better offer, I hope you'll join us."

"It's a lovely offer, and as soon as I know my plans, I'll let you know."

"Wayne says you're seeing someone, you're welcome to bring him."

"That's very sweet. I'll figure out the plan and shoot you an e-mail." I make a mental note to send some pecans and chocolate cake to him at the store to thank him.

"Sounds good. Get home safe, Jenna."

"I will."

He kisses my hand, and I get into my car. And for at least four blocks, I can see him in my rearview mirror, watching me drive away.

15

*B*e prepared for them to not love him."

I'm not in love with him myself yet, but why would they not love him?

"Because they love you and they want the best for you. And he is perfectly fine, but he isn't going to make them jump up and down."

I don't need them to jump up and down. I just want him to be there.

"Why?"

Because he is in my life and they are my family.

"But what is he? You still haven't once called him your boyfriend."

He's the guy I'm dating.

"And?"

And that's enough.

"For them or for you?"

Hopefully for all of us, for now.

"Okay. Remember you said so."

Can I get dressed now?

"I'd check that dog before you get fancy."

Crap.

"You said a mouthful."

This is the moment the unmistakable smell wafts its way up my nostrils.

"CHEWIE!" I run out of the bathroom and into the bedroom. The puppy, who'd followed me upstairs with Volnay when I came up to shower, is sitting on the bench at the foot of my bed. Next to a pile of poop that I presume must have come from a brontosaurus wandering by, based on the sheer size.

The puppy looks neither apologetic nor sheepish. He sits next to his friend, The Enormous Stank Dump, tongue lolling, one string of drool dripping from the tip all the way to the small puddle forming next to him. Great. Remind me to call Ayers and tell them to rename the bench the Shit and Spit Bench.

"DOWN," I say, using my deepest register, in what our trainer calls the Voice of God. "Bad boy." And I toss on my robe and go downstairs to get the proper cleaning equipment. Deep down, I know that this is my fault; we took an abbreviated walk during which Chewie peed but didn't poop, but I was in a rush to shower and change. Brian is picking me up soon to go to Jasmin and Gene's for Christmas Eve. In all fairness, he had taken not one but two enormous dumps on our morning walk, so I convinced myself that he was just done for the day and would do his business on the last walk of the day before bed. But the one thing that every dog trainer has ever told me is that while dogs are responsible for general destructive behavior like plant dumping, shoe chewing, and garbage strewing, when it comes to going to the bathroom in the house, that lands squarely on owners. No dog that has been properly watched and paid attention to and walked appropriately will go to the bathroom in the house except in a dire emergency or illness.

I manage to get the bench cleaned up, and properly doused

with enzyme spray to prevent future occurrences, by which point I'm really pressed for time. I pull on a pair of black velvet jeans, a sparkly gray tank, and a black sweater. A pair of black suede wedges, a wide bracelet made of about fifty thin silver chains, my diamond studs. I pull my hair into a ponytail, slap on some makeup, and get downstairs just in time for Brian to ring the bell.

"Hello, beautiful," he says, leaning in to kiss me. He looks fabulous in dark wash jeans, a French blue shirt highlighting his eyes, with a black and gray tweed sportcoat.

"Hello, yourself."

He comes in, and follows me to the kitchen, where I have packed up my offerings for tonight. Instead of the more traditional Christmas ham, Gene is going with a twelve-hour slow-roasted pork shoulder. Jasmin is making roasted parsnips with pears, and Andrea is doing creamy grits. I'm bringing Swiss chard with chickpeas, and made some Brazilian fudge balls, sort of a cross between fudge and caramel, and insanely delicious.

Brian greets the dogs, who have come over to love him, and I grab the fudge balls out of the fridge.

"Oh, crap, dog, really?" Brian mutters and I turn to see that Chewie has slimed his right thigh sort of spectacularly with slobber. I reach for a dish towel, dampen it a bit under the tap, and toss it to him to get the stuff off himself.

"Sorry."

"It's not your fault. It's not even his fault. I choose to blame Wayne. He's my personal Grinch."

Brian is still pouting about my not coming to Colorado tomorrow. I actually think the reason I invited him tonight was to try and mitigate his disappointment, but clearly he hasn't gotten over it. He knows that Chewbacca is the reason I can't ever spend the night at his place. Volnay would be welcome, but Chewie isn't finished with his training yet, can't really be trusted to not devour anything not nailed down, and by the time he's ready, he'll be way over the forty-pound weight limit regulation for the building. He blames Wayne for my inability to come on the trip with him, since I can't kennel the dog. And frankly, I haven't done anything but let him believe that, even though Wayne, Benji, and Eloise all have offered to take the dogs if I want to go out of town. And he doesn't quite understand why I feel the need to go to Indiana to see the Brands, since there are so many of them and they will have Wayne.

"Wayne is Mr. Christmas. And he would feel terrible if he thought he had somehow ruined yours."

"Wayne is Mr. Magoo, and while I believe he might feel terrible for approximately eleven seconds, I have faith he would get over it just in time to accidentally back over me with his car."

"Look, all fixed." I gesture at his jeans, which are so dark you can't even see where the damp towel was used. I'm desperate to change the subject. I've been feeling so much better about Wayne since the party at Elliot's last weekend, and I want very much to hang on to that good feeling, especially since I'm still a little nervous about tomorrow. We have a three-hour drive down there, a full day of Brand festivities, and then a three-hour drive back tomorrow night. I've never spent that much time with him, and knowing that a full six hours is going to be one-on-one, I want to hold every ounce of happy thoughts in anticipation. "Besides, a little slobber never hurt anyone. He just loves you soooo much."

"If only he could love me less wetly." Brian comes over to where I'm standing. "Now you on the other hand . . ." He leans in and kisses me deeply. And wetly.

"I take your point."

"Before we go . . . I have something for you." He pulls a long thin box from his inside jacket pocket.

"I thought we weren't doing gifts?" I'm mortified. After I told him I couldn't go on the trip, we agreed that we wouldn't do presents. And I took that seriously. I don't have so much as a card for him.

"I know. But then I saw this and I couldn't resist."

"Not fair."

"I never promised to be fair. I'm a lawyer." He grins.

I take the box and open it. Inside is a delicate white gold chain with small diamonds spaced about every inch and a half. "Brian, it's gorgeous. And it's too much."

"Nonsense. It is perfect for you, and you deserve it. Someone in your life should be giving you gifts that are actually what you want and need. And don't require such intense maintenance." He gestures at the dog, and while the necklace is beautiful, I can't help but thinking in a weird way that somehow it is about proving something about himself as it relates to Wayne. But I shake it off, because Brian is putting the necklace on for me, and pulling me to the powder room to admire it. And while it isn't something I ever would have chosen for myself, I have to admit it does look very pretty. I can see why he would have thought to buy it for me.

"Brian, thank you, it's just so lovely. I'll treasure it."

He beams, and we go back to the kitchen to get the food and head to the celebration.

A toast!" Gene raises his glass from the head of the table. "To a happy and healthy New Year for all of us, and a very merry Christmas. Thank you all for being here tonight. I especially want to thank my beautiful wife for everything she is, and for loving me for nearly forty-four years, and for our amazing daughter who brings us such joy and pride. And a moment to remember our beloved Aimee, whose spirit shines on us in these times of celebration, and will support us when things are difficult in years to come."

"To Aimee," Benji says beside me.

"To our wonderful hosts," Brian says from my other side.

"To all of us," Jasmin says.

We're a smaller group tonight. As generous as Jasmin and Gene are at Thanksgiving, they tend to want to be more insular at Christmas; between Jasmin's Catholic upbringing and Gene's devout Baptist one, this night is the part of the holiday they save for themselves. They did a Christmas Eve brunch earlier today with Jasmin's family. They'll go to midnight mass later tonight, and Christmas service at Gene's church tomorrow morning, after which they will stop by the group home to see Benji before heading to Gene's sister's house for a huge extended-family feast. After Thanksgiving, Benji convinced the kids at the home that it would be fun to host a Christmas Day dinner for the kids from two other local group homes, and Jasmin and Gene offered to sponsor the food costs for the event. I'm so proud of him, but ultimately I know it is the kind of idea Aimee would have had, and I can't take credit for inspiring him.

"Hey, you inspire him with the food, I inspire him with the altruism, between us we have plenty to be proud of."

That is true.

So tonight we are just seven. Seven people, and twelve pounds of pork. I pick a piece of the insanely delicious crispy skin and feel it crunch between my teeth. Suddenly the ratio seems perfectly normal. Gene rubbed it with his secret spice mix early this morning, and it's been roasting in a slow oven all day. Andrea's creamy grits are the perfect thing to soak up the thick gravy, Jasmin's parsnips and pears are caramelized and sweet, and everyone praises my chard and chickpeas.

Andrea is sitting with Law, having had not one, but three real dates with the charming doctor since their Thanksgiving hookup, and Brian and I are scheduled to have a double date with them after the New Year. She seems happy and glowy, and even though she and Law have been dating such a short time, they seem very connected. And Jasmin and Gene clearly approve, which makes me wonder if his invite to Thanksgiving hadn't actually been a sneaky fix-up.

I look at Brian and wonder what it is that I don't have that same glow. We've been together longer. He is certainly attentive, but not oppressively so. He's so freakishly good-looking, smart, nice to me. I enjoy his company. We're compatible in bed.

"Compatible is not fantastic."

Compatible is frankly better than a lot of guys I've dated. Including Jack, if you must know.

"Compatible is not sparkly."

Sometimes comfortable is more important than sparkly.

"In pants, yes. In shoes and sex, no."

Oy.

"Twelve hours to cook pork, and twelve minutes to eat it." Jasmin is laughing at us, empty plates everywhere, and people leaning back in chairs, stuffed, but still tempted to reach for more. Law picks a piece of crackling off the shoulder, and Andrea slaps his hand jokingly.

"Leave that boy alone, Dre. He can pick that pigskin all he wants. He knows a good thing," Gene says with a wink.

"Everything was just delicious," Benji says. "I hope you all saved room for dessert!"

Benji brought a fabulous-looking cake made out of twenty layers of crepes with thin layers of vanilla pastry cream in between, the top burnished and brûléed with a crispy burnt sugar layer.

"I'm sure by the time we finish cleaning up, we'll be ready," Andrea says, and we stand to follow Jasmin to the kitchen. Gene motions the men to follow him to the living room, shaking his head at their desire to be helpful.

"Stay out of my wife's kitchen, you'll just make a nuisance of yourselves."

Benji stands, looking torn. Not sure if he should follow the other guys, or stay and help. I know he'd probably rather be with the girls, but he does take a certain pride in his masculinity. Jasmin saves him.

"Benji, will you ask the other men if they would like coffee with their after-dinner drinks?" she asks. He gratefully scampers off with a job, knowing that if they say yes, she will ask him to make it, allowing him to shuttle back and forth and get the best of both worlds.

"Didn't we just do this?" Andrea asks.

"Feels like it, doesn't it. I, for one, am ready for the holidays to be over," Jasmin says. "Takes it out of me more every year."

"You haven't broken a sweat, and you love every minute of it." Andrea laughs, kissing her mother's cheek.

"No coffees," Benji says.

"Okay. Thank you. Would you be a dear and pack up the leftovers? The containers are in the bottom cabinet next to the fridge." Jasmin invents the new job, and Benji gives her a saucy salute and heads across the room to be useful. She turns to me, handing me the now-clean roasting pan to dry and gives me a wink.

Jasmin is right as usual; by the time we are done cleaning, we have earned the desserts, and Benji's cake is spectacular. Everyone loves the fudge balls as well, and soon we are all sated and somewhat sleepy. We all get ready to leave so that Jasmin and Gene can get ready to go to mass. Andrea and Law offer to drop Benji off so that he doesn't have to take the train, and Brian and I head back to my place.

Where we find the contents of his overnight bag, which he accidentally left in the kitchen with the dogs, strewn about, mauled and damp with slobber. There are four neat puncture holes in his tube of fancy Italian toothpaste that he special orders from some New York apothecary, and Chewbacca looks half-rabid with dried toothpaste foam all around his mouth.

Brian is not amused. He also decides not to stay. "It's not just the dog, I have the flight tomorrow, and I haven't completely finished packing, I was going to have to get up early anyway. And as gorgeous as you look, that meal has sort of done me in, I don't think I'm up for anything except sleep."

And I? Try not to look relieved. I help him gather the shreds of his pajamas and socks and underwear, the long-sleeved T-shirt he intended to wear in the morning, the decimated contents of his toiletry kit. His toothbrush is there, with all the bristles mysteriously removed. His comb looks like it went through the garbage disposal. His deodorant is simply gone completely.

"Sorry about the dog, and everything. And thank you again for my beautiful necklace."

"You're worth it." He kisses me, and I believe he isn't angry as much as he is just tired and really overstuffed, and wanting to get organized for his trip.

"Thank you. Safe travels, text me or something if you want while you're gone. But mostly have a great time and please be careful on the slopes. I'd like you back in one piece."

"You got it. I'll call you. And I'll be back on the thirty-first in time for New Year's."

"I'm counting on it." We have decided to just lie low and stay at my place for New Year's, I'm making plans for a yummy meal that we can cook together, and we'll drink great champagne and maybe watch an old movie or two. In addition to Elliot's offer, Andrea and Law invited us to a party being held by one of his friends, Alana and RJ called to say they were having a small dinner party if we were interested, but I frankly don't like being out and about on New Year's if I can help it. It's the one holiday Aimee and I disagreed about. She loved being at a party, all dressed up; I just always wanted to be home in comfy clothes with great food and great wine and no insanity.

Brian kisses me one more time, and heads for home. I change into leggings and an oversized sweater and head downstairs to take the dogs for their last walk of the day. At this hour, we stay on the boulevard, where it is well lit, and keep things pretty brief, although this time I don't head for home till both pups have done a complete toilet. I can't clean up dog poop inside again today. Lucky for me, they both oblige with efficiency and we get home fairly quickly. I've already got everything pretty set to go for tomorrow, another set of fudge balls, two of the chocolate loaf cakes and two pounds of the praline pecans. Eloise-recommended books for the little ones, and iTunes gift cards for the older ones. Six bottles of a locally brewed gin called Letherbee, produced by one of the former bartenders from Lula, and my new house tipple, for all of the brothers. Five bottles of Lillet Rosé for the sisters-in-law. And for Wayne, a signed copy of a coffee table book called *Oeuvre* by an artist named Drew Struzan, who apparently has done many of the most famous sci-fi movie posters, including the iconic ones for the original Star Wars series. George Lucas even did the introduction for the book, and his signature appears beside the author's. Elliot helped me with this one, and I get the feeling that the one hundred dollars I paid for it is way undermarket, but it was kind of him, since Wayne only drinks beer and that is somehow not a festive holiday offering.

I put Chewie in his crate, and lock the kitchen gate, bringing Volnay up to bed with me. Eloise is coming tomorrow afternoon to walk the dogs and feed them, and Benji will do it tomorrow night after his dinner, so they will be fine even if I don't get home till after midnight.

I change into my pajamas and crawl into bed, thinking that tonight I'll easily be able to skip the Ambien.

"*Psst.*"

What now?

"Merry Christmas."

Merry Christmas, my friend. I hope it is very merry where you are.

"It's always merry where I am."

It was ever thus and so.

16

"I can't BELIEVE that Jordan did that," Wayne says first thing as we pull out of the driveway.

"I know. And no one ever suspected?" It's just after nine, and Wayne and I are heading back to Chicago after a very long day. The drive down was uneventful, Wayne told me to sleep, and I used it as a defensive move, faking it for the first forty-five minutes, and finally actually sleeping for the next hour and a half, so by the time I was "awake," we were almost there. We visited with everyone, exchanged gifts, played with the kids, admired new haircuts and clothes and generally got caught up. There was a brief sad moment during grace, when Aimee's oldest brother, Brad, toasted her memory, but then it was all good food and drinks and wrangling eleven kids between the ages of four and sixteen. And then, when the little ones had been banished to the basement rec room to work off their extra energy where they couldn't break something, Jordan popped his sixth beer of the evening and announced that he is gay.

"First I've ever heard of it. I just feel bad for the kid, you know? Feeling like he had to hold that in all this time. I mean, Thom and Jean might have been a little rough on him if they had been here, but jeez, they've been gone since he was pretty little, and you saw how the rest of them reacted. Like he had said he wanted to be an accountant, or was going to buy a Prius. Total nonissue, totally supportive."

"Poor Jordan. He was always something of an odd duck."

"Well, it can't have been easy. To lose both parents a year apart, have to be raised by your older brother, with your nieces and nephews who are practically your same age, that had to be rough."

"I'm sure. But he always seemed pretty good, good grades in school, did well in college, seems to have gotten a first job he likes well enough."

"Yeah. Never seemed depressed really, but disconnected somehow. Aimee never really felt terribly close to him."

"Well, I hope he feels better; it was great how everyone rallied right away and no one acted surprised or scandalized."

"That's the truth, Ruth. A very interesting evening. And the dinner looked pretty good!"

I laugh. They finally figured out to just have a burger in the fridge to throw on for him at these holiday feasts. "It was. Delicious. Wayne, I gotta ask, what is the deal with only eating eleven things? I mean, it's clearly not a political or ethical choice, and you do have something in almost all the food groups, but I just don't really get it."

"You must think it's really stupid."

"I don't really, well, maybe I do, I just wonder where it comes from."

Wayne pauses, and runs his hand over his full-on George Michael stubble that he has chosen for his holiday face. "Well, Elliot said he told you a little bit about how I grew up, and all."

"He did."

"So, there was this old lady who lived in the trailer park, three spots down from us. And I would sometimes do stuff for her; fix things you know, or change lightbulbs she couldn't reach, stuff like that. And when I did, she would make me dinner. She only ever made roasted chicken, pork chops, thin chewy steaks, and burgers. Some sort of potato. Green beans, corn, or carrots. Always an iceberg lettuce salad with ranch dressing. That was it. But it was the best food I ever ate."

I think about what Elliot said about his upbringing, and my heart hurts for him. "It was nice that you had her."

"It was. School food was awful, but I had to eat it, so it felt like punishment. The only meals I ever ate that gave me any pleasure from the time I was about six till my mom died were those dinners with Mrs. Jennings. So those I guess are the only foods I ever associated with being safe and fed and taken care of."

"What about after you left? No desire to explore other stuff when your food was under your own control?"

"When I got to college, I was work study, and worked in the dining hall as a dishwasher, and we didn't get to eat till the end of the night, by which point your safest option is a burger, and everything else reminded me of the free lunches anyway. I guess it just stuck. I know it makes me kind of an ass, but it's just what feels safe to me."

"Oh, Wayne. I had no idea."

"It's not a big deal, Jenny. It is what it is. I manage to keep up my girlish figure!" he says, chuckling, patting his not-insubstantial gut.

"So why the open mind when it comes to desserts?"

"Ahh. That's easy. Elliot's mom ran a bakery. Every day he'd sneak me something she had brought home, something that hadn't sold the day before. Never mattered what it was, it was sweet, so I guess I never had any negative associations with desserts."

"Have you ever tried anything else, I mean since college?"

"Nope. Never really saw the need. There is almost always a burger or steak or chicken or chop on a menu at restaurants. I know how to cook everything I eat. Makes shopping a breeze. And is only really a problem eating at people's houses, but there's always a Mickey D's en route!"

I laugh, since there isn't much else to do. "Well, if there is ever anything you think you might like to try, I'd be happy to go with you or make it for you."

"That's very nice, Jenny. You never know. Maybe this old dog will look for a new trick one of these days!"

My phone rings. It is Brian calling to wish me a merry Christmas.

"Did you make it to Snowmass okay?"

"I did. O'Hare was pretty quiet, but my flight was full. We're all here and we just got back from dinner, so I wanted to catch you."

"Wayne and I are just heading back."

"Well you probably can't talk with him there, huh?"

"I don't want to be rude."

"Not at all. I'm pretty beat anyway. I'll try and call you in the next day or so."

Wayne looks over at me. "If you don't mind my saying, but there's something about that guy I don't really trust."

"Wayne, that guy is your lawyer, if you don't trust him, that's sort of a big deal, globally."

"Not like that, I trust him with the lawyer stuff. But I don't trust him with you."

"I appreciate your concern, but you have nothing to worry about. I can take care of myself."

"I dunno, that Jack was no prize. Thank god you didn't

marry that schmuck. Do you know how horrible it was for me and Aimee to think that you were going to foist him on us for the rest of our natural lives? With his wine snob BS, and his weird obsession with his dental health? And the way he just never let anyone get a word in edgewise, especially you? I'm not afraid to tell you, Jenny girl, that guy was a total tool. You dodged a bullet on that one. That's the truth, Ruth."

I'm stunned into complete silence. But oddly, instead of being angry, I just want to laugh. To think that Wayne felt exactly about Jack the way I have always felt about him? That is like a weird Christmas "Gift of the Magi" moment.

"Well, lucky for all of us, he bailed, never to be heard from again."

"Thank god."

"Not to worry. I'm pretty sure I'm not going to marry Brian."

"Ugh, for sure don't do that. Aimee would come back from the dead just to smack you in the head."

"I totally would."

"We're just dating."

"Exclusively?"

I think about this. I'm not seeing anyone else, but we haven't had the official discussion about it, and a wise woman once told me that unless a man has said the word "exclusive" to you, you should assume he is dating other people.

"She also told you to be sure to provide your own condoms for quality control."

"No, Wayne, we aren't dating exclusively."

"Good. I mean, don't go all Girls Gone Wild or anything, but I think you should date other people."

"Duly noted." I think it somewhat hilarious that Wayne is taking my dating life so personally.

"He's protective of you. The way I would be if I weren't all Ghost of Christmas Past up in here."

Wayne leans forward and presses Play on the car stereo. I'm shocked to hear the strains of A-ha coming out of the speakers.

"Wayne, is this the '80s station?"

"Nope, I made a couple of driving CDs for us." He gestures to a CD case. I pick it up and read his little handwriting. Three CDs. Filled with classics from the '70s and '80s, and all my guilty pleasure faves. Styx, Journey, .38 Special, Men at Work, Fine Young Cannibals, Oingo Boingo, INXS.

"You have *Free to Be . . . You and Me* in here!"

"Well, of course. It was the only record I had until I was fourteen."

"You're killing me."

"Hey, Rosey Grier said it's alright to cry, and frankly, that's the only advice I've ever used consistently as much now as I did as a kid."

"More guys should know that and take it to heart. That it's okay for them to do it and okay for girls. Jack hated when I cried. He always said that he felt like it was inherently manipulative." I'm suddenly remembering why it was so easy to give him the ring back, and wondering why on earth Aimee never said anything to me about him. And then I look at Wayne. And it is clearer than I might like to admit.

"Aimee never cried much, but when she did, I always just let her get it out. I know it makes things better to have the release."

"Yeah. It does." I pause, and then forge ahead. "Noah said sometimes he can hear you crying at night."

"Yeah. Night is when I miss her most. Every night we'd get into bed and trade days, you know? Lying in the dark, what was great, what sucked, what was funny that we've been waiting all day to share. Even when she got home late from some party, I'd wake up and we'd lie there and trade days. And now I get into bed and she's not there, and she's not coming later, she's just gone. No one to trade days with. Makes it feel sometimes like the day didn't happen, you know, because there was no one to witness it."

This brings tears to my eyes. "I know what you mean. She called me every morning. Same thing. To touch base, to plan, to reflect. To have the connection."

"Yeah."

"He was okay, right, I mean, not worried or anything?"

"He's a very levelheaded little guy. He said he understood why you were sad and that you have plenty of people to help you."

"That kid and marrying Aimee are the two things I ever did totally right in my whole life."

"The Best of Times" comes on next. "I'd call these CDs a solid third," I say. Wayne laughs and reaches over and takes my hand. His hand is a little sweaty, but strong, and he holds on, and I let him, and we sing together at the tops of our voices as we head home. "The best of tiiiiiiiimmmmmmmmmeeessss . . ."

I walk in my door at a little after midnight. I'm hoarse from singing; Wayne and I did car karaoke all the way home. As soon as I come through the door, Chewie and Volnay come running down the hall to greet me in a happy jumping pile of dog. There is a note on the side table from Benji saying that they are fed and walked and that he cleaned up the mess in the kitchen, and that I should move my plastic goods out of the lower drawers, which Chewie has apparently figured out how to get into, and that I'm going to need more Saran Wrap and Ziploc bags.

"Dog? In case you were curious? This whole *Marley and Me* act you have going on is not cute, and you are not getting a movie deal." Chewie looks at me quizzically. "And you? Are you not supposed to be training him?" I say to Volnay. She looks up at me as if to say that he is adopted and apparently this is nature not nurture.

"I give up. And I'm too tired to complain. Time for bed." But as I head to the kitchen to get Chewie in his crate, he shoots right up the stairs with Volnay. By the time I get up there, they are both curled up on my bed. I'm feeling a little cramped from the long hours in the car, and decide to leave them there while I take a hot bath. As the tub fills, I think about everything Wayne and I talked about.

"He's not so bad, when you scratch the surface, huh?"

He's got his moments.

"Admit it, you like him."

I'm getting to know him. And I like him more than I did.

"You like him."

I still don't get it. I mean, okay, I can see that he has the ability to be somewhat less constantly irritating than I have previously experienced. But that still doesn't explain him being your grand passion. You loved everything cosmopolitan and sophisticated. Your favorite word was *elegant*. You wanted everything in your life to be beautiful. How did you end up with Wayne? I mean, seriously. Not being a total waste is one thing, I can see that he has some qualities, but that is a far leap to love of your life.

"You'll see."

I strip off my clothes, put my hair in a bun on top of my head, and lower myself into the steaming water. Suddenly I bolt upright.

You don't have some weird creepy fantasy about me getting together with Wayne, do you?

"Okay, GROSS. If there weren't a strict no-ralphing-in-heaven-policy, I would totally throw up right now. I just meant that you will see. You will eventually see why I adored him above all other people including you, and I hope you'll see that you can have that too. With someone else. Because if you hook up with my not-so-merry widower, I will come back from the dead just to cut a bitch."

Thank god.

I sink back into the water, letting the heat soak into my bones and relax my muscles.

"AAAAHHHHH!" I yell as nearly fifty pounds of puppy lands on my chest, then slides half into the tub, freaks out, and scratches the bejesus out of me getting himself out of the tub.

Nothing sexier than an overweight, naked, wet woman with red welts all over her torso and thighs chasing a soaking puppy all over the house. Wayne might not be as awful as I always thought, but this gift that keeps on giving that he has foisted upon my life is not exactly keeping him off my shit list.

By the time I get Chewbacca into his crate, a feat that takes the better part of a half an hour and four pieces of bologna, and clean up the broken vase in the hallway that fell off the table when Chewie slammed into it, my adrenaline is going. Despite the fact that it is now well after one in the morning, I'm wide awake. And I really don't want to take a pill, because it'll throw my whole day off tomorrow if I sleep till noon or something. I lie in bed, Volnay snoring on the pillow beside me, in the dark with my iPad, scrolling to see if there is anything I want to watch on my Netflix queue. Aimee convinced me not to put a television in my bedroom.

"It's dangerous. Bedrooms are for sleeping and sex. TV in the bedroom is not elegant."

But it is nice when you can't sleep. Or when you're sick.

"You have that tablet thing for that. TV in the bedroom is a slippery slope. You should at least have to get out of bed to be a couch potato."

Nothing really sparks me on the queue, but I'm too lazy to get up and go downstairs to see if there is something good on the food channels or an infomercial I haven't seen yet. I check my e-mail and decide to shoot off a note to thank Elliot.

E-

Just wanted to thank you so much for helping me with the book for Wayne. He really was very touched, and I think it was the perfect thing. You're officially in trouble, since now I'm going to have to rely on you for all of his birthdays and Christmases in perpetuity. I really appreciate it, and hope your holiday was joyous.

Best,
Jenna

I look at a food blog I love called *Sassy Radish* for a minute, thinking I might want to try the recipe for sweet potato, parsnip, and carrot latkes with harissa, when my e-mail dings.

J-

It was my absolute pleasure to be of assistance. And frankly, I'm delighted to think you would rely on me for anything. Did you just get back this late? I hope it was a good day, and not too marred by Aimee's absence. I know that holidays always seem to intensify loss. My dad and brother and I always really miss Mom most at this time of year. I hope there was enough happy around you to keep things buoyant, or at least enough booze to make things joyful. Any chance I'll be seeing you New Year's?

E

That's so sweet of him.

E-

Thanks for the thoughts; it was pretty joyful all things considered, even without getting overly boozily lubricated. And I'm so sorry; I didn't realize your mom was gone. Were you able to be with your dad and brother today? Thank you so much for the New Year's invite, I believe the plan is to lie low and have a fuddy-duddy New Year's. Brian is just getting back from skiing that morning, so I don't think he'll be up for a party, I'm fairly doubtful we'll even see midnight. But I'm sure you'll have a great time!

J

J-

I'm actually still here in sunny Missouri, driving back tomorrow. Mom passed away about ten years ago, but thank you for your kindness. Luckily my aunt hosts, dozens of cousins and an enormous ham, turkey with all the trimmings, and I make my famous gingerbread, and we stuff ourselves and sing carols, and we all wear horrific holiday sweaters and do a truly massive White Elephant swap. A good day. And just enough family time to appreciate them, and not get overly claustrophobic in the old twin bed. Sounds like a nice plan for you for New Year's, but you'll be missed.

E

E-

Um, famous gingerbread? I didn't know you cooked. Recipe, please.

Your day sounds quite lovely. Although that many tacky holiday sweaters in one place might give me the heebie-jeebies. Which is probably a bad thing for a Jew to say, now that I look at it.
Going to try and get some sleep, have a safe drive back tomorrow.

HA! Never would have thought of that, but you're right, looking at it is kinda funny.

Sleep well, Jenna.

E

And then, surprisingly, I do.

17

I'm bundling myself up for the walk over to the Library. I've got confirmation that at the moment we are completely without customers, due I'm sure to the icky weather and the New Year's preparations. No one ever needs last-minute New Year's food books. But Chewie has never been there, and the trainer told me at puppy class last night that if there is a place I'm going to want him to spend a lot of time, I should acclimate him as soon as possible. He's already met everyone except Lois, who apparently has baked a new batch of her famous peanut butter dog biscuits in his honor. The store is closing at three, but I want to get there this morning so that I'm home and settled before Brian gets there around two.

And even though the weather is gross, I'm looking forward to getting out of the house. Yesterday was a bad day. Aimee's birthday. She would have been forty-two.

"Younger than you!"

I turned forty-two the week before Aimee died. I didn't even realize it was my birthday until my parents called to wish me a happy day.

Aimee loved her birthday. And she never let anyone shirk on celebrating just because she was smack in the middle between Christmas and New Year's. And god forbid you tried to pull the "I got you one bigger gift to cover both."

"Hey, they are not the same thing. Two different events. Two presents. That's the rule. Anything else is bullshit."

Aimee always popped out of bed on her birthday bright eyed and full of glee and high expectations.

I? Woke up yesterday with a horrible sinking feeling, rolled right over and went back to sleep. I slept the sleep of denial till nearly eleven, by which point Chewie had not only shit on the kitchen floor, he had apparently practiced his Ice Capades routine upon it, managing to get it well and truly spread around, ground into the wide grout on my terra-cotta floor, smeared on the kickplates of half the cabinets. After screaming at the poor dog and smacking him a good one on the snout with the *New York Times* Dining section, I spent a full hour and a half on my hands and knees weeping angry tears of frustration, scrubbing dog shit of a particularly foul nature, much of which had already dried to rock hardness while I was wallowing in bed trying not to think about all the birthdays Aimee would never have.

By the time I was done, my hands were red and chapped from the scalding hot water I'd dosed with bleach, both my knees were black and blue and swollen, and Chewie was cowering in the living room. Where he had peed right by the door, since in my eagerness to get the mess cleaned up, I had forgotten to do so much as let him out into the backyard. And then I really lost it. Spectacularly. Curled up in a fetal position on the living room floor, sobbing so hard I could barely breathe, the dolphin noises coming out of me horrifying both dogs, who ran around and around me, licking any skin they could find and whining.

I eventually got up. Shook it off. Took a shower. Took some

Advil. Then Brian called, and just when I needed someone to tell me that the whole thing was hilarious and a great story to bounce me out of my funk, he launched into another anti-Wayne, anti-dog tirade.

"Seriously, Jenna, I know you don't want to hurt anyone's feelings, but enough is enough. You're a grown woman. If you don't want something in your life, you can do something about it. Half-Brain has to realize that he can't just do these things that have such huge consequences for other people. Give him the dog back, tell him you're sorry, explain to Noah it wasn't a good fit, and be done with it."

"I can't think about that right now."

"Well then, to a certain extent, you get what you deserve on this one. If you don't have the courage to just say what you want and need, you live with the results."

"That's a little harsh."

"Just the way I see it. Sorry you're having a bad day. Really, I am. We're heading out to the mountain. I'll see you tomorrow afternoon and hopefully the dog will behave himself between now and then, and we'll have a very nice New Year's."

And then he was gone. And I? Dove headfirst into a tub of mocha chip ice cream and a bag of salt and vinegar potato chips and ate my way out.

It was, as they say, not a good day.

But today, today is fine. I'll take Chewie to the Library, and tell everyone about the literal shitstorm, and they'll laugh and make me feel better, and then we'll come home and Brian will come back and we'll make the small prime rib I picked up. Brian requested old school New Year's, and I've come up with what I think is the perfect menu. Iceberg wedges with a homemade Thousand Island dressing and bacon bits. Prime rib, slow roasted in a very forgiving technique I developed after years of trying to make it for weddings and parties where the timing of the meal can be drastically changed based on length of ceremony, or toasts, or how well the venue staff can change over a room. Twice-baked potatoes, creamed spinach. I have a stack of crepes already made, ready to be turned into crepes suzette with butter and brown sugar and orange zest and flambéed with Grand Marnier, because if you go old school, something needs to be set on fire. With homemade vanilla bean gelato to cut the richness, of course! I've got two bottles of vintage Krug, a bottle of thirty-year-old Giacosa Barolo red label, and a 1985 tawny port. I spent an insane amount of money over at Howard's Wine Cellar, but hell, what's the point of being a millionaire if I don't drink ridiculously well now and again?

I? Am flipping the script. Erasing yesterday like it didn't happen. It was a blip, an anomaly. And now it's back to normal.

I snap on the dogs' leashes, grab some blue bags for my pocket just in case, and head out. The boulevard is lovely, covered in a light dusting of snow, the sun bright and the air brisk but not brutal. We walk up, both dogs taking opportunities to roll in the snow, and play with the other dogs we pass on the way. When we get close to the Library, I start to get a little clenchy, like maybe one of my attacks is coming on, but I breathe deeply and the feeling passes. I know I'm just nervous to have Chewie at the store. I really can't handle another disaster so soon.

"Hello, Liebchen. And who is this handsome boy?" Lois

comes to greet us. She hands a small treat to Volnay right off, but makes Chewbacca sit and make eye contact before he gets his. It is the perfect thing to do, immediately putting him in training mode and establishing Lois as an authority figure. He takes his treat, follows Volnay to the corner where her bed is, and flops down on the floor next to her as if he is the calmest most well behaved of all dogs.

And my shoulder blades release, and I can breathe.

"He's very sweet for a terrorist," Eloise says, sitting on the floor with Chewie sprawled half in her lap, receiving some excellent head scratching.

"Chewbacca Bin Laden is his AKC name," I say, laughing. "Talk about your dirty bomb!"

"I would have thrown up. Did you want to throw up? I would have literally THROWN UP," Andrea says, putting on her coat. She is leaving early to go get ready; Law isn't picking her up to go to their New Year's party till five, but apparently she has scheduled a half day of beauty prep at the salon. "Happy New Year, everyone."

"Have fun," Eloise says, releasing Chewie and levitating her lanky frame off the floor in one effortless motion, and going to give Andrea a kiss.

"Say hi to Law for me," I say.

"Will do, and don't you have to get going yourself soon?"

"Yeah, probably should head back." I check my watch. It's after eleven. Brian's flight should just be taking off. "Everyone have a very lovely New Year's, and I will see you all in a couple of days." There are kisses all around, more dog treats, and a bag to take home. And all the way back down the boulevard, a prancing proud pup and his adoptive little mama, and their very relieved owner.

The first text comes at 11:30, just as I'm getting home.

Light snow. Flt delayed. Leaving in an hour. B

The second at 12:10, after I finish my shower and personal prep, I'm shaved and lotioned and perfumed, my hair is shiny and silky and smells of almonds and vanilla. I'm in one of Aimee's lounging pajama sets, with the robe, puttering happily, and doing the mise for dinner.

Snow heavier, delayed again. Leaving at 2. Still back for dinner, but maybe not for cooking lesson. B

Well, that isn't the worst thing. I make the creamed spinach, as close as I can get to the memories I have of eating it at Lawry's Steak House with my parents when I was a little girl. My secret is mascarpone, which I stir in just at the end, to up the creamy factor and give it a little bit of tang. I put it in the fridge, since it will reheat beautifully alongside the roast. I pop the potatoes in a 400 degree oven, right on the rack so that the skins will get nice and crispy, and head upstairs to throw on some clothes so that I can take the dogs for another walk to hopefully wear them out a bit. I really want them mellow for tonight, especially Chewbacca. I can't deal with another lecture from Brian.

The third text hits at 2:15, just as I'm snapping on leashes.

On the plane!

The fourth at 2:30, just as we're hitting our stride, finding the perfect pace that gets Chewie working, but isn't too fast for poor V.

Temp dropped, deicing planes. Supposed to take off at 3.

The fifth at 3:07, as I'm handing out treats and getting out of my coat.

Canceled. Will call you in 15.

And just like that, my lovely quiet New Year's at home with Brian and all this good food and good wine goes right down the fucking toilet.

"I'm so sorry." Brian calls just as I'm taking the potatoes out of the oven.

"You can't control the weather."

"No, but I could have been smarter and come back yesterday to be safe."

"It's okay. You know I'm not a big one for New Year's anyway."

"How do you feel about a New Year's Day dinner instead?"

"That would be fine by me."

"I'm rebooked on the morning flight, so barring more weather, I'll be back tomorrow and we can have our date tomorrow night."

"Sounds great. So what are you and the guys going to do tonight?"

"Huge party at the airport hotel bar."

"Ugh. At least I get to be home."

"Well you should go out or something. You said you had other offers, call someone and go play. No use staying home."

"Maybe. I'm actually sort of tired, so I might take a little nap and see how I feel."

"Okay. Well whatever you do, have a good time, and think of me at midnight."

The nice thing about this menu is that it will keep fine for tomorrow. I decide to finish the potatoes, cutting the tops off and scooping out the fluffy interiors, leaving a quarter-inch-thick shell. I mix the scoopings with butter, sour cream, cheddar cheese and chives, add a splash of milk to keep it smooth, and restuff the potato shells, sprinkling a mixture of shredded cheddar and fried shallots on top, and pop them in the fridge. All I will have to do tomorrow is cook the beef, reheat the spinach, and bake the potatoes. I head upstairs to lie down, suddenly feeling dead tired, and probably still recovering from the emotional debacle of yesterday, and I let both dogs join me for naptime on the bed, a very special treat for Chewie, who continues his good boy routine, making me wonder if we might not be turning a corner of some kind.

The phone wakes me just after eight.

"Jenny! Happy New Year!"

"Hi, Wayne. Happy New Year."

"You sound weird, I didn't interrupt anything did I? Hi Brian! Sorry!"

"He's not here, you didn't interrupt anything. He got stuck in Aspen, flight canceled."

"Well then get over here!" I can hear him calling out. "Elliot, Brian's flight got canceled, Jenny is just home alone!" Crap. Then I hear rustling noises on the phone.

"Hey, Jenna."

"Hi, Elliot. Happy New Year."

"And to you."

"Sounds like you're having fun over there."

"That we are; I hear your plans changed."

"Nothing like weather to get in the way."

"Well, we'd love to have you here if you're up for it. Pretty low key, Wayne is here and Georgie, Ronald and Carolyn, and another couple that I don't think you've met."

"You're in full swing over there, sounds like, I think it would . . ."

"Nonsense. I'm doing grazing buffet, no sit-down dinner. We're all just milling around and nibbling at will, and drinking champagne. It's easy and casual, and we'd love to see you."

I pause. In the background I hear a happy noise. And after a four-hour nap, now I'm awake. Everyone else who invited me is well into dinner by now. As if to offer a vote, my stomach growls so loudly that Chewie jumps up and starts running around the bed looking for an intruder.

"I can hear you not saying no, so I'm taking that as a yes. And before you say one more word, I'm sending a car for you."

"Elliot, that's very unnecessary, I can get a cab."

"On New Year's Eve? I think not. Look for a black town car in twenty minutes."

And I can't think of a single reason to say no.

"Make it thirty, I have to get dressed."

"We're not fancy, so don't pull out the ball gown."

"I was thinking the Leia gold slave bikini. Too much?"

"You wear that, you'd better bring a justice of the peace, because I'll marry you on the spot."

"Better not, then. My lawyer is stuck in Aspen, and I'm a strict pre-nup kind of girl."

"Safer that way. I'd go with jeans, then."

"Okay. And Elliot?"

"Yeah?"

"Thank you. I'll see you soon."

God help me. I'm off to Geek Central New Year's.

One of my favorite stories about Aimee, is from the summer we spent touring Europe after college graduation." I'm having, despite myself, a very good time. Elliot lives in a very cool restored Victorian in Old Irving Park, and blissfully the décor is like his office at the store and not full of collectibles and movie posters. He has a great buffet set up with my favorite kind of nibbly foods, cheeses and sweet-and-sour meatballs, a glazed ham with little biscuits to make sandwiches, some sort of savory spinach bread pudding, mini quiches, pigs in blankets. The people are all very nice, very welcoming, and not one of them has head tilted at me. It's actually pretty normal, despite the fact that Georgie keeps coming up to me and giving me odd bits of information about himself. Tonight I have learned that his work as a computer networker is going really well, and that he was just hired to work on a big movie that is filming locally. That he is allergic to shellfish. And peanuts. And dust. And sunscreen. And apparently, you know, everything.

But this small group, even the one couple I've never met before, they don't look at me like I am supposed to collapse or burst into tears at any moment. Instead, they've asked Wayne and me to tell good Aimee stories, and now that I've started I kind of can't stop.

"I was getting ready to start culinary school at Le Cordon

Bleu in Paris, and Aimee was coming back to Chicago to go to business school at Northwestern. We had saved up to spend three glorious months just playing and being young and free. We were in the south of Italy, and Aimee decided we should pop over to Monaco for dinner. There was a restaurant she had heard of, and as we all know, Aimee always knew where the best and newest places were. We took the train into Monte Carlo, and found a small restaurant on a tiny side street just off the center of town. It was nondescript on the outside, but spectacularly elegant inside.

"We didn't have a reservation, but with her broken French, and fabulous smile, Aimee had the maître d' eating out of her hand and we were shown to a quiet table for two. Before we were able to open our menus, they were whisked away, and we were told that the chef wanted to cook for us, and that the meal would be on the house. We giggled, and I told Aimee that she was the only person I knew who could have pulled that off, and hoped she hadn't promised anything unladylike. The meal was epic. Twelve, maybe thirteen courses, each more delicious and intricate than the last. Wines specially matched for every course, and the most attentive service. With every dish we sent effusive compliments back to the kitchen along with clean plates, and I surreptitiously kept notes of every dish and every wine in my little notebook in my lap, wanting to replicate flavors and remember every detail."

Elliot refills my glass with Pierre Gimmonet champagne, a pretty sophisticated choice, and very delicious.

"Thanks, El. Anyway, we were lingering over post-dinner drinks when the chef came out to greet us. He seemed perplexed when he saw us, but recovered quickly, and sat down to join our table for a brief chat. The mystery was quickly resolved. Aimee, in her indomitable way, had tried to tell the maître d' that we were traveling from the states and that she had heard about the restaurant being recommended by M. F. K. Fisher and Alice Waters. Turns out the young man misunderstood and thought that we *were* M. F. K. Fisher and Alice Waters, hence the amazing comped meal." Everyone breaks up; the story was legend in our inner circle, but the people here are hearing it for the first time. And Wayne is nodding and beaming at me while I tell it.

"We laughed with the chef about the mix-up, and offered to pay. He smiled and said it was his pleasure, we had been wonderful guests to cook for, and he hoped we would return someday. So, flash forward. My first week at culinary school, they were honoring some alumni, and we were all invited to attend the ceremony. Imagine my delight and surprise when I saw our chef from Monte Carlo among the honorees! I went up to greet him after the ceremony, and he kissed me three times, then put his arm around me and in rapid-fire French, explained our connection to the other chefs, who laughed heartily at the mix-up. Later, in talking to one of my instructors, I found out that the gentleman I thought of as 'Chef Louis' was in fact Louis Rebluchette, and that the restaurant was his three-Michelin-star Louis, and the meal Aimee and I had so enjoyed would have cost us nearly two thousand dollars if we had been paying customers! After culinary school, I was able to do a six-month series of stages in all of his restaurants, a gig that no recent graduate had ever been blessed with, all because of Aimee's audaciousness."

"That is amazing. And so like her," Carolyn says. "She once got us house seats to the opera by pretending to be one of their board members!"

"She sounds pretty awesome," says Beth, a very nice woman who apparently runs a successful accounting firm during the day, and is a Steampunk goddess by night.

"I was pretty awesome."

"She was exceptionally awesome," Wayne says.

"Thank you, my love."

"Hey everyone, make sure your glasses are full, we are one minute away!" Elliot says. I look at my watch, and can't believe it's already almost midnight.

We gather around the television, glasses in hand, watching Ryan Seacrest, and missing Dick Clark.

"Ten . . . nine . . . eight . . . seven . . . six . . . five . . . four . . . three . . . two . . . one . . . HAPPY NEW YEAR!"

The couples kiss.

Wayne and Georgie indulge in a solid back-slapping man hug.

And Elliot? Pulls me close and plants a kiss right on my lips. His lips are soft, but the kiss is firm, and while no one would ever claim that it was anything other than New Year's friendly, it makes my girl parts go all tingly.

"Happy New Year, Jenna. Here is to a year that is full of all the happy that last year missed." He squeezes my shoulder, and then heads for the kitchen.

Before I can even process what just happened, I am grabbed in a classic Wayne bear hug. "Happy New Year, Jenny! Here's to us. Surviving last year, and surviving next year." His eyes are sparkly with tears.

"Happy New Year, Wayne. I'll drink to that." I raise my glass to him.

"To Aimee," he says.

"To Aimee." I clink his glass with mine.

"To me!"

"Milk and cookies, anyone?" Elliot reappears from the kitchen with a large platter of chocolate chip cookies, and a little wire holder containing a dozen little milk bottles with striped paper straws, that turn out to contain vanilla malted milk shakes.

"Elliot, these are amazing," I say, slurping the bottom of my bottle.

"No one ever thinks about malt in vanilla, but I like it better than chocolate."

"Look at you, sneaky foodie."

"No so sneaky," he says, winking. "C'mere." He takes my hand and leads me to the kitchen. Through the door is a kitchen that appears to be practically as well kitted out as my own. A wall of spices that might actually beat mine. High-quality equipment as far as the eye can see and all of it clearly well loved and well used.

"Elliot! I had no idea!"

"Shhh. Most of my circle thinks that any self-respecting geek needs to live on pizza and cereal. If they find out I cook, I'll totally lose street cred."

"Your secret is safe with me."

"We should cook sometime."

"You got it. Maybe next time Noah is down you and I can knock out some roasted chickens!"

He smiles, a little wanly. "You bet. That will be fun."

"I should go, have to get the dogs out. Thanks so much for a lovely evening, Elliot, really."

"Anytime. I'll go call the car for you."

I head out of the lovely kitchen and make my good-byes to the rest of the group. Georgie, the third musketeer, kisses me wetly under my ear and whispers that he will call me later. I'm not really sure what that is about.

Elliot walks me out and opens the car door for me. "Good night, Jenna."

"Good night, Elliot, thank you for saving my New Year's."

"The pleasure was entirely mine." And then he kisses me again, the same tender kiss as before, and my physical reaction is the same, which I attribute to being full of champagne.

I get into the car, and he closes the door.

"Back to Maplewood, miss?" the driver says, and I realize it is the same guy as earlier.

"Yes, please."

And I'm almost home before I realize that I've completely broken my promise to Brian; not only didn't I think about him at midnight, I haven't thought about him at all, all night.

18

Turns out all the strange attention from Georgie wasn't actually out of nowhere. He called me the week after New Year's, as he said he would. And asked me out. I politely declined. Then I called Wayne.

"Did you give Georgie my number and tell him I would go out with him?"

"What? You said you weren't exclusive. Georgie's a great guy."

"Wayne. I know what I said, but I've been single a long time. Don't you think if I were going to spark to Georgie I would have done it already?"

"I thought you needed a nudge."

"Wayne, please don't try and fix me up."

"But you aren't exclusive."

"I'm also not actively on the market."

"That Brian guy is slippery, he'll trap you."

"I promise you, Georgie is not the guy to prevent Brian from trapping me."

"Okay. I was just trying . . ."

"I know. It's very sweet. Just don't, okay?"

"Okay. Am I still house-sitting with the dogs next weekend?"

"Yes, please, if that's still fine."

"It is. But I wish you weren't going."

"It's just a weekend in Saginaw. Two nights. I'll be back Sunday."

"Weekends like that lead to exclusivity, and you know my vote on that."

"He just wants you to have the right love."

He wants a punch in the mouth. GEORGIE?

"He's trying."

Yes. Yes he is. VERY trying.

"Thank you, Wayne. If I promise to not come back exclusive, can I still go?"

"Yes. I'll be there Friday."

"Thank you."

B rian made it back from Aspen in time for dinner on New Year's Day, demolished the food and wine with me, and asked if I would join him for a weekend away in a friend's weekend home in Michigan in a couple of weeks.

"Boy, do all your friends have extra houses to loan you?"

"Yep. I only hang out with people who have multiple houses."

"Guess I'm going to be off the list."

"You just haven't found your second home yet."

"Yes you have."

"Guess I haven't."

"YES YOU HAVE."

Aimee and I fell in love with an old stone *mas* in the south of France. It used to be a mill, and had a huge main house with three outbuildings on the property. We swore we would buy it and renovate it as our vacation home together. We got close to doing it too, but then she got sick and there went the dream. The Voix keeps telling me to do it anyway, but I know better. It's too much; I can't do it on my own, and wouldn't want to.

I agreed to the weekend away. Wayne agreed to dog sit. Originally I wanted him to just take the dogs to his house, but then he said that he had some sort of massive Terminix bomb thing he wanted to do and that he would just house-sit and dog sit. At that point, despite the fact that I'm reasonably sure that between Chewie and Hurriwayne my entire home will be leveled while I'm away, I couldn't really say no. Plus I really didn't want to know why he was having the house bombed, and once he assured me that whatever the issue was it wasn't transferable to my house, I caved. Thankfully, Wayne needs access to a television at all times, so he will stay in the guest room. The idea of Wayne in my bed just completely makes my skin crawl.

Meanwhile, why can I have a TV in the guest room and not the bedroom?

"Because a guest room is like a hotel room, and guests need a TV. Your bedroom is your sacred space, and you need quiet."

You and your freaking rules.

"You're the one who always listened."

I'm starting to wonder why.

"Because I'm always right."

Well, there's that.

I may be a little nervous about going away with Brian, but I'm very ready for a break. Chewbacca continues to Jekyll and Hyde all over the place, two days of being an angel, followed by a day of eating the furniture. Plus now he has begun humping everything in sight. Volnay put the kibosh on things quickly when he attempted to violate her in her sleep, but my couch cushions, table legs, and guests have not been so lucky. The breeder said we should wait till he is six months old to neuter him, so I have another two months to live with a horny humpmonster. Plus he is apparently in the ninety-ninth percentile for weight and height, clocking in at nearly fifty-five pounds already. My vet said he is likely to end up somewhere in the 125- to 135-pound range when he is full-grown. Great. My dog is going to be MY ideal weight.

Yesterday he did his test run at the doggie day care that Alana uses, and it was gently suggested that I not bring him back. Ever. Something about him getting out of his crate and into the office and eating most of a printer and someone's shoes, and going all date rapey on a shy Bernese during playtime. So embarrassing. Now I have to try and find another place to take him so that he can get some good socializing when puppy kindergarten is over next week. I'm just not really a good dog park person. Probably because I'm not really a good dog person, come to think of it.

I'm up and packed early, even though Brian isn't picking me up till three thirty. Wayne is coming at three. By nine, the dogs are walked, the house is pretty Wayne-proofed. I've moved anything both breakable and valuable into the butler's pantry cabinets, which lock. I've put all of my small valuables and personal papers in the safe. Yesterday I roasted a chicken and grilled a large steak, both of which are in the fridge along with a case of beer. There are carrots and green beans blanched, so he just has to heat them up, and two bags of frozen French fries. I've got a folder ready for him with instructions for all the appliances and electronics.

By ten, I realize that I have to do something, or I'm going to twiddle my thumbs all day. I decide to bake something for Wayne, leave a little bit of delicious for him for the weekend.

In the pantry I look to see what ingredients I have on hand. Bars of bittersweet chocolate and dark cocoa powder put me in the mind for something decadent and rich. And then it hits me.

"Blackout Elevator Cake."

Exactly.

Aimee and I once got stuck in a load-in elevator at an event venue en route to an engagement party due to a blackout. We were there for nearly four hours. The only thing we had with us was the dark chocolate layer cake I had made as a surprise for the groom, who hated the lemon chiffon his bride-to-be had chosen. I meant to sneak it into the party, and serve him a special slice, and then send the rest home with him. He never got it. Aimee and I sat in the dark, eating cake with our hands by the light of our cellphones and laughing and telling stories and sharing our mutual fear that we would have to go to the bathroom before they found us. We did not. But when they finally got us out, our teeth were black from the chocolate cookie crumbs, Aimee had frosting in her hair, I had chocolate pastry cream dolloped in the middle of my bosom, and we both had fudge frosting under our fingernails. We were both half-sick, and the cake was half-gone, and it was one of the best days of my life.

The cake turns out to be the perfect idea. The focus baking requires settles my mind and my nerves, doesn't let other thoughts sneak in. Stirring the pastry cream and putting it in the blast chiller in the island, a total chefly indulgence that I have never once regretted. The house filling with the scent of rich, dark chocolate as the cakes rise in the oven. The treat of the moist trimmings as I even up the layers before spreading the thick custard filling between them. The fudgy frosting smoothed perfectly over the whole thing, and then immediately marred with chocolate cookie crumbs.

Blackout Cake is almost enough to make me want to stay home. But more than that, I think Wayne will be delighted. It weighs about forty-two pounds as I shift it out of the kitchen and onto the counter in the Kitchen Library, shutting the door behind me. Chewie is not just getting heavier by the day; he is also getting taller, and has become something of a counter surfer.

By the time the cake is finished, I'm calm and collected. I forget how much my sense of self is connected to the kitchen, to cooking. From the moment I went to culinary school twenty years ago, right up until the moment Aimee got sick, cooking was my center and the main occupation of my mind. Even when we sold the business, just four months before Aimee's official diagnosis, back when we thought that her permanent fatigue was a result of the relentless nature of the company, I went from overseeing the catering aspect of the company, to a return to the cooking I loved most, hosting dinner parties for friends and family, hanging out at the Library testing new recipes and making customers and staff my guinea pigs, teaching the occasional class with Andrea.

"You have to get back in the kitchen."

I know. I just . . .

"No excuses. You have to cook. You need to get the Notebook out again."

The Notebook has been with me for twenty years. Aimee gave it to me for a graduation present when I finished at Le

Cordon Bleu. It's a handmade journal, must have over four hundred pages, ten by twelve inches, and bound in soft gray distressed leather. It looks like a witch's grimoire of spells, or the kind of notebook Marie Curie would work problems in. And it is about two-thirds full of my chicken scratch, notes for recipes, ideas of flavors that might pair well together, techniques I want to try and improve, drawings of plating ideas. It used to be that when I was stressed, or excited, or sad, or bored, I would go to the Notebook and then to the kitchen.

"It'll cure what ails you."

And maybe she's right. Maybe some of my aimlessness is simply not feeling useful or needed or productive. It's ironic really. We did such a good job of building our business, it didn't need us anymore. And such a good job of training our staff at the Library, it runs like a clock without us. If only Aimee had been as successful in preparing me to live without her.

Here we go!" Brian says, opening the door of the cozy-looking cottage tucked away on a lovely street in the very quaint village. We step inside and he turns on the light. It is a little bungalow, the perfect kind of place for a quiet weekend away. Saginaw is about a four and a half hour drive from Chicago. We got through two of Wayne's '80s driving CDs that he gifted me after our road trip before Brian called uncle in the middle of Adam and the Ants. He's not a car karaoke guy, apparently.

We get the car unloaded, and head out to a place called Jake's for burgers, since it is already after eight, and neither of us is much in the mood to try and cook anything. Back at the cottage, Brian lights a fire, and we open a bottle of calvados that I brought with me.

"This is nice. Thank you for bringing me."

"Thank you for coming. Am I allowed to say that I appreciate the peacefulness?"

I laugh. "You mean because there isn't a huge puppy alternately humping your leg and eating your pajamas?"

"Yes. That."

"Well, the good news is that I signed him up for the next level of training, so we are going to commit to making him a good Canine Citizen, and the vet says the humping and rambunctiousness will go away once I get him neutered."

"Well, I suppose that is something. And finally you found a good use for Wayne. Maybe you could get him to dog sit now and again at home. I'd like to wake up with you at my place once in a while."

I lean forward and kiss him. "I bet that could be arranged."

What we begin on the couch in front of the fire, we continue in the bedroom, and after, I fall into deep and satisfied sleep. The phone wakes me at six.

"Whaddizit?" I whisper sleepily, having tiptoed out of the bedroom and downstairs.

"First off, everything's fine," Wayne says.

"I'm pretty sure that isn't really true if you are calling me at six in the morning on a Saturday. What happened?"

"Well it's a funny story, really . . ."

"Pretty sure that isn't true either."

"Well, the thing is, we're at the emergency vet."

Well, now I'm awake. "What happened? Is it Volnay?" The idea that my sweet old girl might go without me there makes my heart clench.

"No, she's fine. But, um, I sort of left that cake, which was totally awesome, by the way, you should be a professional chef or something!"

"WAYNE!"

"Oh, yeah, anyway, I left the cake on the kitchen counter when I went to bed, and then Volnay came and woke me up at three, and I thought she needed to go out, but it turns out Chewie got onto the counter and ate the rest of the cake, and he looked really uncomfortable, and when I checked online to see if I could, you know, give him some Tums or Pepto or something it said that chocolate is like toxic to dogs so we hightailed it to the all-night emergency place, and they pumped his stomach, poor guy."

Shit. Shitshitshitshit. One weekend. I wanted ONE weekend. I can feel my recent goodwill toward Wayne, well, waning. "Is he okay?"

"Oh, yeah, a total trouper. The doc said he probably prevented most of the damage when he threw up."

"You mean when they pumped his stomach?"

"Nah, I mean when he threw up at home. I dunno if the living room rug is gonna be the same, but it probably saved his life."

"What was he doing in the living room?" Only took me the better part of eighteen months for my rug guy Mickey at Al-Sahara to find the perfect large rug for the living room. In creams and golds and taupes. Which are definitely not going to recover from dark chocolate dog puke.

"I must have left the kitchen gate unlocked when I went to bed."

One . . . two . . . three . . . four . . .

"Anyhoo, he's fine, strong as an ox, doc says not to worry I can take him home, it's just, um . . ."

"Good god, Wayne just spit it the fuck OUT."

"The bill is more than I have left to spend on my credit card, so I need you to give them your card to pay for it or they won't let me take him home."

"Fine. Put them on the phone."

He hands me off to a nice woman named Cindy who explains that in addition to the ninety-nine dollar emergency after-hours visit charge, my pup has received a stomach pumping, activated charcoal, an IV to replace electrolytes and flush his system, monitoring, some tests . . . grand total seven hundred eighty-five dollars. I give her my credit card number and tell her to put the large idiot back on the phone.

"Hey, cool, all set. So don't worry at all, I'm gonna take him home, lock him up tight, clean the rug, we're all good here. You have a great weekend, and sorry I had to wake you, but if I left him here they were going to charge a boarding fee . . ."

"It's fine, Wayne. It's fine. Thank you for taking good care of him." The phrase sticks in my throat, but at the end of the day, even if it is Wayne's stupid fault the dog ate the cake, at least he did all the right things. I've heard of dogs actually dying of chocolate poisoning, and while I would have gladly killed the dog myself more than once in the past month, I find I don't actually want him dead.

"Hey, no problem! I'll see you tomorrow! And Jenny, look, I know that Chewie seems to have been something of a consistent problem child, I didn't really think about it when I got him for you, but if you can't handle him, you know, if he isn't the right dog for you, I'll take him back."

"We'll talk when I get home."

"Okay, just an offer. Have fun. Say hi to the Bri Guy for me!"

I hang up, sit down at the kitchen table, and let my head drop until my forehead meets the cool surface. And then the sweating starts. And the heart racing. And the wobbly legs and the colon spasms and the race to the bathroom. You'd think I ate a whole poison chocolate cake. I'm back in the kitchen, clammy and still sweating and heart fast, but with a somewhat calmer stomach, when Brian comes down, rubbing his sleepy eyes, hair still weirdly perfect.

"Hey. You're up early."

"Sorry. Small emergency back home."

"Let me guess. Wayne burned down the house? Blew up your car?"

"Chewbacca. Ate a whole chocolate cake. Three a.m. emergency vet run, which Wayne couldn't afford to pay without my okay."

"Good lord, it never ends. Is the dog okay at least?"

"Right as rain according to the vet. Strong as an ox and twice as graceful."

"I knew it was a bad idea for you to let him stay at your house."

"Well, I didn't have much of a choice. Wayne's place is being fumigated, and the kennel politely declined our business."

"Still. I don't know which is worse, Wayne or the fucking dog he foisted on you."

"Hey, people make mistakes. Dogs are just dogs. The dog could have died and Wayne did all the right things to save his life, and wouldn't have even told me till tomorrow except Aimee's stupid rules meant he didn't have access to enough funds."

"Leave me out of this one."

Have I told you lately about the general direction in which I would like you to fuck?

"Ouch. You're really not a morning person."

"I still think you should get rid of that damn beast. Hand him back to Wayne with a 'thanks but no thanks' and be done."

And then something weird happens. I stop sweating, all at once, like flipping a switch. My heart rate normalizes. And I start to cry. And I'm not a crier. Especially with guys. Never have been. But all at once the whole thing hits me, and all I can think of is my poor Chewie, so sick and unhappy and I wasn't there. As panicked as I was that something might have happened to Volnay without me, there is something that is now just sinking in. Wayne's offer to take the dog away, Brian's insistence at getting rid of him; my heart hurts.

I look up at Brian through tears. "I LOVE that dog. He's going nowhere. And you'd better figure out how to tolerate him, because me and him? We're a team. We're family. Package deal. And I would really appreciate if you would, one, stop telling me to get rid of him and B., perhaps show the tiniest bit of compassion for my dog who could have DIED tonight."

And that? Right there? Was a beginning and an ending. It was the beginning of a deep love affair with a badly behaved dog, and the ending of my lovely weekend away with Brian.

19

Nancy laughs. I can't really blame her. "That is quite a tale."

"Yeah, I know."

"So the weekend was a bust."

"Not entirely. Brian was somewhat shocked by my outburst, and disappointed when I said I wanted to go home to be with my dog, but we talked on the ride home, and by the time we got back I think he got it. He ended up spending the night at my place that night, and we've been pretty good since then. I got us reservations for EL Ideas for Valentine's Day, which is damn near impossible, and a place he has wanted to eat forever, and he was really excited, so I think it was ultimately a strengthening thing."

"So do you consider him your boyfriend?"

"I consider him the man in my life."

"That's not the same."

"No, it's not. But it feels like enough for me, for now."

"And for later?"

"I'm living in the moment."

"That sounds like a cop-out. But today I think we have bigger issues that it brings up."

"Like?"

"Like this whole distance thing. You fight liking Wayne.

You fought liking the dog. You fight getting committed to Brian. You're keeping things at arm's length, and I'm wondering why?"

"I think I'm fine. I don't just open up right away."

"You've known Wayne for almost a decade. You've had the dog for two months. You've known Brian for six years and have been dating for three months. These are not 'right away' situations."

"What can I say, it is what it is."

"Why do you think you keep having these panic attacks?"

"Because someone I know refuses to hook a girl up with the Xanax." I laugh, but it's forced.

"That isn't an answer. When do you have them?"

"They just come out of nowhere."

"I don't think they do. I think they come when you are scared about being close to someone or something."

"I don't think that."

"You say they started when you were dealing with Aimee's death becoming imminent, your very best friend in the world, leaving you. You told me you had one the first time you went back to the Library after she died, with your adopted family waiting to be kind to you. At Thanksgiving when Andrea and her mom reached out to say that you could lean on them. When Wayne called to say that the dog could have died. You don't see a pattern? That you are scared when closeness is involved? That you're keeping things at arm's length?"

"I really don't." Except that I do.

"Jenna. I know that losing Aimee was, is, so very, very hard. I also know, or at least I infer, that your independence is hard won and protective. That you have always been insular. It was just you, growing up, with older parents who were loving but gave you as much space as your intelligence warranted, and in the process, made you very much a person who did for herself."

"And this is a bad thing?"

"Of course not. Unless you use your ability to do for yourself to keep you from making strong connections to other people."

"Then how do you explain Aimee? I could not BE closer to someone."

"True. But you met Aimee and made that friendship everything for you personally. And your work took care of the rest. You seem to think that if you are weak, if you show vulnerability, if you NEED, that that makes you needy. Unlovable, maybe. But more importantly, I think you have not yet begun to scratch the surface of your loss of Aimee, and unconsciously are working very hard at not getting particularly close to anyone or anything else, because you can't pile loss on more loss."

"Again, this is bad why?"

"Until you address what it means to have lost Aimee, you can't let someone else in your life who might leave you. It's like refinishing furniture. You can slap another coat of paint on top, but it will bubble and streak and never be right. Or you can do the very hard annoying work of stripping away the finish that is there so that you can start clean, and fresh."

"Seriously? I'm getting furniture-stripping metaphors? At one hundred and eighty-five dollars an hour?"

She smiles. "I'm redoing a sideboard."

"Thought so."

"I'd argue it still fits."

"I hear you. I don't really know what to say about it, but

I hear you. I don't think it's true, but you think it's uncon-
scious, so I can't really be sure. I know I'm sick of the whole
world waiting for me to fall to pieces."

"Why?"

"Because I can't."

"Can't what?"

"Fall to pieces."

"Why not?"

"Because."

"Because why?"

"BECAUSE AIMEE IS DEAD."

"And?"

My voice cracks. "And she is the only person I can fall
apart with. She is the only person who can put me back
together. Because she is the only one who has ever known my
secret heart and my dark places and my deepest fears and she
IS FUCKING DEAD. I trusted her. I trusted her with everything I am and was and wanted to be. I trusted her with my
whole heart and she promised to be here and she is GONE. I
can't lose it because she is the only one who could bring me
back." The tears are hot and fast on my cheeks. "Don't you
think I would have dearly LOVED to just go to pieces? I don't
have the luxury. If I let myself go to pieces, I'd never get
myself whole ever again. Who is going to put me back
together? My parents? They're a thousand years old and two
thousand miles away. Wayne? He might not be the devil I
imagined, but he can't remember to put the cake away; he's
going to patch me up when I fall? My staff? I love them, but
they WORK FOR ME. I pay salaries, benefits, I know they
care, but they can't see me all broken. Brian too. Who, pray
tell, do I really have? No one, that's who. I am the most alone

person in the world. But at least I know me. I know what I can do. I can take care of my dogs, and make sure the people around me are taken care of, but there is no one to do that for me. I know it, and it sucks, but it is what it is. I never got the people who get so angry that they sweep everything off the table to break into a million pieces on the floor. Because when they're done with their fit, they are going to have to clean that shit up. My dog craps on the floor, I have to clean it up. Why would I crap on the floor myself, knowing I'd have to clean it up. I can't break into a million pieces, because frankly, I don't want to have to clean that shit up."

"And if Aimee were here, she'd clean it up."

"She'd clean it up. Or we'd clean it up together. Or she'd trick someone else into cleaning it up. And make it better. She'd make it fucking ELEGANT."

"And if you tried to get close to someone else, to let other people in, to like Wayne, to love the dog, to love Brian, they could also leave you, you could also lose them, and Aimee can't clean that up either."

"Every guy who ever broke my heart, every bad grade, every client who yelled, every soufflé that fell, Aimee was there. When my parents moved away, when Jack left, Aimee was there. Now, no one is here. It's just me. Me and my pain and my fear and my loss and my aloneness, and it may not be what I would have chosen, but I know it and I can handle it. Because I don't really have a choice."

"What if you did?"

"Did what?"

"Have a choice."

"I don't."

"Of course you do."

"Well, maybe I should just get on my magical unicorn and fly to this wondrous land of choices you speak of," I say, snarkier than I intend.

She raises an eyebrow. "Feel better?"

"It was kind of a good one."

"Of course it was."

"Fine. You tell me. What fabulous choices do I have?"

"You think about that, about the choices you do have. The ones that might help you find a safe place to land if you fall apart a little bit. And we'll talk about it next time."

Sigh. "Okay."

"And Jenna?"

"Yeah?"

"Here." She hands me a piece of paper. It's a prescription for five Xanax.

"Finally."

"Here's the catch. That is the only prescription I will ever write you for those pills. You get five. Total. Forever. Use them wisely."

Figures.

When I get home, I walk the dogs and collapse on the couch for a nap. My outburst really took it out of me. When I wake up, it's after six, and I'm ravenous. I go to the kitchen, and stare blankly into the fridge. Nothing jumps out at me. I wander into the Kitchen Library and look over the shelves of cookbooks. And there, on the bottom shelf, The Notebook.

I pull it out, feeling the cool, soft leather. I take it into the kitchen and put it on the table. I turn the pages, watching my handwriting change, my tastes develop, my palate getting more sophisticated. I look at every page, reading my scrawled notes, until I get to the last page.

I had forgotten about this recipe idea.

Aimee's Salad Bar Soup

I'd been hanging out with Aimee in the hospice. We were talking about the perfect home-cooked meal. And she said her idea of the perfect home-cooked meal would be a hearty filling stewlike soup that didn't require any work. The opposite of me. And I came home and couldn't sleep and came up with this idea and wrote it down, and while I was doing that she was slipping into the pain that would require so much morphine that we would never have a lucid conversation ever again.

I reach up to wipe tears away to find that my cheeks are dry. And then I get up. I grab my coat and head for the car. In ten minutes I am at the massive Whole Foods on Kingsbury. I go to the salad bar. I fill containers with carrots, celery, sliced onions, shredded cabbage, chopped tomatoes. Garbanzo beans and corn. Shredded chicken, peas, chopped cauliflower, and broccoli. Baby spinach leaves. Cooked barley. I check out, with my three salad bar containers, and head back toward home. I stop at La Boulangerie and pick up a baguette. I get home and don't even take my coat off. I get out one of my big stock pots, and dump all three containers into the pot. From the pantry, a jar of Rao's marinara. From the freezer, a container of homemade chicken stock. I don't even bother to thaw it, I just plop it like an iceberg into the pot. Salt, pepper, red pepper flakes for heat. I crank the heat to medium, give it a stir and leave it. I dump my coat, and head upstairs. I get into a very hot shower, feeling my shoulders unclench in the steam. I get out, dry off and get into comfy clothes, throw my hair in a ponytail. I head back downstairs, pour a glass of wine. I set a place at the table, a French linen tea towel for a place mat, a single large silver spoon, both treasures found at Clignancourt market in Paris. I grab the butter from the fridge, and a half a lemon, a wedge of parm, the cheese grater from the drawer, the baguette. I go to the stove, where the soup is bubbling like mad, giving off an amazing smell. I give it a stir, a quick taste, adjust the salt and pepper. It will taste even better tomorrow, but it is still very fresh and delicious. I ladle out a generous bowl and set it at my place. A squeeze of lemon, a shower of grated cheese. I alternate between bites of hearty savory soup and thickly buttered crusty bread. I eat two bowls. Half the baguette. Finish the wine. And think, whatever else there is, this is good. And would have been just what Aimee wanted.

20

I hate Valentine's Day.

"Valentine's Day is AWESOME."

Valentine's Day is crap. It's always crap.

"Valentine's Day is one of the best days of the year."

You just say that because there are presents involved.

"Well, DUH!"

It never works the way you want it to; someone is always disappointed.

"Not me."

Sure, you always had secret admirers and doting boyfriends, and a loving husband.

"And you had me."

Well, look how that's working out for me.

"Yeah, sorry about that."

Aimee was always my Valentine's Day backup. She sent flowers and cards and silly presents. She coached boyfriends and lovers. The few Valentine's Days I ever liked, I liked because she orchestrated them. But let me be clear, it isn't my day, it isn't my holiday, and I never look forward to it, whether I'm romantically attached or not.

Frankly I'd skip it altogether, but Brian made a point of

asking me to spend the evening together, and it's impossible to tell the guy you're sleeping with on a regular basis that Valentine's Day is "not your thing." I offered to cook, which is the best expression of affection I can think of, not to mention keeping you away from the overpriced and underwhelming "special dinners" at local restaurants. But he hemmed and hawed and it became clear that he wasn't so interested in eating in. I'm getting the sense that some of his foodie claims and interest in learning to cook might have been somewhat exaggerated. So I called in a major favor and got us the last two seats at EL Ideas, a very exclusive twenty-seat BYOB tasting menu restaurant that is about impossible to get into. Aimee and I wanted to go together since it opened, but she just never felt up to it. We used to have a dining adventure together once a month, picking a new restaurant or a wacky ethnic food to try; it was our girls' night out, no Wayne to limit our choices. We ate the city, sometimes going superfancy, sometimes grungy and suspect, but always interesting and a great time to be together and talk life and dreams the way we always did.

I haven't been so excited about getting to EL, even though their reviews continue to be extraordinary and everyone I know who has gone just raves. Going without Aimee seems like kind of a sacrilege, but Brian's been talking about wanting to go ever since one of the partners at his firm went and raved, and it was something I knew I could do, so I'm trying to put on a happy face. But I won't lie. It feels weird. Things have been okay since our weekend away debacle, but not amazing. I feel like he's losing patience with me, and I'm not really sure why, and I'm not really sure that I care. For sadly not the first time since we started dating, I have really been questioning his motives, his desire. I'm still not exercising, so I just keep getting doughier. Certainly not getting younger. Sometimes I just look at him with all his gorgeousness and wonder why on earth he is even bothering with me.

And when I think these things, the Voix alternately yells at me for self-doubt, and tells me that I can do better.

"You CAN do better. He? Cannot."

I thought you were all excited when we hooked up.

"That was before I thought you were going to just hunker down with him in a boring little rut."

My ruts are the only things keeping me sane.

"So be insane."

I'm having conversations with my dead best friend, which is as insane as I would like to get, if you don't mind. I hear the food in the nuthouse is lacking.

"Suit yourself."

I'm supposed to meet Brian at six at his place, even though our reservation isn't until seven thirty. Which makes me nervous. The dinner tonight is my gift to him, it's a very expensive meal, and you have to prepay, it's nonrefundable, plus it's BYOB, so there are the wines to deal with. I've actually spent significantly more on the evening than I would have on a physical gift, but I'm still awkward about the whole present thing. Considering the necklace at Christmas, I'm worried about his giving me something too big. Presents always made me uncomfortable, since I'm just one of those people who's hard to buy for, and I'm always worried about both being disappointed, and worse, that I'll show it, which I know is horribly ungracious. I like giving things, love it actually, but accepting them has just always been sort of hard, and it got worse when we started making serious money. Even before the big sale, when we were just making pretty high salaries, people would give me presents, and the idea that they would spend their money, usually on things I didn't really want, when I could well afford to just buy the right thing for myself, it just makes me tense.

I like something homemade and simple. Something from your heart. Preferably delicious. Bake me cookies, make me jam or pickles. Bring me some fabulous ingredient or nibble you picked up in your travels. Cook me dinner. Share your old family recipes with me. Take me to a new restaurant or food market or equipment store I've never been to. Knit me a comfy scarf in a color you think looks good on me. Anything that is a genuine expression of your affection and doesn't cost a fortune or require you to wrack your brain too hard or get stressed out. And whatever you do, don't bring me candles or bath products.

"You can't have too many candles or bath products."

Wrong. I have a whole cabinet full of that crap.

"I always gave you candles and bath products."

Which is why I have a whole cabinet full.

"Oh."

Exactly.

Volnay is having a rough morning; it's a damp dreary gray day, and her joints are stiff and sore, so I forgo the morning walk and just let the dogs out in the backyard for their morning business. Today I am taking Chewie to his third doggie day care tryout. The second place I tried last week also put him on the no-fly list. Something about getting out of his

crate and eating the wooden gate for the small dog pen, caus-
ing a stampede of miniature pups, and turning the whole
facility into the O.K. Pomeranian Corral. Apparently those
little fellows can hide in a million places, and it took the entire
staff most of the day to find and wrangle them. Sigh. Hopefully this new place will be able to handle him, because he
needs a place to socialize, and I need a place to leave him
when I go visit my folks for Passover in March. Wayne offered
to take him anytime, but I think our tenuous friendship will
survive better if I have trained professionals dealing with my
ridiculous monster. But I am letting Wayne pick him up today
and deliver him back to my place while I'm out with Brian.
It will make my life so much easier to not have to deal with
him, and Wayne seemed eager to help.

My phone rings just as I'm getting Volnay set up in the
Kitchen Library for her breakfast. It's Wayne, calling to wish
me a happy Valentine's Day.

"Ready for the big plans with Brian?" he asks.

"We're just having dinner."

"Okay. If you say so. But if he pulls out a little velvet box,
run away! Run away!"

I can't help but laugh. "I promise, if he pulls out a little
velvet box, I'll run like the wind. How are you doing?"

He sighs. "I'm okay. You know. Sort of shitty, really."

"Yeah. She loved Valentine's Day. And she always made
it good for the rest of us."

"Yeah. She did. So that sucks."

"It does. You need anything?"

"Nah. Elliot gave me a boxed set of the original 1963 *Doctor Who* DVDs last week, and Lois sent over a huge package
of pastries from the bakery this morning, I'm just going to

hunker down and geek way out and go into a mild diabetic coma till it's over."

"Well, it's good to have a plan."

"I thought so. What time do you want me to pick up the pup?"

"I'm meeting Brian at his place at six, but I'd like him to get the full-day experience, so pick him up between five thirty and six, and just drop him at my house. Thanks for doing that, it really is making my life easier."

"My pleasure. And I promise not to let him eat anything other than his dinner."

All I can do is laugh. "I'd appreciate that. And Wayne, I'm around most of the day, so if you need to check in, just give a call."

"I will, thanks, Jenny. You have a good time. But not too good!"

I laugh. "I will."

I get all of Chewie's stuff together, his favorite toy, a bag of treats, a bully stick. The fourth brand of supposedly indestructible chew toys, the previous three having been reduced to bits within hours of handing them off.

He's running around excitedly, panting and huffing the way he does when he's really happy.

"Sit," I say, raising my hand in a fist the way the trainer has us do it. His butt hits the ground. I open my fist to a flat hand and he immediately lies down. I toss him a treat. "Good boy. Now look, three strikes and you are gonna be out, mister man. So please go to this place and be nice and stay in your crate even if you know you can get out and let the little yippy dogs alone and don't eat the furniture and for god's sake DON'T RAPE ANYONE." He barks, and I toss him another treat. I'm really dying to slip him a Benadryl, but with my luck he'll have some allergic reaction, so I'm not giving in to the temptation.

I toss Volnay a treat, and she heads over to her little bed for a nap, and I snap on Chewie's leash and we head out to what I hope is a successful tryout.

The young man behind the desk at Doggie Day Afternoons Day Care looks like your classic skate punk, with peach fuzz on his chin and wide black plugs in his ears, and the never-a-good-idea white-boy blond dreads. But he comes around the counter to greet Chewie with a big smile and lots of praise.

"Chewbacca, rockin' name."

I'm still a little embarrassed to have the Star Wars moniker on the dog, but I give my standard excuse. "My best friend's stepson named him."

"Well, it is very cool. Great-looking Bordeaux, he's gonna be a brute, aren't you boy?"

"He's already something of a handful," I admit.

"No worries, I love these guys. I have a Neapolitan mastiff myself; they're pretty similar. He eating your whole house?"

I laugh. "So that's not unusual?"

"Nah. That's the breed. Bless their hearts. He is full-on Hooch up in your place?"

The rest of my life it's going to be Hooch. Even Benji is orchestrating a team movie night so that he can finally see it. "Yep. Although he hasn't eaten my car yet."

"Most people think that movie was just made-up and exaggerated for cinematic hilarity. But we know better. We know someone loves to play Mr. Destructo at every turn!" He is down on his knees play wrestling, and Chewie is clearly delighted with his new friend. "My mastiff ate the door off the closet where I keep his food when he was six months old. Literally."

"Yikes."

"In his defense, it was a shitty hollow-core door."

"Well, that'll teach your landlord to cheap out."

"Anything I need to know? Besides the obvious?"

"He manages to get out of most crates," I admit.

"Yeah, mine did that a lot. I'll throw my bike chain on his door so he doesn't get out."

"That would be great. And he's only four months old, so, um . . ."

"He's a total horndog leg humper?"

I love this kid. I still want to shave his head and delouse him, but I love him. "Yeah. Legs, furniture, other dogs . . ."

"I'll do a smaller playtime with him; I have a couple good old boy labs and one shepherd who should be able to hang with him and keep him in line."

"Terrific. My friend Wayne is coming to pick him up."

"What's Wayne's last name so I can check ID when he comes?"

This makes me feel really good. Not that I think anyone is out to steal my little monster. "Garland. I gave the girl on the phone his info for emergencies when I made the reservation."

I feel really good about leaving him here, and pray that he behaves himself enough to be invited back.

When I get home, Volnay seems to be feeling better, so I take her for a short walk to stretch her legs. When we get back we log in to the Doggie Day website and catch Chewie playing with a couple of large Labradors. There appears to have been some sort of plush toy massacre, there is stuffing and fuzz everywhere, and something tells me that there has recently been some deadly tug-of-war. I'm just logging off when my e-mail pings.

Jenna-

Am going to be in your neck of the woods to look at someone's collection, thought I'd stop by with lunch if you are up for that. I've been having a hankering for Olga's, but one cannot tackle the wall of schnitzel alone.

Elliot

———————

E-

Have never heard of Olga's, but a lady never turns down schnitzel if it is offered.

J

———————

J-

Prepare yourself. I'll be there around noon thirty. You're about to be converted.

E

I smile and look at Volnay. "Wall of schnitzel, hmmm?"

The bell rings at precisely 12:31.

I open the door to Elliot's grinning face. He is carrying a small foil-wrapped baking dish, a large white paper bag, and a single enormous deep magenta peony. He hands me the flower.

"Happy Valentine's Day, Jenna."

It's the most perfect single bloom I've ever seen, and peonies are my favorite flower.

"Thank you Elliot, it's beautiful, and so unnecessary, and, um, WHAT is that amazing smell?"

"Mmmm." He wafts the bag at me. "Olga's. Kitchen?"

I lead him to the kitchen, and he begins to unpack the bag on the island while I put the flower in a vase. I grab two plates from the open shelving above the counter and hand them to Elliot, who is unwrapping a sandwich the size of Wyoming.

"Holy mother of cheddar, what is that?" I say, gesturing to the sandwich, which is at least six inches tall, and appears to be piled with about five pieces of chicken schnitzel, those amazing pounded pieces of chicken breast, breaded and pan-fried. They are layered on plain white bread, and the smell is just heavenly.

Elliot pats his little belly. "That, my dear, is the famous chicken schnitzel sandwich from Olga's. And despite my vast appetite and my not insignificant gut, even I cannot eat a whole one. Which is why I'm eternally grateful for your letting me come over and share one with you."

"Anything I can do to be accommodating." I laugh as he places one half of the sandwich on each plate, each half looking like enough to feed three people.

"I don't know if you like mayo or anything, I believe in purity of essence myself, but if you want condiments, you'll have to add them yourself."

"Not for me, mayo squicks me out. I use it as an ingredient, but not on sandwiches. But I may indulge in a pickle slice or two, if you'd care to join me."

"The perfect woman. Pickles for sure."

I get us both glasses of ice water, pull out the jar of dill pickle slices, grab a couple of napkins. Elliot has also brought a bag of potato chips, as if we will need anything besides these enormous sandwiches. He brings the plates over to the table.

I place a few of the pickle slices on my half sandwich, and try to get my mouth around the monster. I feel like I'm going to have to unhinge my jaw. Elliot smiles at me, and then removes a couple of pieces of chicken from his own sandwich, eating them with his fingers, to help make the thing more manageable. I follow suit and am amazed at the flavor. The schnitzel is crisp and not greasy, well seasoned with salt and pepper, the chicken moist and flavorful and still warm. I take a bite of the sandwich, the soft white bread the perfect foil, and the little bit of vinegary bite from the pickle cutting through the richness.

"Delicious," I manage to say without spitting pieces of chicken at him.

Elliot rolls his eyes in ecstasy. "I know, right? Such a special treat. And you should meet Olga. One of these days I'll take you there to see the place for yourself."

"Well, thanks for the introduction, this is insanely good."

"My pleasure. Next time we go pork chop sandwich. On the bone, if you can imagine. So, how are you doing?"

"Good. Especially now." This thing is freaking amazing, I'm having a total foodgasm.

"I know from Wayne that Aimee really loved Valentine's Day and made it special for everyone."

Great. This is a pity luncheon. I'm shocked by how much it bothers me that he must be so proud to have worked up this little plan to keep my mind off my crushing grief. The sandwich sticks a bit in my mouth. But he continues.

"I don't know about you, but I always sort of hated Valentine's Day myself. And nothing makes me more irritated than someone who loves it trying to get me to drink the Kool-Aid."

Wait. Maybe not a pity lunch? "Yeah. Aimee was a hearts-and-flowers girl on a normal day, so she went a little batshit on Valentine's Day."

"She used to send me cookie bouquets and crap." Elliot laughs. "And I always thought that for someone so smart, she was really dumb to think that it did anything but annoy the shit out of me." And my shoulders completely unclench. It's the first time since Aimee got sick that anyone has said anything about her that was less than saintly.

"Hey, lets not speak ill of the well-intentioned dearly departed here, people."

"I used to get candles and bath salts. Like the consolation prize to being single was candlelit lavender baths for one. Whoo-hoo!"

"Below the belt, that is below the freaking belt, missy."

"Exactly. It's like when I was little and my mom would send Valentines to school for me, in case none of my classmates gave me any." Elliot shakes his head.

"Brutal! Even my folks didn't do that."

"Yeah. I never got to tell her that perhaps if she hadn't insisted on the homemade bowl haircut and the brown corduroy leisure suit, perhaps my classmates might have handed me a card themselves."

"Ha! You didn't."

"Oh, yes. Yes I did."

"Is there photographic evidence?"

"Yes. And before you ask, no. You do not want to know what you would have to do to see them."

We finish as much of our enormous half sandwiches as we can manage, and I clear the plates. "What's in the pan?" I ask, gesturing at the foil-covered dish.

"I had some people over for dinner last night, and I always buy bread because the table seems empty without it, and in these carbs-are-the-devil end-times no one ever eats it. And my philosophy is that if life gives you stale bread . . ."

"You make bread pudding?" I finish for him, since this has always been my habit and my line when asked.

He smiles. "Yep. I experimented a little, I had some palmier cookies left over as well, and figured they are so crispy, maybe they would work in there."

"Okay, that is a genius idea. Why didn't you tell me you had bread pudding? I wouldn't have eaten so much schnitzel."

"A couple of smart girls I know say there's always room in the dessert compartment." It was always our mantra. He comes over and lifts the foil off the pan. I can see that it is golden and crispy, and the scent of vanilla and butter wafts up at me. Elliot grabs two forks from the bin on the counter and hands one to me.

"I'll grab some plates."

"Don't bother. It's just us," he says, and digs right in. What the hell. I aim for a particularly crusty bit on the edge.

"Oh my, that is amazing," I say. It is perfectly balanced, rich but not heavy, just the teeniest bit of chew left in the bread, vanilla and butter and . . . something else . . .

"Toffee. Crushed-up Heath Bars in the middle."

"Of course you did."

"Couldn't resist."

"Elliot, it's amazing."

"Wait till you have it for breakfast tomorrow!"

And suddenly I feel a little weird, knowing that breakfast tomorrow I wouldn't be alone, and knowing instinctively that I won't be sharing this bread pudding with Brian. And more, knowing that I would never let Brian know that I would totally eat bread pudding for breakfast.

"If it lasts that long," I say, reaching for another delicious mouthful.

Elliot checks his watch, drops his fork in the sink, and kisses me on my temple. "Gotta go, princess. One of your neighbors got some massive collection of comics and action figures in her divorce out of spite, and she can't sell them fast or cheap enough. She doesn't know that her ex has called every store in town and left his info, so he can buy them back from whoever gets them."

"Sneaky," I say, and thank god that the one thing that comes from never being married is never having to become the kind of ugly divorce can bring out.

As he is leaving, he says, "Wayne is going to invite you to come somewhere with us in a couple of weeks, and, just, if you can? I hope you'll come."

"Mysterious."

"He is working up to ask you, I don't want to screw him up, but, just, I really hope you say yes. It will mean a lot to him."

"Good to know."

He winks at me and heads down the front stoop, and I head back to the kitchen to clean up. After maybe one more bite of bread pudding.

"You look beautiful," Brian says, opening the door to his condo. I'm wearing a new dress, the only one of the four I ordered online that fit me. I got as far as the parking lot of Bloomingdale's before my stomach and blood pressure revolted, and turned the car right around, paid my ridiculous twelve dollars for ten minutes of driving around the parking lot and came home instead. Apparently I'll have to tell Nancy that I'm afraid to commit to shopping as well.

"Thank you." I do like this one, a deep olive green, with a very flattering crossed top, long sleeves, and a midcalf skirt, with a wide obi-style belt that makes me look like I have a waist. I'm wearing it with a true indulgence, a pair of Jimmy Choo boots that are actually like a kitten heel pump covered with a long sock that goes to my knee. Or I should say, actually fits over my calf, which is a miracle. They are unusual and, I think, terribly sexy.

"C'mon in."

Brian's place is exactly what you would expect of a single lawyer in his midforties with no kids and no pets. Sleek, modern, open-concept loft space, clean, lots of sharp edges and leather and glass, exposed brick, tall ceilings, and what appears to be an eight-hundred-inch flat screen television.

We head into the living room area and sit on the couch.

"Happy Valentine's Day," he says and hands me a small velvet box. Oh lord. And I promised Wayne I would run away, which at the moment, I really want to do.

"Brian, you really shouldn't have . . ."

"Of course I should have." He is smiling at me in a very self-satisfied way.

I open the box. It is a pair of earrings; oval, sort-of-dark, hot pink stones surrounded by diamonds.

"Brian . . ."

"They're Vietnamese rubies," he is quick to point out.

"Thank you. They're very pretty, but I really can't . . . they're too much."

"Of course they aren't."

But they are. Not to mention completely not my style. "You really shouldn't have." He leans in for a kiss. "Really, Brian. I appreciate the thought, but these are just too extravagant."

He looks wounded, and now I feel bad.

"You shouldn't spoil me so much," I say, because what else can I say, and he beams. But I still leave the box on the table, and don't make a move to put them on.

"How was your day?" he asks.

"Good. I had a nice chat with Wayne, dropped Chewie off at the new day care place, which I think might be a good fit, had lunch with Elliot."

"Good god, that all sounds awful. Geek parade."

"That's not nice. It was perfectly lovely. It's a hard day for Wayne, so it was good to talk with him. And he is the one dealing with the dog tonight so that I can be here. Elliot had some business in my neighborhood and stopped by and brought me lunch."

"Well, sounds dreadful to me, but what do I know. Do you ever worry that you'll be like one of those people who doesn't realize their house smells of old cabbages?"

"I'm not really sure what you mean."

"You do too know what he means, and it's extremely douche-tastic."

"I mean, you know, you go to someone's house and it smells sort of bad, like mothballs or cat pee or old cooking, but it's clear that they don't know because they live there so they are used to it, it just smells normal to them. So like, you're spending so much time with these mouth-breathing super-geeks, that now you don't even know how annoying they are." He smiles, clearly thinking that he is saying something hilarious.

He's laughing, and suddenly I kind of want to smack him.

And the sweating starts. And the heart beating.

"Brian," I say as calmly as I can, "I need you to do me a favor and lay off of Wayne and his friends. I know that I certainly have participated enough in the past, and I feel bad about that now. May I use your restroom?"

"Of course, right down the hall, through the bedroom."

I head for the open door, turn the light on, and lock the door behind me.

"He's a shithead."

Yeah. I'm starting to get that.

I try to go to the bathroom, but nothing really happens. I don't know why I'm so upset; after all, not so long ago I would have said things just as offensive.

"Maybe that's why you're upset."

Probably.

"What are you going to do?"

What can I do? I'm going to put on my game face and go eat a very delicious very expensive meal with him, with a lot of very delicious very expensive wines, and then bring him home, and have some sex.

"Why do you make it sound awful?"

Because it suddenly seems awful?

"What would you do if you knew there were no conse-quences?"

Slap him?

"Ugh. No you wouldn't. You're not Snooki for chrissakes. Let's try it another way. What would I do?"

Good god, you aren't going to make me get a WWAD bracelet or something?

"What. Would. I. Do?"

You would tell him you weren't feeling up to it, blow him off and call me, and you and I would go eat the delicious food and drink the delicious wine.

"I'm not saying, I'm just saying."

Just one problem.

"You can still blow him off even if I'm not your backup plan. Tell him your tummy is upset, and go home. You can take a nice hot candlelit bubble bath."

Bitch.

I can hear Nancy's voice in my head. There's nothing wrong with liking him if you want. But there's also nothing wrong with not liking him either.

I wash my hands, and head back out.

Brian is standing there, looking impossibly handsome and groomed, and for the first time since we began seeing each other, I'm completely unmoved by his attractiveness. Suddenly he just looks like an overgrown frat boy to me. And a mean one. And boring. I can't begin to imagine what I'm going to talk to him about for thirteen courses.

I go back over and sit next to him on the couch. "Brian, I'm thinking, um, I'm thinking maybe this isn't the best idea."

"Aren't you feeling well? It would be such a shame to let the reservation go to waste."

I'm about to say yes, that it's my stomach, but I suddenly remember what was so freeing about the beginning of our relationship, the fact that I didn't have the energy to fake anything or lie or play the games. I was just honest with him, and it made me feel good. And I realize that the longer I spend time with him, the more I get away from that honesty, and the less interesting the relationship gets. So I decide to reclaim it a little. "It's not that. It's just, well, remember at Mythos when we talked about my not knowing what I was up for, relationshipwise?"

"Why do I feel like I'm about to get dumped on Valentine's Day?"

"It's not dumping, Brian, it's just . . . I told you that I'm not in a place right now to do much more than be in the moment." And then I cop out the teensiest bit. "As lovely as this time has been with you, maybe it's just completely the wrong timing. And I don't want to pretend to be something I'm not with you."

"You don't have to keep the earrings."

"Oh, Brian. I think that's the thing. You deserve to be with a girl who would be thrilled about the earrings."

"Look, Jenna, I'm a big boy. I get it. I just thought we were having a good time. I'm sorry if I was pressuring you for more. I knew going in that this was potentially shitty timing in your life."

"As shitty as blowing you off on Valentine's Day?"

"Well, to be honest, I don't really care that much about the holiday, it's sort of a girl thing."

"Forgive me?"

"Of course I do." But his clenched jaw says he really sort of doesn't, completely. And I wonder if I'm going to have to find a new lawyer.

"I'll talk to you in a couple of days or something."

"Okay." He walks me to the door, we hug awkwardly, and I head for the elevator.

Brian's doorman gets me a cab right away, and I give him my address. Then I call Wayne to tell him I'm heading home.

"What happened to your big fancy dinner?"

"Brian and I decided to take a little break."

"HALLELUJAH! I mean, um, sorry?"

I can't help but laugh. "It's okay, Wayne. I just wasn't feeling it tonight, and I guess I have to figure out if it is worth moving forward."

"That's the truth, Ruth. But I thought you pulled all kinds of strings for the reservation at that place?"

"I did."

"And I thought it was all expensive and prepaid and non-refundable."

"It is. But what the fuck. I'm rich. I can afford to blow it off."

"But I thought you really were excited to eat there? You and Aimee talked about it forever!"

"I was. I am. We did. It's supposed to be amazing."

"Well, then, come get me. We're going to dinner."

"Wayne, this is SO not your kind of place."

"Hey. It's your kind of place and you're my friend, and it would be a total waste to miss it. It won't kill me. It's what Aimee would do. Let me throw on a nicer outfit, and come get me."

And suddenly, as much as I was looking forward to pajamas and TV and eating the rest of Elliot's bread pudding right out of the pan, nothing seems like it would be more fun than to spend Valentine's Day watching old Eleven Things Wayne eat at one of the most avant-garde, fine-dining, unusual-plates restaurant in Chicago.

"I'm on my way."

EL Ideas—Chef Phillip Foss
Valentine's Day Menu

freeze pop—honeydew / truffle / bitters
shake and fries—potato / vanilla / leek
black cod—black rice / black garlic / black radish
cauliflower—botarga / anchovy / potato
brussels sprouts—grits / kale / horseradish
apple—peanut / bacon / thyme
french onion—gruyere / brioche / chive
ham—fontina / butternut / green almonds
pretzel—beer / mustard / cheddar
buffalo chicken—blue cheese / carrot / celery
steak—components of béarnaise
pie—lime / graham crackers / cream cheese
movie snacks—popcorn / Twizzlers / Raisinets

Wayne looks as if he is being sent to the gallows. One look at the minimalist menu, which not only lists many things Wayne does not eat, but also gives no indication of preparation, and he blanches behind his goatee.

"You don't have to do this," I say. We've just been seated at a small two top in the eclectic dining space. The restaurant is the reverse of most, in that 75 percent of the space is an open-concept kitchen with a small area for tables. The chef is committed to the experience being open to all, and diners are encouraged to wander into the kitchen at any time, to ask the chefs questions, help with plating, even serve fellow diners. Not your usual high-end fine-dining experience, but I'm excited to see how the meal comes together. Each chef takes charge of crafting one or two dishes, and tonight's menu is inspired by comfort.

"Yes, I do." He smiles wanly, but bravely.

"I'll make you a deal; if you'll take at least one bite of every dish, we can totally stop somewhere for a burger on the way home." I'm less concerned with expanding Wayne's horizons than I am with sending untouched plates back to the kitchen. Every chef's worst nightmare. But I figure if he takes at least one bite of everything, I can pull the chef aside quietly and claim that he had gastric bypass surgery or something that limits his intake volume.

He sits up straight. "I'm all in, Jenny. You betcha. If Aimee could see me now!"

"Oh, I see you big man. And I love you more than ever."

"She'd be very proud, I'm sure."

The sommelier brings over the first of the bottles I dropped off here yesterday, having carefully gone over the menu with my wine guru, Howard, who has sent me with four and a half thoughtfully chosen wines to pair with our meal. We are starting with Vilmart Grand Cellier champagne, my favorite bubble.

Wayne takes one sip, and then his eyes snap open so hard I fear he might have bruised his eyelids.

"Not your fave?" I ask, the delicate minerality thrilling my palate.

"Um, no, it's good, but, um . . . Jenny . . . it's . . ." He is staring at the door. I turn around.

Brian. Is here. With some picketytwick blond pair of legs.

Having a serious conversation with the gentleman at the door. Sonuvabitch. I stand up and head across the room. Brian doesn't see me, as he is focused on the task at hand.

"The reservation is under Stewart. The wines were delivered yesterday," he is saying, in a tone that is less than polite or respectful.

"Yes, sir, but, um, the Stewart party is seated."

Brian looks up. Sees me standing there. Then he turns beet red. "Jenna . . ."

"Hello, Brian, how nice to see you again."

"Hi. I'm Amber!" says the Barbie doll.

"Of course you are."

"Very nice to meet you Amber, I'm one of Brian's clients," I say, smiling, putting subtle emphasis on the client part. And noticing a very familiar sparkle. "My goodness, what beautiful earrings."

"He is such a fartweasel."

"Thanks," she says, beaming at Brian, who has now turned the shade of a good cabernet.

"Are you two eating here tonight as well?" I ask, playing dumb.

"I think, um, there is a problem with the reservation," Brian stammers. He looks over my shoulder and sees Wayne, and blushes even harder, as it registers that I didn't go home to wallow in our relationship ending, as he clearly was counting on.

"Too bad. It's supposed to be wonderful, I'm very much looking forward to it myself."

He shrugs at me, eyes full of gratitude that I am not embarrassing him in front of his backup plan. "We should go, I'm—I'm very sorry for the confusion." He puts an arm around Amber to move her toward the door.

"Brian, feel free to drop my name at Blackbird; they should be able to sneak you in if you like."

"Um, thank you, Jenna, it's good to see you, have a wonderful meal."

"We will."

I return to the table where Wayne is grinning ear to ear.

"Guess that break might just be permanent, huh?"

"Could not be MORE permanent." What a shithead.

"Well, I'll drink to that!" Wayne says, clearly delighted.

We clink glasses and let the meal begin.

21

So then, they bring this thing called 'fries and a shake,'" Wayne says. "And the chef says he was inspired by watching his kids dip their McDonald's fries into their vanilla shakes. And it's like this tube made out of a thin slice of deep-fried potato, like a little potato chip in tube form, and it's filled with this insane potato-vanilla ice cream, and then it's sitting on a bed of these leeks that were like melted in butter and a puddle of hot potato soup. But the thing is? It was hot and cold and salty and sweet and crispy and soft and it was TOTALLY like eating a fry dipped in your shake!"

I may have created a monster. Wayne, to his credit, while he didn't love everything at our fancy dinner, did taste everything, and a few of the courses really blew him away. He loved the riff on a buffalo chicken wing, essentially a high-end McNugget with a blue cheese sauce, braised celery, and house-made hot sauce. The honeydew freeze pop that started the meal, essentially a tiny Popsicle; and the steak, even though it was medium rare, were also hits. He didn't like the black cod, which was one of my favorite dishes, and was indifferent to the cauliflower; but the deconstructed French onion soup and ham and cheese sandwiches were both winners, and of course, he demolished the dessert courses. And more importantly, he was good company, and we shared a lot of lovely memories of Aimee, and each dish he would say what she would have liked or disliked about it, and it was as close to her as I've felt, the Voix notwithstanding, since she left us.

Of course, it wasn't exactly a complete Invasion of the Wayne Snatchers. He also asked the chefs why fine-dining chefs didn't wear hairnets, since they are just as likely to get their hair in the food as cheap places, accidentally dropped a plate of carefully picked celery leaves they were using as garnish, and knocked his wineglass all over the table, and me. Twice. But for the first time since I met him? None of these things bothered me or embarrassed me enough to make me hate his existence.

"That sounds awesome," Benji says. "I'm terribly jealous."

"Well, don't worry," I say, accepting a mug of tea gratefully from Lois. "I've booked the whole place in a few months; we're having a staff dinner there."

The experience was so extraordinary and fun, that I found a date that they had no reservations, and bought out the whole restaurant. Since it is only twenty seats, I figure between the Library gang with plus-ones, me and Wayne and Elliot, and Andrea's folks, we'll have a fantastic time. And as Aimee always said, we can't take it with us. It's going to make me so happy to share a meal like that with my nearest and dearest, and even Wayne is excited to go back and see what they come up with.

"That is amazing, Jenna, thank you. What a wonderful thing to look forward to!" Eloise says, handing me a plate with tiny Linzer cookies.

"I can't think of any group who would have more fun than us," I say, biting into the tender buttery cookie with its raspberry jam filling.

"Can Noah come? I want to make sure he gets exposed to really good food," Wayne asks. One of the things we talked about as he was having his first serious foodie experience was how much he wants to make sure that Noah has a healthy and open-minded relationship with food. Josie is apparently not nearly as restrictive as Wayne, but is still pretty simple in her tastes.

"Noah is very welcome," I say, loving the idea.

"Cool. Maybe he can come to some of our dinners too!" Wayne asked if I would be willing to pick up with him where Aimee and I left off with our monthly adventure dinners and take him to different restaurants so that he could maybe broaden his horizons a little. And I'm strangely looking forward to it. I think part of my joy of the meal at EL was watching him really engage with the food and enjoy it, getting to experience it both for myself, and vicariously through Wayne.

"Wayne, I'm really proud of you for going for it," Andrea says, winking at me.

"Well, I suppose even forty-four isn't too old to embrace change," he says sheepishly. "I still think you can survive very happily with my usual dining options, and I mostly probably will, but I have to admit there were parts of it that were exciting and interesting. I'm thinking of it more like going to the theater or opera or something, like a cultural thing you do once in a while, but you don't sell your TV. You're still not going to get me away from my usual stuff on a regular day!"

"But he has promised me I can branch out a bit for dinner parties," I say, reaching for another cookie. "So you'll all be delighted to know we can go beyond roasted chicken and pork chops for future get-togethers."

"Well, I say amen and hallelujah. Can I get a witness?" Andrea says. "And can you tell me what you did about Brian, that deranged titgypsy?"

"He called me the next day to sort of explain. According to him, Amber lives in his building and they have gone out a few times over the past year, very casual. And he figured that the reservation was prepaid and the wines were already there, and it would be a waste to just have them sit there, so he called her to see if she was free for dinner. And when she came up to his place, she saw the earrings, and assumed they were for her and got all excited and he couldn't think of anything quick enough to explain why he would have them, so he let her think they were for her."

"Because that is a man who wanted some guaran-damnteed Valentine's nookie," Benji says, tsking.

"I agree. It's suspect," Eloise says.

"Regardless, he said he was mortified, that it was completely his intention to tell me later that he used the reservation, that he was going to see if they would refund my credit card and charge his for the meal that night, and that he was going to tell me that he would replace the wines and drop them off to me."

"Whatever, it was shitty," Benji says.

"And that's the truth, Ruth," Wayne says.

"He could have asked when you were leaving if he could use the reservation if he was planning on being all aboveboard and thought you wouldn't mind," Eloise says, handing me another cookie.

"I agree on all counts. And I think he now knows that we aren't on a break, we are just not seeing each other socially anymore."

"Are you going to fire the dumb asspimple?" Benji asks.

"Not yet. I figure he'll want more than ever to keep me really happy for the moment, especially since he'd hate for me to explain to his colleagues why I'd like to make a change, so I'm likely to get some free overtime and attention to detail for the foreseeable future. If it gets weird, I'll just have one of the other partners take over."

A small group of customers wanders in, probably just had lunch at Lula, and the team jumps up to launch into professional mode, leaving Wayne and me in the chairs in the front.

"So, Jenny, since I did the thing that scared me with an open mind, do you think I can impose on you to do the same thing?"

Uh-oh. Other shoe. Dropping. It's been a solid month of not hating Wayne, of actually liking Wayne a reasonable percentage of the time, but something tells me that this is all about to change.

"Sure. What's on your mind?"

"I have an idea for a business."

Oh lord, here we go. "Okay."

"But I think in order for it to make sense to you, you have to come see something with me. Next week is the local Comic Con. Elliot has a booth, so he gets a bunch of passes. I'd really like you to come spend a day with us there. Maybe Saturday? There are events all day, and the big gala that evening."

The *no* is halfway out my mouth when I look at him. His face, today festooned with a strange pencil moustache, is open and eager. He looks like a basset hound begging for a treat.

"He went to your fancy dinner to make you happy. The man ate BRUSSELS SPROUTS for you."

Sigh. "Of course, Wayne, I'd be delighted to come."

He lights up like a Christmas tree. "AWESOME! It'll be fun, I promise."

"I don't have to dress up in costume or anything, right?"

"Of course not. We'll go civilian."

"And this has to do with the new business idea?"

"Yeah. I think I'll be able to explain it better after you come and see."

"Okay, Wayne. It's a date."

"Cool. I have to hit the road if I want to make it to Madison for Noah's science fair."

"Yeah, I should go home. I've got a ham in the oven."

"A whole ham? You must be really hungry!"

"Ha-ha. It's not for me. I'm dropping it off at the fire station on Elston."

"That's cool. How come?"

"I met some of the firemen from that station when we had that huge fire on the corner of California and Logan. Apparently their sergeant just retired, and he was the best cook in the place and they've been having sort of sad meals over there. Lots of pizza and sandwiches. So I said that once a week I'd bring them something."

It feels good to be cooking for someone, and fun to be able to test recipes and indulge my desire to make comfort foods at scale.

"That is very cool. They must love you."

"They seem grateful."

"Now why didn't I think of that when I was single? Cooking for firemen. That is genius," Andrea says, coming over to say good-bye when she sees Wayne and I getting our coats on.

"I think a doctor boyfriend with access to box seats for all the sporting events trumps hungry firemen," I tease her. On

Valentine's Day, Law gave her the key to his condo and asked that they be exclusive, with an option on moving in together when her lease comes up this summer. I've never seen her happier, and I know Jasmin and Gene approve.

"You better believe it. We'll see you guys soon?" Andrea asks.

"I'll pop in with the dogs tomorrow afternoon," I say.

"I'm bringing Noah to Eloise's Quiche for Kids class in two weeks," Wayne says.

"Awesome. Stay warm out there."

We wave at the rest of the team. Lois is pouring hot, spiced cider for a couple of the customers, while Benji demonstrates a double potato masher to one, and Eloise shows another the Michael Ruhlman *Charcuterie* book. They're all eating cookies and looking happy.

When I get home, Volnay greets me excitedly. I can barely get out of my coat before tossing her a treat from the bowl by the door. Chewie is at day care, his third visit, and so far he hasn't worn out his welcome. He comes home exhausted, which has cut down significantly on the household destruction. Unfortunately the bigger he gets, the more slobbery he is getting, and I'm just resigning myself to the next twelve to fifteen years of getting slimed regularly. He's putting on about one to two pounds a week, which feels strangely similar to what I seem to be gaining. Of course, he is also growing taller, but me? Not so much.

My house smells of ham and spice and sweet. I head to the oven and peel the foil off the pan, wanting the mango and ginger glaze to caramelize on the top before taking it over to the fire station. My personal farmer, Paul from Paulie's Pastures, has been filling my fridge and chest freezer with amazing meat and poultry, and this ham is from his organic Berkshires. I have a huge pan of corn pudding soufflé already made, a shaved brussels sprouts and kale salad, as well as a double batch of Elliot's bread pudding, since he was kind enough to share his recipe. I'll drop it all off when I head out to pick up Chewie at four. The ham glaze and salad are both new experiments out of the Notebook, which I'm determined to cook something out of at least once a week. I'm starting slow with the firemen until I find out how adventurous they are. But it feels so good to be cooking for people again, to think about what they would like, what would make them happy, or be surprising.

To feel useful.

Jenna-

I hear Wayne convinced you to join us on Saturday for Comic Con. I'm delighted you're coming, and think you might just have a good time in spite of yourself. I've taken a two-bedroom suite downtown at the Peninsula, since I don't think any of us are going to want to schlep all the way back north to change for the gala in the evening. It's technically black-tie optional, but the optional part includes Stormtrooper costumes and vampire formal, so whatever you are comfortable in will be fine. Wayne and I will share one room so that you can have your privacy in the other to relax and get ready. My guess is that we'll all need a nap in the afternoon before the festivities. Wayne will pick you up at nine.

Heard EL Ideas was quite the experience on many levels.

E

E-

EL was amazing, made doubly so by Wayne's being a total gamer and going for it. I was like a proud mama bird watching her baby fly for the first time. Wish you could have been there.

That is so lovely about the Peninsula, but I can get a room there as well so that you don't have to share with Wayne, no problem. I'm sure it will be a fascinating day!

J

_____

J-

I wish I had been there too! If you're up for going again, maybe one of these days I'll snag a reservation and we can go together. Peninsula is totally sold out; I already tried to get you your own room. But luckily the suite is pretty big, and the two bedrooms are on either side of the living room, so you'll have plenty of privacy, I promise.

E

_____

E-

I meant to mention, if you wanted, I already booked out the whole restaurant for a party later this spring, you are definitely on the invite list! I hope you can make it. And you are welcome to bring a date if you like.

So sweet of you to check for me on the room front, looks like I will once again be imposing on your hospitality.

J

_____

J-

You are never an imposition. And I'll be delighted to join your party. It is very generous of you to offer a date slot for me, but I can't really think of anyone I know who would appreciate the experience appropriately. So I can be Wayne's date. If I promise to keep him in line, maybe we'll get invited to sit at your table. Looking forward to seeing you Saturday.

E

Comic Con is like nothing I've ever seen. Thousands and thousands of people, a good percentage of them in elaborate and extraordinary costumes, all going to movie screenings and lectures and panel discussions and shopping at booths and getting books and pictures signed. Elliot has a huge booth, and despite having hired in extra staff, the place is swamped. He seems pleased with how things are going, and blows off my admonition that Wayne and I will be fine if he needs to work.

Instead, he and Wayne tag team taking me to what they consider prime events. We see a special new director's cut of a movie from the '90s called *Galaxy Quest*, which I actually think is hilarious, even though I'm sure I'm missing a lot of the inside jokes. But I'll watch Alan Rickman do just about anything, and the movie is silly fun, and actually pretty smart a lot of the time. Then we stop in to a conversation between Joss Whedon and J.J. Abrams, which is very interesting. We grab a quick hot dog lunch, which is never a bad idea in Chicago, and then we walk the floor, looking at booths, trying out new games, seeing all the crazy costumes.

We each pick out fun gifts for Noah, and I get some quirky stuff for the Library gang. For Lois, a full apron with the famous Leia gold bikini body, which should look hilarious on her round frame. For Eloise, a complete set of Star Wars cookie cutters, including all the main ships, a Death Star, a light saber, as well as Yoda and Darth Vader heads and R2D2. Benji gets a complete set of the *Buffy* DVDs, and a signed shirtless pic of Spike, who according to Benji is a major gay icon, despite his hetero behavior on the show.

Andrea is getting the new twenty-fifth-anniversary DVD set of *Rocky Horror Picture Show*, and a signed copy of a new memoir by a local writer called *Confessions of a Transylvanian*, since she recently admitted that she spent two years in high school playing Magenta in the live cast up at the Music Box. Having seen that production more than once myself in high school, we had a good laugh about it. Especially when we figured out that, of course, both of us budding foodies were most fascinated by the whole dinner party scene, and wondered exactly how one would properly cook a haunch of Meatloaf.

Everywhere we go, Elliot is greeted warmly, and I'm consistently shocked by how many of the people we meet are scarily normal. Even some of the people who are in major costume regalia, we meet doctors and lawyers and architects and an enormous number of people who work in the computer industry. There are artists and actors and accountants. And everyone is having a helluva good time.

I think back to the parties Aimee and I planned, and how all those tuxedos and ball gowns weren't really that much different, costumewise, than some of these getups. Not as elaborate or out there, to be sure, but not so different. After all, is an hour at Bobbi Brown for the perfect party makeup that much of a stretch from an hour putting on a Klingon forehead or Spock ears? Is searching for the perfect dress, shoes, bag, wrap, jewelry so much different from the perfect jumpsuit, ray gun, ammo belt, and communicator? And unlike most of the regular parties we did, these people are way open to each other and the experience. There don't seem to be gaggles of people standing back to judge the other gaggles. And while a lot of the subsets do seem to flock together, Star Wars over here, Lord of the Rings over there, I haven't overheard one snarky comment about someone's costume. None of the women here, in all of their variety of shapes and sizes, seem to be doing anything other than squee-ing at each other and praising how gorgeous they are. And everyone seems to just own themselves. I've been at hundreds of events looking at a sea of black dresses because everyone thinks it is slimming. But today I've seen a riot of color and skin. Including a 350-pound raven-haired vixen in a chain-mail corset, with cleavage you could park a hovercraft in, surrounded by a coterie of clearly smitten men. I wanted to high-five her.

At one point Elliot was grabbed from behind and lifted into the air by one of the most insanely beautiful men I have ever seen.

"Elliot! You bastard. I can't believe you sold to that shithead from Florida."

He looks really familiar, but I can't place him.

Elliot looks down from his midair posture. "Um, Nathan, this is Wayne and Jenna. Jenna, Wayne, Nathan Fillion."

Nathan puts Elliot down, takes my hand and kisses it. I do not even want to begin to explain the effect this has on me, but let's just say that all the girl parts are awake now.

"Nate, man, I'm a huge HUGE fan," Wayne says, elbowing me out of the way, and shaking his hand so hard I fear his arm may fly off.

"Shiny," Nathan says. I just gawp at his broad shoulders, chiseled features, twinkly eyes. This guy makes Brian look like a Morlock, which I have discovered today are ugly, underground H. G. Wells characters.

"Shiny?" I can't help but ask.

Nathan grins. "Elliot? Did you bring a civilian to the Con?"

"She's doing us a favor. Jenna, Nathan is an actor. You might recognize him from *Castle*? The police show? But he was on *Buffy*, and then had the lead in that show *Firefly* that they were talking about in the panel this morning."

"The creepy priest!" I say, a vague memory coming back from watching the *Buffy* series that Wayne gave me during my surgery recovery.

"Yes. But that was just ACTING," Nathan says, with a gracious smile.

"Sorry. I watched *Buffy* with a lot of Vicodin." Boy I'm really making a great impression here.

"Lucky you."

"Sorry about the blaster, man, but what could I do? It was for charity," Elliot says.

"Yeah, well, next time just call me. I come back from shooting and I'm all outbid, with nary a heads-up from my best connection. Gotta go do a signing, you guys coming to the party tonight?"

"We'll be there."

"Shiny." He winks at me. "Maybe I'll see you. Jenna, don't let these reprobates lead you astray." And then he is gone.

"Why does he keep saying things are shiny?" I ask Elliot. He and Wayne laugh.

"Oh, SOMEONE is going to need a *Firefly* marathon," Wayne says.

"I think so," Elliot agrees.

"You are officially getting Geek inducted."

Lucky me. Of course, if it involves spending time looking at that insanely hot man-muffin? I'm in.

B y four o'clock we're dead tired, and despite comfortable walking shoes, after trolling all over the convention hall for hours, our dogs are barking. The three of us pile into a cab and head for the Peninsula Hotel. Elliot's suite is lovely and huge, and we all agree to meet in the living room at six thirty to head to the gala.

I crash on the soft king-sized bed and nap like the dead for over an hour. Then I take a delicious bath in the large tub, soaking my tight muscles and letting the hot water get the crimps out of my back and neck. I dry my hair and put it up into a simple chignon, do my standard formal makeup, smoky eye and nude lip, and struggle into the two pairs of maximum-hold Spanx I need in order to squish into my only formal dress that fits, a charcoal gray heavy silk, with a 1950s sensibility.

Deep scoop neck that hits just at the outside edge of my shoulders, three-quarter sleeves, very fitted bodice to the waist, and then a wide crinolined skirt to just above the ankle. I always feel like Joan from *Mad Men* in it, even though I know it is much more likely that I look like first-season Peggy. I'm wearing my grandmother's emerald and diamond art deco chandelier earrings, which my mom gave me when I turned forty. A pair of bronze metallic Charles Jordan pumps. A simple pewter beaded clutch. A black wrap shot with tiny matte silver sequins. I head out to the living room.

"Yowza. Hey Elliot! Did you invite Sophia Loren?" Wayne yells. He is wearing an actual tuxedo. Granted, it is too short in both sleeves and pants, revealing white socks and the totally wrong pair of lace-up wingtip shoes, and his bowtie is a clip on, and his cummerbund is on upside down. But he looks elegant in a very Wayne way. He is even clean shaven, albeit sporting what looks like the beginnings of muttonchop sideburns.

"My goodness." Elliot comes out of his room, looking pretty dapper. His Gary Sandy haircut is feathered impeccably, and his tuxedo fits him well. He has chosen a brocade vest with matching tie, which on closer inspection is a black-on-black rendition of the Gotham skyline. And his velvet slippers have the Batman logo embroidered on them in silver.

"Very handsome, both of you," I say, and I can't help but smile. They both are pink from hot showers, and Wayne has shaving cream on one earlobe. Elliot's vest is straining a bit over his tummy.

"Are you ready for the geek prom?" Elliot asks.

"I'm ready," I say. They both offer arms to me, and the three of us head out, and I suddenly have a flash of Dorothy with the Scarecrow and the Tin Man.

The gala is in the large ballroom at the Hilton, and the place is done like every sci-fi and fantasy movie ever made threw up in here. There is a strange mishmash of décor. The tables seem to be paying homage to generic wizardry and witchcraft, with wands and cauldrons, and the place cards looking like little brooms. But there is a bank of blue photo booths that Elliot explains are the iconic TARDIS time machines from *Doctor Who*. The appetizer buffets seem to be based on the Lord of the Rings movies, but the bars are decked out in Steampunk, a sort of amazing hybrid of Victorian and Industrial. And, as you can imagine, the band is doing a classic bar scene from Star Wars thing.

"Wow," I say to Elliot.

"Yeah. More is more," he says.

We get drinks, green something or other with dry ice in it for me, and red beer in bottles labeled TruBlood for the boys, and find our table. Georgie is already here, as are the other couples from New Year's, which is nice. Georgie is wearing one of those tuxedo T-shirts, Ronald and Carolyn are sporting Clark Kent and Lois Lane. They all look kind of weirdly fabulous, and again, I'm struck by how much fun everyone in the room is having. Elliot was right, there is everything from Stormtroopers with bow ties, to pinup girls with lots of tattoos, a very funny zombie version of Buzz Lightyear, a bunch of people in versions of the black patent leather suit from *American Horror Story*, plenty of vampires, even one guy who turned himself into Han Solo in carbonite, which made Wayne and me crack up.

There are some speeches, some awards, some charitable donations. The food is fine, but unmemorable. They wheel out a cake that is a huge replica of Hogwarts. There is dancing, which we thankfully skip, but is entertaining. You haven't lived until you've seen a Cylon dancing with Cinderella. Sadly, my new boyfriend Nathan Fillion is nowhere to be found, but our table is lively and excellent company, and the people-watching is spectacular.

While we are poking at our half-stale Hogwarts cake, Elliot spots a big client he wants to touch base with, Georgie goes to flirt with a large girl in a Catwoman suit that is straining to contain her ample frame, and couples take advantage of a slow song to go dance.

"So, what do you think?" Wayne asks.

"It's fun, Wayne, thank you for inviting me."

"What do you think of the party? From your professional opinion, I mean, the execution and stuff?"

I think about this. "Honestly?"

"Yes, please."

"Well, I think it's fun, but sort of disjointed. It's all over the place. And I know that the convention incorporates everything from sci-fi to fantasy to comics, from Disney to *Twilight* and stuff, but I think there should be a way to unify the event so that it is less chaotic. And you know how I feel about standard hotel catering."

"Guess who planned the party?"

For the first time in years I realized that I hadn't even checked the program to see. "Who?"

"The CMG outfit from LA."

"Okay." Not really sure where he is going with this. "Do you think I should be telling Peerless to bid on it for next year?"

"No. I think you and I should plan it next year."

"I don't follow."

"This is the business I want to start. I want to start an event planning company. But one that specializes in theme events like this."

"Wayne, no offense, but you were never really involved in the business, event planning is really hard, with a lot of moving pieces . . . and if you want it to be worthwhile, you need clients with decent budgets."

"Hear me out. I'm talking about a niche market. Only theme events, catering specifically to the kinds of people in this room. A lot of these folks? Have a TON of money. Georgie? His company does ten mil a year. Ronald and Carolyn must make mid–six figures between them, Beth and John at least that. Hell, look at Elliot!"

"Well, I know that sometimes he does a pretty big sale of a rare comic, but how much can the store really make?"

Wayne laughs. "Um, Elliot is probably worth more than you. The store is his version of the Library; it's his clubhouse, and his office. He has been brokering high-end comic and movie collectibles for over twenty years, and his clients are the richest guys on the planet. He probably does a half a million a month in sales in Asia alone."

My jaw drops open. "I had no idea."

"Look, all those Dungeons & Dragons geeks you remember from high school? They are the Steve Jobses and Wozes of today. Forget the meek inheriting the earth, it's the techno age, the GEEK shall inherit the earth. Computers and technology are where the money lives. And all those geeks, those very rich geeks, they want really cool events and they are willing to spend loads of money to get it right. They want *Buffy* birthday parties, and *Doctor Who* Christmas parties and Star Wars weddings. They want Lord of the Rings bar mitzvahs for their kids, and off-the-chain Tim Burton Halloween parties. And if they could get the details right, they will pay for it. That's what I want to do. I know the details and I'm connected in the geek world for clients. But I don't know shit about parties. YOU know about parties. You would know which cake artist would have made this cool looking AND delicious." He points at my half-eaten cake. "Look, I know I have all kinds of schemes, but I've really been thinking about this one, and I've been going to the fair-to-middling versions of these parties for years. I KNOW that with my connections, and your party planning, in three years? We'd be printing money. Everything from the private parties for individuals to premiere parties when new movies come out? Events at all the Cons? This one isn't even a big one; wait till you see San Diego, the original Con! There were like one hundred and fifty thousand people last year! And so many parties the whole weekend, and they don't ever get that level of awesomeness that you and Aimee always brought to your parties. And I know that she was a big part of that magic, but I feel like it was her taste and elegance and details that were her part. And you have a lot of that, and I have the rest."

I'm stunned. I'm looking at Wayne, Half-Brain Wayne, with his endless idiotic ideas, and his eager puppy eyes, and I? Don't hate this idea.

"But Wayne, you keep saying you and I. But this is your

business, your idea. What if I'm not ready to get back into work like this? What if I don't want to start all over?"

"Look, if you like the idea and you are behind me when it comes to figuring out the financing, and you really don't want to be involved at all, then maybe I'll talk to Andrea or see if I can poach someone from Peerless. But I think it doesn't really work its best without you. I know you only technically have to deal with me for another eight months if you want. I'm asking you to give me eighteen. Give me a year and a half to work together to get this off the ground, fifty-fifty, and then if you hate it, we'll figure out a way for me to buy you out."

I take a deep breath. My heart starts racing, and I wait to see if I'm going to have to run to the bathroom, but I suddenly realize I'm not having an attack. I'm excited. I'm excited at the prospect of a challenge, of meaningful work, of building something again. I smile. "Wayne, I actually think this is not a bad idea, and I'm not saying no. But I'm not saying yes either. I need to look at my contract with Peerless and see what it says about noncompete. And you need to come up with a serious business plan that includes numbers so we know what we are talking about financially for you. I'm not going to let you bankrupt yourself on a risky business venture. I'll give the accountants the go-ahead to pay for consultation for you to develop a business plan, but that's all I can commit to right now. Let's both get our ducks in a row, and talk in a few weeks when we know more."

Wayne leans over and gives me a huge hug. "You won't be sorry, Jenna."

I look at him. "You called me Jenna." It sounded so strange.

"Yeah. Elliot asked me earlier if anyone else calls you Jenny and I realized that I've never heard anyone else call you Jenny and he said maybe that's because you prefer Jenna."

"I usually do."

"You could have said."

I think about this. "I could have. So I guess I don't mind when you do it."

He grins. "Like my own private name for you."

I nod. "Just for you."

"Like you and Aimee called each other schmoopy."

"Yeah, something like that."

"Jenny?"

"Yeah?"

"Thank you. For everything. Aimee always said that her life was infinitely improved by your presence in it, and now I really know firsthand what she meant."

"Thank you Wayne. She always said the same about you too. And I'm starting to see why."

And I am.

"Told you so."

Don't push it.

Elliot's car drops Wayne off first, and then heads for my place. I finally figure out that the town car and driver that he sent for me on New Year's are actually not from a service, but are his, full-time.

"Why the driver?" I ask after we drop Wayne off.

"Never learned to drive."

"Seriously?"

"Seriously. Couldn't afford a car in high school or college, then I moved here and public transportation was fine and cabs when I needed them. Just got used to not driving. And then I met Teddy here a few years back when he drove me for a whole weekend at the San Diego Con, and it turned out he was from here and had family here and wanted to move back, but needed a job to do it. Seemed like a good fit, and infinitely easier on me."

"Wow."

"Yeah, I know, it's a little weird, but Teddy really takes care of me."

"I'm his Alfred," Teddy says from the front seat.

"I'm no Batman." Elliot laughs. "But it's true, Teddy does most of my errands and stuff, and it means that I can work in the car, which is helpful."

"I keep telling him I need a red phone," Teddy says.

"And I keep telling you that's only for the Commissioner," Elliot quips back. It's clear that they genuinely like each other, and I like the thought that Elliot met a nice guy and helped him come home. "Wayne said he talked to you about his new big idea."

"He did. It's a really interesting idea. If his take on things is right. What do you think about it?"

"I think if I'm going to spend six figures hosting a party for the San Diego Con every year, I'd like it to be more awesome."

"You do that?"

"I do that."

"And do a lot of people?"

"Yeah. They do."

"And his thoughts about private parties? Theme weddings and birthdays and stuff?"

"My buddy Ryan did a Renaissance Faire thing for his fortieth. I think he spent nearly 200K. He's trying to figure out how to top it for his forty-fifth next year."

"Wow."

"And the weddings can be even more major."

"So you really think it can work?"

"I think it would need someone to take what Wayne has to offer in consulting on theme and turn it into viable executable plans. I think it needs you, and if you aren't willing to do this with him, then you need to let him down gently. All or nothing. If you let him go it alone, for all his good intentions, it will fail. You have to be all-in on this, Jenna, and no one will blame you or think ill of you if you can't or just don't want to do that."

"It's a lot."

"Yes, it is."

"But if I were in, you think we could be successful?"

"If you were in? I think in five to six years you might very well be able to sell the company again to one of your competitors, maybe even to Peerless again, and settle in for an even more lovely retirement than you are enjoying at the moment. I'll tell you what, if you want to do a sort of a test run, I'll hire you and Wayne to do a party for me. *The Avengers* is coming out, and I always try to do a theme party when comic movies get released, invite my high rollers. I can get a buddy of mine to send you a DVD screener of the movie. You and Wayne plan the party. Carte blanche. Whatever budget you think you need to make it great. See how it goes; if you can find the right people, the right resources, and you don't end up wanting to kill my buddy, that might help you make your decision. Especially if you get nibbles to do more stuff from the people who attend."

"You're a good friend."

"I try to be."

And he really has become a good one to me too.

We pull up in front of my house. Teddy parks and gets out to open the door for me. Elliot gets out on his side to walk me to the door, carrying my small bag of the regular clothes I wore all day and my larger bag of purchases and Con swag.

I lean over and kiss his cheek. He smiles at me and places a hand softly on the side of my face, and then turns and walks down the stoop.

I turn and open the door and walk inside. I drop the bags on the floor, my purse on the table, and my coat on the rack, kicking off my shoes. I hear a whooshing noise and turn to see the orange blur launching himself into the air, and barely have time to brace myself for the impact. He knocks me on my ass, which is protected by layers of crinoline and plenty of fat trapped in a Spanx prison. "Hi, boy, hi, I know, how are you? You missed me, huh?" He is stomping all over me, licking my face, biting my hair, rubbing his big square head on me. I realize it's nearly one in the morning, and since Benji picked him up at seven, this pup is way due for a walk to burn off some puppy energy. I push him off me, and stand up. Then I look in the mirror. I'm a hot mess. Slobber all over my dress, half my makeup is licked off; my hair is pulled into a wild nest.

My doorbell rings.

"Hi," Elliot says.

"Hi."

"What happened to you?"

I preen. "What? You don't like it? I call it 'attacked by

puppy.' It's replacing heroin chic and grunge as the new alternative hot."

"It's a look, alright."

I laugh. "So much for Sophia Loren! Did you forget something? Did I leave something in the car?"

"No, I realized that it was very late and you might need to walk your dogs, and I didn't want you to be out this late alone."

"That's so sweet, Elliot. I do have to walk them. But I think I have to change first . . ."

"And you'll need different shoes." He points at our feet, where Chewie is mangling one of my pumps as if it is filled with peanut butter and hamburgers.

"Oy. Yeah. I guess I will. Do you mind waiting five minutes?"

"I don't mind at all. Waiting is one of my best skills." He smirks at me, and I run upstairs to change.

22

I look down at the little pale blue oval in my hand. One of my five precious Xanax. I've never been a bad flier, but I've already had two miniattacks today, and something tells me that perhaps this is the time. I woke up at four thirty this morning in a cold sweat, my heart fluttering like a little hummingbird. After rapidly downloading the contents of my intestines in a noisy and unladylike manner, I couldn't fall back to sleep, even after my pulse finally settled down. At six I gave up and went downstairs to find that while the dog gate was still locked and Volnay sleeping behind it, Chewbacca was crashed out on the living room couch, and two of the three cushions had been completely mauled beyond recognition. Great. Now he is big enough to jump the fence. I packed him up and drove him to Doggie Days, as much for his own safety as for my convenience, paid the kennel fee, and said I would be back to fetch him Sunday evening, and in an emergency to call Wayne. Andrea is house-sitting to take care of Volnay, and to have a romantic weekend with Law, and I couldn't in good conscience leave the Demolition Pup in the mix. I think she wants to get a dog, but Law isn't so interested, so she volunteered so they could do a little trial run.

Elliot sent Teddy to drive me to the airport and save me a car service, which was very lovely of him. I had a second attack in the middle of the security procedure, and almost gave the

TSA guys a real dirty bomb to discover, but made it through the other side and into the nearest bathroom in time. And after a clammy hour at the Admirals Club, I am now on my plane to SFO, staring at a little bit of numb that is looking very tempting.

"Why are you so freaked out? They're just your parents."

I dunno. I haven't seen them in almost eight months. I haven't seen them since . . .

"Since I croaked? Shuffled off this mortal coil? Bit the dust? Expired? Missed the curve? Became formerly animated? Crossed over? Danced the last dance? Ran off with the reaper? Became living-challenged?"

You talk a lot for a . . .

"Corpse? Ex-parrot? Worm food?"

And this? Right here? Is why I am going to take this pill as soon as the flight attendant brings me my water.

"You're fine. They're your parents. It's Passover. You'll make matzo balls with Eileen and debate the state of the election with Mike, and watch a lot of taped old-people shows like NCIS, and get a cramped back from that horrible guest room pullout bed, and then you'll come home and you'll see them again in the fall for Rosh Hashanah."

The flight attendant delivers my water, and I don't hesitate. I swallow the pill, finish the glass and lean back in the seat, closing my eyes.

"It'll be fine. You'll see. They're fine. It will be a great weekend."

And then I am gone.

One thing about Xanax if you aren't used to it? It makes everything deliciously fuzzy. I don't remember takeoff, and barely registered landing. I floated to baggage claim, was greeted by Jorge, the driver I arranged, who took my bag and led me to a car that was the twin of Wayne's monstrosity. I have to give credit, though; they are comfy to ride in. I watched the world go by, the Voix was blissfully quiet, and I just started to come into focus as we pulled into my parents' Berkeley driveway.

"Sweetheart!" My mom comes to the door and grabs me in a hug, planting multiple kisses on my cheek and neck.

"Hi, Mom," I say, thinking that her hair seems to be getting blonder, and that she is definitely noticeably shorter than the last time I was here.

"Hello, pumpkin." My dad comes into the foyer to give me a hug, his gray curly hair bushy around the sides of his head, scalp shiny above. But his hug is still strong and comforting, and his eyes have lost none of their twinkle.

"Hi, Daddy."

I schlep my suitcase inside and take it to the guest room cum office where I stay when I am here. The dreaded pullout couch is already unfurled and made up, room has been made in the closet, my mom's laptop pushed to the side on the table that serves as her desk to make room for me. There is a pair of dark chocolate squares on a little doily on the pillow.

I unpack quickly, avail myself of the bathroom just outside the door of my room, and get their gifts and the other treats I brought out of my carry-on bag. I've brought a tin of homemade chocolate-covered toffee matzo, which my dad loves even though he's always at risk of pulling off a crown. A second tin of coconut macaroons, my mom's favorite, in a new configuration, an experiment from the Notebook, using large dried flakes of unsweetened coconut instead of the little sugary shreds that are most common. The result, as I hoped, was gorgeous little craggy mounds of golden-brown coconut, crispy on the outside, chewy inside, barely held together with sweet goo, tasting mostly of coconut and not cloying like so many of these traditional sweets. Half of them I dipped in dark chocolate, and half I left plain. I found a great wrap sweater in a shade of green that is going to make my mom's eyes pop while it keeps her warm, since she apparently has no circulation, based on the house always feeling like a sauna. For Dad, an antique harp-shaped multitool, his favorite thing, something that shows old craftsmanship, has inherent patina and beauty but is still enormously functional.

I open the window in my room and turn on the ceiling fan. This is when we begin the thermostat dance. The thermostat is right outside the room where I'm staying. It currently reads 78 degrees. As in, my parents have set the temperature of their house for a level of heat that when it hits that temp outside, SANE people turn on their air conditioning. I turn it down to 70. For the next two and a half days, this shift will occur at least eleven times a day. None of us will speak of it.

I head out to find my folks in their charming kitchen. The Spanish-influenced home was built in the 1920s, and retains the original terra-cotta tile floor in the kitchen, as well as the original tile counters. My parents opened the back wall and added French doors to lead into the back garden, so the kitchen gets wonderful light and breezes on the rare occasion you can get Mom to agree to leave the doors open. It isn't a foodie kitchen or a chef kitchen, but homey and warm, and really the kind of kitchen you want your parents to have.

"Come sit, schnookie," Dad says, patting the chair next to him at the rustic farm table.

"Do you want a cup of tea? The kettle is still hot," my

mom says, getting a mug off of the weird wire mug tree they keep on the counter, and rendering the question sort of moot.

"Sure, Mom, thanks."

One thing about Mom, she might not remember what she had for breakfast or where her keys are, but she remembers how you take your coffee or tea, whether you like a "real" martini (gin) or a "weird" martini (vodka), and whatever it is you might be allergic to. In moments, I have a steaming cup of Constant Comment with precisely one and a half packets of Splenda and a splash of milk sitting in my hands. Of course, as it is a thousand degrees and I'm already sweating, the hot beverage has some-what less appeal, but then I remember Jasmin telling me that in tropical climates they drink hot tea in hot weather to make themselves sweat so that they can cool off. Maybe it will work.

"So, what's going on? How is everything and everyone? How are our grandpuppies?" my dad asks. Thank goodness. These are easy and safe conversations. I tell them about Andrea and Law, about everyone at the Library, about Noah's winning his school science fair, and Benji's new three-month stage at Conlon, a two-Michelin-starred fine-dining restaurant that is owned by my friend Alana's business partner Patrick. Benji is starting in a couple of weeks, and is giddy at the thought of learning from the team there. I also think he already has an epic crush on Patrick, who is very handsome, but also seriously straight.

I relish sharing the adventures of Volnay and Chewbacca, ending with the couch-eating incident of this morning.

"Oh my," Mom says, wiping a tear from laughing so hard. "What a naughty dog!"

"He sounds like a real handful," Dad says, shaking his head. "What was Wayne thinking?"

"Well, it is actually sort of widely held that older dogs can be rejuvenated by the presence of a younger dog, so Wayne just thought it would be good for Volnay to have a puppy of her own. And a friend of Noah's mom raises this breed and had someone back out on a purchase, so . . ."

"So Wayne just jumped in willy-nilly on your behalf," Dad says.

"Because deep down he probably subconsciously knew that you would object, so by involving Noah and making it about giving a home to an abandoned dog, he could justify it in his own mind," Mom says, dipping a little into therapist mode, as she is wont to do.

"I don't know that it was that calculated. And it wouldn't be what I would have done for myself. But at the end of the day, Chewie is sort of shockingly lovable, and it certainly has put a little spring back in Volnay's step."

"Lovable, but hard on the furniture," says Dad, looking at the pictures in my phone of Chewie sitting proudly in the middle of his reupholstery project.

"Well, it's just a couch. I e-mailed the girl who helped me at Montauk Sofa when I bought it, and ordered two new cushions. *C'est la vie*. Besides, as I recall, I had my own moments back in the day!"

"Oh, god, you were a DISASTER," my mom agrees.

"Remember when she thought she'd help the painters?" Dad asks. They were painting their master bedroom when I was about seven, with buttery yellow walls and chocolate brown trim. Ah, the '70s. The painters took a lunch break, and I went in and drew a field of brown flowers on the still-wet yellow.

"The painters? How about the hole she made in the wall next to her bed?"

When I was about ten, I once spent an entire rainy Sunday

reading Nancy Drew mysteries on my bed, absentmindedly picking at a small crack in the plaster on the wall beside me. By the time I finished *The Secret of the Old Clock*, there was a foot-wide hole in the plaster, all the way down to the lathe.

Dad chuckles. "How about when she sent the pork chop into the wall?" At this the three of us crack up.

"It was not my fault! They installed the vent filter backward!" My folks redid the kitchen when I was in high school, getting a Wolf cooktop with indoor grill, and instead of an overhead hood, put in a backsplash downdraft vent that opened up behind the stove. I decided one night to make dinner for us; pork chops to test the grill. I opened the vent, turned it on High, and got to cooking. Already confident in the kitchen and having a little bit of flair, I went to flip one of the chops with a little bit of abandon, but instead of getting my spatula underneath the chop, it hit the bone with enough force to shoot the chop right into the vent. Where it got sucked into the wall, because the filter was in backward, leaving enough space for a prime piece of porcine deliciousness to slip right by. Let's just say it was not an inexpensive or convenient thing to retrieve. And week-old wall-chop is not going to be the latest Yankee Candle scent.

My mom reaches over and squeezes my hand. "I, for one, adore this dog, I think it is the closest thing you'll ever get to having a child just like yourself."

And whatever else it dredges up for me, it is good to be a family again for a little while.

Is the water boiling?" my mom asks

"Yep, ready for balls." We are making the matzo balls for tomorrow night's Seder. She mixed the batter earlier today so that it would have ample time to chill, and now that we have rolled them, it's time to put them in the boiling salt water to cook. My mom brings over the plate with the balls, and I drop them carefully one by one into the boiling pot, reducing the heat to a simmer and covering. We have the brisket in the oven, braising slowly, and a large pot of chicken soup simmering as well. We'll make the vegetables and matzo kugel tomorrow. The table is already set, and all of the various elements, the apple and nut and wine mixture called charoset, the freshly grated horseradish, and other Seder plate necessities are all set. My mom hard-boiled the eggs yesterday, unfortunately, so I expect they will have rubbery whites and powdery yolks surrounded by green. And since even I can't bring myself to make gefilte fish from scratch, Mom picked up some from the local deli. It seems like a lot for just the three of us. But I'm sort of glad we aren't hosting a big event.

"So, how are things with that Brian fellow?" Mom asks.

"Over. It wasn't serious, we were just dating and it sort of ran its course."

"I'm sorry to hear that, he sounded nice."

"He is nice, just, I'm not really in relationship mode right now."

"I would think that now would be the time you would most want to be in relationship mode."

"I'm just not frankly much in the mood. Dating is hard and annoying. All those conversations, where you went to school and your career and all that. It requires energy I just don't have these days. I think dating Brian just proved that I'm not ready."

"Honey, I know it has been a rough couple of years, losing Jack and losing Aimee, and all of it. But you know we worry for you. We want to know that you are happy."

"Well, I think for the time being, we all have to settle for me being content. Happy, I don't know what it will take to get to happy. And I don't know that a man will be involved."

"What about a woman?"

"MOM! I'm not gay."

"Ha! Go, Eileen. Way to put it out there."

"Well, there's nothing wrong with it if you were."

"Of course there wouldn't be, but I'm not." Vey is mere.

"Your dad and I would be fine with it. We live in Berkeley for chrissakes."

"I'm not sure what that means, and I know you'd be fine with it, but I like men."

"Okay. Just putting it out there."

"Is this about Aimee?"

"Oh HELL no."

"Well, the two of you were extremely close, and you were very involved in her sickness, and you don't seem to really be bouncing back from her death, so yes, it has occasionally occurred to us that perhaps there was more than just friendship there."

"Now I know how Gayle and Oprah feel."

"Mom. I loved Aimee with my whole heart, in a totally platonic way. She was my best friend and business partner. We were as close as friends could be for twenty-four years. So I'm not just going to get over it in ten minutes. And a boyfriend isn't going to fix that." I'm snippier than I mean to be, but these are the exact conversations I didn't want to have with my parents.

"Okay, okay, I just wanted to give you an opportunity to talk about it."

"No offense, Mom, but I have a shrink for that, and it isn't you. Don't try to be my therapist, just be my mom. I'm as fine as I can manage to be right now."

"Well, then, I'm glad you have someone you feel you can talk to." And the hurt is very apparent in her voice.

"How are my girls?" Dad wanders into the kitchen.

"Well, according to your daughter, we are as fine as we are going to get." My mom, for all her qualities, has a tendency toward petulant when things don't go quite how she wants them.

"Eileen . . ."

"Mike . . ." Uh-oh. Sounds like there is about to be a "discussion."

"Okay, I'm going to go check my messages." There is a knot in my throat, and I can feel that the tears are going to come for sure if I don't get out of here. I leave the kitchen and head for my room. One of the problems with my family has always been that my folks were so set in their ways by the time I came along, and I'm an only child, so unless the three of us agree on something, it always feels like two picking on one. And yes, often it was me and Dad disagreeing with Mom, on top of traditional mother-daughter tension.

I check my voice mail, nothing. E-mail. Just junk. I log into Doggie Days, but the webcams are showing that it is playtime for the little dogs, no Chewie. I contemplate another Xanax, sitting on the foot of the horrible pullout bed. There is a knock on my door, and then my dad's head pops in.

"You okay?" he asks. And I try to say yes, but the crying starts and then I'm lost. Dad comes in and sits beside me, putting his arm around me and shushing me while I sob into his chest.

"She just worries about you, she wasn't trying to make you upset."

"I know." I sniffle. "She just pushes my buttons."

"Well, she installed them!" he says, making me laugh.

"Good point."

"And I helped, I know. Do you want to talk about it?"

"Not really. And I don't mean to shut you guys out, I just, I've been so sad for so long and so angry for so long and there is not a thing in the world I can do to change the source of my sadness and anger, and talking about it just makes it worse. And I'm sorry that goes against the grain of the sharing dynamic here, it isn't that I don't trust you or think you won't understand, but it doesn't help me."

"We just want you to have a happy life."

"Even if I'm a lesbian."

Dad laughs. "That's your mom. I always knew what you and Aimee had wasn't romantic."

I wipe my face. "Can't you rein her in a bit?"

"I'm sorry, have you MET your mother?"

"Good point."

"For what it's worth, we are enormously proud of you. We are thrilled that you are so financially secure, truly. But we do think that perhaps you should be thinking about how to best fill your days to help you get through this tough time. Maybe find some volunteer work that feels meaningful to you. Or travel. Something to help you refocus your time a bit, and not give yourself so much latitude to stay stuck in your grief."

"Duly noted."

"Your mom went to take a little lie-down."

"How is she? Really?"

"Well, you know, her blood pressure isn't ideal. She doesn't have the energy she used to. We're old people, kiddo, our warranties are up. It's all slowly downhill from here. But she's fine, and we're fine. Don't worry."

He leaves, closing the door behind him, and I lie down,

the stupid pole in the middle of my back, the flat, sad pillows, and I close my eyes against the tears that threaten to come back, and sleep.

After a couple of hours I wake up, still somewhat off and groggy from the Xanax and the emotional discussion with my folks. I reach over and turn the light on next to the couch, as it has gotten dark in the room since I fell asleep. My arm is streaked with dark brown. I bolt upright, wondering if I am bleeding from somewhere. There is more brown on the side of the pillow, on the blanket beside me. Did I shit the bed? Is that possible? I'm checking my face for a nosebleed when a familiar scent stops me. Chocolate. Holy hell, I forgot my mom put chocolates on my pillow, and have apparently napped on them, getting chocolate all over the bed linens and me.

But at least it isn't blood or poop. I'm laughing hysterically when the door flies open. My mom, clearly a little groggy herself takes in the sight.

"Are you bleeding?" she asks, rushing to my side, worry on her sweet wrinkled face.

"Nope. But I would recommend in future that pillow chocolates be well wrapped."

She looks at the mess, slaps her forehead, and then begins to laugh herself. By the time Dad comes in to see what is going on, my mother and I are holding each other, laughing and crying at the same time, which is all you can ask of family. That and forgiveness.

What does the wiseass child ask?" my dad says, leading the abbreviated and somewhat irreverent Seder we tend to prefer when it is just us.

"When are we gonna eat?" I say, accepting my cue.

"Soon!" my mom says.

Things are back to normal after yesterday's tension. My chocolate bed debacle broke the tension, and we cleaned up, went out to Chez Panisse for dinner, came home and watched, you guessed it, taped episodes of *NCIS* while both Mom and Dad fell asleep in their recliners. Today we mostly relaxed, went to the amazing Monterey Market, where I bemoaned the climate of Chicago that makes such variety and abundance fairly impossible. We puttered around in the garden out back, ate casual lunch of cheese, sausage, bread, and fruit with a salad of market finds with herbs from the garden. We made the matzo kugel, reheated soup and matzo balls, threw the brisket back in the oven, and my mom made her famous dome of broccoli, just steamed broccoli florets that have been meticulously arranged in a deep glass bowl with all the heads facing out so that you can actually unmold it in a perfect dome. I've never been able to successfully replicate it.

Our Seder hits all the high points, we wash hands, open the door for Elijah, dip twice. We ask the four questions, name all the items on the Seder plate, and claim the ten plagues. We eat the Hillel sandwich. We ask the questions that the Wise, Wicked, Simple, and Too Young to Know How to Ask children would ask, and we answer. My "wiseass child" is our cue that we are wrapping things up, and are going to get to the best part, the meal.

Mom and I head to the kitchen to retrieve the plates of gefilte fish, each on its classic leaf of romaine with slice of cooked carrot on top. A little horseradish colored magenta with beet juice, and we tuck in. My dad dips his hard-boiled egg in the leftover salt water from the dipping ritual earlier.

My mom slices hers and eats it with the fish. I skip the egg, not being a fan of hard-boiled in the best of circumstances, but definitely not when Mom is making them, bless her heart. The fish is good, was clearly handmade by the deli, fairly light and with clean fish flavor, enhanced by having been poached in a classic fumet broth. The horseradish punches it up perfectly and keeps it from getting boring.

"So glad you could be here, honey." My mom reaches over to squeeze my hand. She's been very solicitous since our discussion yesterday.

"Me too, Mom. And I was thinking maybe I'd try to come again before Rosh Hashanah, if you thought that was good." I realize that even if we are beyond deepness, closeness is still important, and I need to make more of an effort to spend time with them.

"We were actually thinking that we are overdue for a Chicago visit, so maybe this summer we would come there instead, what do you think of that!" Dad says, striking deep fear into my heart. Managing them here in their natural habitat is one thing. Having them invade mine makes for deep mental and physical exhaustion. But of course I can't say that. What I say is, "Of course, that would be fantastic! And I can have a party at the house, invite all your old cronies to come see you and visit." If they are coming, a project like a party will keep us busy, productive, and away from dangerous subject matters.

"Wonderful. We'll make plans soon," Mom says, standing to clear the plates.

We walk out with the soup bowls, and tuck in again. The broth is rich and chickeny, the matzo balls are perfectly seasoned.

"Great balls, girls," Dad says. "Are there more?" My dad can eat a matzo ball in half a second, and while Mom and I have barely dented our first, both of his are gone.

"Are your legs broken? They're in the kitchen," my mom says, and he gets up to replenish his bowl.

"I'm going to get the brisket!" I say, wanting to move this party along.

By the time we have eaten heartily, packed up leftovers and gotten everything cleaned and put back to normal, they are both wiped out. Dad falls asleep watching the news from his recliner, and Mom heads to bed early to read. My flight is at noon tomorrow, so we will go somewhere for breakfast before I have to go to the airport. Two and a half days, but it feels like I've been here for a week. I'm exhausted.

I head for my room, leaving Dad snoring in front of the TV. I check my e-mail.

Jenna-

Hope things in sunny California are good, that your parents are well, and that you are full of matzo. But not too full. I hear it is very binding.

Elliot

This makes me giggle.

E-

Now you know why we sing "Let My People Go" at Passover. Folks are fine, thanks for asking. Full of opinions and suggestions as parentals are wont to be. And planning to descend upon me for a Chicago-based visit sometime this summer, so I'm contemplating moving and leaving no forwarding address.

J

_____

J-

Ohh. The dreaded parent visit. I've managed to avoid that for the last five years, since my dad hates leaving the couch, let alone the state. You can always hide at my house if you want. When are you back?

E

_____

E-

I might just take you up on that!
I'm back tomorrow around six.

J

_____

J-

I'll send Teddy. Since you are getting in around dinnertime, how about coming back here and I'll make us something?

E

E-

Andrea is making dinner at my house to welcome me home. Why don't you join us?

J

_____

J-

If it isn't an imposition, I'd love to. Text me when you land, Teddy and I will be circling O'Hare. Safe travels.

E

And something about that just reminds me how excited I am to get home, and I head right for bed, hoping sleep will make the time go faster.

Andrea, that was really delicious," Elliot says.

"Seriously, woman, that was just specfreakingtacular," I agree. Andrea put out an amazing spread for my welcome home dinner. Lamb shanks that she braised in pomegranate juice with chickpeas and walnuts and fennel. Wide homemade pappardelle noodles with truffle butter and lemon and chives. Steamed thin French green beans. And now we are finishing slices of a dense pistachio cake with a fig glaze, topped with a bittersweet chocolate ganache.

"Well, this is every cook's dream kitchen, I get very inspired," Andrea says, her blush turning her caramel skin almost copper.

"She's been stuffing me to the gills all weekend," Law says. "I keep sneaking to the gym in the morning before she wakes up, to combat it."

"Better get used to it, buddy boy, if I'm moving in." She grins at him, and it is lovely to see the energy between them. Easy and affectionate and connected.

"Sounds like a good problem to have, if you don't mind my saying," Elliot says, using the back of his fork to pick off the last few moist cake crumbs from his plate.

"It's definitely not a complaint," Law says, leaning toward Andrea for a smooch.

"Sounded like it was a hard trip, at times," Elliot says.

"I think they are at the age where little changes start to really add up, and since I only see them a couple of times a year, it makes it more noticeable. My mom is officially shorter than me, which didn't used to be true. They're showing their age, little bits of forgetfulness, and I know they are in their eighties and it's to be expected, and I should be grateful they can still live alone and take care of each other, but it's hard. I don't want to be frustrated with them, but I can't help it. And that makes me feel guilty, especially since I'm not there to help out. But they're coming for a visit sometime early summer, so you will all get to see them."

"CHEWIE, NO!!!" Wayne yells, scaring the bejesus out of me. He leaps from his chair to chase the dog, who has counter surfed to grab the half-eaten shank off of Wayne's dinner plate, and is now tearing through the house with his prize. We all jump up from the table, Andrea and I getting handfuls of treats from the canister, and see if we can wrangle the pup while Volnay gets excited, and jumps straight up and down on her stumpy little legs, barking joyously at this new game.

The good news is that between the five of us, we catch the dog.

The bad news is that we don't manage to catch him before he hides his prize somewhere to enjoy later. We get him back downstairs, and Wayne sets about doing a training session with him to refocus his energy, while Andrea and Law clean up, and Elliot and I do a thorough search for the bone upstairs. Not only is he not allowed people food, but cooked bones pose a real threat to large dogs, especially with his kind of jaw power, and I don't relish the idea of a midnight trip to the emergency vet when he gets a bone fragment caught in his throat.

"I'll have to figure out a way to repay all of your kindness," I say, as we search my closet, feeling strangely intimate. "The airport run especially, I know how tedious that is."

"You could let me make you dinner."

"Anytime," I say, as we shift the search into my bedroom.

"How about next weekend. Maybe Saturday?"

"Sure. That would be great. Let me know what I can bring. Is Wayne coming?"

He pauses, leans down at the corner of my bed, and stands up with the offending bone in his fingertips. He walks around the side of the bed, kisses my cheek almost absentmindedly and says, "No. Wayne is not coming." And heads downstairs with the bone.

I think I have a date with Elliot.

23

A nd how do you feel about having a date with Elliot?" Nancy asks.

"I'm not sure. I mean, I've never thought about him in a romantic way. And he isn't my usual type."

"Your usual type hasn't really been that great for you, if memory serves."

"Does that matter? Are you attracted to him?"

"I don't exactly dream about him. But he kissed me New Year's Eve and there was a not unpleasant response."

"So he isn't your dream guy, but he's worth giving a shot?"

"I don't know. He is sort of a new friend. I mean, I've known him for years, on the periphery, one of Wayne's guys. But recently I've gotten to know him for himself, and I like him. He's smart, and sweet, and he's been very kind to me."

"And you have said you have some things in common."

"Well, he's a foodie and a cook, so we have that. And history."

"Has he been specific about this being a date? Or is that just your assumption?"

"It's totally a date."

"It's my assumption. And I can't very well ask him, because if it is just him being nice or a good friend, it would be very embarrassing."

"You have a date with El-li-ot."

Great. Now the Voix is doing E.T. impersonations.

"Go with your heart, Jenna, it won't lead you wrong."

"I hope not."

"Trust me, once you go geek, you never go back, my friend."

Good lord.

I head straight from my session with Nancy to Brian's office. I haven't seen him in person since the EL Ideas debacle; we've been conducting business entirely by phone and e-mail. But the consultant is finished with Wayne's business plan, and Brian wants to go over it with me. I've scanned it already myself, and the news is clear. Yes, this is a viable business idea. Yes, there is a market for these services. And yes, as long as I'm only involved in specifically what they refer to as "alternative theme" events, I'm not limited by my agreement with Peerless. On the other hand, since Aimee's will specifically forbids any single investment of more than 10 percent of the principal of Wayne's trust, the business model they have come up with would require at least one other significant partner or investor.

"Essentially, what we are saying, is that Wayne isn't looking to launch this at a start-up level," Brian says. "If he were looking to start small, do basic local events and build a reputation, the way you and Aimee built your business, this would be a no-brainer. But he is talking about going from zero to sixty like a Ferrari. He's talking about needing to build contacts and develop resources immediately, not only in Chicago but in Los Angeles as well, and eventually New York. Offices. Staff. Marketing. And company-funded sample events to show what can be done. You are talking about a two- to three-million-dollar launch, and then needing cash infusions for the first two years until projections of profits can start to figure in."

"Zoiks. That is a lot." I knew what Wayne was thinking of would be expensive, but this is bigger than even I anticipated.

"Are you really even seriously considering this? Going back into business? With WAYNE?"

"I have to consider it seriously, in no small part because it is just the kind of crazy idea that could work. And because I promised Aimee that I would really look at all aspects of what Wayne wanted to do, and always consider whether she would encourage him or let him down gently, and so far, I believe this has the potential to be something she would have encouraged, or at least not dismissed out of hand."

"Suit yourself. Bottom line, Jenna, he cannot do this without you. Full stop. Forgetting even the logistics of the event planning industry, which Wayne knows nothing about, he needs your money. He won't get another investor to take a flyer on him, especially if you aren't involved. And from my perspective, if you are involved, you would need to own half of the company, same as you did with StewartBrand. Which means dipping deep into your principal as well. Your investments have done well rebounding from the crash, but you are just now getting back to the precrash level in your principal, which means you have essentially not made a dime in over four years. Obviously you still have plenty of money, but dipping this deep into that principal will be felt, you'll have to pay some penalties, and there will be tax implications of making that much cash liquid. And of course, there is the Wayne element."

"The Wayne element."

"Jenna, you are halfway to freedom from Wayne. A few more months and you can hand him back to us, and not have to deal with him anymore. If you launch this business with him, you are locked in, day in and day out, for a minimum of four or five years. And really, can you imagine him really helping at these events? I just see him knocking over ice sculptures, and tipping over cakes, and generally being a bull in the china shop everywhere he goes. A bull on steroids. With an inner ear imbalance. On roller skates."

"Enough, lawdouche, she gets it."

"I know. But again, Wayne is pretty clear that his area here would be identifying and helping land clients, and consulting on thematic details and event brainstorming, and keeping up with all industry aspects of the target market."

"You mean going to movies, reading comics, and playing video games."

"Yep, something like that."

"You can't really be thinking you are going to do this."

"I can be thinking that. And I'm pretty sure that the only opinion I asked you for on this was legal ramifications and financial obligations. I don't really care about your personal opinions."

"Well, that hurts my feelings, because I still care about you on a personal level, and I think this is a huge mistake for you personally."

I wait for my heart to race, for the sweats to start, for my colon to twist itself into a pretzel. And when none of that happens, I look at Brian.

"I think, that being the case, that perhaps you ought to speak to your partners about who might be the best attorney to work with me moving forward."

"You're firing me? Because I care about you?"

"I'm firing you because I need an attorney who is less personally interested in the decisions I make. I'm a big girl, and I have a dad. And clearly, this is no longer a good fit. I'd appreciate a call from the other partners by the end of the week with a plan that I can review."

"Seriously, I feel like you've completely lost your mind!"

"Careful, Brian. At the moment, I'm asking you be removed from my account. However uncomfortable that may be for you with your partners, I assume you would rather that, than having to explain why I'm leaving the firm entirely. And I will be advising Wayne to shift to the same person I am with, obviously, for convenience."

His chiseled jaw snaps shut, and while I can see a dozen retorts on the tip of his tongue, he doesn't speak.

"Thank you. I'll review this further, and will discuss my decision with my new attorney. You'll get formal word from Wayne on his choice soon, I'm sure." And I get up, and leave him sitting there without another word, and get in the elevator.

"YOU are such a badass!"

Yeah, I know.

"And taking Wayne with you, nice touch."

It's the least I can do, Wayne doesn't like him anyway.

"But still, it was very, well, ME."

Well, someone has to hold that standard, you being all dead and such.

"I love it. So that just leaves one thing."

What's that?

"What are you going to wear on your hot date with Elliot?"

What indeed?

I decide on a charcoal gray wrap dress, so a little sassy, but with my flat riding boots instead of heels, so a little more casual. I toss my grandmother's old Hermès scarf around my neck to limit the cleavage, since at my current weight, the girls are at their most abundant bounciness. Plus the vintage pattern from 1960, showing a large floral arrangement in a gold vase in the center, and smaller bouquets at the corners, is intricate enough that it hides the inevitable drips and dribbles I always manage to land on my chest while eating.

"Breaking out the fancy bib, huh?"

Trying to stay somewhat demure.

"The ladies are extra buoyant today. Plus silk is so much more comfortable for tying you up."

Yep. That's me. I'm going to go to Elliot's for dinner, and he and I are going to reenact our favorite scenes from *Fifty Shades.*

"Ick. I'm SO glad I died before I had to read those."

Well, I'll only read them over my own dead body.

"You look lovely for your first date."

It might not be a date.

"And if it is?"

I'll deal with that when and if it happens.

"I think it's wonderful."

You're just glad I'm not dating Wayne.

"I'm glad you are going on a date with a smart, lovely man, who treats you with respect and affection, who is solid and stable, who would not in a million years get twinkles in his eyes about your money."

It might not be a date.

"Well, if it is, don't be a dumbass."

Meaning?

"Meaning you jumped right into the thing with Brian with wild abandon. And on his worst day Elliot is ten times the man Brian is on his best day."

So you think I should sleep with him.

"I think you shouldn't NOT sleep with him because you are overanalyzing anything in your little brain. If the opportunity presents itself, don't run away, just follow your heart."

Or parts southerly.

"Hey, you know what they say about rescue dogs being perfect and grateful? No one is better in bed than the guy who always had to work to get the girls. I'm not saying."

You're just saying.

"Exactly."

"Elliot, that was amazing." The meal has been spectacular. We started with a salad of fennel, golden beets, and grapefruit. He did a veal roast with a classic shallot-cognac pan sauce, smooth with butter and brightened with thyme and parsley, the meat perfectly cooked, still rosy in the middle, with a great crisp brown sear on the outside. An interesting dish of fregola, toasted pearl pasta that is one of my favorite ingredients, cooked with sweet corn he charred on the grill, and chives. And simple steamed asparagus. Everything cooked perfectly, well seasoned, and full of soul. We ate at the small table in his kitchen, tearing pieces of crusty bread to sop up the sauce, and drinking an exceptional Donhoff Riesling that was the perfect foil to the meal.

"Glad you liked it."

"Truly extraordinary."

"Should we have dessert in the library?" he asks, having cleared the plates to the sink.

"Sure." He pulls my chair out for me, and I follow him to the room, completely paneled with bookshelves and cabinets, with an intricate wood ceiling. There is an old leather couch that looks as if it was made of WWII fighter pilot jackets, that mottled, worn leather that is so soft and has such great patina. A deep chair in burgundy velvet with an ottoman. A coffee table that appears to have once been a file for architectural drawings, stripped to the original steel with a glass top. On the coffee table is a bottle of Madeira, a plate of dark chocolates, a bowl of tiny tangerines. He opens a lower cabinet to reveal that it is a minifridge, and brings over two plates that each have a slice of what looks like flan, dark at the top from being baked with caramel.

He hands me a plate and fork, and pours me a glass of wine.

I take a bite. And my eyes snap open.

"Gâteau de semoule?" I say in disbelief.

"Mais oui, mademoiselle, bien sûr." He smiles. "I thought you might like it."

"I adore it. And I haven't had it in years." The very French dessert is essentially baked crème caramel–type custard, thickened with semolina for an amazing texture and added nuttiness. There are juicy golden raisins, which I believe he has soaked in rum, and the caramel you make for the bottom of the baking dish turns itself into a light sauce when you unmold it. It is the kind of dessert that any French *maman* would make on a weeknight for dessert. Unfancy, unfussy, and completely comforting and delicious. You never see it in bakeries or on menus, it is a dessert you get at a friend's house when you go for dinner. And it is the perfect thing. "Elliot, where did you learn how to make this?"

He blushes a bit. "An ex-girlfriend of mine had a French mom. She was the one who really taught me how to cook in the beginning. I think I dated her daughter for at least a year longer than I would have so that I wouldn't have to give up her lessons."

"And after the breakup?"

"You know French women. You cannot insult their dogs, their housekeeping, their food, or their daughters. I was out on my ear. But not before I got her best recipes."

"Was it worth the extra year?"

"Tonight's meal was made possible by it, so you tell me."

"Works for me." I laugh, picturing Elliot fighting the desire to end a relationship for the sake of the cooking.

"Well, then it was worth it."

We dig into our desserts, finishing the plates with delight and abandon, and then settling back into the couch with our wine. I look at Elliot and I'm shocked by how much I want him to kiss me. The circa 1978 haircut suddenly doesn't seem that odd. The slight underbite strikes me as charming in the way that it would on a bulldog puppy. And I'm the last person to be able to criticize someone for a small poochy belly, since I'm certainly sporting one of my own. His eyes are warm and twinkly, his smile genuine. And he has forgone the usual old T-shirt with tweedy sportcoat look for a pair of dark-washed jeans, a black mock turtleneck, and a gray unstructured sport-coat. He looks somewhat dapper. There is a pocket square involved. And I have to say, I'm seeing him in a whole new light. How comfortable he makes me, how much I feel I can be myself with him.

We talk about everything and nothing. My family, and his. Wayne and Noah. Aimee. Wayne's business idea. We talk and talk, and all I can do is look at him and think no, it isn't the wine or the hour, which is getting later and later; or the loneliness, which I have to admit I suffer from. It's just Elliot and his quick wit and good cooking and sweet smile, and I can feel myself reverting back to all those days when I was younger. Sitting in college dorm rooms, or in my little flat in Paris, or in cars after long events, with boys; waiting to see if all the fun conversation and banter were going to take that turn. Waiting for the kiss that might or might not come, with all its frustrating, exhilarant anticipation.

Suddenly, I yawn. And Elliot laughs. "Poor girl, I've kept you up gabbing way past your bedtime. Why don't we get you home?" I look at my watch, and can't believe it is already nearly one in the morning. He stands and offers me his hand to help me out of the deep, cushy couch. His grasp is strong and warm. I stand and he keeps my hand, leading me out of the library and toward the front door. He helps me on with my coat, and then walks me outside. Teddy is there in the town car, and Elliot opens the door for me, and then walks around and gets in on the other side.

Teddy drives to my house in a mere five minutes, and Elliot and I don't speak. When we arrive, Elliot jumps out and comes around to let me out of the car, and opens my door. He offers me his arm, and I take it, a little shocked that there is actually a strong little muscle in there.

"Do you need to take the dogs for a walk?" he asks.

"No. Chewie is at the kennel tonight because they are coming to install the taller dog gates tomorrow, and I'm running out of furniture. And Volnay never likes a real walk at night, she'll just pop into the backyard for a few minutes."

"Okay. Thanks for coming to dinner, Jenna. We'll do it again?"

"I'd love that." I smile winningly. At least I hope it's winningly and not creepy.

"I have to say, it is so nice to finally have someone to cook for; most of my circle, they just don't really appreciate the foodie thing. And it gets really boring just cooking for me."

"I know what you mean." Um? Is there going to be kissing? Or am I just your foodie buddy?

"Maybe next time we can cook together."

"I would really love that." My heart is fluttering, and I'm a little tingly.

"Well, good night, Jenna. I'll talk to you soon."

"Wonderful."

And then, he leans in.

And kisses my forehead.

And turns and heads back down the stairs and off to the car.

He's just being a gentleman," Andrea says as we sit with our coffee and a plate of cinnamon rolls at my house the next morning. Law lives a couple of blocks from Ann Sather's, and while I'm not usually much of a cinnamon roll girl, these are still warm and ultragooey and impossible to resist.

"No, I think it wasn't a date date. I think it was a friend date, a foodie date. I think he truly just loves to cook and doesn't have enough people in his life to cook for and with, and he isn't interested in me romantically."

"Jenna, be serious. Can you be serious? 'Cause I'm being serious. Of course he is interested in you romantically. You? Are his dream girl. He's a nice guy, he knows what you've been through, he knows you just ended a relationship; you guys have the whole Wayne factor. He isn't going to make a move until he is sure that either it will be welcomed and reciprocated, or at least that it won't make things awkward and horrible. And I mean SURE sure, positive, beyond-a-shadow-of-a-doubt sure."

"Good lord, this is ridiculous. I'm forty-two years old for the love of Pete."

"You're never too old to have boy troubles." She laughs at me and takes a deep drink of her latte.

"Oy. So what do I do?"

"Why don't you just let it develop? Hang out. Spend time with him. Get to know him and let him know you. Give it space and time to become whatever it is going to become. And try to just relax and enjoy the journey."

"So you don't know me at ALL."

She laughs. "Okay, well forget the last part."

I drop the dishes in the sink and pack up the rest of the rolls to bring with me when I head over this afternoon, since I can't be trusted with them alone.

The dog gate guy arrives right on time, bringing with him two new gates. The one for the kitchen is much taller, and I've been assured that even at full size, Chewie will not be able to get over it. It is also made of iron scrollwork; it looks sort of like a reclaimed bit of old fencing, so it isn't an eyesore. He is also installing a wooden gate at the bottom of the stairs so that when I'm home and the dog isn't relegated to the kitchen, he still can't get upstairs. After the lamb shank debacle, I found three other hidden caches of food debris upstairs, so clearly he can be very sneaky when he wants to be. The stair gate doesn't need to be as tall since dogs won't generally jump over something unless there is flat ground on the other side, and is a wooden craftsman-style half door that the gate guy has stained to match the rest of the woodwork in the house.

By the time he finishes, I've polished off two more of the cinnamon rolls. So much for willpower. I'm about to head out with Volnay to go pick up Chewie and take them for a Library visit, when my phone rings. It's Wayne.

"Just left a message for that idiot Brian to move my account to whoever takes you on," he tells me. "It felt awesome."

"Yeah, I know what you mean."

"So have you had a chance to look over the proposal?"

"I have. It's a lot to think about, Wayne, for both of us. I was talking to Elliot last night, and he offered again for us to do an event for him. I think maybe we should give that a try and see what happens." I try not to think about the fact that planning this event will give me an excuse to hang out more with Elliot.

"I think that is awesome, great idea. But we only have a month, is that enough time?"

"We'll find out."

"Cool, Jenny. And look, I know that while this is a surefire winner of an idea, if we do this and you realize that going into business together will damage our friendship, then I want you to turn me down. That's the truth, Ruth."

This makes my heart smile. "You betcha," I say.

24

I think we are ready, team," I say, feeling the butterflies I always used to feel in the moments before the doors open. We are in an industrial loft space, which has been kitted out to resemble the S.H.I.E.L.D. headquarters from the movie. A local company called Chicago Router Works has custom designed and built everything from the bar to the serving trays to the gobo that is flashing the S.H.I.E.L.D. logo on the outside of the building, the only external clue that a party is happening here.

All of the waitstaff and bartenders have been costumed to look like the generic security forces from the movie, black cargo pants and shirts, fake weapons galore. The room is filled with black velvet couches and white leather and chrome chairs to create loungey seating areas, as well as tall café tables with stools. We have covered the entire floor with the embossed metal sheets you normally associate with garages, and the large center bar looks like your typical superhero mission control, with built-in iPads looking like computer consoles, each listing the menu.

I hired an amazing band called Hananiah and the Boys, a four-piece ensemble that sounds like a huge band, and bless their hearts, they were game for my dressing them up. So Hananiah is dolled up as Black Widow, and on the piano, bass, and drum are Thor, Captain America, and the Hulk, respectively.

There are food stations around the room, each representing one of the main characters. The Black Widow station is all Russian themed, with a carved ice sculpture that delivers vodka into molded ice shot glasses, buckwheat blini with smoked salmon and caviar, borsht bite skewers, minipita sandwiches filled with grilled Russian sausages, onion salad, and a sour cream sauce.

The Captain America station is, naturally, all-American, with cheeseburger sliders, miniwaffles topped with a fried chicken tender and drizzled with Tabasco honey butter, paper cones of French fries, mini–Chicago hot dogs, a mac 'n' cheese bar, and pickled watermelon skewers. The Hulk station is all about duality and green. Green and white tortellini, one filled with cheese, the other with spicy sausage, skewered with artichoke hearts with a brilliant green pesto for dipping. Flatbreads cooked with olive oil and herbs and Parmesan, topped with an arugula salad in a lemon vinaigrette. Mini–espresso cups filled with hot sweet pea soup topped with cold sour cream and chervil.

And the dessert buffet is inspired by Loki, the villain of the piece, and Norse god of mischief. There are plenty of dessert options, many of the usual suspects, mini–crème brûlée, eight different cookies, small tarts. But here and there are mischievous and whimsical touches. Rice Krispies treats sprinkled with Pop Rocks for a shocking dining experience. One-bite brownies that have a molten chocolate center that explodes in the mouth. Rice pudding "sushi" topped with Swedish Fish.

At the bar, in addition to the usual fare, you can get custom Iron Man, Thor's Hammer, and Hawkeye cocktails, handcrafted by a team I hired from The Violet Hour. And against the back wall behind the band, the movie is running at a scale that makes it just fuzzy enough to look almost abstract.

I have to admit, the place looks fantastic. Chic, sophisticated, urbane. Theme, yes, but not theme park. We have set up a store at the back for Elliot to sell all of his Avengers-related comics and collectibles, and the movie folks sent loads of T-shirts, mugs, mouse pads, and other gear for us to make fun swag bags for when the guests leave, including each person getting a small loaf of zucchini bread with a coupon for 10 percent off their first purchase at The Larder Library.

Wayne comes up next to me and puts his arm around me. "I think we did it."

"I think we did."

"And we didn't kill each other."

"No we did not."

"And now I have to go over to that couch in the middle of the room and not move for the rest of the night." It was our one agreement. I promised he would never be without food or drink or company if he promised that he would limit his movements within the room. I purposely placed a seating area in a location with a direct shot at the bathroom that does not come within eight feet of any of the stations. Wayne laughed when I suggested he be on lockdown, but on consideration, he agreed that perhaps it would be best for him to not move too freely around the space.

"Looks amazing, guys, you really did it," Elliot says, sipping a Thor's Hammer, a combination of mead and whisky with bitters. "Everything is just perfect."

"Proof that if you throw a hundred grand at something, you can make it fabulous."

"Hey, I have six clients coming tonight that are likely to spend at least half that tonight, and all I need is one of them to cough up the 300K for the one copy I have of Avengers number one, and we are golden."

"Well, here's to that!" Wayne raises his beer, and I toast with my hand. I never drink till an event is over.

Andrea is heading up the team in the kitchen, claiming that it is fun to be back on the circuit for a guest performance, and Benji is like a pig in shit playing sous-chef. Eloise and Lois did all the desserts. And I have to admit, while it has been stressful, and between you and me, the movie was dreadful, it was really a fun exercise figuring out how to make it happen.

Elliot leans over and kisses my cheek. "We'll make a geek of you yet." This makes my knees go all wobbly. I'm still getting mixed signals from him. On the one hand, we've been in almost constant contact, between planning the event, watching the movie, hanging out with Wayne, and two more dinners with just the two of us. On the other, while he is warm, affectionate, and darling, he has not made a move to take us to the next level. Sometimes I wonder if he might be gay.

"He's not gay."

Well then he should kiss me.

"Maybe you should kiss him."

I can't.

"Are your lips broken?"

If he rejects me, I'll die.

"I believe you shouldn't be so flippant about such things with me."

Oh, yeah, sorry.

"Kiss him."

He should kiss me.

"Oy. I'm out. You're on your own."

Yeah.

I am.

The night could not be a bigger success. Running the event is a muscle I may not have used in a few years, but it really is like riding a bike. We've hired excellent staff and trained them properly, the décor gets loads of compliments, the band is insanely great, doing everything from Motown to Lady Gaga to music from the movie. Hananiah can sing anything and I wonder how long it will be before they are snapped up by some label and made famous.

And the food goes over like gangbusters. Andrea and I slaved over the recipes, hunkering down in my kitchen for the better part of a week, making sure everything was delicious and replicable at scale. And I have to admit, it feels good. Really good to have obligations and purpose and activity again. Not that I will give my mother the satisfaction of knowing she might be right. I know tomorrow I'll feel like I was hit by a truck, but for tonight, I'm happy. Actually happy. For the first time in months.

Four people asked for our business card," Wayne says, as he is driving me home.

"Yeah, I got about six requests on my end as well."

"So what do you think?"

"I think I need to think, and in the heat of the moment of a job well done isn't the time. But I promise, soon."

"Okay. That's fair. But even if you say no, which I will totally understand, I'm glad we did this one."

"Me too."

"I think sometimes I get so excited about my ideas, and well, I talk myself into thinking I can do them. But let's be honest, I'm kind of a nightmare. It's good to feel like I actually can do something."

"Of course you can do things. Aimee always thought so."

"She would have hated tonight."

I laugh. "Her worst nightmare. SO . . ."

"NOT ELEGANT," we say in unison.

"The dinner at EL on Saturday is at seven, right?"

"Technically seven thirty, but I called it for seven so we don't throw off the kitchen if someone is late. Cars are coming to fetch everyone else around six thirty." I arranged with a car service to pick up Andrea and Law; Jasmin and Gene; Benji and his plus-one, a mystery boy we are all eager to meet; Eloise, Lois, Alana, and RJ; my friend Naomi from Tipsycake and her hubby John. Elliot said Teddy would bring him, Wayne, and Noah. It should be a great party.

"Noah is VERY excited," Wayne says.

"I'm glad he can come. And I found some fun nonalcoholic beverages for him so that he can get something specific with the different courses like the grown-ups." Whole Foods has some varietal grape juices, as well as some unique soda flavors, so Noah should be able to swirl and swish with the rest of us.

We pull up in front of my house. My back has already started to cramp.

"Thanks, Wayne, and congrats. Great party."

"Great party. See you Saturday."

I get out of the car, wincing as my feet hit the ground. There is a hot bath in my future for sure.

25

I want to thank everyone so much for coming," I start, looking around the small restaurant at my nearest and dearest. Noah, adorable in a tiny sportcoat and tie, holding his champagne flute of sparkling grape juice with total seriousness. Wayne has an arm around his shoulders, and is beaming at me. They're sitting with Benji and his date, Jordan. Apparently when Jordan came in for his business a few weeks ago, Wayne took him to the Library and he and Benji hit it off. Newly out in Indiana, Jordan is apparently much more at ease with himself here in Chicago, and it turns out the conference he was attending was also something of a job interview. His firm is moving him here in a month, and he and Benji seem to be looking very much forward to living in the same city. Ever the one for dropping bombs, we discovered this last night when Jordan arrived at Wayne's for dinner and promptly announced he was going to be staying at Benji's instead. That kid is full of surprises. Aimee would approve enormously.

Andrea and Law are sitting with Lois and Eloise, everyone else scattered around at the small tables, flutes of champagne at the ready. And in the corner, next to the empty seat that is mine, Elliot sits, smiling at me, and making my knees go all wobbly.

"I just want to say that the people in this room have all

done their part to help me get through the past three years, and especially the last six months, and I want to thank all of you." I turn. "Especially Wayne." He blushes, and his eyes go a little shiny. "Everyone, enjoy this spectacular meal, Chef Foss and his team are incredible, and very welcoming, so as we go, feel free to wander into the kitchen and ask them questions or see if they need a hand."

"Or a drink," the chef pipes in.

"Hear, hear," his brigade yells out.

"To Aimee," Andrea says, raising her glass.

"To Aimee," we all say, sipping.

I return to my table, where Elliot is chatting with Alana and RJ.

"Lovely toast," he says. Both he and RJ, ever the gentlemen, stand as I arrive, and Elliot pulls my seat out for me.

"Thank you. Public speaking, as we know, is not my thing," I say.

"Are you sure?" Alana says. "I'd love to have you on *Abundance* one of these days."

"We'll see." Television scares the crap out of me.

"You should do it, Jenna; it would make for a terrific show," RJ says.

"I would watch," Elliot says. "Even if space travel is not involved." He winks at me. My heart skips a beat.

"You like El-li-ot."

And so I do. So you can imagine how infuriating it is that he has not made a SINGLE romantic move on me. I thought for sure when we had dinner the other night to debrief about the party, he would go for it. We were at his house; there was wine and candlelight. But same as always, he and Teddy drive me home, he walks me to the door, and kisses my cheek or my forehead.

"You have to make the first move."

Never gonna happen.

"Fine, stay unkissed."

"I'll think about it," I say, if for no other reason, to shut up the Voix.

The first course arrives, a riff on bouillabaisse, with a deep-fried mussel-stuffed zucchini blossom, a small square of seared rockfish, a crouton topped with rouille, that garlicky red pepper–infused aioli that is the traditional topping, all in a small puddle of saffron-infused fish broth. And we are off to the races.

Can I get anyone anything?" I ask Elliot, Benji, and Jordan once we get back to my place. Jordan was eager to meet Chewbacca after hearing all the tales from Benji, so Elliot sent Wayne and Noah home with Teddy, and the four of us took the car I arranged for Benji back to my house. "Tea?"

"I'd love some tea, thank you," Elliot says.

"Me too," Benji says.

"I'm good, thanks, Jenna," Jordan says, wrestling on the floor with Chewie, who has already eaten half Jordan's shoelace, covered his coat with slime, and given his knee a thorough sexual violation.

"You stay, let me get it," Elliot says, realizing that perhaps Jordan might want a minute alone with me. "Ben? Give me a hand in there?" Elliot moves his head in the direction of the kitchen and the two of them head that way.

"Jordy," I say. "I'm excited you're moving to Chicago. And you know, if you need a place to stay while you figure out neighborhoods and stuff, you are welcome here."

He smiles wanly. "You and Aimee were the only ones who ever called me Jordy."

"Do you hate it?" I ask, thinking of Wayne calling me Jenny against my will.

"Nah. I always liked it. And thanks for the offer, but I think I'm going to stay with Wayne. At least for the first few months. He asked, and I think it will be better for us both. He seems like he could use the company."

"That's very sweet of you. I'm sure he would love to have you around for a while."

He pauses. And despite my natural inclination to fill silence with noise, I let him percolate. Finally he looks up at me. "I miss her. It's weird, I mean we weren't that close, not really, but I always felt like she was the one in the family that really got me. She always looked at me like she knew the contents of my head."

"She loved you very much. And she always hoped you would move here."

"Yeah, she said that once, when I was in college. If I ever wanted to come here to live, I could stay with her as long as I wanted."

"She was very proud of you."

"Yeah." His eyes fill with tears. "I talk to her. Is that crazy?"

"Not at all. I talk to her all the time. Every day." Suddenly this doesn't seem so insane.

"It's weird, it's like she's my conscience or something."

I nod. "I know what you mean. I call it the Voix. Like the voice of god. She's in my head."

"I like that. The Voix. She would love that, all French and everything."

"Yeah. I know."

"I feel like whenever I'm scared about something or making a decision, she's like both the angel and devil on my shoulders."

"For me too. She'll always be with us. And Jordan, she would've been very proud of your coming out, how you handled it with the family, your being brave enough to be yourself."

"She's the only one who knew. I told her when I was in high school."

I'm shocked. I didn't think there was anything in the world Aimee ever kept from me, but she never shared this. "She never told me."

"I asked her not to. I wasn't ready for it to be anything major, I didn't want a cheerleading squad, no offense."

"None taken. You're right. If I had known, it would have been impossible to prevent the two of us from trying to get you to come here and go dancing at Berlin and try on our clothes," I tease him. He laughs.

"It does make me feel better to know she kept my secret. I mean, I know she told Wayne. But I expected that, considering."

That bastard. What a faker at Christmas, and on the way home, acting all surprised. "Considering what?"

"You know, how they were. So connected. In tune. In love."

"True enough."

"I didn't like him at first," Jordan admits, almost sheepish. "I was a freshman in high school when they got married, had barely figured out I was probably gay and certainly had no idea how to deal with it emotionally. Wayne just reminded me of all the guys in my high school that were the reason I was staying firmly in the closet."

"I can see that."

"And he was a little weird."

"Still is."

"But the thing is, I don't know anyone with a bigger heart. I always used to hang back at holidays, you know, they reminded me of Mom and Dad, and I used to feel very guilty about how little I actually thought about them, how fuzzy my memories were getting. And Wayne would always come find me, figure out something to do away from the bustle, we'd offer to go pick up last-minute stuff, or he'd say he needed a burger and ask me to go with him. He was always really good about sensing when I needed to get away for a little while."

"That sounds like Wayne."

"Of course, then he'd come home and knock over the punchbowl of eggnog into the fish tank."

"He only did that once." I laugh, remembering.

"Poor fishies," Jordan snorts.

"You seem to be doing okay. But if you ever need anything, anything that you would have gone to Aimee for, I hope you know you can come to me."

"Thanks, Jenna, I know. And I will. Promise."

He gets up off the floor, and comes over and gives me a hug.

"So you and Benji?" I ask.

He blushes. "Early days. We're getting to know each other. I like him. He's a very good cook."

"I'm delighted for both of you."

"Tea for four?" Benji says, carrying a tray back in from the kitchen.

"We brought one for you just in case, Jordan," Elliot says.

"Well, if you all insist," he says, taking a mug.

The four of us sip our tea, Elliot and I on the couch, Volnay snuggled between us, Benji and Jordan on the chairs facing us, Chewbacca on the floor demolishing a plush toy like it hurt his feelings. We wax poetic about the meal, about how much fun everyone had, especially when we sent some bourbon back to the chefs and we all got in the kitchen to play.

"I have got to figure out how they did that PB&J dessert. That was INSANE," Benji says.

"The chef says you are welcome to stage there when you are done at Conlon," I say, having arranged that for him earlier.

"Seriously?! Jenna, that ROCKS!"

"Well, I expect it to be easier to get reservations in the future."

Suddenly he and Jordan both get very quiet. Elliot nudges my hand.

"Um, guys, if you want to take the car, I know it's been a long night. I'll have Teddy come fetch me," Elliot says, giving the youngsters an opening to leave.

"Thanks El, that's awesome," Benji says, jumping up.

We all get up to say good-bye, sending them off into the night. Elliot comes back in to help me tidy up.

"He seems okay," Elliot says.

"Jordan? Yeah. I think he is."

"Is it weird to see him with Benji like that?"

"A little. But good weird."

"They are sort of adorable together."

"Yeah, they are. Young and pretty and new."

"Well, young isn't anything to be excited about. New either, when you think about it."

"I suppose." I look over at him. He's wearing dark jeans, a blue button-down shirt under a sweater vest. His hair is feathered perfectly, shiny clean. He's washing out the tea things in my sink, and I like the way he is so at home here. Now if only he would just kiss me already!

"No supposition about it. Would you go back? Be twenty-three again? You couldn't pay me enough to even consider it." He laughs.

"I suppose."

"So," he says, turning to me as he wipes his hands on the dish towel. "Where are you with the whole business plan? Do you think you are going to do this with Wayne?"

I sigh. "I change my mind ten times a day. On the one hand, I do genuinely believe in the potential of the idea. On the other, it is a tremendous amount of work, and I don't know if I'm really up for the energy it takes to have a start-up. When I launched Fourchette, I was twenty-four. I don't know if I'm up for all of that again. And Wayne and I have finally seemed to figure out what we are supposed to be to one another; it hasn't been easy. I'd genuinely hate to go into business with him and have that screw up our friendship." I can't believe those words just came out of my mouth, and even more than that, that I really mean them.

"But?"

"But, it would be nice to feel productive again, to have someplace to go, problems to solve."

"To be cooking again, literally and metaphorically."

I smile at him, this odd man who somehow really gets me. "Exactly."

"Well, I know you'll figure it out." He looks at his watch. "Pumpkin time for me. I'm going to call Teddy." He wanders out of the kitchen to make his call. And as much as I want to yell out for him to stay, to follow and grab him and kiss him, my feet are cement, my tongue lead.

Elliot comes back into the kitchen. "You'll have me out of your hair in ten minutes." He smiles.

"You aren't in my hair." My heart, maybe.

"You're kind to say so. And I know that we've just eaten half of Chicago tonight, but I've been having a craving for my Burgundian stew. It's a long, slow cook. Thought if you were up for it I'd grab the makings in the morning, bring them here and we could cook? Maybe watch an old movie while it simmers?"

"Absolutely, I'd love that." Thinking of the two of us all morning in my kitchen, cooking together, hanging out all afternoon while the house fills with homey scent. Eating together. And suddenly I think that maybe, after a whole day together, maybe one of us will have the courage to take things to the next level.

"Great! And it makes a vat, figured I'd invite Wayne and Noah to come eat with us, there'll be plenty if you wanted to include anyone else."

Sigh. So much for romance. "Sure, that would be great. I'll see if Andrea and Law want to join us."

"Great." I hear a dim honk outside.

"My coach is here." We walk out onto the porch together and Elliot slides his coat on. "Good night, Jenna. Thank you for everything. I'll see you around eleven tomorrow." He leans in to kiss my cheek, and suddenly a totally-out-of-nowhere uncontrolled force spins my head around, and I catch his lips on mine. And I lean into the kiss, just enough to make him know that I'm kissing him on purpose.

Elliot pulls back, a look on his face that I've never seen, shock? Disgust? I'm an ass. I could kill the Voix, this is all her fault.

I have to cover. "Gosh, neck spasms are a bitch." Yeah, that sounds believable.

"Jenna."

I can't, I just can't hear that he doesn't think of me that way, or doesn't want to ruin the friendship. "So, yeah, stew party, that will be great! Thanks Elliot, see you tomorrow!" And I turn and nearly run back into my house, closing the door on my mortification.

"At least you tried!"

I am going to fucking kill you.

"Too late."

My doorbell rings. Crap.

I open it, and Elliot is standing there, that look still on his face. I stare at my shoes. "Jenna?"

Oy. I look up. And suddenly the look doesn't really look like horror. It kind of looks like something else.

And Elliot takes a large step toward me, grasps my face in his hands and kisses me like I am the cure for everything that has ever ailed him.

"I'll see you tomorrow."

Eight Months Later

Last month, on my birthday, Wayne shared with me the letter that Aimee had left him. Much of it was very personal, and made me somewhat uncomfortable, even though I knew how much they loved each other. But the part that surprised me was at the end.

"*My love, you know that Jenna is the other half of my soul, same as you. And I know that you guys have nothing in common, but I need you to be her best pal for me. To fill that space that I am leaving in her heart. She doesn't have the support system you do, and she'll turn in on herself and be sad for way longer than she should unless you make it your mission to keep her out in the world, to give her some purpose. I'm putting her in charge of a lot of your finances, Brian will explain the details. I'm doing this so that she can't avoid you or blow you off. In the beginning it will probably be really annoying for both of you, but at the end of the day I know that the more time she spends with you, the better her life will be. Don't let her off the hook. Don't edit yourself. Bring her every harebrained scheme, every wild thought that crosses your mind, all the things you would have told me about. You guys will find your way, together, I have faith.*"

And so we have.

W ell, hello there," Nathan Fillion says, as I open the door.

I step aside so that he can come into the studio space Wayne and I rented. "Thanks for coming."

"How can I resist a gig that brings me to one of my favorite cities, AND requires that I get ordained?" He laughs. Damn this is a good-looking man.

"Well, we thought that no *Firefly*-themed wedding would really be complete unless the happy couple were married by Captain Mal himself." Our fifth event since launching Dagobah Productions, this wedding for three hundred is following the *Firefly* theme to the nth degree. And at a cool 500K, we've spared no detail. Including the fifty grand, plus first-class travel, to hire Mr. Fillion to come serve as clergy. He was an enormously good sport when I asked Elliot to reach out to him to see if he was up for it, and apparently said yes in a heartbeat. I think Elliot may have sweetened the deal with a piece of memorabilia or two; no matter how I needle him, he won't say.

"Well, the Captain is here, officially ordained by the Universal Life Church of the Interwebs, and ready to rock."

"Shiny," I say, winking at him.

"She learns fast, this one," he says, looking behind me.

"So she does." Elliot walks up behind me, kisses my cheek and shakes Nathan's hand. "Good to see you, man. Thanks so much for this."

"Happy to help."

I interject. "Chloe over there with the headset? She'll show you to your dressing room. You should have everything you need there, but if not, let her know and she'll take care of you. I'd say we are about three hours out," I say, waving at Chloe, our floor manager for the event, and she comes over to take Nathan to his dressing room.

"Everything looks terrific," Elliot says. "You should be very proud."

"I think we did good, partner." After another month of waffling back and forth, Elliot and Wayne both realized that the thing holding me back was the enormity of being half responsible for the business. So Elliot came in as a third, mostly silent, consulting partner. It took some of the financial burden off of Wayne and me, and allowed us to put some key staffers in place from the beginning that eased the time pressure on me. Elliot handles the technical business aspects, Wayne does client relations and theme consulting, and I do food and basic event organization.

We took three months to research getting our team together, set, lighting, sound, and costume designers we poach from the thriving local Chicago theater scene, makeup artists we fly in from LA. I put Naomi at TipsyCake on monthly retainer that allowed her to hire a cake artist who is also a serious sci-fi and fantasy fan, and she will be in charge of all cake design. I attended the big Comic Con in San Diego with Wayne and Elliot, and we had a booth where we both solicited new clients and had a small recruiting station, finding some really terrific staff to help get us up and running.

"I think we're finding our stride."

"I'm off to get some other work done, but I'll be back later. Late dinner after?" He knows that I never eat at events, so we've taken to grabbing a bite and debriefing at the end of the evening.

"Absolutely." I lean over and kiss him.

"Knock 'em dead, sweetheart." And he heads out. It's still early days for our relationship. Despite the lovely kiss, and all I thought it meant the night of the EL Ideas dinner, it took three more weeks before he kissed me again for real. And another few weeks before we did more than kiss. Apparently Elliot is a gentleman who believes in taking things very slow, especially when embarking on a romance with a slightly broken, still-grieving, often-confused good friend. And throwing the whole business partnership into the mix was a wrinkle neither of us anticipated. But we are officially together, and so far, it's been well worth the wait.

"Told you so."

You know, that is one of your least attractive qualities, that whole "I told you so" thing.

"Yeah? What else are my least attractive qualities?"

Well, the dead thing isn't terribly adorable.

"Point taken."

Can I go run this event already? I have a bride all dolled up as Zoe waiting to wed her Wash.

"Listen to you, all geeked out."

Occupational hazard. And totally your fault. If you hadn't given me custody of Wayne, none of this would have happened.

"I know! Isn't it wonderful?"

Yes.

Yes it is.

Elliot opens my door for me and offers his hand to help me out of the car. I stand and take his arm, and we walk across the sidewalk and into the quad.

"I still can't picture you and Aimee in these hallowed halls," he says. "All that ivy. Seems too staid for you guys."

"Well, I think we both agreed it is better to be the cool kids on a quiet campus than the fuddy-duddies at a party school."

"There is a certain Jenna-and-Aimee logic to that." He laughs. We see Wayne and Noah on the other side of the quad and head over to see them. The rest of the gang is already seated, Andrea and Law, newly cohabitating and snuggled up happily. Benji and Jordan; their romance flamed out as quickly as it started and seems to have left them the best of friends. Lois and Eloise, and Eloise's new guy, Joe, a lanky fair-haired architect who came in to buy a housewarming gift for a client, took one bite of the caramel chocolate cookie bar she offered him, and was smitten. We adore him and look forward to their eventual enormous children. Jasmin and Gene are here, and the rest of the seats are filled with a combination of students and faculty.

Elliot takes Noah's hand and they go to sit with the rest of the gang in the front row. Wayne looks at me.

"Ready?" he asks me.

"Yep," I say, and head for the podium.

I will never get used to standing in front of crowds, talking about Aimee. And you all have the lovely words her husband Wayne put down in your programs. So I know I don't have to list her accomplishments for any of you. We are here today to honor my dearest and best friend. Some of you knew her well; most of you never met her. Here is all you need to know about Aimee: She was the kindest, best friend, best person anyone could hope to know. This school was the reason we knew each other. It changed everything for both of us. So it means the world to know that Aimee will have a permanent place on this very special campus." I turn to look at the small statue behind me. Tucked in a quiet corner of the quad, in a small nook in one of the stone buildings, a three-foot-high bronze depicting Aimee as a child of maybe three or four, sitting on a quilt, reading a book to her bedraggled and beloved bunny rabbit. Wayne found the picture of Aimee in a box of old pictures when he went to the Brands' for Easter, and everything clicked. The innocence of childhood. The connection to literature. No boobs. No Star Wars theme. It was perfect, and once we scoped out the particular spot and made sure it was small and not an impediment to theatrical productions, I signed off on the commission.

"I want to thank all of you for coming today, and to thank the University of Chicago for introducing me to my best friend." I turn to Wayne, reach out for his hand. And look out into the faces of everyone I hold most dear. "Who introduced me to all of my best friends."

Wayne and I hug, and the dean says a few lovely words, and then our group leaves to have champagne and little tea sandwiches back at the Library.

"It was a lovely ceremony," Andrea says, refilling my glass with bubbles.

"Yeah, she would have approved, I think." I take a sip. "So how are things going here, is it different knowing it is yours?" I sold the Library to Andrea last month. It made no sense for me to hang on to it, and I know that she wanted more security for her future. She promoted Eloise to manager, and told her that when she is ready, they can talk about partnership.

"Not so much different, just, you know, settled." She smiles. "We certainly miss seeing you as often as we used to, so the new venture must be going well."

"So far so good. We're building a client base, the events we've done so far have been well received, we're fully booked for the Chicago Con, and already have an event booked for next year's San Diego Con."

She grins. "Um, you mean an event for your *boyfriend*?"

I blush. "And business partner." I look over at Elliot, who has Noah on his shoulders. He catches me looking and winks.

"His hair is SO much better."

Yeah, I know.

"How'd you get him to change it?"

I may have had *WKRP in Cincinnati* on the TV while I was cooking one night when he came over. He looked, pondered, lightbulb went on, and he asked me if maybe he should update his hair. The rest was history.

"Sneaky minx. You sprang Gary Sandy on him and let him make the relevant connections like it was his idea. Evil genius."

I learned from the best.

"You bet your ass."

"Hey, Jenny, I'm gonna get Noah back to Madison, he has school tomorrow. But we're on for our usual Thursday meeting," Wayne says.

"You betcha." I smile at him.

"Thanks for today, I think we did it the right way."

"I think so too. Thanks for not letting go of the idea. You were right, it was a nice way to honor her."

"Well, I think we finally figured out that our ideas really can work when we both have the same goals."

"Yes, we certainly have."

And that's the truth, Ruth.

From Jenna's Notebook

〜

Food is one of the ultimate expressions of love, and for Jenna and the people in her life, it is a central occupation. Here are some of their best and most favorite recipes!

Aimee's Biscuits

SERVES 4 TO 6

Hey, I was never much of a cook when I was alive, and haven't gotten better since my untimely demise. But even Jenna has to agree that my biscuits? Are fluffy little nuggets of delicious that cry out for butter and jam or honey, or mustard and ham. I strongly recommend you make these with a small 1 ½ inch cutter. First off, they get the right ratio of crispy outside to soft inside, and they are easier to eat.

2 cups flour, sifted with:
4 teaspoons baking powder
½ teaspoon salt
½ teaspoon cream of tartar
2 teaspoons sugar

½ cup vegetable shortening or leaf lard, cut into small cubes
and very cold

⅔ cup whole milk

Preheat the oven to 350. Sift the dry ingredients into a large bowl. Add the cubed shortening or lard, and toss to coat. Using a pastry cutter or two butter knives, carefully cut the fat into the flour mixture until it resembles very coarse crumbs. Do not overwork; having some larger pea-sized pieces is okay. Slowly add the milk, and mix briefly until you see the last of the flour mixture become incorporated. Do not overmix.

Flour a board and pat the dough into about ½-inch-thick slab. Using a floured 1 ½-inch to 2-inch circular cutter, cut dough into biscuits and place on a greased pan about an inch apart.

Bake 10 to 12 minutes. Eat while still warm.

⌣

Jenna's Carbonara

SERVES 1 TO 2

You need comfort food? Look no further. This one-pot pasta meal is the perfect thing for a cozy dinner for two, or a post-breakup binge for one.

¼ pound pancetta, chopped finely

2 tablespoons dry vermouth or white wine

8 ounces linguini or spaghetti

3 egg yolks

¼ cup Parmesan, grated finely, plus more for topping

½ tablespoon Italian parsley, chopped

Salt and pepper

Bring a large pot of water to a boil and salt it well. Cook pasta to al dente according to the directions on the box. Drain the pasta when done, reserving about ½ cup of the pasta water to use later.

While the pasta is cooking, in a very large skillet set over medium heat (do not use nonstick here), cook the pancetta, stirring occasionally, until the fat has rendered and the bacon is browned and crispy. With a slotted spoon, remove the pieces of bacon to a dish. Pour off the fat and reserve. Deglaze the pan with the vermouth, being sure to scrape up all the bits until they dissolve into the wine.

Toss the pasta into the skillet. Cook over medium-high heat for a minute, tossing constantly to coat, and adding a tablespoon of the reserved pancetta fat if you like. Turn off the heat.

In a large bowl, whisk together the egg and the Parmesan cheese. Slowly whisk in half of the pasta water. Add the contents of the bowl to the skillet off the heat, along with the bacon and chopped parsley, stirring all the time. Toss well. If too dry, add the rest of the pasta water and continue to toss until everything is well mixed. Season with salt and pepper to taste, and serve with more grated Parmesan.

Jasmin's Pan de Coco

SERVES 8

This traditional unleavened coconut bread is unusual, and very delicious.

1 cup coconut milk

2 tablespoons whole milk

½ cup unsweetened coconut flakes

2 cups all-purpose flour, sifted with:

½ teaspoon salt

½ teaspoon baking soda

Preheat oven to 300°F, and grease a large baking tray. Sift the flour with the salt and baking soda into a large mixing bowl. Add in the coconut milk and the regular milk and mix until combined. Oil your hands, and knead in the bowl for about 5 minutes, it will be somewhat sticky. Portion into four equal pieces, and form each into a roughly 6-inch disk on the baking sheet. Sprinkle the breads equally with the coconut flakes.

Bake 12 to 15 minutes until a skewer comes out clean. They will still be fairly pale. Let cool. Just before serving, put pan under broiler for 2 minutes to toast and brown the tops.

Jenna's Jade Slaw

SERVES 12

Jenna developed this in her earliest days when Fourchette launched. She needed a signature slaw, and always hated gloppy mayo-based versions. This is a perfect side dish for barbeque, or any rich, hearty meal. Bright and crunchy, a great buffet item.

1 head green cabbage shredded as finely as possible (think angel-hair pasta, not spaghetti!)

2 heads fennel, sliced paper thin

2 green apples, julienned fine

1 large jicama, julienned fine

2 hearts of celery, sliced fine

½ cup sliced almonds, toasted

For the Dressing:

¼ cup rice wine vinegar

2 tablespoons sugar

1 tablespoon soy sauce

1 tablespoon grated ginger

⅓ cup canola oil

½ teaspoon ground grains of paradise

Pinch salt

Mix dressing ingredients together till well emulsified. Toss veggies and apples with dressing till thoroughly coated. Let sit a minimum of 1 hour for flavors to blend, then taste for seasoning and balance, and toss with almonds just before serving.

Jenna's Lunch Pasta with Cauliflower, White Beans, Roasted Garlic, & Pancetta

SERVES 4 TO 6

Jenna knows that her best healing happens in the kitchen. This warming pasta is great for a crowd. She adapted the recipe from her pal Alana, making a vegetarian side dish heartier as a main course with pancetta and white beans. (For more of Alana's recipes, check out Off the Menu, *available from your favorite local bookseller or online retailer!)*

2 heads garlic, papery skins removed, top quarter of heads cut off and discarded

6 tablespoons, plus 1 teaspoon extra-virgin olive oil

1 head cauliflower (about 1 ½ pounds)

Salt and ground black pepper to taste

¼ teaspoon sugar

1 pound small-shaped pasta, Jenna prefers orechiette

¼ teaspoon red pepper flakes

2 to 3 tablespoons juice from 1 lemon

1 tablespoon fresh parsley leaves, chopped

2 ounces Parmesan cheese, grated (about 1 cup)

¼ cup chopped walnuts, toasted

¼ cup pancetta, cubed

1 15-ounce can cannellini or other small white beans, drained

Adjust oven rack to middle position, place large rimmed baking sheet on rack, and heat oven to 500 degrees.

Cut one foot-long sheet of foil and place garlic heads, cut-side up, in center. Drizzle ½ teaspoon oil over each head and seal packet. Place packet on oven rack and roast until garlic is very tender, about 40 minutes. Open packet and set aside to cool. This can be done up to three days in advance.

Place baking sheet in oven to heat. Trim outer leaves of cauliflower and cut into small florets, discarding the tough center stem. Place cauliflower pieces in a large bowl; toss with 2 tablespoons oil, 1 teaspoon salt, pepper to taste, and sugar.

Remove baking sheet from oven. Carefully transfer cauliflower to hot baking sheet and spread into even layer, placing cut sides down. Return baking sheet to oven and roast until cauliflower is well-browned and tender, 20 to 25 minutes. Transfer cauliflower to cutting board. When cool enough to handle, chop into rough ½-inch pieces.

While cauliflower roasts, sauté the pancetta in a large skillet until browned. Remove from skillet with slotted spoon and pour off all but 1 tablespoon fat. Add beans to the skillet and toss to coat with the fat, then cook over medium-high heat till warmed through. Bring 4 quarts water to boil in large pot. Salt water well, and cook pasta according to package directions, until al dente.

Squeeze roasted garlic cloves from their skins into small bowl. Using fork, mash garlic to smooth paste, then stir in

red pepper flakes and 2 tablespoons lemon juice. Slowly whisk
in remaining ¼ cup oil, and stir in ½ cup cheese.

Drain pasta, reserving 1 cup cooking water, and return
pasta to pot. Add chopped cauliflower, beans, and pancetta to
pasta; stir in garlic sauce, along with ¼ cup cooking water,
and parsley. Adjust consistency with additional cooking water
and season with salt, pepper, and additional lemon juice to
taste. Serve immediately, sprinkling with remaining ½ cup
cheese and toasted nuts.

~

Wayne's Favorite Cider-Brined Pork Chops

SERVES 6

*When you only eat eleven things, they better all be good!
Jenna developed this recipe especially for Wayne, and it is his
favorite. You'll like them too.*

8 tablespoons kosher salt, plus more for seasoning chops
2 tablespoons freshly ground black pepper, plus more for
    seasoning chops
4 cups apple cider, plus more as needed
6 1 ½-inch-thick center-cut or loin-cut pork chops, bone in
6 tablespoons grapeseed oil

To make the brine, dissolve the salt in ½ gallon of warm
water in a large bowl. Add the pepper, pour in the apple
cider and mix. Drop the pork chops into the brine and add
enough additional apple cider so that the chops are mostly

submerged. Cover and refrigerate for at least 8 hours and up to 24.

To prepare the chops, preheat oven to 400 degrees. Remove chops from brine and dry well with paper towels. Rub them with 2 tablespoons of the oil and season well with salt and black pepper.

Heat the remaining oil in two oven-safe (cast iron preferably) skillets and brown the chops, three to a pan, for 4 minutes a side. Place skillets in oven for 6 to 8 minutes and then remove chops to a warm platter. Cover loosely with foil and allow them to rest for about 10 minutes.

Lemon Chili Green Beans

SERVES 4 TO 6

When you are sick of the same old same old "tender crisp" steamed green beans, try these. They're full of flavor and a bit of heat; Jenna thinks you'll be a convert.

1 pound French thin green beans (haricot verts) trimmed
1 tablespoon chopped shallot
Juice and zest of one lemon
1 tablespoon grapeseed oil
2 tablespoons butter, divided
¼ cup dry white wine
½ teaspoon red pepper flakes
1 tablespoon chopped fresh tarragon or parsley
Salt and pepper to taste

In a large sauté pan over medium-high heat, melt 1 table-spoon butter with the grapeseed oil. When it stops foaming, add the shallot and red pepper flakes, and cook until lightly browned. Add green beans and cook until they begin to get a little color. Put in the wine and lemon juice and cook until it has reduced almost completely, by which point the beans should be tender. Toss in the remaining butter and stir until it has created a sauce. Season to taste with salt and pepper and add the chopped herbs at the last minute.

Fig Tarts with Pistachio Cream

SERVES 4

These simple little desserts are very elegant and special. And what Jenna made the night she and Brian first got together . . .

1 recipe of your favorite pie dough or store-bought crust, rolled out and cut into 4 6-inch circles

1 pint fresh figs, washed and cut into six wedges each

4 amaretti cookies, ladyfingers, or other hard cookie, smashed to crumbs

4 teaspoons Demerara sugar, like Sugar in the Raw

½ teaspoon cinnamon

¼ cup fig jam

½ cup heavy whipping cream

1 teaspoon sugar

1 tablespoon canned pistachio paste (I like Love'n Bake)

Preheat oven to 400°F.

Place the rounds of dough on a parchment-lined baking tray about 1 inch apart. Divide the cookie crumbs between the rounds and spread out, leaving about ½ inch around the outside edge. Divide the figs between the rounds, making a pretty spiral design with the wedges on top of the crumbs, again leaving about ½ inch at the edge. Fold the edges up around the figs, pinching where necessary. Mix the cinnamon and sugar. Sprinkle the tarts with the cinnamon sugar and bake until golden brown, and the dough is cooked through, about 14 to 18 minutes. Let cool on a rack.

Mix the fig jam with 1 tablespoon water and heat in your microwave until melted, about one minute. Strain and paint the strained jam on the figs, avoiding the crust if possible.

Before serving, whip the cream and sugar to soft peaks. Fold in the pistachio paste and top the tarts.

Jenna's Morning-After Dutch Baby Pancake

SERVES 2 TO 4

All the things you love about a pancake, but easier since you just make one large one in the oven as opposed to all that flipping. Jenna likes it with butter, lemon, and confectioners' sugar, but it stands up to maple syrup or jam just as easily.

½ cup all-purpose flour
½ cup whole milk
2 large eggs

3 tablespoons unsalted butter, plus more for serving

1 tablespoon sugar

Pinch salt

Confectioners' sugar (to taste)

Fresh lemon juice (to taste)

Preheat oven to 425°F. In a mixing bowl, whisk together the milk, eggs, flour, and tablespoon of sugar and pinch of salt. Melt the 3 tablespoons of butter in a 12-inch skillet or ovenproof dish over medium-high heat on the stovetop, until it is sizzling and the foaming stops. Pour the batter into the pan or dish and put the pan immediately into the oven. Bake for 20 minutes or until the pancake puffs up and turns golden brown. Drizzle with melted butter if you like, sprinkle with the confectioners' sugar and lemon juice. Watch it quickly deflate, and serve immediately.

Jean's Thanksgiving Yeast Rolls

SERVES 10 TO 12

Jean wasn't the world's most passionate cook, just like her daughter, Aimee. But Jenna got addicted to these wonderful little rolls when she went home with Aimee for Thanksgiving in college, and now she is thankful for them every year. Your leftover turkey sandwiches will never be the same.

2 packages dry yeast dissolved in 1 cup warm water

1 cup shortening

1 cup boiling water

¾ cup sugar

2 eggs, beaten

2 sticks butter, melted

1 ½ teaspoons salt

6 cups all-purpose flour

Put shortening in a large bowl and pour over boiling water to dissolve. Add sugar, salt, eggs, flour, and dissolved yeast. Mix well, put in a lightly greased bowl, cover tightly with plastic wrap, and refrigerate overnight.

On a lightly floured board, roll the dough ½-inch thick. Cut with a biscuit cutter. At this point, you need to decide what kind of bread you desire . . .

For basic rolls, pour half of the melted butter in the bottom of two roasting pans, place the cut rolls on top and then paint the tops with the remaining butter. Let rise 2 to 3 hours at room temp and then bake at 350°F for 18 to 24 minutes until golden brown.

For fun cloverleaf-style rolls, use a smaller biscuit cutter, dip two or three rolls in melted butter and stack, then place the stacks on their sides in buttered muffin tins, let rise 2 to 3 hours and bake at 350°F for 20 to 25 minutes until golden brown and cooked through. (For Parker House style, make the dough into small balls, three per cup, rest of instructions the same.)

For lovely rings of breakaway bread, dip each piece in melted butter and stack sort of willy-nilly in 2 greased Bundt pans. Let rise 2 to 3 hours till doubled. Bake at 350°F for 30 minutes or until browned.

Eileen's Lemon Cream Tart

SERVES 8

Jenna's mom may love Thanksgiving, but she finds the traditional pies a little too heavy. This bright creamy tart is the perfect substitute.

For the Crust:

1 cup all-purpose flour

¼ cup powdered sugar

Pinch salt

½ cup cold unsalted butter, sliced thin

For the Filling:

4 eggs

1 ½ cups sugar

½ teaspoon salt

2 tablespoons lemon zest

½ cup lemon juice

½ cup butter, room temperature

1 cup heavy cream

1 tablespoon sugar

Preheat the oven to 425°F.

Combine the flour, powdered sugar, salt, and butter in a mixing bowl and blend together using a fork. Press into a greased 8-inch tart pan with a removable bottom. Place the crust in the freezer for at least 15 minutes. Bake the crust for about 12 to 15 minutes, until crust is golden brown. Remove from the oven and let cool.

Whisk together eggs, 1 ½ cups sugar, and salt in a heavy-bottomed stainless steel pan. Add zest and lemon juice; cook over a medium heat, whisking constantly until thick, about 6 to 8 minutes until the mixture coats the back of a spoon. Remove from heat and stir in the butter a little at a time until fully incorporated. Cover with plastic and refrigerate until cold.

Whisk together the cream and sugar to stiff peaks. Pour the lemon filling into the prebaked tart shell and spread evenly on the bottom; top with the whipped cream. Keep chilled until ready to serve.

Eloise's Potato Gratin with Prunes

SERVES 12

Eloise first brought this dish to a staff potluck. Everyone was skeptical about the combination, but it turns out that potatoes with prunes is insanely delicious. Perfect with pork or poultry, it has now become everyone's favorite, and soon to be one of yours. (With thanks to David Bouley; adapted from his grandmother's recipe as dictated in the middle of a cooking class.)

5 pounds starchy potatoes, peeled and sliced thin on mandolin

2 leeks, chopped

2 scallions, chopped

2 tablespoons flat-leaf parsley, chopped

2 cups half-and-half

3 cups cream

1 clove garlic

Nutmeg

Salt and pepper

1 cup prunes, halved or quartered

1 stick butter

Preheat oven to 350°F.

Rub gratin dish with the cut side of the clove of garlic. Butter the dish liberally. Sauté leeks and scallions in 4 table-spoons butter till soft but not browned. Put potatoes in pot and add half-and-half and cream, the garlic clove, and a good grating of nutmeg. Bring to a simmer, and cook 5 minutes until slightly thickened and potatoes become flexible but not cooked through. Ladle half of the potato mixture into the gratin dish, followed by the leeks and scallions and sprinkle the prunes evenly over the top, and then the parsley. Add the rest of the potatoes. Fill with cream and half-and-half mixture just to the level of the potatoes. Discard the rest. Dot the top of the dish with remaining butter and bake 40 minutes to an hour. Cook till well browned and softened all the way through. Should be creamy, but thick and not soupy. You can hold in a 200°F oven nearly indefinitely.

Lois's Poppy Seed Cookies

SERVES 10 TO 12

These little cookies are simply addictive, the perfect accom-paniment to tea or coffee.

3 eggs

1 cup sugar

¾ cup cooking oil

¼ cup orange juice

¼ teaspoon salt

¼ cup poppy seeds

2 cups sifted all-purpose flour

Preheat oven to 350°F. Beat eggs till foamy, then add sugar, oil, juice, and salt. Add poppy seeds and flour and mix till well blended. Drop by heaping half teaspoons (I know it looks like not enough, but trust me) 1 inch apart on ungreased sheet pan. Bake 15 to 18 minutes, until just golden around edges, but still pale in the center. Remove immediately from sheet to rack and cool.

Benji's Butternut Squash Soup with Fried Ginger

SERVES 10 TO 12

Benji is in the throes of the most exciting time as a chef, experimenting to find his own personal style, and putting his mark on holiday traditions.

4 pounds cubed, seeded, peeled butternut squash

3 boxes chicken stock or a gallon of homemade stock

1 pint heavy cream

2 medium (or one large) yellow onions

1 stick butter

Fresh-ground nutmeg

¼ teaspoon Espelette pepper, ground or paste (optional)

Salt and pepper to taste

2 tablespoons pickled ginger, drained and dried on a paper towel

4 tablespoons grapeseed oil

Sugar

Sauté onions in butter till soft, add squash. Add chicken stock to cover by about 2 inches. Cook over medium heat till very soft, about 35 to 45 minutes. Blend with immersion blender or in stand blender till very smooth; for extravelvety soup strain through chinois or fine strainer. Add cream and season to taste with salt and pepper and fresh nutmeg.

Heat the oil till it is shimmering, and fry the pickled ginger until it is slightly browned and crispy. Remove from oil and drain on paper towels, sprinkling with sugar. Use to garnish the soup.

———

Lois's German Potato Salad

SERVES 6 TO 8

Lois might only be half German, but this potato salad is the real deal!

3 pounds Yukon Gold potatoes peeled and cut into large chunks

1 red onion, diced as fine as you can

⅓ cup rice wine vinegar or other mild white vinegar

½ cup canola oil

Salt and pepper to taste

1 bunch chives, chopped very fine

Boil potatoes in salted water till fork tender . . . do not overcook or they will get waterlogged. Soak onions in vinegar. Drain potatoes thoroughly, and pour over vinegar/onion mixture and oil, and mix gently, trying not to break up potatoes. Let sit at room temperature, tossing occasionally until cooled. Taste for salt and pepper. Garnish with chopped chives. This salad is better if it never gets refrigerated, and there is nothing in it to go bad or get rancid, so it is the perfect thing to bring to an outdoor party where food is likely to sit out.

Alana's Chicken with Chorizo and Chickpeas

SERVES 6 TO 8

It is so nice to see Alana and RJ so happy, and still cooking together. (If you haven't done so already, you can check out their story in Off the Menu *by Stacey Ballis, available in paperback, audiobook, and for the e-reader of your choice from your favorite local bookseller or online retailer.)*

4 ounces Spanish chorizo, sliced ¼-inch thick (this is a cured sausage red with paprika, do not substitute fresh Mexican

chorizo here; if you can't find Spanish chorizo, use a stick of
pepperoni)

3 pounds chicken thighs (bone-in, skin on)

Salt and pepper

1 can chickpeas, drained

1 box frozen artichoke hearts, thawed

2 small red onions, sliced

2 garlic cloves, thinly sliced

2 sprigs fresh thyme

¾ cup dry sherry

2 cups chicken stock

1 cup diced plum tomatoes

2 teaspoons Espelette or Aleppo pepper (If you can't find these,
substitute sweet paprika, but try to get the Espelette, it is
worth it!)

¾ teaspoon crushed red pepper flakes

Handful fresh basil, torn, for garnish

Put a large deep saucepan or skillet over medium heat. Cook
the chorizo, stirring occasionally, until chorizo has rendered
its fat and is brown and crispy. Remove chorizo with a slotted
spoon or spatula to your slow cooker, leaving the fat in the pan.

Season the thighs with salt and pepper on both sides. Add
the chicken pieces to the skillet and brown well on both sides,
especially making sure to render the skin so that it is crispy
about ten minutes total. Remove the chicken pieces and set
aside.

Remove all but two tablespoons of fat in the skillet. Add
the onions, garlic, artichokes, and thyme. Season with salt
and cook, stirring occasionally, until vegetables are soft, about
five minutes. Add the sherry, tomatoes, paprika, and red pepper

flakes. Stir well to dislodge any browned bits and simmer for one minute. Add this mixture to your slow cooker, put in the chickpeas and stir to be sure it is all well combined.

Nestle the thighs in the mixture in your slow cooker. Put in enough chicken stock to come up to the thighs, leaving the top ¼ inch uncovered. Cover the slow cooker and turn on high for at least 3 hours. You can then turn to low and hold till dinnertime, or cook on low for up to 8 hours. Before serving, season to taste with salt and pepper and garnish with basil. Serve.

If you don't have a slow cooker, you can cook in a covered Dutch oven at 350°F for 1 ½ hours.

Jenna's Dark Chocolate Pudding

SERVES 6

RJ is a pudding aficionado, and this deep, dark grown-up pudding that Jenna makes is right up his alley.

½ cup plus 1 tablespoon sugar

½ cup Hershey's Special Dark cocoa powder

5 tablespoons cornstarch

Pinch salt

1 teaspoon instant espresso powder

1 quart half-and-half

3.5 ounces dark chocolate, 80 to 90 percent cacao chocolate, chopped

1 teaspoon vanilla

Sift dry ingredients. In a large saucepan, pour in the half-and-half and whisk in dry ingredients. Cook over medium heat, whisking until pudding starts to bubble and thicken, about 4 minutes. Remove from heat and stir in chocolate and vanilla. Whisk until chocolate is fully melted and incorporated. Pour into six ramekins and chill until set. Serve with lightly sweetened whipped cream.

Benji's Spicy Carrot Dip with Dukkah

SERVES 12

Benji knows that especially around the holidays, everyone can get a little sick of the usual cheese tray or veggie platter with hummus. This sweet and spicy dip is a great new addition to your repertoire. Paired with the Middle Eastern spice-and-nut mix called dukkah, it makes for a fabulous appetizer. If you are worried about people assembling their own, you can make them as crostini ahead and serve on a platter.

For the Dip:

2 pounds carrots, peeled and cut into 2-inch lengths

6 tablespoons extra-virgin olive oil, plus more for dipping

3 tablespoons white wine vinegar

5 teaspoons harissa

¾ teaspoon ground cumin

½ teaspoon ground ginger

Kosher salt and pepper to taste

In a large saucepan over high heat, cover the carrots with water and bring to a boil. Reduce the heat to medium and simmer until tender, about 20 minutes. Drain the carrots and return them to the dry saucepan. Cook the carrots for 30 seconds or so over medium heat to dry them out. Remove the pan with the carrots from the heat and coarsely mash them with a fork or whisk. You want a coarsely ground carrot puree, not too smooth. Stir in the olive oil, vinegar, harissa, cumin, and ginger, and then season the mixture with salt and pepper.

For the Dukkah:

1 cup shelled roasted pistachio nuts

1 cup shelled roasted sunflower seeds

1 tablespoon whole coriander seeds

1 tablespoon whole fennel seeds

1 tablespoon whole cumin seeds

¼ cup toasted sesame seeds

½ teaspoon crushed red pepper flakes

1 tablespoon sea salt or kosher salt

1 teaspoon black pepper

Toast spice seeds. Toast sesame seeds separately. Crush spices to coarse powder and mix with salt, pepper, and pepper flakes. In mortar and pestle or coffee grinder, crush pistachios and sunflower seeds, leaving some pieces.

To serve: slice a baguette into ½-inch-thick rounds. Dip each round lightly in extra-virgin olive oil and then in the dukkah. Spoon the carrot dip on top.

Praline Pecans

SERVES 8

Jenna knows that these are insanely easy to make and very addictive. They also have a longer shelf life than anyone has willpower, and they freeze beautifully. You can multiply this recipe almost infinitely.

1 stick butter
2 egg whites beaten till foamy
4 cups pecan halves (1 pound)
1 cup sugar
Flaky salt

Preheat oven to 350°F. Toss nuts with egg whites until they are well coated. Sprinkle with sugar and mix well. Melt butter on a large sheet pan. Spread nuts over butter. Bake at 350°F for 10 minutes, then reduce heat to 250°F and bake 30 to 40 minutes stirring every 10 minutes till dry.

Gene's Twelve-Hour Pork Shoulder

SERVES 10 TO 12

Jenna, for one, can't get enough of ham. But if you're looking for a great alternative for your holiday table, or just want a terrific dish for a dinner party, you can't go wrong with this slow-roasted pork shoulder. Don't let the

*skin-on aspect scare you, by the time the shoulder is done you
have ultracrispy crunchy cracklings that are essentially pig
candy.*

2 tablespoons fennel seeds, toasted

2 tablespoons kosher salt

1 teaspoon Espelette pepper (You can substitute Aleppo pepper,
  or sweet paprika, but try to find the Espelette, it is worth it.)

½ teaspoon ground grains of paradise or black pepper

2 fennel bulbs, in 1-inch chunks

6 medium carrots, peeled and in 1-inch chunks

3 onions, roughly chopped

1 bunch fresh thyme, tied with cotton twine

1 10- to 13-pound pork shoulder on the bone, skin on, scored in
  diamond or square pattern (You can ask your butcher to
  prepare it just this way for you, he'll know what you are
  talking about.)

Grapeseed or other flavorless oil

1 bottle wine (if you want to drink white with the dish, use
  white, same for red)

1 pint chicken stock

Preheat your oven to 500°F.

Smash the fennel seeds, salt, and peppers in pestle and mortar or pulse in a food processor until you have a coarse powder.

Put all of the chopped vegetables and thyme sprigs into a large roasting pan. Sprinkle with salt and pepper. Pat the pork shoulder with oil and place on top of the vegetables. Now get the spice rub massaged into the skin of the pork, getting it into all of the scores. Put the pan in your preheated oven for 30 minutes, then turn the heat down to 250°F, and cook for 9 to 12 hours. The meat should be soft and yielding and you can pull it apart easily with a fork or tongs. Pour all the wine into the roasting tray an hour before the pork is done.

Once the pork is out of the oven, let it rest for half an hour before removing it to a large board. Pull off the cracklings, and scrape extra fat from the underside of the cracklings and remove large pieces of unrendered fat from the surface of the meat. You can either pull the meat apart into large pieces, or serve whole with a tongs and a large fork for your guests to pull apart themselves. If you are pulling the pork yourself, serve the cracklings on the side, if you are serving whole, simply place the cracklings back on top of the roast once you have defatted. Hold in a 200°F oven until you want to serve.

Remove the thyme sprigs from the pan, and use a slotted spoon to put all of the vegetables in a medium saucepan. Defat the pan juices and add to saucepan. For a chunky sauce, use a potato masher, for smooth, an immersion blender, and add enough stock to achieve the consistency you want. If your sauce needs brightness, try adding a couple of tablespoons of balsamic vinegar. Season to taste with salt and pepper.

Swiss Chard and Chickpeas

SERVES 6 AS A SIDE DISH

Jenna tends to bring vegetable side dishes when she goes to dinner at Jasmin and Gene's, since they lean toward rich hearty soul foods. This is a great winter side dish that Jenna

*developed when her fourth CSA farm box in a row contained
a pile of Swiss chard. You can substitute kale or other hearty
greens if you don't have chard.*

2 large or 3 medium bunches Swiss chard, any color or combination
1 can chickpeas, drained and rinsed
2 tablespoons olive oil, plus more to finish
1 teaspoon Worcestershire sauce
1 tablespoon white balsamic vinegar (or white wine vinegar)
½ cup chicken stock
Salt and pepper to taste
¼ teaspoon red pepper flakes (optional)

Separate the stems from the leaves of the chard, and chop
the stems into ½-inch slices, and tear the leaves in 1
½-inch pieces. Heat a skillet over medium-high heat and add
the oil. When the oil begins to shimmer, add the chickpeas
and sauté until they begin to get a little golden and crispy
on the outside. Add the chard stems and cook for a minute,
then sprinkle the Worcestershire sauce and vinegar over
the top and cook until nearly evaporated. Toss in the
chard leaves and gently combine with the stems and
beans, then pour the chicken stock over. Mix in the red
pepper flakes if you like a little heat. Continue to sauté until
the leaves are cooked, and the stock is mostly gone. Season to
taste with salt and pepper, and finish with a drizzle of fruity
olive oil.

Lois's Peanut Butter Dog Biscuits

YOUR YIELD WILL DEPEND ON HOW LARGE
YOU MAKE THEM, BUT ASSUME ABOUT TWO DOZEN
LARGER OR FOUR DOZEN SMALLER BISCUITS.

*Who says that you shouldn't bake for your furry pals? The
bonus? If you're like Jenna and having willpower problems,
baking for dogs ensures that you can keep your homemade
treats around and not impact your waistline. Adapted from
whiteonricecouple.com, a foodie blog that is as fabulous for
people as it is for dogs.*

2 ¾ cups whole wheat flour

1 ¾ cups all-purpose flour

1 cup spelt flour

½ cup flax seeds

2 tablespoons brown sugar

1 teaspoon sea salt

3 eggs

1 cup peanut butter

⅓ cup vegetable oil

1 cup water

Combine flours, brown sugar, flax seeds, and salt in a mixing
bowl. Add eggs and peanut butter and mix until incorporated.
Mix in oil. Add enough water until dough is smooth and
workable.

Cover the dough and set aside for 15 to 20 minutes to relax.

Preheat oven to 375°F and line a couple sheet pans with
parchment paper or Silpats.

Roll out dough to about ½-inch thick. Cut to desired shape then put on sheet pans. Base your shapes on the size of the dogs you are dealing with. Volnay likes a delicate, small round about 1 ½ inch in diameter; Chewbacca likes a large 3 x 1 ½-inch rectangle. But if you have dog bone cutters, have at it.

Bake for approximately 40 minutes, or until biscuits are slightly browned and fairly hard. (They will harden a touch more when cool.) Set aside to cool, then treat the pups liberally.

Wedge Salad with Thousand Island

SERVES 4

You might think you don't like Thousand Island dressing, but this homemade version is nothing like the gloopy bottled stuff, or overly sweet stuff you get at the salad bar. This is old school delicious, and a wonderful surprise for your guests.

1 head iceberg lettuce, cored and cut into 4 wedges and kept cold

8 strips thick-cut bacon, cooked crisp and crumbled

1 cup good-quality mayonnaise, Hellman's is best

½ cup Heinz chili sauce

2 tablespoons sour cream

1 teaspoon lemon juice

1 tablespoon sweet pickle relish

2 tablespoons finely chopped celery hearts

1 teaspoon Worcestershire sauce

Pinch red pepper flakes (optional)

Salt and pepper to taste

Mix all the dressing ingredients together and keep chilled. To serve, place a wedge on a chilled plate, dress with 2 tablespoons of the dressing and a generous sprinkle of bacon bits. Pass more dressing on the side.

〜

Jenna's Blackout Elevator Cake

SERVES 8 TO 12

For all chocolate lovers, the ultimate chocolate cake. Just don't feed it to your dog.

For the Cake:
- 1 ½ cups all-purpose flour
- 1 cup Hershey's Special Dark cocoa powder
- 1 ½ teaspoons baking powder
- 1 ½ teaspoons baking soda
- 1 teaspoon salt
- 2 cups granulated sugar
- 2 large eggs
- 1 large egg yolk
- 1 cup sour cream
- ½ cup unsalted butter, melted
- 2 teaspoons vanilla extract
- 1 cup brewed dark roast coffee
- 2 ounces dark chocolate, melted

For the Filling:

- 1 cup whole milk
- Pinch salt
- ¼ cup sugar
- 1 large egg
- 2 tablespoons cornstarch
- 2 ounces bittersweet chocolate, finely chopped

For the Frosting:

- 4 ounces bittersweet chocolate, finely chopped
- 11 tablespoons unsalted butter, at room temperature
- 1 ⅔ cups powdered sugar, sifted
- 2 teaspoons vanilla extract
- 1 teaspoon instant espresso powder
- Pinch salt
- 1 package Nabisco chocolate wafers, crushed

Make the Cake:

Mix dry ingredients including flour, baking powder and soda, salt, cocoa powder, and sugar. Whisk to combine.

In separate bowl, combine eggs, sour cream, butter, melted chocolate, and vanilla. In bowl of standing mixer, add wet ingredient mixture to the dry. Mix for one minute until combined. Pour in coffee and mix until smooth. Divide evenly into two 9-inch cake rounds that have been greased. Bake at 350°F for 30 to 35 minutes until toothpick comes out cleanly.

Make the Pastry Cream:

Warm milk and salt in a saucepan on medium-low heat until steaming. Meanwhile, whisk egg, sugar, and cornstarch. Pour hot milk slowly over egg mixture, stirring continuously. Pour entire mixture back into saucepan and cook over medium heat until thickened. Pour hot pastry cream over chocolate. Stir until smooth as chocolate melts. Chill in the refrigerator until set. Place in between layers of cake once both cake and cream are completely cooled. Very important: Assemble cake before making frosting. If your kitchen is warm, store the assembled cake in the fridge while you make the frosting.

Make the Frosting:

Melt chocolate in a double boiler or in the microwave. Cream butter in bowl of standing mixer. Add sifted powdered sugar and espresso powder and salt, and cream again. Finally, pour in vanilla and melted chocolate, mix until smooth. Frost cake before icing is cooled, because it will harden at room temperature and be difficult to spread. While the frosting is still fresh, press cookie crumbs around the outside of the cake.

Serve with vanilla ice cream or very lightly sweetened whipped cream.

Aimee's Salad Bar Soup

SERVES 1 TO 8

A perfect fall or winter last-minute dinner. Just dump and heat up. Use what you have. Done in 30 minutes, but even better the next day, or the third. A little crusty bread on the side, maybe a green salad, it will be all you need and a cure for what ails you.

8 cups assorted veggies from your salad bar, in fairly equal proportions. I use the following, but you should use what you like. (I don't like mushrooms in this soup, they make the broth sort of muddy.)

Shredded red cabbage

Kale

Carrots

Celery

Chickpeas

Red onion

Zucchini and/or yellow squash

Broccoli and/or cauliflower

Peas

Chicken (If they don't have it on the salad bar, try a rotisserie chicken. Also good with leftover meats if you have them around.)

1 jar of your favorite marinara or tomato basil sauce (I love Rao's), or a jar of tomato puree

1 large russet potato, peeled and cubed

1 cup small whole wheat pasta, like ditalini or orzo, or a grain like barley or brown rice

¼ cup flat-leaf parsley, chopped

Pinch of red pepper flakes (optional)

Salt and pepper to taste

Water or chicken stock

Lemon and Parmesan cheese to garnish

Dump all of the veggies excluding the potato into a large stockpot. Add the jar of marinara or tomato puree and enough water (or good chicken or vegetable stock if you have it on hand) to cover the veggies by about 2 inches. Stir well, and bring to a simmer over medium-high heat. When the soup is bubbling, add the red pepper flakes if you like, and salt and pepper to taste. When the broth tastes great, add the pasta and potato and cook for another 12 to 15 minutes. When the potato and pasta are cooked through, taste again for seasoning, and let cool before storing in fridge or freezer.

If you have any leftover cooked veggies in your fridge, you can add them when you add the pasta and potato.

Use what you have! No jarred pasta sauce? Grab a large can of crushed tomatoes. Have some fresh herbs on hand, or some slightly sad wilty veggies in the crisper? Use 'em up. Prefer a grain to pasta? Try barley or farro or brown rice. Want it soupier? Add more water or stock. Heartier and more stewlike, add less.

———⌣———

Elliot's Valentine's Toffee Bread Pudding

SERVES 12

If life gives you lemons, you make lemonade. Preferably with vodka in it. If life gives you stale bread? Make bread pudding.

Elliot knows that the way to Jenna's heart is through gestures like bringing her enormous sandwiches and a pan of this homey and comforting dessert.

4 cups whole milk

1 cup heavy cream

5 large eggs

4 large egg yolks

8 to 10 cups stale cubed bread, preferably French baguettes, about 1 ½ to 2 loaves

1 cup chopped chocolate-covered toffee (about 4 to 6 Heath Bars, chopped)

1 cup sugar

Pinch salt

1 vanilla bean, split and seeds scraped out

6 tablespoons unsalted butter, melted

8 palmier cookies (optional)

Preheat your oven to 375°F and butter a 9 x 13 deep baking dish or roasting pan. Toss your cubed bread in the melted butter in a large bowl to coat all of the pieces.

Mix the milk and cream in a medium saucepan with the scraped vanilla seeds and the pod, and put over medium-high heat. Cook just until a thin skin forms and you can see small bubbles around the outside edge. Do not let boil. When the milk reaches this point, remove it from the heat and remove the vanilla pod.

Whisk eggs, yolks, sugar, and salt in a large bowl. Add 1 cup of the warm milk mixture, whisking quickly to temper, then add the rest of the milk and whisk until completely combined and the sugar melts.

Put half of the cubed buttered bread in the bottom of the pan. If using the palmier cookies, crumble them in an even layer over the bread. Sprinkle the toffee pieces evenly over the layer, then top with the rest of the cubed bread. Pour the custard over the bread, pressing down to help the bread absorb. Let the pan sit for at least 30 minutes to absorb the custard. Can be made to this point and then refrigerated overnight if you want to make it the day before an event.

Place the baking dish in a large, deep roasting pan, and fill halfway up the side of the baking dish with boiling water. Bake for 40 to 50 minutes in the water bath until a skewer in the center comes out clean. Serve warm or cold, with ice cream, whipped cream, or sweetened crème frâiche, or caramel sauce if you like.

Fire Station Ham

SERVES 16 TO 20

You don't need a houseful of hungry firemen to enjoy this ham; it's the perfect thing to make for Christmas, Thanksgiving, or Easter, or for a Super Bowl party!

1 whole bone-in ham, about 12 pounds (You can use spiral sliced if you want, but I find that they tend to be less moist than whole hams you slice yourself; see if your butcher can get you one if you don't have good access at the grocery store.)
1 8-ounce jar mango chutney
2 ounces ginger jam or ginger syrup
2 tablespoons finely grated shallot

1 cup light brown sugar

Zest and juice of 1 orange

½ cup strong Dijon mustard, I prefer Maille brand

3 tablespoons tomato paste

2 tablespoons hoisin sauce

Salt and pepper

½ teaspoon red pepper flakes

Preheat oven to 350°F. If you are using an unsliced ham, score the skin and fat of the ham in a diamond pattern. Place the ham in a roasting pan, and put 1 cup of water in the bottom.

Mix all glaze ingredients in a bowl. Spread the glaze all over the ham, being sure to get it into the scores. Cover the pan loosely with foil, trying not to touch the surface of the ham, but still sealing in the edges. Bake for 2 hours. Remove foil and bake an additional half an hour or so to caramelize the glaze. You can hold in a 200°F oven for up to two more hours before serving.

Corn Soufflé Pudding

SERVES 12

Nothing goes better with ham than corn pudding, and this version is surprisingly light.

2 cans creamed corn

2 cans whole kernel corn (do not strain or drain)

16 ounces sour cream

2 sticks butter, softened

2 boxes Jiffy corn muffin mix

3 eggs, separated

¼ teaspoon cream of tartar

Pinch salt

¼ teaspoon ground white pepper

Preheat oven to 350°F, and butter a 9 x 13 baking dish. Mix all of the ingredients except the egg whites and cream of tartar in a large bowl. In your standing mixer, beat the egg whites till they are foamy. Add the cream of tartar and beat to stiff peaks. Fold a third of the egg whites into the corn mixture to lighten it, and then fold the rest in carefully, trying not to deflate the mixture too much.

Pour the batter into the baking dish and bake for 45 to 55 minutes until golden brown and a skewer in the middle comes out clean.

Coconut Macaroons

MAKES UP TO 24 COOKIES

These unusual cookies use larger dried flaked coconut instead of the usual shredded sweetened coconut, for a much more sophisticated and less cloyingly sweet dessert. Adapted from Alice Medrich.

4 large egg whites

3 ½ cups unsweetened dried flaked, not shredded, coconut (also known as coconut chips)

¾ cup sugar

2 teaspoons pure vanilla extract

Slightly rounded ¼ teaspoon salt

Line 2 cookie sheets with parchment paper.

Combine all of the ingredients in a large heatproof mixing bowl. Set the bowl directly in a wide skillet of barely simmering water (if your bowl bobs in the water, simply pour some out). Stir the mixture with a silicone spatula, scraping the bottom to prevent burning, until the mixture is very hot to the touch and the egg whites have thickened slightly and turned from translucent to opaque, 5 to 7 minutes. Set the batter aside for at least an hour to let the coconut absorb more of the goop. (You can also make it to this stage and store in the fridge for up to three days before baking.)

Preheat the oven to 350°F. Position racks in the upper and lower thirds of the oven. Using 2 tablespoons of batter, make heaps 2 inches apart on the lined cookie sheets. It is okay if some of the goop is left over in the bowl, but try not to have the goop puddle at the base of the cookies. Bake for about 5 minutes, just until the coconut tips begin to color, rotating the pans from top to bottom and from front to back halfway through the baking time to ensure even baking.

Lower the temperature to 325°F and bake for 10 to 15 minutes, until the cookies are a beautiful cream and gold with deeper brown edges, again rotating the pans from top to bottom and from front to back halfway through the baking time. If the coconut tips are browning too fast, lower the heat to 300°F. Set the pans or just the liners on racks to cool. Let cool completely before gently peeling the parchment away from each cookie. If they are sticking, place them in the fridge or freezer for 10 minutes and try again.

The cookies are best on the day they are baked—the exterior is crisp and chewy and the interior soft and moist. Although the crispy edges will soften, the cookies remain delicious stored in an airtight container for 4 to 5 days.

───────⌣───────

Lamb Shanks with Pomegranate and Walnuts

SERVES 6

Andrea knows that this homey dish is the right way to welcome a weary traveler home. An easy dish for a dinner party, you can make it the day before and reheat; the flavors only get better.
Adapted from Daniel Boulud's Braise *cookbook*

6 lamb shanks (buy foreshanks if you can get them, ask your butcher)
4 ½ tablespoons grapeseed oil
6 garlic cloves, peeled and chopped
2 sprigs fresh sage
1 ½ teaspoons ground sumac
¾ teaspoon red pepper flakes
¾ teaspoon fennel seeds
3 medium red onions, sliced
2 medium fennel bulbs, sliced
1 ½ tablespoons tomato paste

4 cups pomegranate juice

2 15-ounce cans or 1 28-ounce can chickpeas, drained and rinsed

¾ cup golden raisins

¾ cup chopped walnuts

2 tablespoons pomegranate molasses

Seeds of 1 to 2 pomegranates

2 tablespoons chopped flat-leaf parsley

2 tablespoons chopped fresh mint

Preheat oven to 275°F. Season shanks well with salt and pepper. Heat oil in a large Dutch oven over high heat and sear shanks well on all sides till browned, 12 to 15 minutes. Remove to a platter, and reduce heat to medium. Add the garlic and seasonings to oil and cook, stirring for one minute, but be careful not to let burn. Add veggies and cook till softened, about 10 to 12 minutes. Stir in tomato paste and cook 3 minutes. Add juice, chickpeas, raisins, walnuts. and molasses. Return shanks to pot and bring to a simmer. Cover and braise in oven for 1 ½ hours, turning shanks twice while cooking. Remove lid, turn shanks again, and cook uncovered till lamb is caramelized on top and sauce is thick, about another hour. Reduce oven to 200°F and hold shanks, uncovered, until time to serve. Serve with fresh seeds, parsley, and mint sprinkled on top.

Truffled Pappardelle

SERVES 6 AS A SIDE DISH,
CAN DOUBLE EASILY IF YOU HAVE A LARGER PARTY

*This is one of the easiest dinner party side dishes on the planet.
It comes together in a flash, but has big wow factor.*

1 pound wide pappardelle pasta
1 3.5-ounce tub truffle butter
Zest of one lemon
3 tablespoons finely chopped chives
Salt and pepper to taste

Cook pasta to al dente in well-salted water. Reserve 1 cup of the cooking liquid, and strain pasta, returning it to the pot off heat. Add the butter, chives, and lemon zest, a pinch of salt and good grinding of black pepper, and ¼ cup of the reserved pasta water, and mix until all the noodles are well coated. If the pasta seems a little dry, you can add more of the pasta water. Taste for salt and pepper and serve hot.

Pistachio Cake with Fig Glaze

SERVES 10 TO 12

*This nutty cake is simple and not too sweet and works well
for both a fancy dinner dessert, or a casual brunch offering.*

5 ounces ground pistachios

½ pound unsalted butter (plus 1 tablespoon melted extra for greasing the pan)

½ vanilla bean

1 ⅓ cups powdered sugar, plus extra for dusting the cake

⅓ cup all-purpose flour

5 extralarge egg whites

3 tablespoons granulated sugar

½ cup fig jam (you can substitute apricot)

Preheat oven to 350°F. Cut out a circle of parchment paper to fit in the bottom of a 10-inch round cake pan. Brush the pan with a little melted butter and line the bottom with the paper.

Place the rest of the butter in a medium saucepan. Slice the vanilla bean lengthwise down the center, using a paring knife to scrape the seeds and pulp onto the butter. To make sure not to lose any of the seeds, run your vanilla-coated knife through the butter. Add the vanilla pod to the pan, and cook the butter until the butter browns and smells nutty (about 6 to 8 minutes). It helps to frequently scrape the solids off the bottom of the pan in the last couple of minutes to ensure even browning. Set aside to cool. Remove the vanilla pod and discard.

Mix pistachio flour with the confectioners' sugar in a food processor until mixed. Transfer to a large bowl. Place the egg whites in the bowl of a standing mixer fitted with the whisk attachment. Add the granulated sugar and mix on high speed 4 to 5 minutes, until the mixture forms very stiff peaks. Transfer the whites to a large mixing bowl.

Alternate folding the dry ingredients and the brown butter into the egg whites, a third at a time. Remember to scrape the bottom of the brown-butter pan with a rubber spatula to get all the little brown bits.

Pour the batter into the prepared cake pan, and bake for 40 minutes to 1 hour. Cool on a rack 30 minutes. Run a knife around the inside edge of the pan, and invert the cake onto a plate. Peel off the paper, and turn the cake back over onto a serving platter. Heat the jam with 2 tablespoons water until you have a liquid glaze, and pour over the cake. If you are serving as a brunch or tea dish, leave like this. For a dinner party dessert you can add a layer of bittersweet chocolate ganache over the glaze, or serve with a scoop of ice cream.

Elliot's Roasted Veal with Cognac Shallot Sauce

SERVES 4

Elliot knows that the way to a chef's heart is through her stomach, and this classic and simple French roast with a pan sauce is the perfect thing to make for her.

1 loin of veal (2 to 2 ½ pounds)

3 sprigs thyme, leaves picked

1 tablespoon grapeseed oil

1 ½ tablespoons sherry vinegar

3 tablespoons cognac

3 tablespoons walnut or hazelnut oil

3 tablespoons unsalted butter

3 tablespoons chopped shallots

1 ½ tablespoons fresh thyme leaves

3 tablespoons fresh parsley, chopped

Preheat oven to 375°F.

Season loin with salt and pepper, rub with thyme. Heat oil in large ovenproof skillet and sear the loin to golden brown on all sides. Roast in oven until medium rare. Remove the cooked loin to a plate. Rest covered with foil.

Put the skillet back over a burner on medium-high heat, add the nut oil, and sauté the shallots until they are translucent. Then reduce the heat to medium low and deglaze the pan with the cognac (add cognac off heat to prevent flare-ups), being sure to get all the browned bits from the bottom. Once the alcohol has burned off, add the thyme, and whisk in the butter until you get an emulsified pan sauce. Add the thyme, and taste for salt and pepper. Serve over the sliced veal, and sprinkle with parsley.

Fregola with Sweet Corn and Chives

SERVES 4 TO 6

This unexpected side dish is a fun change from the usual potatoes or rice.

Kosher salt

1 ½ cups fregola pasta (a large toasted pearl shape, you can substitute Israeli couscous but you'll lose a little of the fabulousness)

2 ears corn, shucked

2 tablespoons extra-virgin olive oil

Freshly ground black pepper, to taste

¾ cup chicken stock

¼ cup freshly grated Parmigiano-Reggiano

2 tablespoons chopped chives

Bring 3 quarts of water to a boil and add 1 tablespoon of salt. Set up a small ice bath nearby. Cook the fregola in the boiling water until somewhat tender but not cooked through, very al dente, about 10 to 12 minutes. Drain the fregola, refresh it in the ice bath, and spread it on a tray lined with paper towels to dry.

Preheat the grill or a cast iron skillet.

Brush the ears of corn with the olive oil, season with salt and pepper, and place on the grill or in the skillet, turning every 2 minutes until all sides are nicely browned or charred and the kernels are just beginning to burst. Remove the corn and, when the ears are cool enough to handle, cut the kernels off the cob with a sharp knife.

Combine the blanched fregola, sweet corn, and the chicken stock in a 12- to 14-inch sauté pan and cook over high heat until the stock boils and is mostly absorbed into the grain, about 5 minutes. Add the grated Parmigiano-Reggiano and salt and pepper and toss over high heat for 1 minute more. Stir in the chives and serve hot.

Gâteau de Semoule

SERVES 8

This is an old-school French dessert that is enormously comforting. And since Elliot knows that Jenna went to culinary school in France, it is the perfect dessert to woo her with.

¾ cup plus 12 tablespoons sugar

2 teaspoons butter, melted

3 large eggs

4 cups whole milk

1 vanilla bean

Pinch of sea salt

¾ cup plus 1 tablespoon fine semolina

¼ teaspoon freshly grated nutmeg

½ cup golden raisins, soaked in ¼ cup hot water or a liqueur of
    your choice (optional . . . I often substitute dried cherries or
    currants or leave it out altogether . . . toasted pine nuts are
    an interesting substitution as well)

Place a rack in the center of the oven and preheat to 400°F. Have a 6-cup soufflé dish or charlotte mold ready.

Place 12 tablespoons of the sugar in a medium skillet. Cook over medium heat, swirling the pan as the sugar dissolves. Once it has turned golden, quickly scrape the caramel into the dish or mold, swirling to coat the bottom. Once the caramel has hardened on the bottom, brush the sides of the dish with melted butter.

Whisk the eggs in a bowl. In a medium saucepan, combine the milk, the remaining ¾ cup of sugar, and the vanilla bean (split lengthwise and seeds scraped into the pan). Whisk over medium heat until small bubbles form around the edges. Remove from the heat, cover and let steep for 10 minutes. Remove the vanilla bean.

Return the milk to medium heat. When small bubbles form around the edges, add the salt and slowly sprinkle in the semolina, whisking constantly. Once it is incorporated, stir with a wooden spoon until thickened, about 10 minutes. Turn off the heat and quickly whisk in the eggs. Stir in the nutmeg and raisins. Pour into the prepared dish and bake until puffed and golden, 40 to 45 minutes. Serve warm from the dish, or cool and unmold. To unmold, run a knife around the sides, set the bottom of the dish in boiling water for 5 minutes, then turn it out onto a cake plate.

Elliot's Burgundian Stew

SERVES 8 TO 12

Elliot and Jenna are taking things slow ... even in the kitchen. A dish like this will make your house smell delicious all day. It'll serve a crowd handily, but don't let the volume dissuade you from making it for two; it freezes beautifully.
Adapted from The New American Cuisine *cookbook (1983)*

12 ounces diced slab bacon or salt pork
2 medium onions, chopped
1 cup chopped celery heart, with the leaves

4 carrots, peeled and cut into 1 ½-inch chunks

2 leeks, white part only, chopped

2 small turnips, diced

1 ½ pounds lean pork shoulder, cut in 1 ½-inch cubes

1 ½ pounds beef shoulder, cut in 1 ½-inch cubes

1 ½ pounds kielbasa sausage, in 2-inch chunks (use a good local
butcher version if you can get it, grocery store versions can
break down and get mushy)

Bouquet garni of 3 sprigs parsley, a celery stalk with the leaves,
3 sprigs fresh thyme, 2 bay leaves tied in cheese cloth or just
wound with butcher's twine

8 cups good beef stock

3 large russet potatoes, peeled and cut in eighths

1 small green cabbage (use Savoy if you can get it) cut in 8
wedges, with the core intact to hold the wedges together

2 cups flageolet or cannellini beans, soaked overnight

3 tablespoons demi-glace or condensed beef stock (optional)

Salt and pepper to taste

In a large heavy-bottomed wide Dutch oven, cook bacon slowly over medium-low heat to render the fat and make it crispy. Drain bacon and reserve for serving. Add onions, celery, carrots, leeks, and turnips to the hot bacon fat and sweat vegetables slowly about 10 minutes. Add all the meats and bouquet garni to the pot and cover with the beef stock. Raise heat to high and bring to boil. Skim the foam, then reduce heat to low and cover, and simmer gently about 1 ½ hours, the meat should be tender, but not falling apart. Add the beans and cook about 15 to 20 minutes. Stir in the demi-glace if you have it. I like to cook it to this stage, cool it down in the pot, and then refrigerate overnight for up to two days. If you are making and serving it the same day, just continue immediately with the next steps. The day you want to serve, bring to a simmer over medium-high heat, add the potatoes and cook about 15 minutes. Nestle the cabbage wedges down into the broth and cook covered another 10 minutes. Taste to be sure all the vegetables are cooked through and the meat is the right level of tenderness, and season the broth with salt and pepper. Turn on low and leave until you want to serve; it is fine to be on low for 3 to 4 hours.

To convert for a slow cooker, once the vegetables have been sweated with the bacon fat, transfer them to your slow cooker; add all of the rest of the ingredients except the cabbage and cook for about 8 hours on high. Add the cabbage about 1 hour before serving.

To serve, have the crispy bacon bits for people to add to their taste, and crème fraîche mustard sauce to put on top:

  2 cups crème fraîche
  3 tablespoons Dijon mustard
  2 tablespoons lemon juice
  4 tablespoons chopped chives
  Salt to taste

Mix all ingredients together and keep chilled until service.

Read on for a sneak peek at another
delicious novel from Stacey Ballis

Off the Menu

Available now from Berkley

Through the fog of those last ephemeral floaty moments before I fall into deep sleep, I suddenly feel a stirring in the bed next to me. I smile, knowing that as delicious as sleep is, there is something unbearably wonderful about the need for tenderness and contact. I roll over and let my tired lids open, forcing myself back from the brink of the sleep I desperately need, to attend to my sweetheart, who I need more. He looks at me with what can only be described as a perfect combination of love and longing, and tilts his head to one side, dark chocolate eyes sparkling wickedly in the darkness.

"Yes? Can I help you?" I say, my voice slightly roughened with exhaustion.

He lets his head tilt slowly to the other side and he reaches for me with a tentative teasing touch, then stops and just waits.

"You are very demanding, you know that?" I can't help but laugh.

But what can I do? He is the love of my life. A smile appears on his face and he reaches out again, this time more assuredly, tapping my hand with gentle insistence.

"Okay, okay!" I give up. I can deny this boy nothing.

As soon as he hears that word, he pounces, all twenty-six pounds of him landing with a thump on my chest.

This dog will be the end of me.

"I know, I know, boy, you need some extra-special love time, because you were at doggie day care all day while I was working to put kibble on the table."

Dumpling rolls over in my arms so that I can scratch his oddly broad chest. He is, to say the least, one of the strangest dogs anyone has ever seen. Which of course, is absolutely why I adopted him. I don't really know for sure what his lineage is, but he has the coloring and legs of a Jack Russell, the head of a Chihuahua, with the broad chest and sloping back of a bulldog, wide pug-ly eyes that bug out and are a little watery, and happen to mostly look in opposite directions. His ears, one which sticks up and one which flops down, are definitely fruit bat–ish. And when he gets riled by something, he gets a two-inch-wide Mohawk down his whole back, which sticks straight up, definitively warthog. He's a total ladies' man, a relentless flirt, and the teensiest bit needy in the affection department, as are many rescue dogs. But of course, he is so irresistibly lovable he never has a problem finding the attention he desires.

He is also smart as a whip, and soon after I got him my dear friend Barry took him to train as a therapy dog so that the two of them could work occasionally in hospitals and nursing homes and with disabled kids. He has the highest possible certification for that work, and was one of only two dogs out of fifty to pass the test when he took it, proud mama me. Barry is an actor and cabaret performer, and on the days when he is not in rehearsal he often volunteers to "entertain the troops" as he calls it, singing standards for the elderly, doing dramatic readings of fairy tales for kids with cancer, and teaching music to teenagers with autism. He'd seen someone working with a therapy dog at Children's Memorial Hospital, and when he found out how meaningful that work can be, he asked if he could borrow Dumpling and see if he was the right kind of dog. Dumpling turned out to be more than the right kind of dog; he turned out to be a total rock star, and has become a favorite at all of their stops. The fact that Barry has snagged many dates with handsome doctors and male nurses using Dumpling as bait is just a bonus for him. Dumpling loves the work and I love knowing that he spends at least one or two days a week out and about with Barry instead of just lazing around and getting too many treats from his pals at Best Friends doggie day care.

Dumpling is the kind of dog that makes people on the street do double and triple takes and ask in astonished voices, "What kind of dog IS that?!" His head is way too small for his thick solid body, and his legs are too spindly. His eyes point away from each other like a chameleon. One side of his mouth curls up a little, half-Elvis, half palsy-victim, and his tongue has a tendency to stick out just a smidgen on that side. He was found as a puppy running down the median of a local highway, and I adopted him from PAWS five years ago, after he had been there for nearly a year. He is, without a doubt, the best thing that ever happened to me.

My girlfriend Bennie says it looks like he was assembled by a disgruntled committee. Barry calls him a random collection of dog bits. My mom, in a classic ESL moment, asked upon meeting him, "He has the Jack Daniels in him, leetle bit, no?" I was going to correct her and say Jack Russell, but when you look at him, he does look a little bit like he has the Jack Daniels in him. My oldest nephew, Alex, who watches too much *Family Guy* and idolizes Stewie, took one look, and then turned to me in all seriousness and said in that weird almost-British accent, "Aunt Alana, precisely what brand of dog *is* that?" I replied, equally seriously, that he was a purebred Westphalian Stoat Hound. When the kid learns how to Google, I'm going to lose major cool aunt points.

Dumpling tilts his head back and licks the underside of my chin, wallowing in love.

"Dog, you are going to be the death of me. You have got to let me sleep sometime."

These words are barely out of my mouth, when he leaps up and starts barking, in a powerful growly baritone that belies his small stature. The third bark is interrupted by the insistent ringing of my buzzer.

Crap. "Yes, you are very fierce. You are the best watchdog. Let's go see what the crazy man wants."

Only one person would have the audacity to ring my bell at a quarter to one on a weeknight.

Patrick Conlon.

Yes, *the* Patrick Conlon.

Owner and executive chef of Conlon Restaurant Group, based here in Chicago. Three local restaurants, Conlon, his flagship white tablecloth restaurant, housed in a Gold Coast historic mansion, which recently received a coveted second Michelin star. Patrick's, a homey high-end comfort-food place in Lincoln Park, and PCGrub, his newest endeavor, innovative bar food in the suddenly hot Logan Square neighborhood, dangerously close to my apartment. He also has Conlon Las Vegas, Conlon Miami, and is in negotiations to open PCGrub in both those cities, and a one-off project looming in New York as well.

But even if you have never eaten in one of Patrick's restaurants, you have probably seen him on Food TV, where he has two long-running shows, *Feast*, where he demonstrates home versions of his restaurant recipes and special menus for entertaining, and *Conlon's Academy*, which is a heavily technique-based show for people who really want to learn professional-level cooking fundamentals as they relate to a passionate home cook. Maybe you have seen him guest judging on *Top Chef*, snarking and sparring with Tom Colicchio, Padma getting all giggly and tongue-tied in his handsome presence. Or judging on *Iron Chef America*, disagreeing charmingly with Jeffery Steingarten at his curmudgeoniest. Or on a booze-fueled tour of the best Chicago street food with Anthony Bourdain. Or giving his favorite foods a shout-out on *The Best Thing I Ever Ate* or *Unique Eats* compilation shows. Or maybe you have read one of his six bestselling cookbooks. Even more likely, you have seen him squiring an endless series of leggy actresses and pop princesses and supermodels on red carpets, and read about his latest heartbreaking act in a glossy tabloid. And yes, before you ask, that latest angry power-girl single by Ashley Bell rocketing up the country charts about "settin' loose the one who cooked my goose" is totally about him.

Why, you might ask, is a world-famous chef and gadabout television celeb ringing my bell at a quarter to one in the morning on a weeknight? Because I am his Gal Friday, Miss Moneypenny, executive culinary assistant, general dogsbody, and occasional whipping post. I help him develop his recipes for the shows and cookbooks, and travel with him to prep and sous chef when he does television appearances and book tours. I also choose his gifts for birthdays and holidays, order his apology flowers for the Legs, as I call them, listen to him bitch about either being too famous or not famous enough, and write his witty answers to the e-mail questionnaires he gets since few journalists like to do actual note-taking live interviews anymore. I let the endless series of the fired and broken-up-with he leaves in his wake cry on my shoulder, and then I write half of them recommendations for other jobs, and the other half sincere apology notes, which I sign in a perfect replica of his signature, practiced on eleventy-million cases of cookbooks and glossy headshots that he can't be bothered to sign himself.

And on nights like these, when he has a date or a long business dinner, I drag my ass out of bed to make him a snack, and listen to him wax either poetical or heretical, depending on how the evening went.

I quickly throw on a bra and my robe, while Patrick leans on the bell and Dumpling hops straight up and down as if he has springs in his paws, and joyously barks his ill-proportioned tiny little head off, knowing instinctively that this is not some scary intruder, but rather one of his favorite two-leggeds.

Cheese and rice, why are the men in my life so freaking demanding tonight?

"I. Am. Coming!" I yell in the vague direction of the door, turning on lights as I stumble through my apartment.

I open the front door, and there he is. Six foot three inches, broad shoulders, tousled light brown hair with a hint of strawberry, piercing blue eyes, chiseled jaw showing a hint of stubble, wide grin with impossibly even white teeth, except for the one chipped eyetooth from a football incident in high school, the one flaw in the perfect canvas of his face.

Fucker.

I gather up all five foot three of my well-padded round

self, with my unruly dark brown curly hair in a frizzled shrubbery around my head, squint my sleepy blue eyes at him, and step aside so he can enter.

He leans down and kisses the top of my head. "Hello, Alana-falana, did I wake you?"

Patrick doesn't walk as much as he glides in a forwardly direction. Most women find it sexy. I find it creepy.

"Of course you woke me, it's one o'clock in the good-manned morning, and we have a meeting at eight." I cringe at my accidental use of my dad's broken-English epithet. A lifetime of being raised by Russian immigrants, who murdered their new language with passion and diligence, has turned me into someone who sometimes lapses into their odd versions of idioms. The way people who have worked to get rid of their Southern drawls can still slip into y'all mode when drinking or tired.

He turns and puts on his sheepish puppy-dog face.

"Oops. So sorry, sweet girl, you know I never keep official track of time."

It's true. Bastard doesn't even wear a watch. It would make me crazy, except he is never late.

"It's okay. How may I be of service this, um, *morning*?" He'll ignore the emphasis on the hour, but I put it out there anyway.

Patrick reaches down and scoops Dumpling up in his arms, receiving grateful licks all over his face. Damned if my dog, who is generally indifferent to almost all men, doesn't love Patrick.

"I had a very tedious evening, and a powerfully mediocre dinner, and I thought I would swing by and say hello and see if you had anything delicious in your treasure chest."

"Of course you did. Eggs?"

"Please."

"Fine."

Patrick follows me to the kitchen, carrying and snuggling Dumpling, whispering little endearments to him, making him wiggle in delight. He folds himself into the small love seat under the window, and watches me go to work.

Between culinary school, a year and a half of apprentice stages all over the world in amazing restaurants, ten years as the personal chef of talk show phenom Maria De Costa, and six years as Patrick's culinary slave, I am nothing if not efficient in the kitchen. I grab eggs, butter, chives, a packet of prosciutto, my favorite nonstick skillet. I crack four eggs, whip them quickly with a bit of cold water, and then use my Microplane grater to grate a flurry of butter into them. I heat my pan, add just a tiny bit more butter to coat the bottom, and let it sizzle while I slice two generous slices off the rustic sourdough loaf I have on the counter and drop them in the toaster. I dump the eggs in the pan, stirring constantly over medium-low heat, making sure they cook slowly and stay in fluffy curds. The toast pops, and I put them on a plate, give them a schmear of butter, and lay two whisper-thin slices of the prosciutto on top. The eggs are ready, set perfectly; dry but still soft and succulent, and I slide them out of the pan on top of the toast, and quickly mince some chives to confetti the top. A sprinkle of gray fleur de sel sea salt, a quick grinding of grains of paradise, my favorite African pepper, and I hand the plate to Patrick, who rises from the love seat to receive it, grabs a fork from the rack on my counter, and heads out of my kitchen toward the dining room, Dumpling following him, tail wagging, like a small furry acolyte.

"You're welcome," I say to the sink as I drop the pan in. I grab an apple out of the bowl on the counter and head out to keep him company while he eats. I'd love nothing more than a matching plate, but it is a constant struggle to not explode beyond my current size 14, and middle-of-the-night butter eggs are not a good idea.

Patrick is tucking in with relish, slipping Dumpling, who has happily returned to a place of honor in his lap, the occasional morsel of egg and sliver of salty ham. Usually I am very diligent about not giving the dog people-food, but I don't have the energy to fight Patrick on it, especially since I am feeling a bit guilty about how little time I have had to spend with the pooch lately. Barry is out of town playing Oscar Wilde in a Philadelphia production of *Gross Indecency*, so it has been all day-care all the time for the past three weeks, and another three to go. So a little bit of egg and prosciutto I can't argue with. Patrick manages to inhale his food and pet Dumpling nearly simultaneously with one hand. With his other hand, he is fiddling with my laptop, which I left open on the table when I went to sleep, after a night of working on new recipes for his latest cookbook. He pauses, and looks me right in the eyes.

"Damn, girl, you make the best scrambled eggs on the planet." Patrick is a lot of things, but disingenuous is not one of them. When he lets fly a compliment, which is infrequent, he makes eye contact and lets you know he means it very sincerely.

I let go of my annoyance. "I know. It's the grated butter." I can't stay mad at Patrick for longer than eighteen point seven minutes. I've timed it.

"I know. Wish I had thought of it."

"According to the *Feast* episode about breakfasts for lovers, you did," I tease him. I'm not mad about this. It's my job to help him develop recipes and invent or improve methods. And since I am petrified at the idea of being on camera or in the public eye in any way, shape, or form, he is most welcome to claim all my tricks as his own. Lord knows, he pays me very, *very* well for the privilege.

"Well, I know I *inspired* the idea." He's very confident of this, thinking that I came up with the technique to enhance his dining experience when he foists himself upon me in the middle of the night, which I also think he believes I secretly love.

He is enormously wrong on both counts.

I came up with it for Bruce Ellerton, the VP of show development for the Food TV Network and senior executive producer of our show. Bruce comes to Chicago periodically to check in on us since we are the only show that doesn't tape in the Manhattan studios, and he and I have been enjoying a two- to three-day romp whenever he is here or I am there for the past four years. We are, as the kids say, friends with benefits, and I like to think we enjoy a very real friendship in addition to an excellent working relationship and very satisfying sex. We have enough in common to allow for some non-bedroom fun, and easy conversation. We also have a solid mutual knowledge that we would be terrible together as a real couple, which prevents either of us from trying to turn the relationship into more than it is. We stay strictly away from romantic gestures; no flowers or Valentine's cards or overly personal gifts. If either of us begins dating someone seriously, we put our naked activities on hold.

Or, I'm sure we would, if either of us had time to actually date someone seriously.

Bruce's favorite food is eggs, so I developed the recipe for him one evening when bed took precedence over dinner and by the time we came up for air, take-out places were shut down for the night. Patrick is blissfully unaware of the special nature of my relationship with Bruce, so I just let him think they are "his" eggs.

"You inspire all my best ideas. Or at least you pay for them. So was tonight business or pleasure?" I crunch into my apple.

"Biznuss," he says around a mouthful of toast and egg. "The New York investors want to push the opening back a few months. Michael White is opening another place around the same time we were going to, and everything that guy touches is gold, so we don't want to end up a footnote in the flood of press he will get. Mike is a fucking amazing chef, so I don't want to invite any comparisons. Let him have a couple months of adulation, and then we'll open."

Patrick, to his credit, is a chef first and a television personality second. He keeps a very tight rein and close eye on all of his restaurants, develops all the menus in close consultation with his chefs de cuisine, who train the rest of their staff in his clean and impeccable style. For all his bluster, and as much as he has the vanity to enjoy the celebrity part of his life, the food does come first, not the brand. He is at the pass in each of his Chicago restaurants at least once a week, and checks in on his out-of-town places once a month or so. And he is secure enough to recognize when someone else is really magic in the kitchen and to not want to muddy the media waters. Having eaten at almost all of Michael's restaurants over the years, I can't blame Patrick for wanting to bump his own stuff to let the guy have his due. The words *culinary genius* come to mind immediately and without irony.

"So, late spring then?" I'm mentally adjusting my own schedule, since whatever Patrick does inevitably impacts my life not insignificantly.

He takes the last morsel of toast and wipes the plate clean, popping it in his mouth and rolling his eyes back in satisfaction. "Yup."

"I'll go through the calendar with you tomorrow and we can make the necessary changes." Crap. I have eight thousand things to do tomorrow, or rather, today, and this was not one of them.

"Sounds good. You just tell me where to be and when and what to do when I get there!"

I wish. "How about you be at *your* house in ten minutes, and go to sleep . . ."

He laughs. That is not good. That means he is choosing to believe that I am joking so that he can stay longer. There is not going to be enough caffeine on the planet to suffer through tomorrow. Er, today.

"So guess what started today?" He smirks at me, pushing his empty plate aside and moving my computer in front of him.

"I can't begin to imagine."

"EDestiny Fall Freebie Week!"

Oh. No.

"Patrick . . ."

"Let's see what fabulous specimens of human maleness the old Destinometer has scraped up for our princess, shall we?" He chuckles as his fingers fly over the keys, logging into the dating site with my e-mail and password, settling in to see what new profiles the magical soul-mate algorithm has dredged up for me. It should be the last thing I would ever let him do, or even tell him about, but my ill-fated brief stint as an online dater somehow became part of our business practice. And it is my own damn fault.

Dumpling nuzzles under Patrick's chin, another betrayal, and I clear Patrick's plate and flatware, and go to wash dishes, while my bosshole in the other room yells out that there's a very nice-looking seventy-two-year-old bus driver from Hammond, Indiana, who might just be perfect for me.